XTREMUS:
A BIONICAN QUEST IN THE WAKE OF CYBERGEDDON

PETER WIESNER

MONTAG

DEDICATION

This work is dedicated to all those who develop and use technology for protecting our natural environment and preserving our cultural heritage, as well as safeguarding our privacy and personal space.

CHAPTER ONE
THE BIONICANS

As the sun shines through the raggedy palms along the steep beachfront palisades, unclothed Bionican men and women covered with body paint and body piercings dance to a heavy, steady drumbeat that intensifies as the sun goes down. Bonfires, lit earlier in the day, come to a full roar, shooting flames high into the darkening wake of the sun's descent. Embers float to the ground as the undulating shadows of the dancing figures streak across the blanched shell of a high-rise building that once proclaimed the power and the glory of the Cyber Age.

Condor, tall and powerfully built, crosses his arms watching the dancers extend their arms upwards to greet the night. Observing them intensely, he moves through the crowd, sporting his Birkenstock sandals that are standard issue for hackers. His naked bronze skin, covered with tattoos, ripples over lean muscles accentuated by the bonfire light. He unfolds his arms and strokes the stubble on his prominent cleft chin. Like all hackers, his shaved head distinguishes him from the hairy-headed users he commands.

Draper, a skinny hacker with a missing tooth, approaches Condor.

"You do *not* want a repeat of last year."

Condor nods, his eyes reflecting the crackling bursts from the bonfires. "I will make sure that things do not get out of hand."

Digi Diva, the only female hacker in the group, is a tomboy, on the thin side, part Mexican Irish, Japanese and French. She is the only hacker, in fact the only woman in Bionica, who insists on wearing jackboots instead of the prized Birkenstocks that are reserved for the hackers. Each day, when she puts them on, Digi hums the Old Nancy Sinatra tune, *"Well, these boots are made for walking, and that's just what they'll do. One of these days these boots are gonna walk all over you."*

Like all the other hackers, Digi is shaven bald and bare-breasted, covered with tattoos; her angular features accentuate her quizzical expressions. Still trying to prove her value, she reminds her colleagues, "We are running out of replacements. We cannot afford to sunset any deviants." She is boyish and military in her manner, and has a tendency to flash her prominent teeth when she wants to make a point.

"They will not go anywhere I do not *want* them to

go," Condor replies.

"A user is a user is a user abuser," Digi wisecracks, trying to impress Condor with her charms. The other hackers laugh because they know that Digi has a thing for Condor, but they also know that many of the choice female users already have had his thing. Digi tells herself that Condor secretly lusts for her, but does not respond to her for professional reasons.

"*Must* be my buckteeth," she mutters privately to nerdy Phiberoptik, who lost all of his teeth because of gum disease.

"Nah, you just have a *gross* overbite." He stretches out a toothless grin that forces Digi to tamp down her silliness. Phiberoptik, low on the hacker totem pole, also has a thing for Digi but is too shy to do anything about it.

Digi tries to regain the moment. "Seriously, we have to keep them in line so that we do not jeopardize D-train production. We *need* to meet our quotas."

All business, Condor looks at her, "Eric will be here soon. He will deliver clothing and food."

"And meat, I hope," Pengo laughs, with the approval of the other hackers – Phiberoptik, Draper, and Jim the Greek.

Daytrain, D-train for short, is the staple crop that the Bionicans use to keep plugged into "The Well"—a database that contains all of the digitized knowledge developed during the Cyber Era.

As the leaders of the Bionican Chosen People, the hackers are keenly aware of their history and mission. They know that The Well is the only remaining repository of information that survived Cybergeddon – all other digitized information disappeared when the eco terrorists unleashed the deadly virus that destroyed the world's information infrastructure. Right now, their job is to make the Bionican users stay plugged-in to keep The Well's endangered database alive.

"*Use* it or *lose* it," Phiberoptik pipes in, "that is our motto."

"Remember, we Bionicans are the only ones who should have complete access to The Well," Condor reminds his colleagues. "That means we have to control access by our users, so that they do not surf what is forbidden." While all users are D-train addicts, hackers avoid it because if they come addicted, they lose their ability to hack The Well. They know that they cannot keep the users in line if they act like users.

"Once the users are hooked, they cannot get enough. That should never change," Condors says to his hacker colleagues. "The Greeks want to pull secret information from The Well, but we *cannot* allow that to happen. Now we have to deal with their children."

"Yes, a few of their children have come to us, wanting to become users," Phiberoptik reminds the group of a continuing challenge. "We have to make sure that we train these new users properly."

"We cannot let them have uncontrolled access to The Well," says Condor in all seriousness. "Our duty is to protect The Well. There is always the possibility of using its information to develop weapons of mass destruction."

Unlike the hackers who were responsible for political and economic terrorism that culminated in the *Makeitso* virus, Condor and his fellow Bionican hackers are comparatively a docile lot, engineered to be trustworthy, loyal, helpful, friendly, courteous, kind, obedient, cheerful, thrifty, brave, clean, reverent, and trustworthy – up to a point.

"This is no time for user friendliness. If they screw up, we *have* to kill them," Pengo adds.

"I am not so sure they would know what to do if they had access," Digi Diva says, bringing up the old download problem.

"Let us make sure that The Well remains read-only," Condor says, ending the discussion.

Condor returns to his seat on a throne-like chair, made from carved wood, to supervise the solstice celebration that is now in high gear. Condor positioned the chair on the embankment to provide him with a panoramic view of the proceedings attended by hundreds of users who have gathered in front of the bonfires. He knows from experience that when users step up their utterances, it is time to watch out.

"*Small* is beautiful," one user cries out in a squeaky voice.

"Reduce, recycle and reuse," another user offers as his slogan for the day.

"Reduce, recycle, reuse *and recover*," the user corrects himself. Condor smiles because things are going well; the users are sticking to the script.

"*Long* live the Diggers."

Condor is looking for more. "Who, what, where, and how?" Condor yells at him.

The user shouts out the right answer, "The American Diggers, 20th Century, San Francisco – they gave things away for free because human beings are the means of exchange."

So far, so good, but Condor knows more is coming.

"*Down* with Western Civilization. *Down* with the Earth despoilers."

Condor yawns. He has heard these phrases many times before and hopes that his users will exercise more originality during the Teach-In scheduled for the next day.

The users start turning up the volume of their breathy pronouncements.

"They *poisoned* the waters."

"They *killed* off the birds."

"They *murdered* the wild animals."

Just then a vulture circles above, taking notice of the goings-on. The users continue to drone on.

"We are *here* to testify."

"On this day of the summer solstice."

"We are the only ones left to remember."

The users keep adding to their litany. The single utterances overlap and grow into a collage of words that becomes a rumbling howl. Annoyed, Condor makes the throat cutting gesture to silence them. The howling stops but the dancing continues.

One user woman with long stringy hair breaks the silence, "Long live Xtremus."

Condor knows this is off topic. Talk of it can lead to even more dangerous topics, like religion. Condor has to act fast before the group gloms onto these themes and spins out of control.

"Let us not go there today. Keep up the pace. Keep moving." He raises his clenched fist to signal that freelance testimonies are off limits.

The users obey and continue to dance and moan through most of the night until they collapse from exhaustion. Next morning, they rise out of the smoke of fading bonfires and turn to each other for acknowledgment. Hesitating as if they have forgotten something, the users wander off in small groups and sit under the palm trees waiting for the next phase to begin.

Condor approaches them. Pounding his fist into the palm of his hand, he shouts out, "The time has come. The time has come. The time has come." The users know what is next. They form a circle around a sacred obelisk chiseled from stone, chanting the name of the legendary Julia Butterfly Hill, one revered for her vigil that saved a 1000-year old tree named Luna. Their chanting evokes a collective vision of La Tigresa, another tree-minded heroine, whose legendary striptease disarmed evil loggers.

One frightful woman, covered with scars from self-inflicted wounds, releases a handful of monarch butterflies into the air. So begins the Teach-In awaited by everyone. Each user has been tasked to memorize a quote from The Well.

Condor roars, "Refresh, refresh, refresh." All users concentrate their mental powers on what they have absorbed from The Well.

Soon Condor escorts Larry, one of his users, to the front of the group. The little man with a goatee proclaims, "Jerry Brown, the Great Moonbeam Visionary, saw two scenarios vying for the fate of humankind: an industrialized, computerized world of 12 billion people surviving as a global ant heap, or a transformed civilization based on wisdom, restraint and caring."

As he listens to Larry, Condor's thoughts wander to

mental images of the world that once was – great elec-trified cities with crowds of people and cars in constant flux. Bionica, once called Santa Monica, was the home of the great RAND Corporation, which now lies in ru-ins, its offices torn apart and hundreds of filing cabinets filled with precious knowledge, upended and ransacked by eco-terrorists. Just a stone throw away is Silicon Beach, where the cyber geeks once surfed and skate-boarded along the Speedway in view of the ruins of the Santa Monica Pier. Nearby, the remains of a giant Ferris wheel, once powered by the sun, is frozen shut with rust.

Condor wonders whether humanity could ever re-trieve this past. Whenever he tunes into The Well to fathom the end of the past, he hears terrifying sounds of the endless riots and armed rebellion that led to Cy-bergeddon. This time he shuts out these noises so that he can concentrate on minding his users.

The teach-in continues. An old woman, wearing a tattered hoodie, stoops in front of Condor and bellows out a quote from Edward Abbey, spiritual father of the Earth First movement, "Sentiment without action is the *ruin* of the soul."

Maya, a radiant young woman with long black hair, quotes the Greenpeace activist, *"Instead of going out to shoot birds, I should go out and shoot the kids who shoot birds."* Ty, a thin gaunt man with empty spectacles, looks up and declares, *"The only real good technology is no technology at all. Technology is taxation without representation, imposed by our elitist species upon the rest of the natural world."* Sammy, a short youth with a red headscarf, quotes Paul Ehrlich, a 20th Century ecologist, *"Giving society cheap, abundant energy would be the equivalent of giving an idiot child a machine gun."*

A shrill voice exclaims, *"Remain* a parasite or *become* an Earth warrior." The borrowed words continue as the group forms a circle chanting, "We are Earth warriors. We are Earth warriors. We are Earth warriors."

Maya rises to speak and asks, "What is Koyaanisqatsi?" There is a long period of rehearsed silence until she gleefully supplies the expected answer.

"It is Hopi for unbalanced life, life in turmoil, life disintegrating."

As the users holds hands and sing old traditional folk songs and plaintive American Negro spirituals, Condor keeps on watching and staring ahead. As the sun sets, Sammy begins to sing, *"Sometimes I feel like a motherless child"* while the exalted users roll their eyes skyward and surrender to the moment of collective bliss. After the song ends with *"a long way from home",* a deep silence sets in, punctuated by sporadic wind whistles and insect noises that become louder as the darkness of evening intensifies.

A voice from The Well breaks the silence. It speaks the common mind through a breathy woman's voice. No one is sure who she is or was, or whether she is real or synthetic. Condor looks around to make sure his users are on task, ready to receive the spoken word with a single mind. The increasingly preachy voice from The Well quotes the Indian philosopher, Jiddu Krishnamurti, *"On this day, all authority of any kind, especially in the field of thought and understanding, is the most destructive, evil thing. Leaders destroy the followers, and followers destroy the leaders. You have to be your own teacher and your own disciple. You have to question everything that man has accepted as valuable, as necessary."*

Every user can recite Krishnamurti's immortal words by heart, at least for that moment. And when that moment passes, they forget what they heard, but they know they can always play it back. They understand that to *question everything* is to allow deconstruction from The Well into their hearts so that every question can be asked and answered as many times as needed until the withering void of bliss sets in. The users are transfixed by Krishnamurti's words that have been heard many times before. He emerges as an apparition and continues to speak to the crowd in his female voice.

"Freedom is not a reaction. Freedom is not choice. It is man's pretense that because he has choice he is free. Freedom is pure observation without direction, without fear of punishment and reward. Freedom is without motive. Freedom is not at the end of the evolution of man but lies

in the first step of his existence."

The users rise to sway and dance as Krishnamurti completes his oratory; the prophet raises his arms to create an arc, and so do the dancers to the rhythm of the drumbeat that punctuates his words. Then the stream of words is completely displaced by drumming as the pace of the dancing escalates into a juggernaut of joy that gradually dissolves in a denouement that brings all movement to a close.

Condor stands by, scanning the exhausted crowd of the post-apocalyptic proletariat. After the daylong teach-in, the users prepare to log off. The sun lowers beneath the horizon and the brain drain begins. Condor gives the expected cue, a downward gesture of his flattened right hand, which prompts the users to chant "ohm" to close down The Well network and revert to the drives in their own heads. Once this is accomplished, they fall to the ground for a good night's rest.

The Well will only release those who have participated wholeheartedly and sincerely. The few who failed to log off must remain in place and continue chanting silently into the dark, hoping to avoid the neurasthenia that sets in once their connection to The Well goes into overtime.

When the teach-in comes to an end, Condor maintains his aloofness. With his arms crossed, he looks with disdain at the few users who have been unable to log off.

This has been his event to manage and he wants to maintain his standing among the hackers for running a tight ship. He will not tolerate illegal exiting. Straggling users must meet all networking requirements before they can exit from the teach-in.

The naked bodies of the users gyrate into the darkness as their heads swirl into the rapid-fire cleansing hallucinations that are necessary for exiting. With the waning bonfires glimmering in their eyes, they breathe heavily and sink to the ground, thankful that they have been released for the night.

The users snore themselves into deep sleep, and Condor has a few moments to check out his animated tattoos. Like the other hackers, he was born with a turnkey, hardwired knowledge of The Well, with tattoos all over his body documenting his privileges. But what distinguishes Condor from his colleagues is that the tattoos on his arms undergo constant change.

Condor keeps watch over his animated tattoos. He checks his right arm for its daily message. Today, his arm shows Socrates at the Parthenon speaking to his pupils. Condor can barely make out Socrates' words, but after a few tries, makes sense out of the rolling text, "All I know is that I know nothing."

Condor's preoccupation with his tattoos brings to mind his long-deceased mother, who was responsible for his having them.

Whispering, Condor asks, "*Where* are you now, Mother? *How* are you able to talk to me? You tell me I am special and different from the others, but what are the tattoos saying to me? *Mother*, tell me more. I know I am different. Why am I here? What is my destiny?"

He stares at his tattoos wondering what they will tell him next, but nothing happens. The tattoos are done for the day.

Several days later, the tattoos provoke Condor again. This time, it is a quote from John Milton, which he has heard before. So this time he lip-synchs, *"He who reigns within himself and rules passions, desires, and fears is more than a king."* Condor strokes his arm as if to squeeze meaning from the moving message. "Mother, what is Milton saying to me? What is it that I am supposed to do differently?"

Condor is not sure that The Well approves this quote. To avoid trouble, he begs The Well to forgive him in advance.

"Will I go on the right path?" he mumbles expecting to get an answer from The Well. As he strokes his tattoos, they become illuminated. Taking this as a positive sign, Condor smiles and ponders what lies ahead of him. Soon the tattoos trigger trivial advertising slogans related to drinks from the distant past, drinks that he has never had. Unlike phrases from philosophers, pop-up advertising taglines cause him no anxiety.

"Take tea and see."

"Things go better with Coke."

"It's the real thing."

These mid-20th Century advertising phrases make him thirsty and give him ersatz sensory experiences from the drinks he has tasted only in his dreams. Although he has never had these drinks in real life, he is able to taste tea and Coke through his imagination.

There is a gaping emptiness in Condor's life. He longs for the day when he will understand and experience what makes him whole. He wants to be transported to a world where the desires of his dreams are real. In frustration, he scratches his tattoos, and they respond by showing him an image of himself climbing huge boulders by the sea. He sees himself struggling to avoid being swept away by the waves of the sea. He flexes his arms and grips the air to embrace the feelings unleashed by his hallucinations and to feel at home. Still in the end he feels only frustrated and unfulfilled. Perhaps, he wonders, he must leave Bionica to realize his future.

When Condor thinks about his future, he finds himself imagining the world before he was born. He is aware of the time when millions of privileged people were connected through The Well, each of them actively involved with each other through brain implants. During those heady days, The Well was at it is peak; things were different then because information could be developed and exchanged freely without censorship. But that changed with the abuse of cyber power that led Cybergeddon. Anyone who was a *somebody* became a *nobody* overnight.

Condor reminds himself, "We are special because we had updated virus protection, and it is our duty to safeguard The Well. We cannot allow another security breach. That is why The Well is read-only, free from digital viruses and cyberterrorism. Our job is to protect that freedom."

Condor does not question his role in safeguarding The Well, but secretly he wants to escape from this birthright and his obligations. He is afraid of voicing his desire to be free, afraid of what might happen to him, and afraid of losing his hacker status and privileges.

As Condor struggles with disturbing questions, his thoughts shift north and east to the Greeks, who live in Macedonia – a territory stretching from Malibu across the Santa Monica Mountains to the reaches of the Pacific Palisades, Calabasas, Bel Air, Beverly Hills, Hollywood, Chatsworth, and Pasadena.

Condor has heard about the "polis" in Chatsworth and the Greek museums in Pasadena, but he has never visited them. He also knows about the lavish Greek plantations in Calabasas, worked by slaves from the LA basin.

The Goths control human trafficking. They provide the Greeks with slaves and distribute Daytrain throughout the LA basin, an area populated by isolated communities of brown people that barely survive through foraging and subsistence farming. Goth warriors, led by the G-spot Biker Femmes, kidnap and enslave these unfortunate basin folks by luring them with D-train, as well as trinkets and sexual favors. When necessary, the Femmes terrorize the brown denizens into submission through a combination of lethal martial arts and the skillful application of sadomasochistic paraphernalia.

The G-spot Femmes, led by the notorious Gonorrhea, are widely feared and admired for their ruthlessness and discipline in keeping the Daytrain and slave trade going. They also procure virile men for Greek women and are on the forefront of sexual warfare and the promotion of female fertility and superiority. They have built their reputation by calling out notorious Lotharios to prove their manhood in public and sacrificing losers in the name of Lorena Bobbitt to Freyja, the Norse goddess of sexuality, fertility, gold, war, and death.

Rather than getting their hands dirty, the Greeks let the brutal and uncouth G-spot Femmes and their male counterparts do the dirty work associated with slavery, sex trafficking, and the Daytrain trade.

For Condor, the growing popularity of Daytrain is a mystery. He does not understand why anyone on the outside would have an insatiable desire for Daytrain without having full access to The Well. But he accepts the fact that the Bionicans depend on the Daytrain trade and that The Well does not want him or anyone to tamper with it.

"The Well teaches us that the Greek users cannot have access to the sensitive areas of The Well. My job is to stop them if they try." This pronouncement makes him feel better because he knows it pleases The Well.

Condor remembers fondly participating in a Bionican raid led by his mentor, Simon Girty. They targeted an abandoned home with a huge private library and 20th Century oil paintings of men in business suits and women in formal evening gowns covered by cobwebs. When they entered the library, they came across books stacked to the ceiling covered with dust.

"Let's roll," Girty commanded his gang and then pulled books by the armful from the shelves and tossed two of these at Condor's feet – Ray Bradbury's *Fahrenheit 451* and Tom Wolfe's *Bonfire of the Vanities*.

Condor remembers Girty asking him, "What do you think these books have in common?" Condor doesn't know, shaking his head.

Girty answers for him. "So if you don't know, then

what do you think we should do with them?"

Wearing his best brown shirt, Condor knows the answer. "Burn them. Burn them all! They are all useless. Long live The Well!" And so the books are piled high and burned along with the house and everything in it.

At that time, Condor was still an adolescent and had so much to learn; he looked up to Simon Girty, who was then the chief hacker of the Bionicans. He admired Girty's British accent, acquired through his immersion in the BBC and recalls Girty telling him that the Greeks are useless and dangerous, and that it is every hacker's job to prevent them from learning the secrets in The Well.

Condor recalls Girty lecturing him. "Do not be fooled by their love for learning. What they want is power. The Greeks are far more dangerous than the Goths because the Goths can be bought, whereas the Greeks want to change how we think."

Condor is ashamed to acknowledge how much he once admired Simon Girty, who became branded as a traitor when he deserted Bionica. Condor certainly does not want to end up like him.

Taking a walk around the perimeter of Bionica, Condor imagines the bright, shiny buildings with balcony views of the ocean bay. Now all he sees are ruins – rubble and debris surrounding a few raggedy palm trees that survived. The pervasive stench of raw sewage is everywhere. When it comes to water and waste disposal, it is back to the basics in Bionica. Condor heard that the Greeks are shitting pretty with their new cesspools, viaducts, and indoor plumbing, but he is proud that the Bionicans have gone back to the basics – simple latrines and open sewers.

Condor looks among the ruins for relics of the past that he might have seen during his hallucinations or in his cryptic animated tattoos, but he never finds anything. He wanders back through a field overgrown with Daytrain plants that are just now giving off a pungent odor signaling that harvest time is near.

Bionicans do a lot of file sharing. Like "googlers" in the past, these social netwits "snorkel" each other to find content and then they download the content from the domains of others. This leaves precious little time for grooming each other for the fleas and lice that cover their bodies along with welts and scars from insect bites.

Condor looks up noticing the exchange between Dirty Nellie and Frizzy Jennie, who are wearing shifts they made from D-train hemp. Both users try to impress Condor with their Well throughput. Jennie, the younger of the two, flirts with Condor now that she has caught his eye. Condor looks away, recalling what had happened before when he lingered too long with her. He learned the hard way that prolonged sexual contact with users erodes his authority. Romantic intimacy is not on his playlist. He walks away as Nellie and Jennie continue to chatter.

"Please let me know what I need to know about breathing," Nellie asks her friend, as she adjusts her flip-flops and the straps on her hemp dress.

"Here are some lessons from Yogi at Tantric Central," Jennie replies. Guided by her virtual mentor, Nellie does her deep breathing exercises, her heavy breasts expanding with each breath to breach the top perimeter of her dress.

"Anyone want to trade?" Nellie puts out the word that she wants to share her "experience object" with other users. "I need someone to get some water." Old Nellie has trouble walking and for her, even the simplest chore is a source of pain.

Jennie steps forward. "I will help you, but I want you to let me in on the latest deal in Online Shopping Heaven."

"Why not ask Condor?" Nellie smiles, "I am not sure I can do that. The Online Shopping Heaven is even off-limits for me. Condor does not want too many of us poking around."

"Oh please," Jennie pleads in a girlish voice. "I need

to have access to make progress on my self-help work."

Nellie relents, "OK, I will do what I can for you this time. But, I will not do it for free, this will cost you."

Jennie smiles, "I know. I will not tell anyone else."

Nellie laughs, "I am doing this for you because you are nice. I do not, would not, do this for everybody."

On most days, Nellie and Jennie can be found walking the virtual Agora to ply their knowledge with their peers. Jenny and Nellie lecture each other on their respective subjects. It makes no difference if they share knowledge in the Agora; that is not the point of their online education since users have no way of applying what they know. The important thing is that they respond positively to the temporary knowledge that comes their way from the other users.

The Agora has dozens of forums where users expound on some subject area, such as Undressing for Success, without knowing anything about it. They do this because they are keeping The Well database alive through their continuous involvement. Without them, The Well dies.

"Use it or lose it," Nellie says within an earshot of Condor. "Like the Book People in *Fahrenheit 451*, we keep the knowledge alive."

It does not matter that Nellie never read *Fahrenheit 451*. The fact is that she does not read. She is merely repeating a Well "knowledge object." The old itch and scratch method, built into the system, determines which knowledge area needs attention and which knowledge needs to be sunsetted. After they retrieve content, users talk up the knowledge objects to increase their relevance. This gives the appearance that the information in the Well is current and up-to-date.

The topic shifts to Condor.

"He is my favorite," Jennie exclaims "But he is so quiet when he does *you know what* with his thing," she adds with a prudish blush.

Nellie agrees. "He is the only one who is not so cocksure about everything."

"Yes, the rest believe they know everything there is to know." Jennie points to her head and laughs. "But you know, there are a few tricks that I had to teach him, after dark."

"And the others just call us 'stupid users' – they have no respect, especially Phiberoptik, who tried to bite me from behind. And that female – Digi Diva, they say she once belonged to the G-spot Bikers. She was friendly with that vicious bitch, Gonorrhea. Can you imagine, women with jackboots? It is not womanly."

"I just *love* my crocs."

"And she has a thing for Condor."

"I cannot imagine he would go for a woman who likes to crack heads. I think that is a man's job."

"They brought her on because they want someone

who is willing to crack women as well as men. She is better at it than the guys."

"We better watch out. The guys tell us we are safe so long as we stay in Online Shopping Heaven. They have no respect."

"Condor is different. There is something in his eyes. He is so curious, so questioning...so manly."

Nellie laughs, "You should know. You spend enough time studying him using the abs app from The Well."

Jennie responds, "I think he is looking for something that he has not been able to find in The Well – it is as if he has come to the end of what he can know from it."

Condor notices two men who have stopped working to chat, and he cracks his whip in their direction.

Today it is Frank's and Bill's turn to bring the water, which they carry in large metal cans suspended on shoulder poles.

"Better get moving," Connor barks, "We need all the water we can get."

Condor inspects the drinking water by stirring it with a stick. It is unusually brown.

"Ugh!" Condor says showing his displeasure.

Frank replies, "That is all there was. There must have

been a storm."

This is a good excuse. Bionicans are always expecting bad weather even though the local climate is always sunny and dry.

"Look guys, if we drink this water, we are going to get sick, maybe even die."

"This water is all that we could find," Bill protests. "Can you not get special dispensation from The Well so that we can drink this stuff safely?"

Condor pauses for a moment to consider Bill's suggestion.

"Make sure that everyone who drinks this water is in good standing with The Well. Also make sure that they have taken enough Daytrain. So long as the users take it, we will be OK. The Well will keep them immune from disease. For those who lose contact, or who are not in good standing, their death will not be pretty."

Frank interrupts Condor, mimicking the sacrifice mantra from The Well.

"We all have to do our part for The Well. We have to be ready for the ultimate sacrifice for The Well," Frank says sarcastically, thumping his chest.

"When The Well is not happy, no one is happy," Bill adds his bit to this volley of bravado.

"Leave well enough alone," Frank finishes with a laugh. This is not the first time Frank and Bill have gone through this routine.

Condor does not like user humor but tolerates it. While other hackers would have punished Frank and Bill with a lash of the whip across their backs, Condor believes that his job as a hacker is to keep Bionica on an even keel, and this sometimes means turning a blind eye to the user's attempt at lame humor.

"What do you think humor is? A joke?" He cracks the whip above their heads.

"All right, all right for crying out loud," Frank protests. His pal, Bill, withdraws into obedience like a dog waiting for a bone. Within earshot, several Bionican children find some human bones.

"What is this?" a child asks, bringing a bone to his Mother, Una, who closes her eyes, scanning The Well for an answer.

"It is a femur bone from a human leg," she declares. "It belonged to one of our ancestors. Our ancestors are all around us; you should not play with them. It is disrespectful. Instead, listen carefully to what is inside you."

The child closes her eyes and tries to concentrate. "There are just a lot of chatbots in my head; I do not know which voice to listen to."

"You are too young to understand. Just keep on listening and there will be a voice just for you – your special voice.

After his shift, Condor continues his roving inspection tour through the ruins of Bionica. He visits the interiors of the gutted Santa Monica Place, once a shopping mall. As he passes the Mall, he sees several Bionicans inhabiting the empty, windowless stores along the garbage-strewn Mall promenade once famous for its juggling acts.

The users scurry off clattering their flip-flops as Condor cracks his whip after them. He continues on his rounds in the market area where users have set up their stalls. Two male users argue about their spots in the mall where they have displayed their scavenged goods, including tools, building materials, and rope. A group of female users show off the materials they found in an abandoned store. Since there are no outside customers willing to buy stuff from smelly Bionicans, the users just end up trading stuff with each other.

Condor walks down an alley where several users have put up shanties built out of found materials. Each is decorated with items taken from stores that were ransacked after the Great Plague annihilated the merchant class.

"I see you have doubled your collection of little plastic ponies," Condor picks up a yellow little pony that heads the lineup. "What will they do for us this month?"

"They are all about loyalty and kindness." Martha is beaming because she knows that she can get away with loving her little ponies without being hassled by The Well.

Condor smiles wanly and then passes by the next group of shanties. The first is stuffed with Disney souvenirs, another with plaques and trophies from Hollywood. There is a collection of t-shirts that promote charity runs to fight breast cancer, diabetes, and childhood obesity. He passes by an old woman who is rearranging her collection of sex toys by the bucket full. These are harmless enough.

Condor then stumbles upon the piece de resistance – a shanty decked with religious paraphernalia, as well as a heap of Christmas decorations featuring a line-up of Santas and reindeer. The owner of this budding religious shrine, Little Eddie, fusses with his nativity scene. He holds up to inspection a crucifix retrieved from his piles of religious articles, completely unaware of Condor standing over him,

"You better watch out!" Condor shouts at him.

Startled, Eddie looks up and says good-naturedly. "Hey, I know that tune. *You better watch out. You better not cry; you better not pout I am telling you why. Santa Claus is coming to town.*"

This catches the attention of The Well. Condor

knows what comes next – the dreaded Asshole Tattoo on Eddie's forehead – a scarlet red letter "A" followed by a trompe l'oeil hole oozing with bloody excrement.

His face turning red, Condor lifts the whistle hanging from his neck and blows it furiously three times, getting the attention of three burly users harvesting Detrain nearby.

"Get rid of that religious rubbish!" he orders the three men, who leap on top of Little Eddie's shrine and hack everything to pieces and toss them into the alley for everyone to see. They spare nothing – Mary and Joseph, Baby Jesus, and the Three Wise Men. They decapitate all of them, flinging their heads in the direction of the onlookers, who turn away, not wanting to be associated with any religious relics.

"*Nobody expects the Spanish Inquisition!* The next time we will have your head." Condor spits and wags his warning finger at the cowering Eddie, who slips away after the A-hole tattoo and its stench fade. Condor is sick of dealing with user nonsense and looks forward to the next brain purge that will help clear out user rubbish.

Condor keeps on walking north past the arcade of personal services. This time he passes on Touchy Feely, a new age massage parlor that specializes in *everything* from tip to toe. Feeling out of sorts, he comes across several stragglers hanging out on formerly stylish Montana Avenue. "You know damned well this area is off-limits for users," he yells, waving his arms. Only hackers are allowed north of Wilshire where the better people once lived.

Condor heads to his private headquarters at Our Lady of the Sea – an abandoned and repurposed Catholic church within shouting distance of the Promenade.

At the church's entrance is a vestibule with a stained-glass window depicting the figure of Christ, whose head is no longer there. The terrorists punched out a long time ago. Condor admires a stash of relics from the Cyber Era, including Bill Gate's personal Y2K t-shirt, the Lisa Apple mouse from Steve Jobs' first personal computer, and The Virtual Boy, which was the first portable 3D video game console developed and manufactured by Nintendo, and the Worlds of Wonder Julie Doll.

Then Condor inspects his favorite collection, bones – human bones – that he keeps hidden in a hidden ossuary. His plans to construct a full skeleton made up from the bones of all of the users whose bodies were left for the boneyard vultures to pick clean. Condor has so far managed to keep this taboo passion for bones a secret, even from the noses of his beloved three pigs.

Condor keeps three pet pigs in the chapel that he has named after ancient search engines – Google, Bing, and Yahoo – loyal pets who scamper up and down the church aisles looking for Condor, waiting for their turn to accompany him on his rounds. The three pigs are adept at locating users and finding things that Condor needs. This time, Condor picks Google to help him check up on his users.

"Let us see how things are going with the D-train," he mumbles to Google who acknowledges the command with a squeal and runs ahead of Condor as they make their way to the D-train depot where dozens of men, watched by a group of women, are unloading weed-like plants from an old truck that wheezes to a halt. As the men sort out the D-train that has been trucked in from Malibu, Gertrude steps forward as the leader of the group of four tasters – including Martha, Maria, and Theresa – to sample the flavor of today's load.

"What is the taste of the day?" Gertrude, a gaunt woman with long hair asks the other tasters "Please, anything but meat." They shout out possible flavors – including carrot bread, tofu, and flapjacks – while Theresa, an older woman with missing teeth, keeps quiet. The women keep on popping-up with words for foods that they have never eaten. After a few tries, Gertrude arrives at a consensus flavor, healthy broccoli. When Gertrude and the others complete this daily ritual, she always says the same thing, "After all - You are what you eat."

Seeing this, Condor and Google are satisfied that things are on track and looks on as Gertrude and her three colleagues continue to trip on food. Gertrude exclaims, "*They* were wrong, wrong, wrong, when it came to the food groups because they included meat." In agreement, Martha agrees while stroking her little pony. "Eating is a holistic spiritual exercise," she says, stroking her little yellow pony. Maria concludes the discussion by asserting her favorite bon mot, "Food and meditation - perfect together."

"Never mind food," says hefty Martha, interrupting Maria, "I just want to keep myself warm. Tasting food may be love, but to smell things is divine. I adore the smell of perfume and English soaps," she says with an air of authority that anyone should question since, in reality, she has no idea where England is. "Chanel No. 5," she exclaims seductively, "I wear five drops when I go to bed." To top Gertrude's virtual food admonition, she says with loud emphasis, "You are not just what you eat. You *are* what you smell."

Maria, whose ears are covered by charred golden earrings, contributes to the collective wisdom, "They say that Daytrain consumed with a sincere heart will prolong your life."

"How do we know that this is true? I have forgotten how old I am and how long my life has been. That is why I am always young again," says Teresa breaking her silence.

Gertrude snaps at her, "Shut up. You probably never knew. We all grow old before our time." Meanwhile, Condor, overhearing the squabbling among the women tasters, keeps looking at his wrist looking for a watch he never had.

"Whatever will happen next?" Teresa says, looking at Condor, who is no mood for romance.

In response, Condor says, "Stay happy. Emphasize the positive. Negators will die. Happy days are here again. Eat your Daytrain and you will be young forever. It is guaranteed."

Teresa mutters, "He is right. There is nothing more to talk about. When it comes to Daytrain, you feel what you eat. Happy thoughts mean happy meals. Sometimes I dream of steak and meatballs. That makes me all meat."

"You had better keep that to yourself; eating meat is not part of the Bionican way. The Well would not like to hear that in your thoughts." Condor says before leaving the scene with Google in tow.

CHAPTER 2
SAFEGUARDING THE WELL

Sitting around a table in an empty lot strewn with debris, Una, Sasha and Nancy care for the young ones while other women take turns extracting nectar from the Daytrain plants and processing the stalks, first into flour and then into dough for the baking of D-train bread. Jennie and Nellie who happen to walk by, join them. The constant crying of the infants provides a backdrop to the women's discussion regarding the challenges of raising children in Bionica.

Some of the older children are in the background playing. "Here we go, make it so," they grab their heads and fall to the ground, playing dead.

"It is just as well that they make a fuss because then we know that they are there," says Sasha, a young woman with a mustache, to her older companion, Nancy.

"If they are not acting up, they sometimes just vanish," Sasha says lowering her voice, referring to the disappearances of Bionican children over the past years.

"We need to have more, but we also have to watch out to make sure that the Greeks do not steal them. That is how they get their slaves," says Una, giving her daughter a protective hug. The child is still clinging to the human bone she found.

"We cannot use force alone to protect the children because that makes them rebellious. We have to teach them by example; they have to learn to keep quiet when necessary, like when the Greeks or even the Goths are out prowling. We cannot just depend on The Well to keep the children on the path."

"But what about the strays?" Sasha asks, "What do we do with them?"

Sasha is referring to the influx of the young bloods from the outside – needy kids from the LA basin as well as the privileged boys and girls who want nothing else in life but to experience Daytrain for kicks on the pretext of wanting to discover its secrets. Nancy knows that strays are needed since without the influx of young converts, the Bionican community would wither away.

"There is no birthright in Bionica; even the strays deserve a place on the path. The Well provides for all," she proclaims. "We are the mothers of us all. It is up to us to get all children to act responsibly," Nancy explains. "Kids have to learn that there is more to The Well than porn, music, and more porn."

"And the men do not help. The men are useless when it comes to teaching the children. They are nothing but pigs," Sasha grumbles.

"Except for fathering children, we do not need men. We can learn from The Well although everything that we need to know. I would rather have a Daytrain high than an orgasm with a man any day," says Nancy. She laughs out loud and continues in a lower voice, "The Well entrusts to us what is most important and it leaves the rest to the men."

The women continue their volley of complaints, knowing full well what comes next.

"The Well is chauvinistic."

"Long live women's liberation!"

"Sisterhood is powerful!"

"Down with that token tootsie," Nancy laughs, referring to Digi Diva.

"The Well cannot make us feel any worse than we already do."

Jennie, who has kept quiet during this medley of complaints, finally pipes up. "But Condor is different. I think he cares."

Nellie laughs, "I should know; women love him too much, but he has some surprises coming. He has no idea who we are."

There is a long silence and then the women act to forestall trouble. They shout in unison, "All is well that ends well. All is well that ends well. Three cheers for The Well." The women get their shot of endorphins now that they are off the women's liberation bandwagon.

At the end of every lunar month, the Bionicans gather on the Mall around the sacred obelisk to begin the maintenance process, purging all useless and unwanted memories shared through The Well. This process is done separately for men and women. Today is the brain-drain day for men. Mikvah for women is next week.

Before the purge, the men line up around a water truck used for irrigating the D-train fields. This Great Wash is their only opportunity for individual hygiene. Each man is hosed down, and the men wait until they are dried so that the purge can begin.

Taking command, Condor juts out his chin and announces, "As you know, we all have to come clean; we must eliminate what is impure, improper and archive what is unimportant. I will tune in on each of you to make sure that the cleansing process works well. If a problem occurs, raise your right hand so that I can help you tune in, turn on, and drop out as required. Understood?"

Shortly after all the Bionican men nod yes, the antivirus cleansing begins. Eyes are closed as each mind communes with The Well to clear the network connections and the inner memory reserves that inevitably permeate consciousness; everyone knows that dirty thoughts make dirty links, which make for dirty minds.

This time, however, things do not go smoothly. Little Eddie is in trouble again, just days after Condor's men destroyed his religious shrine. Condor has been expecting problems with him and is convinced that something has to be done now that the scarlet A-hole tattoos are not only on his forehead, but also all over his body. The stench is unbearable. Condor tries to prevent a plumbing catastrophe by working with Little Eddie to shut down the faulty connections, but that does not work. Little Eddie starts to moan. Seeing that he cannot save him, Condor jumps into action to prevent his stench and pain from seeping back into the network; his skin starts to disappear as the tattoos take over completely, indicating fatal errors that would be bad for everybody on his network. Condor knows all too well that if he allows Little Eddie to go beyond the breaking point, he and all the other Bionican purgers would soon be covered with A-hole tattoos.

Little Eddie screams on top of his lungs, "And God said, let us make man in our image, after our likeness. And let them have dominion over the fish of the sea, and over the fowl of the air, and over the cattle, and over all the Earth, and over every creeping thing that creepeth upon the Earth." Condor recognizes that this is heresy and that any invocation of God goes against the evolved Bionican dogma that rejected Unitarianism in favor of Eco Utilitarianism.

Accessing his administrative responsibility, Condor whispers the patch words into Little Eddie's ears, hoping that this will work since he has always had a soft spot for Little Eddie because of their shared left-handedness. He repeats this patch over again hoping that the passage from Genesis will go away.

"At least introduce a note of irony if you cannot get off the topic," Condor whispers. But the patch does not work. Quaking and shaking, the Little Stinker Eddie continues, *"And God blessed them, and God said unto them, be fruitful, and multiply, and replenish the Earth, and subdue it: and have dominion over the fish of the sea, and over the fowl of the air, and over every living thing that moveth upon the Earth."*

As the scripture gets pushed into The Well, the other purgers become increasingly agitated. "Stop him before we are all lost," someone cries. Condor knows he has to act quickly to avoid a descent into chaos; the longer he hesitates, the more dangerous Little Eddie's incantations become. Condor can feel the scarlet nausea growing inside him; this tells him that he must act decisively.

In a panic, he summons the Bionican mission statement, "Allow them to do no harm to the general good," which has been implanted in his mind since birth; like all babies, his tiny brain was originally connected to The Well through crude electro-signalers in the birthing labs that were popular before Cybergeddon. Since The Well was designed to save the earth from man's imminent destruction, it has no tolerance for any religious doctrine that justifies man's dominion over the environment.

Condor's intervention has no effect on the delirious Little Eddie who continues his religious rant, *"And God said, behold, I have given you every herb bearing seed, which is upon the face of all the Earth, and every tree, in which is the fruit of a tree yielding seed; to you it shall be for meat."* The word "meat" causes paroxysms on the verge of pandemonium because the knowledge networks in The Well teach that rampant meat eating destroyed the planet. *We are meat. We do not eat ourselves. Therefore, we do not eat meat,* so instructs The Well. Knowing this, and with his increasing helplessness to stop the purging network overload, Condor's nausea creeps up to his throat from his stomach and he fears that the dreaded A-hole tattoo will come for him next.

Condor's meta-messaging safety system reminds him about a key imperative of The Well. Those who stray from the path are a threat to the Earth and must be eliminated. The Well allows for errors that it can correct, as long as the proper connection can be maintained. However, once a user error causes grave, uncorrectable disruption and disharmony, the connection as well as the user must be terminated to preserve the safety of the Bionican community.

Unable to stop himself, Little Eddie drones on, *"And to every beast of the Earth, and to every fowl of the air, and to everything that creepeth upon the Earth, wherein there is life, I have given every green herb for meat, and it was so."* The crazed freak's eyes roll around in their sockets, unaware of the fatal errors his recited Genesis passages are causing.

"He just wants to be a martyr who blurs the line between church and state, and knowledge and faith," a terrified user yells. Another user yells out, while making the sign of the cross, "If we do not stop him now, they will take over again, and they will try to destroy The Well."

"We are helpless without the safety of The Well," another user cries.

Condor is well aware of the dangers of Evangelical Creationism, the most virulent form of ancient religious knowledge. The evangelicals did not help matters during the Great Plague when they welcomed Armageddon with open arms as the long-awaited Rapture, where the good would rise into a promised land and the bad would burn alive in the streets for eternity.

Seeing that Condor has lost control of Little Eddy, who is now laying supine, a backup group of hackers race towards Little Eddie with a deep-red cushion ringed with tassels, and carefully place it under his babbling head. The cushion is used to execute users who go haywire and threaten to infect The Well networks – an especially dangerous proposition during the lunar purges. Knowing that he has no time to lose, Condor holds the Emergency Hammer that is part of every purge; he examines its jagged metallic edge, and is confident that it will do the job. Carefully he taps into The Well and recalls the protocols for successful user elimination: 1. Crack open the user's head at the precise spot that liberates the brain from the parietal bone. 2. Send the disable message *free at last* directly from the affected brain to The Well, thereby disabling the distress signals being experienced by the other users. 3. Disconnect the brain by severing the brain from the spinal cord.

The first part of the elimination protocol, cracking the bone skull properly, takes special skill and lots of practice. Cracking it incorrectly and damaging the brain make it impossible to send the *free at last* disable messages. A botched crack can result in the destruction of all the brains on the local neural network, or in this case, all the Bionican men who are participating in the Lunar purge. So, in short, Condor knows that the consequences of a botch would be disastrous. Luckily, fully certified hackers go through extensive training on how to successfully sever damaged neural connections using sacrificial pigs as their subjects. Condor knows how to proceed.

As the hackers gently role Eddie from supine to prone, he continues to quote from *Genesis*, "*Thus, the heavens and the Earth were finished, and all the host of them.*" After the hackers position Eddie's head, Condor raises the Emergency Hammer with both hands and bashes the user's parietal bones at the sagittal suture with a sweeping downward motion to his head; the blood spurts out of the skull, exposes the brain, covers Condor's face and spills down his hands.

Miraculously, Little Eddie rises to his feet and extends his arms to the heavens, muttering his final statement on Earth, *"Father, forgive them for they know not what they do,"* and then collapses into the waiting arms of Condor, who holds him up momentarily and then lets him drop to the ground. Condor attaches two wires from his portable data surge to Little Eddie's exposed brain and types – Z:\>MOUNT>freeatlast.exe_. Then he reaches down around the base of brain and grabbing onto the spinal cords, yanks the brain out as it pulses still.

A wave of relief flows out to the connected users with the *free at last* command as the blow to Little Eddie's brain gets equated with a decisive blow against the spread of "tautological monotheism" through The Well. Following a chorus of cheers, one user steps forward to speak for the group. "Oh thank you, great hacker Condor. May your aim always stay true should this happen again." Silently, the users realize that this could happen to any of them. They know that the penalty for transgressing The Well is death and so they are grateful to Condor for helping them walk the straight and narrow.

Shaken, Condor reassures everyone that justice has been served. "Extremism in the name of a healthy planet is no vice; no pain is too great to save a wild creature. Let us plant a tree where evil strikes. It is time to move on. The Earth needs you." Condor exults in the completion of this mission, perhaps taking more pride and pleasure in the eradication of Little Eddie than is the norm.

"Let us recycle his body," one user exclaims. And so, assisted by those hackers who came to his rescue, Condor loads Little Eddie's body on a small wagon and pushes it to the Bionican Boneyard at Silicon Beach. They toss it over the Great Firewall, which was constructed out of giant Hummer transport vehicles that were torched by the Earth Warriors, a group of eco-terrorists, who were devoted to zero carbon emissions. Little Eddie's broken body lands under the gaze of swirling vultures and on top of the thousands of the picked-clean bones, of those who ran afoul The Well before him. Within seconds, the waiting vultures swoop down for their next meal. Little Eddie was not the first, nor would he be the last who would have to die to protect the safety of The Well.

"If there is no discipline, we are all lost," Condor says to himself. "And even the birds have a right to eat. We can take from Nature only if we give back to Nature. Everything that goes around comes around." Condor repeats the cliché that has ricocheted in his mind since it was planted in his baby brain. Soon all that remains of Little Eddie are his scattered bones piled on top of the Bionican bone heap. Condor cannot wait to add a few of Eddie's bones to his growing skeleton collection.

After the messy purge, Condor meets with his fellow hackers to conduct a post- mortem on the latest sacrifice for the protection of the integrity of The Well.

"I heard that he was going to recite the entire Old Testament, from *Genesis* onwards. It is a good thing you stopped him, or the thought contagion might have included the New Testament," says fast-talking toothless Phiberoptik, putting his arm around Condor's back. Phiberoptik – lanky and gaunt-faced, bald on top, with a beard that comes straight down to his waist – always seems to have the right thing to say.

Draper, a skinny hacker of few words, joins in, "You are one hell of a guy, Condor – just one clean blow and the breach was essentially over." Although Draper is not fat, he has a blemished and dimpled round face with tiny features for a man his size.

New to the squad, Digi Diva earned her stripes by dispatching a female runaway user two months ago. She flashes her buckteeth as she compliments Condor. "It is a job and someone has to do it," she chirps and slaps him a high five. Condor is feeling much better about how he handled Little Eddie.

"I am pleased with the endorsement, but we cannot afford to dispatch too many more, or our population will go subcritical," Condor responds with measured self-righteousness. "We have to wait for new recruits before we purge again."

Jimmy the Greek says nothing. He can keep silent because everyone knows he knows the odds about practically everything. Jimmy is of medium height and has a blonde curly beard that bounces off his breast. He rarely cracks a smile. The hackers like Jimmy because as an ex-Greek he knows what the Greeks are thinking, and when they might attack next. There is sometimes the suspicion that he has not abandoned his Greek loyalties and is, in fact, a spy. Still, The Well accepted him as a hacker and as a trusted member of the squad.

Pengo puts the best possible spin on things. He is very tall and tends to crane his head down so that people can hear what he has to say. His skin is dark brown. Droplets of sweat on his brow glisten when he turns toward the sun. Sometimes he looks you straight in the eye; other times, both his mind and eyes wander. He is a good-natured, task-oriented hacker with a lot of patience. Pengo also loves a good cliché, especially those related to manliness, like "standing tall," and "man the torpedoes."

"This," Pengo says with the conviction that this statement is his and his alone, "is as good as it gets." Pengo is keen on self-help. "Hey guys, do want to go over the seven habits of highly successful people?" he proposes.

The other hackers groan good-naturedly.

Phiberoptik pipes in, "I would be happy to hear about Steven Covey if you all are willing to let me sing the best of Abba and tell you about their wonderful country, Sweden, and the history of its Kings and Queens. Or, I can give you a tour of all the different neighborhoods of 18th Century Stockholm."

The rest of the hackers laugh at Phiberoptik's offer. Laughing the loudest is pock-faced Draper, who is the tech guru constantly running vintage code from the 20th Century computer revolution, grooving on the intricacies of software development

"Now what about you," Digi Diva says to Jimmy the Greek, "why do you not ever try to impress us and quote us some statistics from the past, just for the fun of it."

Digi Diva perversely modifies her request, "What about statistics from today?"

Jimmy is annoyed, "You know the answer to that. There are no current statistics. We no longer know anything about the world today. Make no bones about it; that is why we have to safeguard the past."

Digi begs to differ. "You all say you have a special relationship with The Well. That may be true, but it takes teamwork to keep things going. We have to look ahead."

"That is all well and good. But we hardly have enough time to keep a lid on things." Jimmy the Greek replies agitated.

Condor, who has not said much in this exchange, uses Jimmy's comment to expound on his pet concern – The Greeks.

"We must protect The Well from the Greeks. If we do not, they will use information from The Well to develop weapons of mass destruction. They may tell you that they will not make the same mistakes again because of their devotion to ancient wisdom based on their books, but do not be fooled. They cannot stand us and they do not like the way we smell. But, they love our Daytrain and keep on sending us their unhappy children, hoping that they will become users hooked on D-train, who will betray us by giving their Greek parents what they want, total access to The Well."

"And why is that?" Jimmy feeds Condor the line that will conclude the rant.

"The Greeks understand that knowledge is power. They want our knowledge so that they can have the power to control our future. They want the secrets of The

Well and they want complete control over our Daytrain."

"*That is* for sure," Pengo says. This gets a laugh from the group.

"And they want our children."

"We sure dropped the ball when those kids disappeared," Digi says.

"The Goths probably sold them to the Greeks." Eyeing Jimmy, Draper adds," You should know, you were raised by them."

Jimmy looks away, not wanting to discuss his past.

"Nothing we can do now," Pengo sighs.

Condor does not say anything. Everyone knows Condor fathered the kids that disappeared, but discussing his prolific paternity is taboo. Besides he cannot tell whom to trust anymore. Things like Little Eddie reciting *Genesis* do not just happen. They have to come from somewhere or someone – probably Simon Girty. Only a hacker could program that information into a user.

It is a full moon, time for the hackers to take stock of the users. Together they drink from a common pitcher filled with mead, one of the last pleasures still allowed by The Well. Jimmy the Greek is off in a corner consulting his beads so that he can understand what he needs to think about next.

The hackers gather together into a circle. They raise their arms skyward to invite The Well to talk to them. After an interminable pause, The Well tunes in. This time, the message from The Well is different. "Beware, one of you will betray the movement. Who will it be?" The hackers look at each other nervously, wondering what is going on.

"Yes, one of you will betray the movement," The Well continues. "There is no way of predicting who this will be or how it will be done. But, it will be done."

All the hackers know that if they ever got caught betraying The Well, the penalty would be death by disconnection and good old-fashioned head cracking. It is the duty of every hacker to destroy any other hacker who betrays the cause. Contrary to the rule that allows one hacker to disconnect a user, the decision to destroy a hacker has to be unanimous among all Bionican hackers.

Feigning innocence, Digi Diva wonders, "Why would anyone want to betray The Well?" There is grumpy silence. Everyone knows that she and Girty once had an affair.

Pengo shoots back, "You of all people should know. Your renegade hacker, Simon Girty, betrayed The Well and he got away with it, maybe with some help from you."

Simon Girty still holds the record for the largest number of cracked user heads. With the help of the Goths, he escaped from Bionica when it became apparent that he had overstepped his authority by committing unauthorized killings of users in an attempt to disrupt The Well.

"I tried to stop him. She doesn't want to talk about the real reason for Girty's defection – Gonorrhea – leader of the G-spot Femmes and estranged daughter of Olin, the chief warlord of the Goths. Digi had introduced Girty to her, much to her later regret.

"I am sorry I had anything to do with him, but I was young then," Digi says looking away embarrassed. "Now he is with the dirty knights," she says, referring to secretive bandits who, in league with the Christians, are disrupting the Bionican trade and jeopardizing their food shipments.

The affair Girty had with Gonorrhea after he ditched Digi Diva, helped him to discover his inner sadist. Unlike Digi, the wild and crazy Gonorrhea was impressed by his bravado and applauded when he told her about decapitating a user on the spot for minor trespasses that were correctable. When his unbridled cruelty came to light, Girty fled from Bionica to catch up with Gonorrhea. Having burned his bridges with The Well, he was hell-bent on bringing The Well down

This was not news to anyone. Every time the hackers meet, they denounce Simon Girty and swear to kill him if the opportunity arises.

Without thinking, Condor blurts out, "Someday I

will go north to The Valley to find that dirty cyber punk and slay him to make him pay for his sins." This declaration surprises the others because it is not customary for any hacker to leave the Bionican community, no matter what.

Jimmy the Greek stops consulting his beads and looks up at Condor, hesitating before he speaks.

"Condor, though you are a valiant warrior and a loyal defender of The Well, the odds are against your maintaining purity of mind if you ever leave Bionica – even for the noble purpose of killing Simon Girty," warns Jimmy. "Without us there are no guarantees."

"OK, let us accentuate the positive," says Condor. "We must remember that the real purpose of this hacker gathering is self-development. Today was a difficult day. Somehow Little Eddie was corrupted with words from *Genesis*, and then The Well told us that there is a traitor among us. Tomorrow let us lighten things up when we get together for some badly needed fun." The hackers clap and cheer *hoorah* in support.

The next day, Condor and his hacker buddies gather around for a social event, free of users, in the restricted Miramar Hotel lobby. Condor takes his place in one of the many dilapidated armchairs as a cloud of dust puffs up from beneath him.

"I guess we can start when the dust settles," Condor remarks while the others snicker. Condor announces, "It is time for the dream machine."

"What is it this time?" asks Pengo, his arm raised, ready to make a suggestion.

"You had your turn the last time," Condor replies.

"Maybe this time we can do something educational, maybe a documentary about The Well when it was created in 20th Century Sausalito as a cluster of electronic villages," Pengo suggests.

The rest of the group is silent. Jimmie the Greek yawns.

"What about a visit to Ancient Greece and Ancient Rome?" Jimmie asks to no one in particular.

Digi Diva is offended by this suggestion. "Everyone knows that the ancient world is off-limits. If we start going there, we will only be playing into the hands of the Greeks. Besides, The Well only has clips from old Hollywood movies."

Phiberoptik clears his throat to get attention. "I wonder what else is available in the premium entertainment channels of The Well. Maybe there are some important things that we need to know that The Well forgot to teach us?"

Digi Diva, opening up a can of worms, wonders.

"Does anyone here know how all this in Bionica got started?"

Pengo cautions, "I am sure everyone knows that Bionica started with a good reason. That was the first thing – a good reason. Before that there was something called the Universal Genome Project that reduced every living thing and every person to DNA. This led to the use of genetic algorithms to incorporate technology into physiology. Scientists discovered that people were just like some birds. In fact, they discovered that there was hardly a genetic difference between the crow family (corvids) and the parrot family (psittacines); and that these birds share certain instinctive and cognitive traits with us humans (hominin clade)."

Phiberoptik interrupts, "The Well says that, just like birds, we should imprint people with knowledge that would last a lifetime."

"No more teaching or learning through life; instead everyone is imprinted and connected to The Well, and everything that anyone needs to know is always online." Digi Diva exults.

"Just like birds," Draper says, prancing around the room while flapping his arms.

"If you understand flight so well, what prevents you from flying?" Phiberoptik teases him.

Pengo laughs, but then continues to kiss The Well's virtual ass. "The Well is great. We can send and receive information through The Well. We can tell The Well what we are doing, and what we need, and The Well responds. Our brains are so much better because of The Well. We must remember: *a mind is a terrible thing to waste."*

"It is the collective unconscious realized in our neural networks," Digi Diva exclaims, "and today that is where we are. Here, at the height of our achievements, there is no place to go, nor more resources to exploit, and no more errors to make. We have achieved the singularity. Everything good is unified," she says in a tone that indicates that she has said this many times before in search of the endorphins she craves.

Hanging in the lobby of the Miramar is a life-sized digitized portrait of Raymond Kurzweil, who winks every time singularity is mentioned. The last time she made him wink ten times is when she recited ad libitum the ten digital wonders of the world associated with that term. This time Digi, crunching her teeth in frustration, restrains herself from singing the praises of Raymond, who only winks once because Draper steps in to take the floor. "Except we cannot go backwards," Draper asserts with a schoolmaster's bravura. "This is the end of the line," he says, treading on thin philosophical ice. "All we have to our names is a huge..." Draper pauses in mid-sentence, feeling a sudden pain in his head inflicted by The Well as a warning sign. "Database," he still manages to blurt out. "Yes, all we have is a database. Otherwise the game is over."

Chastened by the pain, Draper is careful about what he says next. The Well does not want him or anyone to admit that its system no longer generates new knowledge. Its database carefully selects knowledge from the past and hides or eliminates controversies and ambiguities.

"To have something that is new you have to know what is old. It is our connection to The Well that restores our faith," Draper says. This statement, while not exactly pleasing to The Well, is ambiguous enough that it eases his pain. So Draper suggests they sing the praises to The Well. Together they sing off-key:

The Well's got rhythm.

The Well's got music.

Who could ask for anything more?

Old man trouble I do not mind him.

You will not find him around my door.

The Well's got starlight.

The Well's got sweet dreams. Who could ask for anything more?

The more the hackers praise the virtues of The Well, the better they feel. They start by saying something mildly heretical and then shift gears to say something praiseful. The Well, which at first penalizes their brains with shocks of pain, always appreciating mid-point corrections, rewards the hackers by increasing the neural endorphin flow that compensates for the original pain. At the end of this passive-aggressive routine, The Well offers extra doses of neural endorphins as the reward for toeing the line.

"Sure, we have intellectual freedom up to a certain point, but it is an illusion that we have to keep to ourselves. We are at the mercy of a system that we cannot understand," Condor intones, trying to keep the discussion within bounds.

"The Well is a work in progress and that we all play an important role in making it work," Digi Diva says as she smiles at Condor with a seductive wink. Condor admires the tone Digi's maxillary sinuses lend to her voice; it adds a certain charm to her buckteeth.

"Yes, we have to pick up the pieces because the scientists and engineers who built The Well did not finish the job."

"The Great Plague changed things. The system went down." Condor looks at Draper to see what he has to say.

Draper pauses and then mutters. "Maybe it is all for the better. The Plague got rid of a lot of useless people who were a burden on the environment. We can't allow that to happen again."

Condor gives Draper a friendly nod and then tries to end the discussion. "We do not know everything that is going on in the world. All we know is what we have in our heads."

To which Digi Diva says, "Does it matter? What do we care so long as we can travel through space and time with just our minds? We should be grateful for that." This thought makes her feel better as The Well gives her a generous jolt of endorphins.

Pengo and Phiberoptik try to get things on a lighter note.

"Remember when we time traveled to ancient Egypt riding a camel to the pyramids?"

"Or when we had front row seats at a medieval joust?"

"Or when we flew in a B29 during World War Two?"

Digi interrupts the string of memories, laughing. As the only female in the group, she has strived to be one of the boys, pretending to be on board with the male-oriented fantasy trips.

"Ah, it is still a man's world," she says. "Sure it is just pyramids, jousts and B29 bombers, until it is not. When you guys get into full gear with your fantasy connections to The Well, there are always the trips to brothels, exotic pleasure islands with Gauguin, and all those classic, disgusting porn movies from the so-called Golden Age of Porn." Frustrated with the male-oriented playlist of her colleagues, she continues, "Remember what happened when I suggested, just for the hell of it, that we go to a fashion show from the 1950s, or visit a literary salon in Paris from the 1920s?"

The guys groan.

Sensing that things were getting out of control, Condor tries to close the discussion. "We have to remember that these fantasy experiences are just permutations of cinematic images stored in The Well through the network of all users. Sometimes trips have to be cut short because of vestigial intellectual property restrictions, like those in place for all the Disney properties."

The group groans upon hearing Condor use fancy words that are obviously not his.

"We all know that The Well collection is limited, but that is all we have," Digi concludes. "And because that is all we have, it makes our job protecting it all that more important." The Well gives Digi still another boost of neural endorphins.

After Digi has the last word grinning like an idiot, Condor raises his right hand to signal to end the party, even though the customary fun never began. As so often before, the nerdy hackers got hung up on talking about experience rather than taking part in it.

At the end of their communion, most in the group go to their private rooms on the concierge floor of the Miramar, a rare privilege for the hard work that they do. Condor, on the other hand, sets off to spend some quiet time with his pigs – Google, Bing, and Yahoo – at his nearby church hideout. On his way, he thinks about his fellow hackers and realizes that their world is forever limited to The Well. If push ever comes to shove, the hackers will acquiesce and take comfort in The Well. They will never venture out to see if they are right or if they are wrong. They will never see if there are any other riches in the world that could be exploited to help The Well become even better than it already is. Thinking about these things leads Condor to see that sometimes limits are a good thing, and sometimes they are not. Thankfully he was not online with The Well when he ventured these critical thoughts, because it is likely that he would have triggered a fault in the security network if he had connected.

Condor arrives at the church, happy to be with his pigs, which approach him wanting to be fed. After giving them slop from a bucket, he sits at the pipe organ and goes through the motion of hitting the keys to make sounds. But this organ has been silent as long as he can remember, and so this instrument makes no sound besides the thump of his fingers against the keys. When he tunes into The Well and requests organ music, he is unable to access any. Apparently, organ music is not on his playlist. Google tries to help out by oinking when Condor hits the keys, but it is no good. Even The Well is useless because it has a ban on organ music and does not support pig vocalization.

Alone, Condor starts to feel the onset of depression. He has no one to talk to about his organ, not even Digi Diva, who is the understanding sort. So instead he resorts to internal cheerleading by talking to himself.

"I cannot let any of them find out how I feel. They believe that turning to The Well can cure everything. I know that is not true, and I have got to find a way out of this. If they discover how I feel, I could wind up like Simon Girty, who went over the top in his user killings because of his doubt and depression. It did not help when the Bionicans blinded his mother, Athena, because of her stubborn opposition to virtual enjoyment and her insatiable desire for consumer goods.

"I am nothing like Simon Girty," Condor says aloud, but deep down he knows better. It felt good each time he cracked the skull and severed the spine cord of users who ran afoul with The Well. "I only kill for the greater good," Condor proclaims whenever he feels pleasure at administering death. Each time he kills, the pleasure increases during the act, followed by a period of depression that he reverses by thinking more about the enjoyment of killing. Having the power to take away the most precious possession of a sentient being allows him to assert a singular pleasure of his own. He imagines users as useless sheep in a useless dream in which he uses an assault rifle to mow down several at once, exulting in the peace that comes after the deed is done.

"I will not ever do that," he assures himself. "I am a professional hacker. They imprinted me for this work when I was a baby for this work, and that is why I am the leader of my squad. I will remove any and all pleasure from performing my duty. And I will only do what is necessary and demanded of me by The Well." But, Condor knows that the day will come when he will be expected to kill again, just like he had to do with Little Eddie, and he thinks about the unbridled pleasure that this will bring.

Exasperated, Condor lies down and tries to stop thinking about killing users. After a brief silence, a strange woman, shimmering above him, appears to him in a hallucination.

"I can see your struggle. Come to the sea. I am waiting for you there."

Just near the edge of Bionica, Condor hikes down a rugged path through sandy cliffs overlooking the ocean. Faded and dilapidated danger signs warn hikers to stay off. Ignoring the signs, Condor continues to climb down the path. Halfway down the cliff, Condor trips on a wire cage that spills open and lets loose a torrent of human skulls that fall in a long row of piles along the trail. He takes cover to avoid being hit. As Condor reaches the beach, and the fog clears up and the crashing surf sounds intensify, he notices that some of the fallen skulls are formed into a giant a peace sign. Confused by the symbolism, Condor continues to walk along the beach and approaches a pile of large boulders on the edge of the sea. He sits on one of them, cradling his head in his arms a few minutes later, he gets up to remove his clothes.

Condor sees a figure emerging the remaining patch of fog. It is an old woman. "Do you not recognize me?" She asks. "Look at your tattoos."

Condor stares at the tattoos on his forearm and sees that they are morphing into the face of the same woman he has just met in a hallucination. She appears to become progressively younger as she speaks. The image of the woman in the tattoo mimics the same change. Soon there is only a young woman who stands before him.

"I am Julia," she says. "You should know me."

"Mother?" Condor asks.

She ignores his question and stares at him, pausing before she speaks.

"I want you to listen carefully. There are great things in store for you. You are to go on a quest. Listen to the dwarf. Listen to..." Her voice fades out as she disappears just as quickly as she appeared. Blinking into the sun, Condor looks around and all he sees is a beach. There is nothing else. Terrified, Condor comes to his senses, puts on his clothes and goes home.

Walking among the Bionican ruins, Condor watches the circling vultures and pines for the opportunity to satisfy the bird's appetite. For a long time, Condor has spent his spare hours wandering aimlessly among the ruins of his youth, connecting to The Well to learn about all the different places. While walking, he spouts his tattoo-inspired phrases to himself in the hopes that someday he will fully understand them and what happened to all the people in Bionica, but instead his mind goes in circles like the flight path of a vulture. He wishes he could fly away somewhere, away from the pain of knowing what has come to pass in the wake of the dark and violent past. Maybe there is some brighter place where he could go, a place that is not touched by the destruction in Bionica that he sees everywhere. His frustration clouds his yearning for peace. He feels the strength of his anger rise in his arms and braces himself for an opportunity to raise his fists and to strike someone down, anybody who would get in his way. He is unable to shake these feelings even after he returns to the Mead House to be with the other hackers.

"What is on your mind," Digi asks him, noticing his ill-defined angst.

Although she has grown to admire and even savor Condor, there are aspects of his recent demeanor that trouble her. He does not answer right away, but then replies.

"A lot of things that you do not understand," he responds.

"Try me."

"What would happen if we gave up, if we allowed our secrets to flow into the world? Would that matter anymore?"

"You know we have no way of knowing this; our sworn duty is to uphold," Digi reminds Condor.

"Uphold what?"

"The secrets of The Well."

"What are these secrets? Why do they matter?" Condor says.

"If we knew what those secrets were, we might not uphold our sworn duty."

Condor pauses a moment and then gives in, "I see your point."

Digi slaps him on the back and grins, giving full view of her full moist lips and sparkling teeth. He feels her full bosoms brush against him and tries to imagine the shape of her sternum and the flow of her ribs as they connect to her thoracic spine. Condor recoils, afraid of what might happen if he follows Simon Girty down this path. Digi tries again, this time putting her hand chastely on his scapula in a coy display of affection that she hopes does not go unnoticed. Condor removes her hand and slaps her on the back.

"You are one of us – one of the guys. I can count on you," he grunts with reluctance.

"I wish I could be *more to you* than that," she says. "You may think I am all wet, but to tell you the truth, I really am. I have that *thing* for you."

Condor feels uncomfortable hearing this, and instinctively tries to protect his from hers. "I am tired; I better pack off. Remember what happened to the last guy that you became *more to*? He got lost. I do not want to become another Simon Girty."

As he leaves, Digi looks on and shrugs her shoulders. It was worth a try, and she thinks she will have another shot.

Condor has a recurring dream. It begins in splendor and sunshine – a formal garden party in a mansion overlooking the sea. People are dressed to the nines, men in black tuxedos and women in long formal gowns, clothing that no one wears anymore. Condor is stark naked, but none of the guests pay attention to him as he moves through the crowd to a large patio area where several men, wearing gardenias in their lapels, vie for hors d'oeuvres served by the help,

Seated around a small round table, three young women in white dresses nurse brightly colored drinks. They are trying on each other's hats and giggling when they nod and wave their approval to Condor as he passes them. Nearby, three young men, presumably their husbands, are trying to get laughs by imitating animals that are now officially extinct – the lion, the tiger, and a polar bear. Then they take on the roles of Dorothy cohorts, the Cowardly Lion, the Tin Man and the Scarecrow in "The Wizard of Oz."

"Do you think we will come across any animals?" the Lion asks shivering.

"Only animals that eat straw," replies Tin Man.

Then the three prance arm-in-arm chanting, *"Lions and tigers, and bears, oh my. Lions and tigers, and bears, oh my. Lions and tigers, and bears, oh my."*

This charade falls flat. Unimpressed, the three women turn around and feign laughter. They would rather watch Condor standing there nude in full salute and size him up, blushing and gossiping behind their tilted hats. Condor, feeling self-conscious, moves along. But he knows that his nakedness is what ensures his survival and the survival of his future progeny.

As he continues through the dream, Condor sees two males wearing tuxes leaning against a stonewall overlooking the sea below. Barely audible under the pulsating sounds of the ocean surf, they sound like adults talking about investments and trade. However, when Condor takes a closer look, he realizes that they are only boys playing adults; their precociousness is prefabricated. Both of the boys have brain implants that feed them data. The implants enable the boys to process data without understanding what it is that they are discussing as they move from topic to topic. The boys stop talking when Condor approaches them.

One of the boys, the younger of the two, asks, "Where are your clothes? You are not one of those eco-terrorists, are you?"

Drink in hand, an old woman in a long black dress appears from the crowd. She assures the boys, "Do not worry. He is just on a quest. He is one of you." She takes Condor's arm and leads him away to a quiet spot, clasps his hand and looks straight into his eyes.

"Is everything all right?" she whispers to him, "because if everything is not all right, *make it so!*" Condor recognizes the phrase, and he knows that this is the same phrase that the eco-terrorists used to trigger the deadly *makeitso.verb.exe* computer virus that killed off everyone with implants, except for the virus-protected Bionicans.

Telling Condor to step aside, she heads toward the

crowd and shouts at them, "Is everything all right? If not, then make it so." No one responds – a dead silence, as if someone has just killed the electricity and extracted all movement and sound from the air. She shouts again, "Is everything all right? If not, then make it so!" Her shrill, menacing tone has a chilling effect.

One cries out in disbelief, "I am being hacked and I cannot access my account with my password." Others blurt out password letters and numbers in desperate attempts to reverse the brain attack. Running around wildly, several men, their arms flailing, overturn furniture and tear down the artwork that graced the plush estate, including the portrait of a young woman that Condor thinks looks just like his Mother. The three young women, who only minutes earlier had admired each other's hats, giggling and gossiping together, lose their balance and, writhing in pain, cry out in one final gasp before slumping to the ground. Condor runs to them and makes a half-hearted attempt to help them, but seeing them foam at the mouths, unable to breathe, he turns to the spot where the two young boys had been and sees that they, too, are under attack. The boys' brains pour out of their skulls through their ears, noses, and mouths.

The old woman shrieks at the convulsing crowd cackling with glee, "Your virus protection is gone. Your passwords are compromised. All your brains belong to us."

Color drains from the bodies of the boys, who clutch their heads in a vain attempt to keep their thoughts from hemorrhaging in the air. A man cries out, "They are attacking my brain." Another whimpers, "This is the end." before slumping to the ground.

Condor tries, but he cannot help them. The virus spreads from electronic to human systems through a dormant viral infection, possibly through a systems update that caused all systems demolish rapidly. As the only remaining guest unaffected by the voice commands, Condor hears the old woman's voice again. He is alone, and her words rattle in his head, *make it so."* His dream path becomes panoramic. When he closes his eyes, he sees the victims' heads explode into a stampede of extinct creatures – lions and tigers and bears – kicking and clawing their way out of the mansion. Even in the dream, he does not know for sure if his head will explode. Then he realizes that he is a Bionican and that he will be spared because all Bionicans received virus protection.

Shaking and sweating, Condor wakes from his dream, and though he regains his composure, the uncertainty and sense of unworthiness that he felt in the dream persist. He wonders what the dream means and whether it points to what is in store for him, and what he has to do. Perhaps there is something that he has to learn from the past.

On his next free day, Condor goes out to walk off the recent changes that he has been feeling. He extends his walkabout beyond the Bionican perimeter at the foothills of the Santa Monica Mountains, a place where even hackers are discouraged to go. There, as he expected, he encounters still another woman, the third of his visions. This time she is an old woman in a black dress, sitting on a rotten tree stump.

"Are you Athena who was banished from Bionica long ago?" he asks.

She looks up, her eyes milky and unseeing and responds to his question as if she has known him for a long time.

"They did not like that I took the name of the Greek virgin goddess of wisdom, war, and the arts and crafts. And so all I have left is my voice."

"Ancient Greece is taboo," Condor says, "Why did you risk everything?"

But Athena is deaf as well as blind and cannot hear him, and so she does not answer, and instead lectures him in her clarion voice, "You cannot understand what you are missing. It is like explaining sight to someone who is blind. It is like explaining hearing to someone who cannot hear. It is like..."

Condor clears his throat in an attempt to slow her down.

"There were so many *things*." Athena pauses for emphasis and continues with a rapid-fire description of domestic bliss and the wonders of consumer pleasures long lost in his world: "… a family eating together at a dinner table, a basket of fruit from the grocery store, a steaming cup of coffee, a woman combing her long brown hair with a natural bristle brush, a sunset observed from a picnic blanket, a couple in a tender embrace on a bed with duvet covers…"

Condor cuts her off, "Enough, enough. I know that I have missed things; I do not need to hear more. We all have lost things, but we have gained things as well." His voice is a rebuke of angry disdain and impatience. She has hit a nerve. Tears come to his eyes as he realizes how much he has been deprived of the things that he has never possessed.

The old woman speaks to him intently, "You think you will live forever even though you know that is an illusion. If they do not kill you off first, you will be forced to leave Bionica and wander like me. You know they put out my eyes with a burning chemical because I saw too much, and they punctured my ears with red-hot stakes because I heard too much. And finally they disconnected me from The Well, so that I would be forever alone, but they *will not* silence me."

Condor now remembers the story of the woman who sat before him on the rotten tree stump. She is the mother of Simon Girty, who questioned the pleasures of virtual enjoyment that The Well provided. By destroying her sight and hearing, the Bionicans believed she would never be able to see and hear what she talked about, and that she would die in a state of enforced delusion, alone in her own thoughts.

As he stares at her with her story in mind, she says, "Someday you will be old and helpless like me. Before that happens you ought to find your mother and see what she has to say. She will tell you. She will set you straight, like I did with Simon." The old woman's voice trails off as she fades and disappears from Condors sight.

After finishing his disturbing walkabout, Condor is at a loss for what to do. He knows that he cannot show his doubts, so there is only one thing left, and that is to get back to business. The good news is that today is his rendezvous with Eric, the Goth, with whom he has been trading for several years. Although his fellow hackers tell him that all Goths are cheats and liars, Condor enjoys dealing with Eric. They meet every month like clock-work and have become close friends.

Eric arrives in an old pick-up truck full of goods.

"Here is what you ordered," Eric tells Condor.

Condor counts his ordered goods as his users unload everything, including the food, the machetes, the ropes, as well as the shovels and the many other gardening tools.

"And here is the special package that you requested." Eric hands Condor a large wrapped container of disallowed meat that he and his fellow hackers have been expecting. Condor puts it aside.

Like many Goths, Eric fancies to be Anglo-Saxon, but is a racial mixture. He is of medium height, bronze-skinned, a bit on the stocky side. He has a winning smile and readiness to shake everyone's hands, something that few Bionicans feel comfortable doing. Proud of his recent success as a trader, he shows Condor his new outfit – buckled strap trousers, a black t-shirt, and a studded biker jacket topped off with a black cap.

"Nice," says Condor.

"I got these from a group of Greek kids that work out of an abandoned steampunk warehouse in North Hollywood."

"Business must be good to be trading with kids and coming up with threads like those."

"Good D-train sells," Eric replies.

"Speaking of the devil, here is the stuff." Condor points to the loading platform piled high with bricks of

Daytrain, ready to be loaded into the back of Eric's truck.

"100 keys of D-train. That should keep the slaves and the kids happy."

"Not only them. D-train use is increasing everywhere. Not just the Greek kids, but even our people, even those officially registered under their tribes with full Goth status are starting to use it. That is great for business."

Condor is aware that there has been an increasing demand of D-train. He doubts that the Bionicans can keep up production. They will need to recruit a lot more outside kids to become users to grow and cultivate enough D-train to keep up with the increased demand.

Eric then asks Condor a question that he has never asked him before.

"Condor, how come you do not smell like the others?

"The other Bionicans smell because of their use of D-train to get on The Well and because they work with it daily. It is a double whammy. Not only do their brains get fried, the oil gets into their hands, skin, and breath. I am special because I do not touch the stuff. I can access The Well without D-train. And while I am sharing things that I should not, I am also special because my tattoos move."

Eric was not aware that the Bionicans needed to use D-train to get on The Well. Condor explains why Bionica, because of its even temperature due to its proximity to the sea, is a perfect place to grow D-train.

"We Bionicans have the right vibes to cultivate D-train, thanks to The Well. We talk the talk better than anyone else," Condor brags. Then he moves his forearm in front of Eric's eyes.

"Take a look at her." As Condor shows Eric his tattoos, one of his tattoos begins to move. It is the face of a flamboyant young woman on his forearm.

"Who *is* she?" Eric marvels, not aware that Condor's tattoos had such remarkable kinetic properties.

"They say she is my mother – my mother who has been dead, but I am not sure for how long. I have had these tattoos long before I can remember."

"So what good are these tattoos?"

"As long these tattoos move, I know the Daytrain is good and that you will be coming back to us for more. You know, Eric, It's the stuff that dreams are made of – today and in the future. You guys need us."

Eric teases Condor, "What future? You know that Bionica is history. The future is with us –the Goths. *We* have the energy and vitality, and *we* have the numbers. Maybe you should join us."

Condor teases back, "Me, a Goth? I have the connection right here," Condor says with mock pride pointing to his tattoos. "I am equipped to make the world a better place while you guys are a bunch of meat-eating savages."

Eric laughs. "This from a man who just bought a package of meat for his hacker squad," Eric responds. They both laugh because of the Bionicans' hypocritical consumption of meat.

Condor continues to rib Eric, "You Goths cannot keep up with the Greeks. They know a lot of stuff that you do not. They think they have the answers for everything,"

Eric agrees, "They are arrogant bastards, but there is no doubting their intelligence. Still I do not like that they look down on us because we do all the dirty work. But there is one exception."

"Oh, who?"

"It is Medea. She is very smart and powerful. She is Greek but chooses to live among the Goths."

"And she likes you?" Condor teases.

"I wish she did."

Condor laughs, "So even as she lives with you, she looks down on you, eh? You Goths are not much better. You are also snobs when it comes to us. You think we Bionicans are the scum of the earth."

Eric says, "But you and I are friends, are we not?"

Condor smiles, "Maybe it is because we both cannot stand the Greeks. And besides, the Greeks will never get anywhere without us because they, just like you, want our Daytrain."

Eric agrees. "Yes, Greek demand is up. We are looking to expand the D-train trade to other communities, but the Christians and the Knight Bandits are getting in the way."

"The Christians?"

"Yes, the Christians. And, what is more, they are working with your Simon Girty and the Knight Bandits. They want to convert everybody, and that is not good for business. We are doing our best to stop their teachings. Last week we captured a cart loaded with a hundred bibles, and we burned them all."

Condor says, "I am more worried about the Greeks. They want to control The Well."

Eric looks puzzled. "I do not get it."

Condor tries to explain, "The Well knows everything that is worth knowing. It has knowledge that the Greeks want but should not have. My duty is to make sure that nothing leaks."

Eric laughs. "I do not think the Greeks are all that interested in The Well. They have their own knowledge – in their books. All they are interested in is using your Daytrain for kicks, just like the Goths. They do not want to use it to access The Well and to steal your precious secrets."

Feeling defensive, Condor starts to brag. "We do have important secrets that we keep hidden in The Well. For one, we have a process for growing Daytrain that is so secret that we are not even sure what it is. Only The Well knows for sure, and it only tells us what we need to know to get to harvest."

"I heard that it is also the soil, the sun, the wind."

"Some say it is a special wind, the Santa Anna breeze, but there are other reasons.

"Oh, then what are they?"

Condor rips off a part of the sticky green plant with sacks of nectar hanging from the stems. He plucks one off and offers it to Eric, who squirts the contents into his mouth.

"This is the stuff that dreams are made of." Eric beams as the D-train takes effect. "Everything around me is vibrant, as if saw I it for the first time, like a baby. Nothing bothers me now. I am completely at peace. Nothing will go wrong. Come on, why not join me in a toke?"

"You know I cannot and I will not. I took an oath not to touch the stuff."

"You do not know what you are missing."

"I do, but if I go against the code, that will jeopardize the entire D-train supply line. You would not want that to happen."

"This is some of the best stuff I have tasted. What is the secret?"

"Condor says with mock seriousness, "We infuse the plants with our hopes and dreams; when you take Daytrain, your feelings reflect *our* hopes, dreams, and desires. This is why *our* Bionican Daytrain is so good. It is in a class of its own, better than anyone else's. Daytrain is to Bionica as wine is to Napa."

"Wine? Hopes and dreams? Napa?"

"I am just kidding. That is just what jumped into my head from The Well."

"Oh you Bionicans. You and your useless Well. What is the point of having a lot of knowledge that nobody can use?" asks Eric as he punches Condor playfully.

"The Greeks have been trying to get us to let them into our secrets about The Well and our cultivation of Daytrain. If for no other reason, they want our technology so that they can take over – the Goths included."

"But you guys have no way of sharing what you know, not with your lunar purges."

"They would have to join us."

"And become smelly Bionicans?"

"That is the price of admission."

"No way. The Greeks do not want to give up their fancy lifestyle to get down and dirty with you guys."

"But yet their young people keep on coming to us and becoming users, even though we smell."

"They will do anything for Daytrain, right?"

"I guess so. We make the stuff that dreams are made of."

They both laugh.

Condor then asks, "So, what is with the Goths? What do you guys do for fun?"

"Another poetry slam. We all have to recite a personal poem. If your poetry stinks, it is..."

He makes the throat-cutting gesture.

"Curtain time."

"I cannot figure you guys out. One minute you fight like dogs and then you recite poetry to each other. What is it all about?"

"It is all about power. Remember, the word, not just the written word, is mightier than the sword. Not only do you have to fight, but your poetry has got to be good, too. If your poetry is lousy, you die. And if you cannot or will not fight, you die."

"We Bionicans are a lot more supportive of each other."

"Hah. You say that because you are a hacker. You are part of the ruling class. But you are just as quick to bash in the heads of the poor user who finds religion."

Condor gets defensive. "But, we have no choice. We cannot allow religious thought to destroy our community. It is our form of justice."

Eric continues, "We Goths believe in poetic justice. If your poetry is good, you live. If we think your poetry is not very good, we boo you, and you must leave the stage in shame. If you have courage and you insist on reading your poetry and it becomes good, or even epic, then you can take any lover from the audience that you want, plus you are plied with mead and showered with D-Train. If you have courage and insist on reading your poetry out loud and it becomes truly bad, then you die. It is that simple. For the Goths, words have consequences. *Live free or die."*

Condor snorts. They have come to the end of their talk at the same place where they always end – Goths are better because of this, and Bionicans are better because of that. Neither one of them takes the banter too seriously. Eric starts to packs up the bushels of Daytrain.

"Time to go to The Valley," he says.

"See you, good friend," Condor replies before returning home.

Condor hears the voice of the old woman again, "Go see the dwarf. Go see the dwarf." His animated tattoo flashes, "Berk the dwarf." Condor has heard about this Berkovitz. He is a technology guru who occupies the former Mormon Temple, several miles east of Bionica on Santa Monica Boulevard. Before Cybergeddon, the Mormon Temple was a repository for the LDS database of all the people who received implants. Eco-terrorists hacked this database and used it to spread the virus that killed off the electronic elite.

"You should see the stuff he has at his place," Digi Diva's says as her eyes get big and round. The Mormon Temple is a repository of hardware and technical information left over from the Cyber Age. No one is sure of the size and scope of his collection of various computers and storage devices. The Greeks selected Berk to organize and rehabilitate whatever technology remained.

The Bionicans consider Berk and the Temple off limits for all Bionicans. For that reason, Condor seeks an exemption from his colleagues. "I have reason to believe that I should see Berk about the things that I have been thinking about," Condor says to the group. He does not expect to receive their blessings.

Digi Diva speaks for the group. "Going to see Berk is a very dangerous thing to do. You know he is not certified. Some say he is a stooge for the Greeks, helping them access The Well." Digi clenches her hands for emphasis. "We have been warned to stay away from him because of how often he has compromised Well security."

"Besides, he is a hardware nut who wants to put software in a hardware prison again," Phiberoptik sputters. "Everything I have heard about him says that he wants to destroy the neural network connections we use to access The Well. He is not on our side."

"He is a dangerous lurker," Draper intones, using up the few remaining words allocated to him for the day to describe Berk. The Well begins to limit the thought allocations for all the hackers on the topic of Berk.

Pengo's lisp goes into high gear. "I know that he can penetrate The Well firewall, and I believe that he is behind the religious fervor that has started to infect some of our users – like Little Eddie."

"For all we know, he wants to take over The Well so that the Greeks can steal its secrets. I think they are looking for trouble in the name of what they call civilization," Digi Diva adds.

Jimmie the Greek warns Condor, "Do not go near him. Chances are that once you are there, something will happen to you and when you return you will run afoul with The Well, and then we will have to run the neural network termination on your brain and throw you over the wall to the birds."

Condor knew that this is what the team was going to say. He assures his colleagues that he will not go to the temple and that he will stay away from Berk and that he will continue to work with his team to resolve whatever problems come up.

"We hope that you will not go. Deep down you are one of us, you are a team player," Digi Diva says betraying only a moment's hesitation because in truth she is not so sure which way Condor will go.

Nighttime, Condor is alone at his place. Lying down on his old lumpy mattress, he is sweaty and unable to fall asleep. His brain feels like it is going to pop. He tries to conjure positive thoughts that will put him right with The Well, talking out loud to be heard. "I do not want to become a traitor like Simon Girty. I want to serve the greater good."

In his mind he sees bare-breasted Digi lifting the Emergency Hammer and smashing it down to crush his skull; then her colleagues, his former friends, toss his body over the wall for the vultures' next meal. He knows that this is a future that he can still avoid.

"I do not want to end up like that," he whispers to himself. "Still, I must pursue the truth that was revealed to me in my dreams." Hearing this, The Well is prompted to start up his migraine. He knows better – sticking to the right talking points avoids problems with The Well. So, he blurts out, "I do not want to betray my fellow hackers. I have taken an oath." This lessens the pain a bit. He has to remember that even when he is disconnected from The Well, he is close enough to its center that it can still sense his thoughts through phantom channels.

In the morning, to sort things out, Condor leaves for the Marina del Rey ruins just beyond the southern edge of Bionica. The inland water areas around the Marina del Rey ruins expanded greatly after climate change, causing the ocean to flood the Los Angeles lowlands.

The Marina is a favorite spot for meeting Eric, the Goth, for Daytrain deals and for the stuff he wants for his Church. This time he is alone. Condor uncovers a small fiberglass motorboat and fuels it from a hidden stash of precious contraband gasoline provided by Eric. He starts the motor and sputters off around the harbor, slowly navigating through the half-sunken boats and debris. A few ransacked boats bob in the water, but they are obviously not seaworthy. He moors the boat at a remote pier and sits down by the water, putting his head between his knees. He tries to ward off the inevitable migraine that sets in when his travels have taken him too far from The Well's center.

The shrill sounds of his mother's voice pierces past the pain and into his brain. "You must contact Berk. It is your destiny and your only chance. He will help you."

Condor's migraine intensifies. "Am I destined to die?" he moans, clasping his head in desperation. He gets up and walks along the pier, first in one direction and then another hoping to find a clear signal to shake off the pain and his mother's voice, but nothing happens, except for the drone of Julia's voice which becomes increasingly loud, "Do not be afraid, you must follow your destiny. You must go to the redheaded dwarf. You must learn from him. He will save you."

Condor stands still and hesitates as Julia's voice goes up a notch. "Listen to me. I am your mother. Although I am dead, I love you the way only a mother can love. A dead mother's love is better than none at all. You are safe so long as you obey me. I will take care of you."

Confused, Condor takes a deep breath and is pleasantly surprised when he realizes that his migraine is gone. That is when he realizes the extent of his mother's influence.

CHAPTER 3
BERK, THE DWARF

Back at the Church, Condor summons his favorite pig, Google, to help him locate Berk's place. "Search for dwarf, Berk, California Temple."

Google looks puzzled. Condor then asks the pig to refine his search by adding "red hair." That does it. Google charges ahead, following the all-knowing little blue ball that will take Condor to his destination. As Google scampers out of the Church, Condor follows down an alleyway and through an opening in the fence leading up along old Santa Monica Boulevard to the Los Angeles California Temple. On top of this concrete building Condor notices the angel, Moroni, high on the temple's tower. Once having faced east, Moroni is twisted and turned around so that now he points his trumpet west in the direction of the setting sun.

Dozens of brown people tend to the vast manicured lawn leading to the entrance of this magnificent building, one of the few that were spared destruction during the uprising. Armed guards in uniform are posted at all the entrances and walk in pairs up and down the pathways outside. An antique sprinkler system, a marvel of 20th Century technology, keeps the grass green all year around. The grounds include Canary Island Pine trees, Palm trees, Bird of Paradise trees, Olive trees, and rare Chinese Ginkgo trees. As Condor and Google approach, Condor sees their images in a large reflecting pool graced with two beautiful and still operating fountains. A guard approaches Condor and asks for his identification. Knowing that he cannot reveal his hacker credentials by connecting to The Well and revealing his whereabouts, Condor freezes for a moment. As his tattoo starts to pulse, he instinctively knows what to do next. He shows his tattoo that reads, "Xtremus." Seeing this, the guard replies, "Berk is expecting you" and stamps his hand.

Condor and Google follow the guard through the huge metal front doors that lead to a series of long-abandoned ordinance rooms where the story of Creation was told to visitors a long time ago. Condor feels uneasy; he is not sure what to make of the Christian imagery that confronts him as he moves from room to room. The guard opens the door of a chamber where he sees a large white-haired head bobbing among stacks of obsolete computer hardware from the 20th Century. At first Condor thinks that he has found the wrong dwarf, but soon realizes that age has caught up with him and that his red hair, which has whitened with age, is a thing of the past. Google wanders off after locating the dwarf.

Berk's shortness brings his head to about an inch above Condor's belly button. The dwarf's ruddy face has a broad nose and heavy features punctuated with small eyes that open wide when he starts to speak. His deep sonorous voice defines and controls the room and their meeting.

"And who are you?" Berk bellows. Condor tries to talk but falters as he attempts to introduce himself, but he is beaten to the punch.

"You know I am Berkovitz. I am the only Jew and the only dwarf around here. Everyone knows me. Perhaps a better question is – what do you want? Are you here to look at my Schwanz?"

Condor does not know what he is talking about, and so he clarifies his purpose, stammering, "I am on a quest. I am supposed to meet you, perhaps to learn from you."

"I have a lot to do; why should I make time for you?" Berk barks at Condor's towering figure that is cowered by the strength of Berk's commanding voice.

The covert voice of Condor's mother butts in, "Tell him who you are and that I am your mother, the founder of Xtreme Marketing; tell him that you are my son created from one of Julia's ova."

Following Julia's instructions, Condor takes a breath.

"I am Condor. I am the son of Julia, founder of Xtreme Marketing." Condor goes on to explain who he is and why he has come. Berk interrupts him and acts as if he already knows all this, though his expression softens, yielding a more friendly, "Ah, yes."

"Yes, I remember Julia, your Mother. She was *quite* a pistol!"

Berk then asks Condor to follow him into another room, a room that he has turned into a laboratory for retro technology, full of all kinds of video and audio electronic devices as well as motors, generators, and piles of circuit boards amidst vectorscopes and testing equipment with flashing lights. Explaining to Condor his work on electronic penetration, Berk's voice accelerates, as it always does, when he talks about his equipment.

"I am basically a RAM guy, but I must say I am proud of my vintage collection of direct-access media storage devices. I have old video recorders and players, CD-ROMs, DVD players. But I am proud to own the original VAX-11 computer as well as modems that were used for the first prototype of The Well. I have more recent vintage stuff like these personal communication devices, some nanotechnology devices as small as a pin and others as large as this suitcase cell phone."

"Does any of it still work?"

He laughs, "I have the animal magnetism to make anything work. As for the machines in this room, I can get them to work if I want to, but there is no point. Nobody uses this stuff anymore. Plus the machines and the computers are pre-Energy Star. They need too much power. They can't compete with you energy-efficient Bionicans. I do not have to tell you, you know exactly what I am talking about, you guys just communicate out of thin air; no electricity is even needed."

"Yes we do. We are always plugged in. Our wires are never crossed," Condor says with pride.

"Except when you leave Bionica and your connection becomes weak as it is now. Besides, you live in an informational ghetto. Do you not know that all your information is dead, archived, gone, defunct?"

Condor doesn't like Berk deriding The Well and comes to its defense. "The Well contains a lot of useful information that we need to keep safe."

Berk throws his hands up. "Safe from what? Safe from whom?"

"Safe from the Greeks or anyone else who wants to destroy the world. That is my job."

"Don't be ignorant. No one wants to destroy the world. We can talk about that and your job, later. First let me show you some of my tools that *do* work." Berk takes him to his work bench and shows Condor his prize possession, an acetylene torch that still fires up, one that he has used over the years to create strange shapes out of scrap metal.

"What else do you have here?" Condor wonders, still unimpressed. Berk shows him another room full of electronic sex toys. "These are my prize possessions, which I occasionally sell off to Greek women who are not finding satisfaction in their marriages." He picks up a dildo and turns it on. "Believe it or not, they all work, and I have a stash of nickel-cads to keep them going for a fortnight, but this is only a sideline. I have more important stuff."

Condor looks blankly at Berk, who takes a deep breath and continues with mock exasperation because of Condor's failure to fully appreciate his collection.

"I have information that was once recorded on physical media. I have books, photos, newspapers, cassette tapes, reel-to-reel tapes, VHS tapes, records, compact disks, eight tracks, and film. This is a rare collection – definitely museum quality. Do you want to take a tour?"

As Condor nods, Berk takes him for a tour of the facilities. His first stop is the print room – a huge hall lined with shelves and piled neatly with books, photographs, and newspapers.

"This, my dear boy, is a library."

"How do you find things here?"

Ever hear of the Melvil Dewey Decimal Classification System? It is all here on tiny cards in these wooden drawers."

There are hundreds of drawers. Berk opens up one of them and pulls out a card and reads it, "Here is one,

From Papyrus to Hypertext: Toward the Universal Digital Library By Christian Vandenthorpe. Funny, a book on digital libraries," Berk laughs out loud.

Condor does not get the joke. "Why is that funny?"

"They were publishing books long after nobody read them, and what is even funnier is that these books are about the information age, and today this card represents the only printed copy of this book in my library. The book burners probably destroyed all the other paper copies of this book, except the one in my rare book collection, and I doubt whether an electronic version was ever created. Do you not get the joke; it is a book about building a library without books."

Still unclear to him, Condor shrugs. "Are there not other kinds of books, like plays or novels?"

"No, I did not try to save those books; the only books that I saved for this collection deal specifically with the history of storing data and information. There is no art, drama or literature here."

Berk drags a chair to a bookcase and jumps on it so then he can reach for some books.

"Here is one of my favorite authors, Harold Adams Innis. What beautiful writing! Listen to what he wrote; it is like music."

Berk reads a passage from *The Bias of Communication* in a nasal monotone. "*The bureaucratic development of the Roman Empire and success in solving prob-*

lems of administration over vast areas was dependent on supplies of papyrus. The bias of this medium became apparent in the monopoly of bureaucracy and its inability to find a satisfactory solution to the problems of the third dimension of empires, namely time."

Condor's face goes blank because he doesn't understand what this passage means, but Berk is not deterred. "Ever hear of Marshall McLuhan? He wrote about the global village and said things like, *The medium is the message* and *The new electronic interdependence recreates the world in the image of a global village.* He was brilliant."

Condor interrupts, "Why do you do all this?"

Berk is annoyed by Condor's impudent question. "I do this for my clients, but what is more important, I do this for me. I am the world's foremost data and information expert, collector and fixer upper; I am interested in anything that stores and retrieves data and information. And I believe that if you cannot store it on an impartial medium, then it is not there."

Condor objects. "But the data in The Well is stored in the minds of Bionicans."

"That does not count. Nobody else is allowed to get to your Bionican stuff to evaluate and verify the data. When your brains are drained, you are running on empty. Besides, The Well is inaccessible to everyone but a Bionican. Your ephemeral stuff is censored; so what use is it?"

"We are protecting the world from the misuse of dangerous content," says Condor defending Bionican policy. "The Well will release all the content when the world is safe for information."

Berk ends the discussion with a dismissive gesture. "But if for some reason y'all die, then the content dies as well. That is why the Greeks will not allow the Goths to kill you Bionicans," Berk laughs. "The Greeks are convinced that you guys, with your neural networks, have the secret key to technology. But, I for one know that your content is irrelevant. It no longer applies to what is happening now. All your data is obsolete because The Well is mired in the past. Nothing is ever updated."

Condor looks confused, wiping sweat from his face. He believes that The Well's database has intrinsic value and that to question it is blasphemy. But despite his reservations, he still wants to hear out what Berk has to say.

Berk continues, "I only collect what I know and I know what I collect; I like to restore data transmission and storage devices."

Condor does not get it. It is crazy to fool around with equipment that one uses or even knows about.

"Let me show you my head end. It is like, I will show you mine, if you show me yours," Berk laughs at his in-joke.

Berk does not expect Condor to understand the 20th

Century cable TV term "head end" and motions him to follow him up a stairwell to another room full of equipment that judging from the flashing lights and buzzing noises appears to be functioning.

"Is this not beautiful? Still going after all these years. Do not make me explain how I power them all because I will not tell you. The power source is a big secret, but the one thing I can tell you is that the information that flows through this system goes way up the tower of this temple, right to that the statue of the angel Moroni standing on top of it."

"What does the angel have to do with it?"

"Do you not get it? Inside Moroni is a transmitter. I can pump out high-speed bandwidth in the direction of Bionica through his trumpet. I stream VOD – Video on Demand. When you and your hacker friends connect with The Well and go on a flight of fancy, here is where we give a helping hand."

This is the first time Condor has heard Berk using the word, we. There is more to this story, he suspects.

"You mean the videos that we see in our minds do not come from The Well?"

Berk strokes his chin. "You have grown up with the idea that The Well is something you and others in Bionica have in your heads or that it exists in the ether. This is partly true, but stuff still has to feed into The Well. That is where I come in; I am your common carrier, pipeline, and gatekeeper all rolled into one."

Condor is perplexed. "You mean to say that you make the videos for The Well?"

"Not on your life. I do not deal in content; content has a life of its own. I am the hardware systems guy. I only transmit data. I thought you knew about this. What kind of hacker are you? Do you not know anything about storage, retrieval, and transmission?"

Condor does not respond; there is a long silence. Berk notices that Condor is staring blankly at his equipment.

"So, you do not know anything about equipment."

Condor is interested in the flashing equipment and starts fiddling with some knobs. Berk runs towards him. "Hey, go easy there, big guy. You are going to break this stuff if you are not careful." Berk slaps his hands. "Please ask me before touching anything."

"Now, Condor, I want to show you something special." He takes Condor into a small room decorated with cheesecake pictures cut from magazines of a woman who looks just like his mother, Julia.

Condor becomes agitated. "Where did you get these? Why do you have all of these?"

Berk calms him down. "Condor, your mother left these for me so that I could share these with the world when the right time comes, and now that you have come to me the right time has come."

"What does that have to do with me?"

Berk explains, "Condor, I hate to break it to you, but your mother has been dead for many years. She died long before you were born, but she left many things for you so that you can know her and learn about you so that you could fulfill your destiny. I know that she has been talking to you."

Condor does not like it that Berk knows about his private contacts with his mother.

Berk tries to assure him. "It cannot be helped. I am your godfather, entrusted to make sure that you become the standard bearer."

"Huh, the what?"

"You know, the bearer of the standard, the keeper of the faith, the carrier of the torch, the man of the hour – all those things."

Condor shakes his head agitated. "But what will happen to me? Just by being here, I have placed myself in great danger. The other hackers will crack my skull and sever my connection from The Well. It is true that I see many things, and I want to possess what I see in my imagination. But, seeing those things hurts because I do not know why I should want something that betrays The Well, and I am also so sick of seeing so many things that do not make any sense to me."

Condor's train of thought is interrupted when he hears his mother's voice, which now takes on a peremptory note. "Stop this self-indulgence. Listen to Berk!"

"I can see your Mother is online again." Berk gives Condor a knowing look.

Condor nods with a smile.

"There is something I would like to discuss with you. Are you ready for it?

"Yes, I know you want to talk about my quest."

"Yes, your quest will be to determine the future of The Well. If you are successful, you will also be able to answer questions about your heritage."

Condor is intrigued. He has always wanted to know more about himself and his special gifts. He likes the idea of being selected.

Berk continues to explain his proposal. "We need you to become a real leader, not just a run-of-the-mill hacker. Your mother has gone to great pains to prepare you."

"What do *you* know about my mother?"

"Umm...where should I start? Ah yes. It was shortly before the Great Plague when the world was completely different from what it is today. Your mother bears responsibility for the plague and what happened, and she also bears the responsibility for what will happen to you. Your job is to redeem her. Now, let me tell you about what you should know about your mother."

Condor interrupts, "I already know her. I have seen her appear. She is a voice in my head; she talks to me and has been telling me what to do."

"Now take it easy. We all have issues with our mothers. Maybe this voice is just a mother pop-up ad."

Berk pounds his fist on the large wooden table in the center of his room. "Look here, you idiot, from this point on, you must tell the voice in your head to go away. If you are to think for yourself, and if you are to redeem her, her voice must go."

Condor hears the voice of his mother chattering away about the importance of being your own person. He tries to shut her out, never able to do that before, but this time, the more he focuses, the quieter the voice gets. "Go out into the world and reunite with me" is the last sentenced that he hears before she fades out and disappears.

"I cannot hear her anymore," Condor says proudly.

Pleased, Berk pinches Condor's thigh. "You have got to free yourself from the bonds of The Well and the bonds of your mother's voice. Otherwise, you are never going to be a self-realized *Mensch*."

Condor looks at him dumbly.

Berk repeats the word, "Mensch, Mensch, Mensch," without eliciting a glimmer of understanding from Condor; he is clueless when it comes to Yiddish expressions, a verbal treasure trove never been included in The Well's database. Berk realizes that it will be a mitzvah and a half to bring Condor up to speed.

Berk tells Condor that he is willing to become his mentor. "Look, my job is to tell you what no self-serving, inside-your-head voice can do. Come to me tomorrow, and we will discuss your quest and your mother."

Next day Condor, accompanied by Google, returns to the temple and is taken to the Celestial Room where Berk is waiting for them. "Make yourself comfortable," Berk says to Condor and then turns his head to make evil eye contact with Google that makes the pig cower and squeal. As promised the day before, Berk tells Condor about his mother's exploits and adventures and how her contemporaries regarded her.

"She was an eco-activist like her namesake, the venerable Julia Butterfly Hill, fighting for the rights of all creatures against the onslaught of human civilization. Your mother climbed and hugged trees in defiance of the logging industry, and she fought for the dolphins and the timber wolves. She was an advocate of minus growth and backed a worldwide plan for family management..

Julia was also the darling of the cyber intellectuals because of her education and erudition. She was one of the remaining few who had read classic philosophy in the original Greek and Latin, and who understood economics. Influenced by Ayn Rand, she described her groundbreaking ideas on Twitter, exposing millions to her book, *Meine Kraft*, in which she turned Friedrich Nietzsche on his head. She later tweeted about Schindler's Lisp, which led to a re-evaluation of slavery and its value in economic development. She is responsible for all the learned quotations that have been swimming in your head since you were born."

As Berk tells Condor about his mother and her exploits, he explains what certain terms mean because Condor has a limited context for learning new things. Being in the Temple and unable to connect to The Well, there is no way for Condor to evaluate the new terms and to assure himself that his thoughts are on the right path.

Berk pokes at him and goes into a rant, "You suffer from traditional information glut. You think you have it all sorted out because you are limited to your context. But *the times they are a changing*, they have always been changing. The Well cannot stop that."

After taking a deep breath, Berk continues with a rhetorical flourish, "*Water, water, everywhere, nor any drop to drink. There was fifty-seven channels and nothin' on.* Maybe we can change all that. Our Civilization is like a cluttered basement; some things just need to be cleared out – The Well included."

"But, there is a lot of good information in The Well,"

Condor begs to differ.

"Just what I like, a young lad with loyalty. I think you will find that you just happened to back the wrong horse."

"Horse? Since when have there been horses? It thought they were all eaten years ago."

"Nah, they still have horses up North. Besides; it is just a figure of speech. I am not talking about actual horses. I am saying that your loyalty to The Well is misguided, since The Well is isolated, censored and controlled, and for that reason it is fundamentally flawed."

Berk then goes back to his main topic, Condor's mother. "She was a great communicator who created countless voices and visions; she inspired people everywhere, both online and in the flesh."

"*And* I must add," Berk says with a knowing emphasis and a glint in his eyes as he points to a semi-nude pin-up of her, "She was one hell of a good looker who knew all the secrets of the user Interface. What a gal!"

Condor is not sure what to make of Berk, or whether to trust him.

"How do I know my mother trusted you?"

Out of the blue, Condor feels the sting of pain and hears a rumbling in his head; something is trying to get his attention. It is The Well's voice, sounding more petulant than usual, warning Condor that he has been away from Bionica too long and that he will lose his standing if he does not return immediately.

As The Well tries to establish Condor's location, random packets of data make their way into his brain. The snake of Creation appears on the wall, and then disappears. A movie snippet of a devil figure, roaring with laughter, is followed by images of collapsing buildings and screaming bodies hurled through the fiery winds of a mushroom cloud. Condor is not used to these kinds of hallucinations, and they frighten him.

"Do not worry. The Well is just kicking up a fuss." Thinking that Condor's blood sugar might be dropping, Berk offers Condor an apple after biting a huge chunk out of it. "Look Condor, we have a lot to talk about, and it is time for us to eat. I could go for some pig chops right now. Would you like to have some with me?

"But, meat is not allowed," Condor interrupts, forgetting his hypocrisy with the Goths. "The Well will not allow it; recreational meat eating led humanity to ruin."

Ignoring Condor, Berk takes a look around the room and spots Google, Condor's beloved pig, which has been wandering around while Berk and Condor were talking. Berk gets on his toes and lifts an antique spear off the wall and chases Google down. With a strategic thrust, he bores it into the pig's gut. With its blood spurting out everywhere, Google squeals in horror and tries to escape as Berk continues to twist the spear inside the animal, releasing more spurts of blood. Dying Google looks at Condor in dismay, pleading for his life, but Condor just

stands there too frozen to act as he watches his favorite pig begin his journey into pork chops. Google dies
betrayed and sacrificed. Berk arranges to have Google's
body brought to the Celestial Room for preparation.

"Best thing in the world, roasted pig," says Berk, ignoring kosher laws, licking his chops as he turns the spit
over a huge fire pit at the end of the Celestial Room. Berk
looks up to Condor and proclaims, "In Valhalla, there
was a pig named Sæhrímnir, which was eaten every evening and came to life again the next day. So, maybe there
is hope for Google, yet."

Condor looks down at his feet in shame.

"Look here, Condor, this is my Valhalla, and I am
going to invite you to a feast the likes you have never had
before."

After setting the table, Berk sorts out the vegetables
from the temple garden and throws them into the boil-
ing pot. "We are going to have a real meal fit for kings."

He makes Condor sit down and then says to him,
"Eat, if you know what is good for you, friend."

At first Condor is reluctant to eat from the body of
his pig friend, but with each delicious bite and swallow
he picks up courage and slices himself another helping.

He imagines Google's friendly squeals while running towards him as he entered the Church, but this memory fades as he dismisses any feelings of regret that he might have. The pig just tastes too good. As his stomach fills, Condor reaches a point of no return. For him, Google is now merely an afterthought. He no longer cares whether they will kill him for eating unauthorized meat. He will not reveal it himself, though he wonders what would happen if his hacker buddies ever find out.

"They do not have to know," says Berk, reading his thoughts. "You hold all the cards, but I am betting that you do not know how to keep your mouth shut. You have been a slave to The Well for so long. You had better stick around me for a while to learn the facts of life. Going back to Bionica now will just get you killed."

After the pork banquet, Berk continues to tell Condor about his mother, but this proves to be difficult. Condor's education is potholed. There is so much that he does not know. He keeps on interrupting Berk. "What do you mean by that? I do not understand what you are saying."

"I think I have the stuff to help you understand." Berk takes Condor into a small room and points to a box full of stuff. "There is a time capsule that your Mother left behind, just for you. You must spend a while with it to learn about your Mother's world. I wonder if you will be able to understand it. I just do not know where else to begin."

"A capsule? What do you do with it?" Condor says, again betraying his lack of understanding.

"You need equipment to play it back. That is where I come in; I am an expert on vintage playback devices. I just love that equipment; this is why I am indispensable. The world needs me to unlock the past that does not exist in The Well. Media playback is my trump card." Condor is intrigued. There is so much that he does not know, and Berk promises to unlock his mother's media time capsule in good time.

"To understand some things, you have to understand other things," Berk says. "I will let you know when it is time to unlock your mother's capsule."

And so the regular visits to Berk's Temple continue. Condor sneaks out just before sunrise and returns when his shift with the users starts. This way he keeps his visits a secret from his fellow hackers, who are unaware of his disconnection from The Well, thinking instead that he must be sleeping late. Throughout it all, Condor manages to do his regular hacker duties without interruptions, but Digi Diva senses a change and is suspicious.

"You do not seem to be as plugged in. What is going

on?"

Condor has an answer that he prepared with Berk's help. "I am trying to reset my neural connection myself so that I can do my very best work. I know that it will take time, but I think it is worth it. Trust me.

Digi is suspicious. "Be careful. You know what the consequences are if you set up your connection parameters incorrectly." She still admires Condor's physique and does not want anything bad to happen to him, and so she puts her hand on his shoulder, hoping that this time Condor will succumb to her affections. At first, Condor flinches as usual, but then he realizes that things have changed. Eating pig chop has paved the way for his desire to bite her sweet skin as well, and so on impulse, right there and then, much to her surprise, he decides to go for her. Digi beats him to the punch and plants her buckteeth into his right shoulder, leaving 32 impressions of her impressive bite. Digi and Condor have a quick *Go-For–It*. Afterward Digi sighs, the only other time she had a Go-For-It was with Simon Girty.

"How was it for you, are you satisfied, I mean really satisfied?"

"Yes," answers Condor tersely on an occasion that would warrant more of a response. It bothers Digi that he does not ask her whether she was satisfied, but *she* does not communicate this to Condor and instead continues to cater to him.

"Do you like my breasts?" she says pointing to them as she covers them with a cloth. She knows that Condor is into size – everything has to be *big*.

Condor answers and then comes up with the question that has been on his mind. "Yes, I like them very much. But tell me, how do *I* compare to Girty?"

Digi has been expecting this. She thinks for a moment and then answers, "You know, Condor, size does not matter. It is what you do and who you are that counts." Condor was expecting to hear something else that would make him bulge with pride. Digi tries to carry on, her buckteeth radiating with happiness. "So, this is our first time," she says forcing a smile, hoping that their liaison will keep Condor on a short leash and allow her bite marks to sink in. She thinks that she and Condor could become soulmates and that all that stands in the way is his reluctance to commit.

"You know, dear Condor, we all have needs. You will never be happy with any woman if you do not understand this. Please let me in."

Condor turns away from her and says nothing.

"You know where to find me if you want to talk," she says, putting her hand on Condor's shoulder. "You know," she says, brushing her body against his, *"I don't want no tears in the end, when it's over."*

"I need some time to think," he says. With a smile, Digi hopes for Condor to come around. But what Digi does not realize is that their first Go-For-It would be their last.

Condor's lessons at the Moroni Temple continue. At Berk's request, Condor brings another of his other pigs, Bing, to be served up. This time it is Condor turn to do the honors, and he takes an antique double-bladed ax to whack the throat of his second most-beloved pig and then helps Berk prepare the carcass for their next meal.

They roast the pig and eat. Condor resumes his studies with Berk; however, the pace is slowed by Condor's knowledge gaps. Every time Berk tries to tell the story of Julia, Condor asks Berk to explain and clarify. "Let us start again from the beginning," Berk says raising his arms and then folding them across his chest before reciting the long-rehearsed story about Condor's mother, Julia, one more time.

"Listen carefully, this is the last time I am going to tell you this story. Your mother wanted to inspire subsequent generations to reclaim what had been lost – the desire for desire and not a desire for things. When she was young, Julia worked as a brilliant marketing person. She and her Cyber Sirens sold "cloud goods" that users could experience only through their imagination, and there was no need to manufacture them; they only had to get programmed into the cloud. According to Julia, the Earth's environment could no longer sustain the level of manufacturing needed to satisfy the insatiable desire to own material goods. Things that were once needed to make day-to-day living more comfortable, such as shoes and clothing, were no longer necessary when people began to be genetically engineered with thicker skins to feel comfortable being naked. As a result of the expansion of goods within the cloud, an elite group of extremely wealthy people began to experience life entirely through their networked imagination. They believed that by staying hidden and connected they would remain cyber safe from all the unrest that was happening in the rest of the world."

Condor nods, pretending to understand.

Looking Condor straight in the eye, Berk explains, "The concept of Xtreme stretches experiences beyond traditional limits: Xtreme Sports, Xtreme Beauty, Xtreme Products, and then Xtreme Marketing. Young people went for the 'X' concept in a big way. They talked about Xtremus as a way of life."

"The Xtremus message was clear: push the limits. As Steve Jobs once said, *Reach beyond accepted boundaries and accepted ways of doing things. Do not do what is expected. Do more. Take risks.* People accepted the Xtremus way of doing things as young people pushed the limits. As a result, the rules, laws, policies, and conventional ways of doing things started to break down."

This "breakdown" interests Condor although he does not follow everything that Berk says, and so he tries take detailed notes. Berk mutters, "Do not get lost in the details. To survive you have to stay with the big picture." Berk continues his lecture flipping through visuals. He has given this talk many times before.

"Not everyone took to the Xtremus Way as an alternative to traditional consumerism. Non-adopters clutched their physical possessions like children clinging to their favorite toys. When persuasion ceased to be effective in recruitment, eco-fear and eco-violence took over. At first, the Xtremus zealots only used the threat of violence, but soon actual violence itself came to be associated with Xtreme Marketing."

Berk pauses then munches on leftover pig and after spitting out pieces of gristle he continues his lecture.

"Instead of serving as role models for abstinence, Julia and her followers perversely confiscated and expropriated houses, cars, fancy home electronics, heirloom jewelry and other collectibles. They urged consumers to abandon their urge to own things so that the Church of Useless Consumption could be eradicated forever. Julia did this with a vengeance through her confiscation campaign, amassing warehouses filled with people's possessions, including jewelry, brand name shoes, fash-

ion forward clothing, and piles and piles of home electronic devices. But instead of following the dictates of
Xtremus herself, Julia became addicted to a lavish lifestyle that was kept from her followers who wanted to
believe in the material-free idealism of her youth. When
they found out what she had become, they hated her for
betraying the Xtremus cause and compared her to the
shoe-obsessed Queen Imelda bitch that once ruled the
Philippines."

Condor, now a bit less spellbound, starts to wonder
where this story is going.

Berk barks at him, "Pay attention, dear boy. I am giving you more than just a sound bite. That is the problem
with you and your hacker friends; all you can deal with
are short bits of information. Lousy 'knowledge objects'
collected into huge databases by all those Web Farts who
populated The Well."

Condor, starting to get uncomfortable, begins to
fidget.

Annoyed Berk asks, "What is the matter? Am I boring you?"

"No, I would like to learn more about Julia; it is just
that I do not know how much time I have here. I am
still afraid that somehow, someday, The Well is going to
catch up with me. If I go against The Well, they will crack
my skull, and I will die alone in pain and the birds will
eat me."

"You have nothing to worry about if you keep on eating pig meat. It will make you stronger than the others. Besides, your tattoos give you a license to break away."

"But does that mean I cannot go back to Bionica once I break away?"

"That is right. You cannot go home again."

Berk goes on. "You have a lot to learn. The first thing you must do is to keep trying to understand your mother, Julia. To fully appreciate her, you must accept her contradictions. Just as you think you understand what she is all about, you learn something more that makes you wonder and reassess whatever you felt for her before. It does not matter if you love or hate her; she will help you understand the world as it might have been and as it might someday be again. But if you chose this path, there are no guarantees, and there is no turning back."

Berk picks up Julia's time capsule and finally shows it to Condor as promised.

"Ok, now I will show you the stuff I have to make this capsule work, including my secret source of electric power."

Berk hooks up the capsule to a playback module and tinkers with the connections. After some futzing, it works. Condor is excited to see a super HD image of his mother instead of just a hallucination. She is a beautiful young woman.

"This is cool," Condor marvels, "is that my mother?"

"Good retro usage," Berk says as he turns knobs on the video player. The screen camera zooms in on Julia, ending on close shots of her mouth and eyes. And then her lips begin to move.

"Condor, my dear son, this message is for you. I am tired now. Soon I will die. And the funny thing, my boy, is that you have yet to be born, but I am sure that someday you will be there for me. I will not be around physically to guide you then, and that is why I am leaving you this time capsule and a blueprint for your future. The dwarf, who has promised to live forever, will be there to guide you. You are probably asking yourself, why? Please be patient and listen carefully as I try to explain to you why I did what I did, and why you must do what you must do. I hope you will learn to understand."

She pauses to give Condor a chance to respond. Her voice continues. "If you do not do as I say, you are on your own and you will be lost. As your mother, I do not want you to live aimlessly. You must act as if there were a new future, one that only you can imagine. You must pay attention to everything that happens around you. Only then will you know the path that you will need to take."

Julia continues with her lecture. "It all started when the economy went sour. Instead of encouraging the desire for desire and wanting more, technology replaced work and consumption. There was more time for leisure and entertainment. It was painfully boring. People were glued to their machines and lost face-to-face contact. As more and more people took to their machines, fewer people ventured out in the world that was becoming polluted with poisoned air and poisoned thoughts. Many people kept on saying that there is no turning back. There is no place to go. The party is over."

Berk is pounding his fist into his hand, excited by Julia's rant. Condor is clueless as he watches the recording.

"I created the Movement where we made it a practice to hack Twitter sites and insert slogans designed to rekindle desire. First, I did it for the money that I was getting from the advertisers and the manufacturers, but soon I understood that my mission was to make people afraid that they might be missing something. Although I wanted to help people, I knew I had to hurt them first."

Restless with all this history Condor asks the dwarf, "What does this all mean? What does she want me to do?"

Then, as if his Mother could hear him, the camera zooms out and looking in his direction, she says, "Condor, pay attention. Do not be selfish. There is a world out there for you to discover."

Condor sinks into his seat. Berk, pulling himself up to be at eye level with Condor, assumes the demeanor of a stern father trying to make his son listen.

"Listen to your mother. Stop whining and pay attention."

Julia's voice becomes louder as if competing for Condor's attention and continues to lecture.

"The challenge for Xtreme Marketing was to create an atmosphere of fear and longing. Pain and only pain, makes people feel real, and that is when you can get their attention. Sometimes you have to use thugs and goons to convince people what is good for them, and that is exactly what I did when I started the Xtreme Marketing movement, which the people later called Xtremus. My success created many enemies, and I know the day will come when they will crucify me. This is why I will give birth to you long after I am gone. Your destiny is to rekindle Xtremus in your time and place. If I am a Queen, your destiny is to be King. Xtremus is the way."

Berk jabs Condor to get his attention while the Julia recording keeps going.

"I would take what she has to say about your destiny with a grain of salt. Xtremus is not the way. Xtremus is obsolete."

Condor's mind wanders, thinking about the possibility of him as King of the Bionicans, of the Goths, and even of the Greeks. His mind wanders as Julia continues the lecture, her voice becoming increasingly insistent.

"As your mother, I assure you that if you follow my example, you will experience my love in ways you cannot imagine."

After a pause, Julia's voice resumes. "Will you swear,

my son, to do the right thing? Will you swear it?"

Berk waits for Condor to decide whether to swear allegiance to her.

As Condor pauses, the dwarf advises him, "It is good that you pause. I would think twice about doing that. You might want to reconsider what she is asking you to do when you learn more about her ideas about economics and consumption."

"But she is my mother. I do want to honor her memory."

"Ok, then swear allegiance, but you might be making a mistake in swearing allegiance to your mother so soon. So let's get on with it, if that is what you want."

Turning towards Berk, Condor raises his right hand and says, "I will do my utmost to honor my mother, her work, and her memory." He repeats this phrase, as if in a trance.

Berk shouts, "Enough!" and Condor breaks out of the spell.

When he finishes, his mother's voice re-enters his mind approvingly. "Now that is a good son of mine. Soon Xtremus will rule the world again."

Berk is at a loss. While he has always admired Julia for her spunk, he is disgusted by Xtremus. He admonishes Condor for not taking his advice to learn more about his mother and her plans before swearing allegiance to her.

"I know that I am partially to blame here, but you

are messing with something that you do not understand. When your mother was a young woman, she produced a promotional video that explained Xtreme Marketing to potential clients. I will show you that later, but first let me explain. She was one of the Young Turks in The Stimulus Think Tank established to increase commercial traffic in the Cyberpolis. The problem was that people were no longer purchasing goods and services on the network. This trend threatened the very economic structure that sustained the development of the global Cyberpolis. Without purchasing activity, the system was sure to collapse. Times were bad, very, very bad. There was what they called unemployment. People were not able to trade their time for money to buy what they needed."

Condor is confused. "People had to work for money? Why was there not enough money for everyone? Couldn't they just make more and hand it out to everybody?

Berk shakes his head. "If everyone gets what they need and want, nobody ever gets enough. There has to be pressure and relative poverty to achieve prosperity."

Berk pulls out different denominations of currency from a drawer and explains how much each is worth and how much time the average person had to spend to earn a certain amount of money. He also pulls out some frayed credits cards and some early 21st Century Bitcoin images and shows them to Condor, who is still bewildered.

"Bitcoins were supposed to be virtual, but believe it or not, some were minted. See, I am the proud owner of a limited edition," Berk brags as he flips the coin.

"Money was very important, and everyone had to have it to buy things, but then they became obsolete when fashionable people received implants so that they could make transactions entirely through their brains."

"But that did not impress your mother. She was beyond any form of money; she did not believe in it. She believed that the life of the mind extends beyond meta-economics. *If you think rich, you are rich* — that is what your idealistic mother preached throughout cyberspace. Her image was everywhere, imploring users to seek out virtual satisfaction away from the physical world by acquiring goods of the imagination; this was not a tough sell because the manufacturing of advertised goods had stopped a long time ago. But she took it one step further; instead of purchasing virtual goods, you only had to imagine the virtual goods, and that was the same as being rich. With her teachings, we could all be rich in our minds. We could have everything that we ever wanted. All we had to do is imagine it."

Berk's face gets serious as he continues to talk. "Faced with the prospect of a complete consumer resistance, your mother declared that something drastic had to be done to force people to do the right thing. There was no other choice, and so the means justified the ends in Julia's mind. Let me show you some more video, as I promised."

Berk activates the play unit by inserting the Julia 1 Data module, called "Xtreme Marketing Promo." Julia appears in the video denouncing the late adopters and freeloaders who benefit from the system without buying into it.

"We are in a crisis, and we must fight for the Cyberpolis. We must fight for it in our homes and in the streets; we must persevere when we log on. No stone shall be left unturned in our battle for holistic consumption. Through you, the age of Xtremus will rise."

Condor has not experienced fully the joys of material ownership and so he asks, "How is it different to possess than to imagine things?" Berk looks at him out of the corner of his eye and says, "Consider your pigs – would you rather imagine eating them or would you like to taste their charred meat instead? Understand that eating something means having full possession of it."

To prove Berk's point, Condor brings his only remaining pig, Yahoo, to the Temple. When he sees Condor brandishing a huge knife, Yahoo whimpers and hides under a pile of papers knowing what is coming. "I see what you mean," says Condor smacking his lips that are watering for meat. Condor corners Yahoo, thrusts a knife in the porcine throat, and when the scratching and squealing ends, says, "The deed is done; the conversation is over. I understand the difference. Perhaps I swore prematurely, but nevertheless I swore an oath to my mother. Now, let us cook and eat this pig."

Condor helps Berk put Yahoo on a spit over the fire pit in the Celestial Room. While the pig roasts, Berk jumps on the table, strokes his chin, and struts about, pointing his finger at Condor as the flames cast a huge shadow of the diminutive Berk on the wall.

Berk bellows, "Now is the time to tell you the details of your quest. You are to live with the Goths in The Valley for no less than five years. You will have a chance to apply your hacker skills to a new community. You are to marry and have a child. Then you will escape the Goths, and you will live with the Greeks where you will receive further instructions from our people."

Condor isn't so sure. "If the Goths find out that I am a Bionican, they will kill me."

"Do not worry. You have a lot of things in common with the Goths. You are naturally a violent man who holds no qualm killing users. What makes you think I did not know of your blood lust? I know much more than you can see. I know that you are no intellectual and that books are foreign to you. The Goths are just like you. They will take to you so long as you become their warrior, and you promise to fight for them. And like most Goths, you do not take Daytrain and you love to eat meat. So you will fit right in. But for now, we eat. I think Yahoo is ready." Berk says sniffing the air

Condor approaches the table with carving knives in each hand and eagerly cuts up Yahoo and puts the pig's pieces on a serving dish. They both eat happily in silence until Berk looks up to talk after finishing his chop. "If you succeed, there will be something in it for you," Berk says with a wink. With a dirty man's smile, Berk whispers into Condor's ear, "The Goths have something you want – the girl of your dreams." But Condor is not sure that any Goth girl could be the girl of his dreams, as either what he wants or what he needs. After burping, Berk suggests that they continue their conversation in the antechamber adjoining the dining area where they can sit comfortably.

"Look, Condor," says Berk, "I know that your mother is now the girl of your dreams, but we are going to change that. As your matchmaker, I say you can only have one dream girl at a time. Your mother is only a stepping-stone. You need to get yourself your own real live dream girl and marry her. Once you do that, you will reinvent yourself; that is your destiny. To blend in with the Goths, you will need a new name. I hereby pronounce you *Siegfried* – a perfect name because it recalls the mythical German warrior hero of the Nibelungenlied who slew a dragon."

Condor agrees but wants to know how to do this.

Berk explains, "Changing your name is as easy as changing your password."

"Huh?"

Berk smiles, "You are a hacker. You ought to know how to do this. Just repeat your new name three times, then say your old name, and then repeat your new name three times again."

Embarrassed, Condor obeys. "I am Siegfried. I am Siegfried. I am Siegfried." After hesitating, he says again, "I was Condor. Now I am Siegfried, Siegfried, Siegfried."

"By Jove, I think you have got it," says Berk with pride. "Now you are no longer a hacker, nor a Bionican. It is time to let go; you are now all on your own. Kiss Condor goodbye and say hello to Siegfried. Your job as Siegfried is to win the heart of Tara, daughter of the great warlord Olin. Your mother would not have it any other way."

"OK, now I am Siegfried," he says, getting used to the idea of being renamed Siegfried. "But before I do this, I must consult The Well again. I need to sign off."

But before Berk can object to this terrible idea, Siegfried closes his eyes to tune in The Well. Nothing happens. It turns out that by being renamed, Siegfried loses his password and all of its privileges. The change of name also has a physiological impact. Siegfried's animated tattoos disappear, and his skin turns a pasty white.

Berk says, "Siegfried, now close your eyes and imagine yourself as you used to be." Siegfried pushes the "undo" part of his brain, and that enables him to regain his previous identity as Condor. His tattoos start to materialize and his weak access to The Well returns.

Berk explains, "See, you can toggle from one personality to another, but being Siegfried will only help you when you are living with the Goths. You also need a third identity that will be acceptable to the Greeks. Let me think. For your time with the Greeks, I name you Jason. The name, Jason, will resonate with the Greeks because they have been waiting for quite some time for someone to bring home the fleece. The Greeks will celebrate your arrival as it is foretold to them, plus they could use someone like you."

Siegfried looks puzzled.

Berk explains, "The Greeks will want to know who you are and what you know; they will want to dip into The Well, and they will want your help in doing so. When you finish with the Goths, your real job is to see what the Greeks are up to and to make sure they are not capable of serious mischief. We want you to work with them to build up something that will do justice to your mother's legacy."

"We?"

"Let me tell you, *we* is a useful construct. It is for me to decide what it is, and for you to find out why. If I feel comfortable with we, so should you."

"Okay," says Siegfried still feeling uncomfortable with this explanation.

Before Siegfried can think about it anymore, Berk goes to a flipchart and draws a triangle. He points to each of the three corners where he writes, "Bionican," "Goth," "Greek." He then looks at Siegfried.

"Guess which stands for what?" Before Siegfried can answer him, Berk blurts out the answer, "The Bionicans are the Super-ego, the Greeks the Ego, and the Goths the Id. Our job is to bring these forces into harmony."

Berk notices that Siegfried is puzzled by his psycho-babble. "Someday all this will become clear to you. Take some time to think about it. We shall then see when you are ready to move on."

Siegfried, his possession of Digi Diva now a distant memory, is at first frightened and then exhilarated by the prospect of battling his way to the woman of his dreams. He warms up to the idea of possessing her, not in his imagination, but in reality.

"What is the girl's name again?" he asks Berk.

"Tara, Tara. It is Tara." Berk replies.

"Tell me more about this Tara. What is she like?"

"What she is like is up to you. You will have to re-invent her in your mind if you want her," Berk says clasping his hands together. "You have a lot to learn if you are to succeed in love. So, it is time to continue your education. You must learn to become more red-blooded, more intuitive, less verbal but more communicative. You cannot be arrogant and aloof the way you were with the Bionican women. You have a long way to go."

Berk then explains the next steps.

"Here is a gold talisman of the boar, Gullinbursti. When you first make contact with the Goths, you must give this as a present to Olin, their warlord. Once he accepts this, which he will, your job will be to live among the Goths and learn their ways."

Berk hands Siegfried a map for locating the Goth headquarters in the Simi Valley, near the Santa Susana Mountains, west of what was once the San Fernando Valley.

"Remember, Siegfried, your main job is to find a way to become a leader of the Goths, and then determine whether the Greeks are on the right path. If the Greeks are false, you must kill their top thinkers. Then you must return to Bionica as Condor and gain access to The Well, which will accept you back if you show that you have killed the right people. If the Greeks are righteous, you, having taken the new name of Jason, and your bride, Tara, will have the power to lead both the Goths and Greeks into the future. When you finish your mission, we will hold a gigantic celebration in your honor right here in the Temple, for then you will truly be King of all."

But Siegfried thinks there is something missing. After a pause, he turns to Berk, "After my years with the

Goths, how am I going to be introduced to the Greeks. How will that happen?" Berk, looking somewhat impatient, pauses, "You are right; I did leave something out. As you are getting yourself established in the Goth world, you will come across Medea, the herbalist, who has strong connections to the Greeks. She will be expecting you."

"Who is she? I heard my friend, Eric, mention her."

"I know Medea well and she knows me well, too. She appreciates the fact that just because you are little like me does not mean you are small. She is very wise. She is very important, very powerful. She will help you understand your quest and to deal with changes that come with it, and you must listen to her. And a final word of advice, do not take any wooden nickels."

"What are wooden nickels?" Siegfried wonders.

"Never mind, you would not know anyway."

CHAPTER 4
ON THE ROAD

"I am Siegfried. Condor is dead. I am Siegfried. Condor is dead. I am Siegfried. Condor is dead." Siegfried waits for his new identity to seep in. Once he declares his new name for the third time, he feels the part.

Well, almost. First, he has to let his hair and beard grow to Goth proportion. That takes weeks. Once his hair is long enough, Berk provides him with Goth clothing and instructions on Goth dress code. This new wardrobe now includes woolen trousers and a sleeveless leather vest designed by the Greeks and manufactured by the Goths.

"Hey, here is something that is in fashion with the Goths."

Berk hands him a black top hat decorated with chicken bones, which he tries on for size.

"Fits perfectly, you make a perfect Goth. It goes with your beard."

As Siegfried embarks on his journey, he lifts Berk and

hugs him goodbye in a rare display of affection. Momentarily, Berk acts like a concerned father proffering some advice. "Try to learn something from this journey. Keep your eyes and mind wide open."

Siegfried is anxious to get going. Carrying a rucksack packed with provisions, he climbs up an embankment to a stretch that was once the San Diego Freeway. Making his way through the motionless tangle of abandoned trucks and cars, he carefully avoids the large cracks and holes of the road surface. Winding north he sees the gutted buildings of UCLA, which was once the center for crowd-funded research that focused on the needs of the now-defunct entertainment industry. Looking back, he sees Bionica receding into the brown and yellow haze caused by the bonfires that were lit during the latest teach-ins. Soon Siegfried is so far off that he can barely see Moroni, perched on top of the towering Mormon Temple.

Continuing through the Santa Monica Mountains, Siegfried passes the ruins of the Getty Museum. This proud building on the mountaintop was destroyed by roving bands of born-again performance artists, intent on destroying Satanism in the art world.

As he sees his homeland recede into the horizon, he has second thoughts about leaving Bionica. "Will I miss being a hacker? I had the power of life and death as long as I stayed with The Well. I could kill to fit the bill. Now that is all gone."

The inner voice of his mother is still there. "What on earth are you thinking about? You must keep your mind on the task. You have your destiny to fulfill. There is no looking back."

His fellow hackers appear in a vision, condemning him in a chorus of voices. "Traitor! We know that you and the dwarf have betrayed The Well. When you return, and return you must, we will crack your bone skull and chop you to pieces for everyone in Bionica to see. We will throw you to the vultures."

Siegfried takes a deep breath, looks back one more time and forces a final disconnect to Condor. Off in the distance he imagines columns smoke billowing from his secret Church sanctuary where he collected his sacred objects and where his late pigs used to roam. He is certain that the hackers would have been ordered by The Well to burn it down. In his mind's eye he sees his pig, Google, pleading for its life and wipes away his tears at the thought of his loss. It is all over now. He is not sure about his quest and wonders what possessed him to leave his cozy life in Bionica. With every moment that he continues to entertain doubts and negative thoughts about his quest, he feels the nausea of not being connected to The Well. Siegfried knows that he has to accept his new quest to avoid pain, and since there is no going back, he clenches his fists with resolve to reinforce his new identity and mission in life.

"I am Siegfried. I am Siegfried. I am Siegfried. I am on a quest."

Saying this makes him feel a bit better. He will do anything to avoid the nausea of The Well, even if it means killing somebody.

Up ahead he hears the distant roar of motorcycles. Siegfried leaves the highway to avoid running into a Goth patrol. He no longer has access to GPS through The Well to help him navigate. Instead, he looks for familiar items and clues that have always helped him find his way through the ruins of Bionica. Searching his neural networks, he finds an outdated app flashing in his head that that does not account for blocked roads and destroyed buildings. Apparently the maps apps have not been updated since the Great Plague. He decides that he will just have to find his way without any network support.

As he walks, the freeway comes to a dead end where a huge pile of cement was strewn by an explosion that occurred years ago. He climbs over long-dead human carcasses of dried skin and bones in rotted clothing that were stacked into pyres but never burned. Climbing over the piles of mummified bodies evokes memories of killing Bionican users who strayed from the path. He gets off the freeway to find an alternate route.

According to recalculation of his GPS, Siegfried continues on Sepulveda Boulevard that will take him to his destination. After walking for several miles, Siegfried has visions of songbirds and the opening lines of Keats' *Ode to a Nightingale* pop up in his mind.

My heartaches and drowsy numbness pains
My sense, as though of hemlock I had drunk,
Or emptied some dull opiate to the drains
One minute past, and Lethe-wards had sunk.

The rest of the poem mumbles through his head as he feels a pinch of sadness.

"It sounds good but I do not understand it. I have never seen that immortal bird." There are no nightingales or any other songbirds in his world.

Siegfried hears what could be the song of a nightingale and is convinced that this is a hallucination, but then he sees what it is – robotic bird perched on a tree, a stone throw away from its solar charging nest. These solar-powered birds, built by Autobahn Society as an alternative to real bird watching, have taunted travelers with their songs for years, and with time, hikers grew accustomed to these substitutes and learned to cherish them.

Siegfried climbs the tree to take a better look at the bird. It is the first bird that is not a vulture that he has ever seen. As he gets closer, the bird increases the tempo and pitch of its song. Annoyed by the simulacra, by the fakiness of this tiny bloodless machine, Siegfried grabs the bird and crushes it in his fist. Its artificial feathers dissolve into the wind when Siegfried releases the bird circuitry from his grip.

If Siegfried could choose another life, he would like to be a huge bird of prey, soaring high in the blue sky. He has no desire to be a songbird because he would have to spend all of his time afraid to die and to sing when there is no one there to listen.

After walking for some time, Siegfried comes across an old sunburned American Indian in full headdress dancing and chanting in the middle of the road. Siegfried watches him for a while. Noticing Siegfried, the Indian stops dancing, turns towards him and stares at him with a smile. Siegfried fixes on the Indian's black eyes buried in his round leathery face.

"My name is Red Cloud. Do you want to join me? I am the last of my kind. All of my people are gone."

"I cannot stop. I must keep moving. I am on a quest. I have a mission."

"Do you not know that the moments pass no matter what you do? There will always be that moment of silence when you will forget why you are here. Meditation is very important," Red Cloud says in his deep, deliberate voice.

"I have no time to meditate."

"Oh yes, no doubt you have better things to do. Do you want to know when the world will end?" Red Cloud asks, his impassive face staying put, as only his lips move.

Without explanation, Siegfried blurts out, "I am a warrior, and I am looking to join the Goths."

There is a long pause by Red Cloud. Then he says,

"The world has already ended. We are no more. You are wasting precious time with your mission. Your ancestors made us many promises, more than I can remember. But they only kept one. They promised to take our land, and they took it."

"But I must go; it is my destiny," Siegfried protests.

The old Indian smiles, "You have a lot to learn. Once you might have been a good Indian, but there are no tribes left for you to join; you are a young man with a questionable birthright. Look at the sky."

Siegfried looks up. "I do not see anything"

"There is the land, sky and sea that once were."

"Yes, but what is there to see?"

Red Cloud looks at him, "Is not there anything that thrills your spirit?"

"Spirit? Is not that like religion?"

Red Cloud replies, "Native peoples do not have church religion but we believe that it is good and true to worship something. Isolated thoughts will strangle your spirit."

Siegfried is suspicious. He remembers how he had to kill Little Eddie for quoting scriptures that threatened the stability of Bionica.

The Indian realizes that Siegfried is spiritually blind and gives him some parting advice, "I see that you think I am quoting scripture. It is not about the Christians or about the Bible. There is freedom when your thoughts are born. The clouds will tell you everything if you listen."

Red Cloud points his finger at the sky and then north-ward with the movement of the clouds in the steady wind.

"If you must go, follow the clouds, that is where your path leads."

Putting his head back down, Red Cloud resumes his dancing, and Siegfried is left to continue on his way.

Alone, Siegfried walks aimlessly. All he hears is a steady buzz of insects.

"Do not allow words to hollow out your resolve; you must be like a fortress," he thinks to himself. He puts the Indian out of his mind, and the buzz of doubt goes away.

Siegfried walks on aimlessly for many hours, first along old Highway 101 approaching Westlake and then along a byway overgrown with weeds and strewn with vintage litter. He is hungry and thirsty. As his stomach growls, he wipes his brow and blinks at a sign in front of what was once a gated community called *Alamo Estates*. In the middle of the road is a guard station. The sign in the window reads, "No solicitors."

Through the broken glass Siegfried looks inside guard station and sees a skeleton, still in guard uniform, who waived through visitors during better times. Free to tres-pass, Siegfried enters the community and walks by rows of abandoned houses with faded "for sale" signs stuck in the ground, a reminder of the Great Real Estate Bust. This neighborhood, like so many in the neighborhoods sur-rounding Los Angeles, was depopulated as a result of the mega plague caused by Cybergeddon. Today, there is no sign of life in the neighborhood. There are no lights and no sounds except for the rattling of a shutter when the wind blows.

Parched, Siegfried picks a house to break into hoping to find something, anything, to drink and eat. The place is dusty but intact. The apparent owner of the house, also now only a skeleton, is reclining on an easy chair; the bones of his pet dog are at his feet. Around the dead man's neck is a crudely printed sign, "I am a pseudo-intellectual." There is a hole in his skull. Siegfried wonders whether the dead man was forced to make this sign before he was executed.

Luckily there is a case of soft drinks in the basement as well as a box of canned sardines and bags of potato chips. Siegfried is not concerned that all of these have exceeded the sell-by date on the bottles and packages. He snaps open the cans, drinks the flat warm sugary liquid and eats the salty smelly fish. They are not nearly as good as in his imagination in which all soft drinks are cold, sparkling and delicious, and the fish is mild and tasty. Still he is starving, so he eats up and then looks around the house. There are photos mounted on the wall of what must have been the house's occupants and their relatives, mostly grandchildren. There are also faded prints from art museum exhibitions. He comes across tall shelves full of books choked with dust.

Siegfried recalls that during the summer solstice celebration in Bionica, piles of books were burned to prevent the rebirth of technology. This is the first time in a long while that he has seen books outside of Berk's temple.

Even though he can read a little bit, he still thinks books are for burning. He scans the bookshelf for titles of possible interest and comes across one by his mother, *Xtremus for Dummies*, as well as *A Handbook on Goth Body Piercing*. There are also self-help books on American Goth counterculture, such as *Explorations of the Dark Side of Life* and *Makeovers for Goth Maidens*. One section contains old European works, such as translations of *Beowulf*, *Romance of the Rose*, a *Portable Blake*, and several books based on the Arthurian Legends. He knows his reading skills are still spotty though much improved by Berk's tutelage. He tries to sound out the words on the books, but this level of effort eliminates reading pleasure. It was so much easier to download electronic content from The Well.

Siegfried reaches for a set of books on the bottom shelf. His eye glances across several titles: *Gulliver's Travels*, *Utopia*, *Looking Backward*, *1984*, *Fahrenheit 451*, *Brave New World*, and *Childhood's End*. He recalls hearing about some of them through The Well. One title catches his eye, *The Silent Spring*, a book by Rachel Carson, who raised public awareness of the environmental harm of pesticides. Another is *A Friend of the Earth*, a book by T. Coraghessan Boyle that dramatizes environmental destruction.

On the top shelf, out of reach and guarded by a spider's web, there are classic Greek works by Homer, Plato, Aristotle, Tacitus, Herodotus, Aeschylus, and many others.

"What good are these?" Siegfried mutters to himself as he thumbs through the pages. Siegfried notices that stacked under the books is a manuscript held together by a huge paper clip. He looks at the table of contents that makes reference to Bionica. His curiosity is aroused. He starts looking over the manuscript. The author, Wiesner, seems to be quite upset about the use of implants and their impact on Society and about weapons of mass destruction. Reading on slowly, he comes across several rather gloomy statements about the end of the world as a nice place to live. The author writes that computer technology will eventually overcome human beings, with statements like "technology is the handmaiden of human obsolescence." Siegfried is not sure about the significance of this writer from the early 21st Century because there is no book version of what he wrote. Maybe this manuscript was an earlier version of this work that may have been published online. Maybe all the copies were burned. Perhaps this loose-leaf version was retrieved electronically from the global electronic network. Perhaps there was a later version that did a better job of predicting the future. Who knows whether this author ever published this manuscript! Maybe it was simply retrieved and printed from his website. Even to Siegfried, the "book" is what gives importance to ideas, even in a world where there are no more new books and where all contemporary communications is online. The more important the book, the warmer the fire feels when it is burned.

Siegfried, of course, cannot fully appreciate what books once meant to people. For now, he prefers the manuscript because it provides better kindling than the bound volumes.

Siegfried is cold and is anxious to get a fire going. He finds kerosene lighter fluid in the kitchen and builds a pyramid of books in the fireplace. He uses the loose-leaf manuscript to start a fire and then watches the rest of the books go up in smoke. As he sees the flames shoot up, he has visions from each charred book in which voices from the burning words compete for his attention.

Each book thrown into the fire has a voice trying to convey the essence of its meaning. As the books burn, a quick succession of random words or sometimes even a single word taken from the book jacket scream out at him. _The Structure of Scientific Revolutions_ by Thomas Kuhn is summed up through two words, "paradigm shift." Karl Marx's *Das Capital* screams out "dialectic." Sigmund Freud's *Civilization and Its Discontents* sighs, "sublimation." *Being and Nothingness*, by Jean-Paul Sartre, ends up yelping, "existentialism." Jacques Derrida, *Positions*, makes a French peep about "deconstruction." Like other Bionicans, Siegfried likes to learn by osmosis, and as the voices from each book call out to him, he realizes that there is no better way to learn what is inside a book than by burning it.

Once the fire is lit and enough books have been burned to create a glowing pile of warm embers, Siegfried snuggles up next to the fireplace and starts to imagine what he would like to read, if he could read. He realizes that he does not know what he would like to read. The number of books, even just in the shelves of this dead man's house, are far too many.

After his stay in the house, Siegfried hits the road again at daybreak. "El Camino Real," the sign says. Siegfried continues along this royal road for most of the day and after passing several abandoned neighborhoods up in the hills, he comes across a freshly painted sign that says "El Rancho de Esperanza." Siegfried sees cattle grazing in the distance and follows a dirt road that leads to an adobe style ranch house. An older man chopping wood is there to greet him.

"Hi there, I am John Smith. I thought you would never come."

"You were expecting me?"

"Of course, you are on a quest, right? Everyone with a quest comes this way; it is a given. Why do you not come in so that we can talk?"

Siegfried gives him a blank stare and then follows John Smith into the house where they settle down for cool drinks in a courtyard surrounded by cactus plants and flowers.

"Conchita likes to garden," the old man brags. "Where are you heading?"

"I am on my way to Simi Valley to join the Goths."

John Smith looks at him and says, "That simple, huh? All you have to do is head in the right direction, kill someone, become a Goth, marry the woman of your dreams, and become their leader. Take some advice from me. You have got to prepare yourself. You need some moral and practical preparation. The first thing you have to do is appreciate poetry."

"Poetry?"

"Yes poetry, words that have a life of their own. The Goths love poetry; they love it so much that they want to remember every word. They hate writing. Under no circumstances let them catch you writing anything down."

"I do not write," Siegfried says with pride and arrogance.

"You do not write? Oh, how wonderful! I take it that

you must be a Bionican, one of those osmosis guys tied to The Well. I know all about your handicap. You fooled me with your long hair and your beard. But if you do not write you cannot be a Greek, and if you do not love poetry, you cannot be a Goth; and so you must be a Bionican."

"You know all about The Well?" Siegfried asks.

"I was on the team that developed The Well; we discovered how to create nano-neural circuitry in a biological medium, like your brain. What you call The Well is in your brain networked with the other brains in your community. Boy, do I hate saying, The Well. Let us leave well enough alone for now," he says laughing. "I know that you and the other neural nitwits in Bionica have this Well network in your heads, too; that is how you are able to receive, communicate and share information. At the time this was a real breakthrough."

"So how did the Bionicans come into the picture?" Siegfried has never been sure how he and his fellow hackers became the guardians of The Well.

"All the original Bionicans were programmed from birth through The Well. By the time the Great Plague happened, we already knew there could be a cyber attack to kill off those with brain implants. We made sure that the Bionicans, who were among those with brain implants, received virus protection from Petri dish inception. The facts of life in Bionica are that none of the original Bionicans, including you, were reared by your birth mothers and fathers."

"But what about me? Why am I special? Why did my tattoos move?"

"You were extra special because of your connection to Julia. She insisted on HD tattoos – straight out of Pixar – so that she could stay in touch with you. We made sure that you would never become addicted to Daytrain because we knew that someday you would be called upon to transform how The Well is used. We wanted someone in the group to have the power to escape from the rules that the hackers were programmed to follow.

"She is your mother lode. Is not that the case with all mothers?" John says with a smirk.

Siegfried stares, losing eye contact with John.

"Right, your mother was a very powerful person. She died trying to preserve her influence over the Xtremus even after death. You must learn to filter her out. I do not think you can trust her," John continues. "Her postmortal possessiveness is pathological."

"Berk told me just that same thing. He also told me that I am to prevent The Well from being compromised. I do not understand why my next mission is to live with the Goths if the Greeks are the ones to watch out for."

"You need Goth experience to succeed in the Greek world, and you need to test your strength against theirs. It is that simple."

Siegfried thinks there are still many potholes in his

understanding of the road ahead.

"What about Daytrain? Why are the Goths against using it?"

John smiles, "The Christians are against it, and many of the Goths are becoming Christians, even as their leadership resists conversions. They tried to forbid it, but there were just too many of them converting. As for the leadership, so long as Greeks and Goths are making profits on Daytrain alike, the stuff will keep flowing. It is that simple."

"And my role?" Siegfried asks again.

"Your challenge, as I understand it, is to penetrate the leadership of the Greeks and become part of it. You will have to make sure that they do not destroy The Well. If they do, they could again unleash the virus of the Great Plague, which is now dormant. That would certainly kill off the Bionicans, who are the most susceptible to a returning virus, and that would destroy The Well entirely in a decisive blow that would destroy our budding post-cyber culture forever."

"What about the Goths, the Christians and the Greeks, how would they suffer under the virus?" Siegfried asks.

"I think the Greeks believe that only they would survive," John says. "And then there would be no one to stop *The Others* – all those who are not part of our larger community." Siegfried is well aware of the other survivors below Pico Boulevard, from Hollywood and Vine across Crenshaw, and then all the way down Pico to Bundy Avenue.

"You Bionicans are lucky because they will not go near you because of the smell, while we – the Goths and the Greeks – have to work together to keep The Others out. We need them to provide us with field and house slaves. The G-spot Femmes are also good at procurement and supply desperate Greek women with Goth men, whom they   train to be pliant and sufficiently affectionate. You know, slaves are our blessed volunteers. We need them to keep our way of life, and we must do everything in our power to keep the peace and to prevent the return of Cybergeddon. You, my boy, will play an important role to help us to do that."

While they are talking about the return of the Great Plague, Conchita brings John and Siegfried some nachos and salsa. As she puts the plates down, John asks, "Where is the guacamole?" As she goes back to get some, her husband continues to lecture Siegfried.

"If you are to be successful, you need to branch out and take responsibility for your thoughts and actions. Living with the Goths is a fine place to start. You need to understand the Goths in order to understand the Greeks. You may find the Goths ignorant, but watch out. The smarter ones will eat pseudo-intellectuals alive. Thankfully you are not one. Remember, the Goths keep the

Daytrain trade going, which now supports their civilization as we know it."

The rancher continues, "After you join the Goths, you will become involved in their Daytrain trade, which has now spread throughout the Valley. Daytrain was first used to pacify the Bionican users, and now young people from everywhere, the Goths, and the Greeks, and even the hackers use the stuff. You are going to help sort things out. And remember one more thing, with all the sectarian intrigue between Goths and Greeks, the Christians are making a come-back."

Siegfried nods, "I know all too well about that. We had to sunset some of our best users because they were infiltrated by scripture from *Genesis*."

John Smith then turns to Siegfried and looks him straight in the eyes. "See those cattle way out there. One of them is Big Ben Time Watcher, my prize bull. I raise them for the Goths. I deal with Goths regularly; they provide me with the stuff I need. I lead a simple life, and they are a honest lot, but I tell you, do not cross them. You also have to watch out for misunderstandings. The Goths kill fist and ask questions later."

"So you get along with the Goths?" Siegfried wonders. "Or do you just trade with them?"

"Hell, I married one, Conchita is a Goth."

"Is that a Goth name?"

"No, she is a brown person, but she is a Goth at heart.

She does not like it that I read; hell, I have to hide my books so that she can pretend not to find them. She thinks anything but gardening is a waste of time."

"But why do the Goths hate books?"

"They do not hate books. They hate the people who make a show of reading. I think they have trouble reading. Many are dyslexics. You see, when we put everything online, there was no reason for people to read. They thought it was too much trouble to decipher words. They wanted pictures, and we gave them pictures; then they wanted sounds, and we gave them sounds. And then they wanted pictures and sounds all together, all the time. And then Cybergeddon took away their movies. So now, those who do not read depend directly on experience to shape what they say and think. The Goths are a very uncivilized lot, but I like them." John says wiping his mouth as he turns to order his dispirited wife, "Conchita, get us some more grub."

Conchita returns with a plate of nacho leftovers, and John whispers to Siegfried, "You know what they say, *how you gonna keep 'em down on the farm after they've seen Paris.*" Siegfried does not know what they would say. He does not even know what a Paris is.

They go inside to eat; the food is coarse but filling. The rancher confesses that he likes the poet Robert Burns and quotes him a line.

The lovely lass O'Inverness,

Nae joy nor pleasure can she see
For, e'en to morn she cries, Alas.
And aye the saut tear blin's her e'e.

He stands up and makes a grand gesture and sighs. "I am the last of the Robbie Burns Society."

Siegfried starts to think that he does not like this rancher by the name of John Smith, but he realizes that the rancher knows a lot about the people in his mission and so he continues to pump him for more information.

"What about the Greeks?"

"Well what *about* them." John Smith snorts back. "They are more like the Romans."

"The who?"

"The Romans. They are bound for glory. What do you want with them?" John Smith asks.

"I thought you knew about the Greek's weapons of mass destruction?" Siegfried asks.

"Weapons of mass destruction?" Smith asks.

Siegfried is slow in his reply, "You know…things like nuclear bombs and chemical and biological weapons, things that were used to blow things up and to make people sick and die. As hackers for The Well, we worried that the Greeks would use The Well to develop these weapons."

John Smith laughs out loud, "You are a bit late. Mass destruction has already taken place. Don't you know about Cybergeddon? Siegfried is confused; of course, he knows about Cybergeddon. John Smith pauses and then resumes in a lower voice.

"From what you tell me, you are on a mission, as part of Project Pygmalion. Everyone knows that. I am supposed to talk to you, just as you were supposed to talk to Red Cloud and Berk before that. Everything is pre-ordained. Somebody has to set you straight; everyone you meet will try. Ignorant, you are a very dangerous man."

Siegfried has never felt like a dangerous man, and he takes this as a backhanded compliment. Basking in the glow of self-importance, Siegfried does not press John to talk about Project Pygmalion and the purpose of his mission. Instead, he is anxious to know what comes next.

"What advice would you give me?" Siegfried asks.

"Hell, I do not have much advice for you, except maybe that if you come across the Bead Lady, which I know you will, listen to her carefully. She will teach you a thing or two of what you need to know to be among the Goths. She is a cherished being. As for living among the Greeks, then you are on your own. You will have to learn from them."

"Where does the Bead Lady live?"

"Just continue north until you hear her singing. She loves birds, and the birds love her. Please be kind to her."

Siegfried thanks the rancher for the food and advice, and heads down the hill to the major road going north.

CHAPTER 5
THE BEAD LADY

After leaping over a fence and climbing over a pile of demolished cars, he stumbles across another dried human body lying flat in the middle of the road.

"It must have been run over by a Goth truck," he mutters to himself, noticing the tire marks. He continues along the path to another highway looking for a place to rest and find drinking water. A real live rabbit darts ahead of him. He bends over, picks up a stone and slings it after the darting blur of fur. He misses. In response to the "ping" of the stone careening off a rock, a rattlesnake hisses his rattler to reprimand Siegfried's trespass. He ignores the snake and continues to stir things up by kicking small rocks lying in his way.

As he walks, he hears the faint voice of a woman singing but cannot make out the words of the song. Following the sounds, Siegfried makes his way down the garden path, surrounded by hedges that bulge in all directions.

The sounds bring him through the thicket to a simple log cabin where a young woman, sitting in a lotus position, strings beads and sings about what she is doing. She is dressed in peasant garb with garlands in her hair in her wonderful garden of vegetables, fruits, and berries. To Siegfried's astonishment, there are real songbirds and hummingbirds and yellow butterflies surrounding her.

"This must be a vision," Siegfried says to himself. He does not like to be fooled. He blinks and still she is there – petite and pert, a bronze woman with hair that continuously changes color from strawberry blonde to jet-black.

"Who are you?" Siegfried asks, interrupting her singing.

"I am the last Hippie Madonna – a mixture of all the races of mankind. All my beads are beautiful. And might I ask, who are you, young man?"

"I am, Siegfried, on my way to join the Goths," he explains.

"And why would you want to do a thing like that?" she asks, looking straight into his eyes, as she puts her finger to her lip after flipping her long hair. As the strands of her hair move, they change colors from blonde to red, and from brown to black. Looking closer, Siegfried realizes that her face morphs as well. One moment she is a fair skinned damsel, next a beautiful dark skinned Nubian, and then a graceful geisha. But even as her hair and skin change, her mouth and voice remain the same.

Siegfried explains, "I am on a mission. I need the Goths to put me in touch with the Greeks."

She sighs. "Oh, you are a special one. I have heard that you were coming. I know you are looking for a girl," she says with low-voiced irony. "Hmm…let me, uh, guess, you are looking for Tara, the daughter of Olin, the Goth warlord. That is what my beads say." She shows him a necklace and puts it around his neck. "Each bead tells a story; you just have to listen. Let these beads do the talking for you. They have your future written in them," she says. She explains that her gift of divining the future is only possible through these special beads. Siegfried recalls that some of his fellow hackers used beads to track time and to plan for the future. Perhaps this bead woman is the source of that knowledge. It was something that he never understood.

He asks, "Who are your people? What is your name?"

"Oh me, oh my, what a lot of questions so early in the day. I am half Goth and half Greek, but I am a mixture of all human races. I am a universal donor. My mother was a beautiful and talented Greek girl who married a strong and handsome Goth. She taught me to read and to grow organic vegetables. My father taught me the beauty of poetry and the meaning of valor. My father was not like the other Goths; he wanted to learn to read just as my mother did and he kept that secret from the other

Goths. When they found out about his books, they beat him and burned his eyes out so that he could no longer read. Even though he could not see, my parents lived together in love. Today, they are both dead, killed by the renegade Bionican, Simon Girty, who wanted to convert them into Believers and failed to persuade them. I see in the beads that someday you will kill him for me. As to my name, since my parents died, I have not been able to remember my real name; they never wrote it down. Another blind Goth, my aunt, taught me to see the future with the beads."

As three little bluebirds land on the Bead Lady's shoulder, she suddenly becomes a brunette. Amazed, Siegfried looks at the birds, real songbirds. He has never seen birds this beautiful so close before. She starts to sing parts of a mid-20th Century tune:

So be like I, hold your head up high 'til you find the
bluebird of happiness
You will find greater peace of mind, knowing there's a
bluebird of happiness
And when he sings to you, though you're deep in blue
You will see a ray of light creep through
And so remember this, life is no abyss
Somewhere there's a bluebird of happiness.

"These bluebirds are my friends. I am known as the Bead Lady, but some people call me the Bird Lady because I love birds and they love me. The birds bring me the seeds for my garden. I am known for my tasty vegetables and my ability to foretell the future. Since I have told you your future, do you want to eat one of my tomatoes?"

The bluebirds fly out of the garden. The Bead lady offers Siegfried a tomato, something that he has never eaten except in his imagination when he was tuned into The Well. Good tomatoes are hard to find, even in the imaginary realm. With a real tomato in hand, Siegfried takes a bite and wonders whether he can penetrate the essence of the tomato without relying on Daytrain. He waits for the sensory experience, but his taste buds fail to report delight. He grimaces. Just as it was with the soft drinks, the real thing does not live up to the imaginary equivalent offered through The Well.

"You must be open to new flavors. Good things come to those who wait," she says, inviting him into her home as she flashes her breasts that move to and fro in her diaphanous blouse.

The first thing he sees as he enters the cottage is a giant mandala made out of beads. Scattered through the house are thousands of beads neatly sorted in piles.

"Each bead has its unique message," the Bead Lady explains.

The Bead Lady picks up a group of beads from under her bed and lets Siegfried feel them. As his hands explore each bead, she begins to speak, conveying a sense of doom.

"Here in these beads is the story of Condor, the hacker. Above all, Condor does what his mother tells him. He longs to touch the things she shows him; because, like her, he wants to own them."

"I know your Mother, Condor; I mean Siegfried," she corrects herself, lowering her voice for emphasis.

"Your mother is the voice in your head. She sent you on a terrible quest. I warn you that she does not love you as a good mother should."

Stunned, Siegfried remains silent. He is afraid that the Bead Lady may know too much, but despite initial misgivings, he is attracted to her.

The Bead Lady continues on a more practical note. "So you want to know more about the Goths because you want to join them. Is that what you choose for yourself?"

Siegfried nods. He is attracted to her sweet face and is drawn to her because of what he can learn from her. But, the more attractive she becomes, the more he distrusts her. It is all very confusing for Siegfried. Does everyone know about his quest, he wonders.

The Bead Lady goes on to tell him about the Goths as if she were reciting an encyclopedia. She uses little clay figurines to illustrate her talk.

"The Goths roam the bumpy and dusty highways on trucks and motorcycles up and down the dry stretches of the San Fernando Valley right across Sepulveda to the

Great Wall along Pico Boulevard. These mobile barbarians control all these roads and fuel supplies in the area. That is the secret of their power."

Uninterested, Siegfried changes the topic.

"I like your hair."

"My hair? Which hair color would you like? As you see, each time I cock my head, the color changes." Siegfried reaches to touch her hair, but she pushes him away.

"Why do you not stay with me and forget this so-called quest," the Bead Lady asks. "If you cannot pay enough attention to learn about the Goths, how can you expect to succeed? The quest is just going to kill you in the end. I know this from my beads. Give me a chance to prove this. I will show you tonight."

As the night falls, the Bead Lady lights twenty candles to represent each of the digits of a normal human being. "Some people are born with more," she explains, referring to the effects of the dark biological experimentations of the past. "So I keep a few extra candles handy in case you grow any extra overnight." Next day, the Bead Lady serves Siegfried fresh vegetables and succulent fruit to charm his novice palate on the assumption that the best way to a man's heart is through his stomach. She hands him a succulent apple that seems to promise him everything with the first bite.

She whispers in his ear, "Please stay with me; I cannot let you go. If you go, you are doomed. We are all doomed but why rush it? So stay with me instead. The beads say that you will never reach your goal. So you will not reach your goal because it will change by the time you achieve it. Let me make you happy. "Just call me Beadina," she whispers into Siegfried ear."

"Beadina," he whispers back obediently without thinking about what she has said.

When she hears her name, Beadina breaks into the Dance of the Seven Veils, removing each of the veils carefully as she tantalizes Siegfried with totally flexible arms and legs that she bundles into a whirl of limbs and exposed breasts that flash by his face – not just two, but four, six, countless breasts there for the taking. Siegfried is taken aback as Beadina, the contortionist, turns herself into a human pretzel, emanating seductive aromas from her nostrils, so that Siegfried is unable to resist the invitation to visit her pelvic cavity chamber of delights.

Seduced and conquered by her unrelenting logic and charms, Siegfried spends a wildly amorous night with her and her magical tresses. He leaps after her shapely redolent rump and thighs and is engulfed by the crescendo of their embrace. Her expressive hands embrace his strong shoulders, and she uses her graceful but powerful arms to draw him to her breasts. He suddenly hears the drums of the summer solstice, keeping the beat of his carnal beatitude.

But things are different in the morning light. Beadina

senses that something is off- kilter.

"Are you experiencing post-coital tristesse?" she asks him matter-of-factly. He does not know French but realizes that she has hit a nerve. He is having second thoughts about this precipitous affair. He feels satisfied, almost too satisfied, which invites the thud of dissatisfaction to descend on him. The word "happy" strikes him the wrong way; it conjures up that all-too-familiar nausea that had kept him in line as a hacker. He is convinced that happiness is bogus and cannot and will not waylay him from his duty to pursue his quest.

The Bead Lady smiles to reassure Siegfried and tempts him with another juicy red apple, like the one she had given him the night before. She looks at Siegfried intently as she warns one more time, "If you continue on your present path, you will lose everything, but if you must go, beware of Medea." Siegfried is taken aback.

"Medea?" Siegfried wonders. "The dwarf had mentioned her. Tell me more."

"She is very powerful. She wants to bring back money. She has foreknowledge of what will happen to you. It is part of her Project Pygmalion. She thinks you are an actor in her play."

"Why should I care?"

"All the world's a stage and all the men and women merely players," the Bead Lady whispers to him.

Not familiar with Shakespeare, Siegfried does not

get the time-honored impact of her words and suspects that she is making fun of him.

"Are you toying with me?" he asks her.

"No, my dear lad, I am probably your only friend in the world. What I want for you is what I want for myself, and all I want for myself is for you to want me. I want you to want me as I want you."

As she says this, the Bead Lady's hair turns gray. .

His mother suddenly appears to him in a vision. "Do not let her fool you," she warns, "She is trouble. She will get in the way of your sacred quest."

As he hears this warning from his mother, his old hacker self takes over. He feels nauseous and stares at the Bead lady, expecting her to react. Instead, her gray hair turns blonde and frizzy; her face becomes more babyish and her voice more childish.

"Will not you stay with me? I need you. Please do not go. Please, baby, I can make you happy."

Siegfried feels nauseous and wants to leave. He knows he has nothing to give, and it makes him angry that she thinks he would change that for her.

"I must go," he says.

"How can you go? I have shown you everything." The Bead Lady screeches, grabbing his arm and tugging at his shoulder while her chameleon hair erupts into a firework of beautiful colors. She deludes herself that she can still seduce him.

"You cannot go. Not after last night when I let you take me, when we became one. I will not let that happen," she demands.

Siegfried pushes her away.

Her voice becomes angry and petulant, "You will never experience happiness unless you are free from disembodied influences. No real man hears voices. Real men have their own voices that respect and protect women."

In a sudden flash of anger, Siegfried reacts to the Bead Lady's attack on his manhood.

Grabbing her by the hair, he asks, "Why are you doing this to me?"

"You are enslaved by your voices. I feel sorry for you."

"I do what I have to do. Do not get in my way, I warn you," Siegfried says with a hollow voice.

"You sure are teaching me a lesson," she says sarcastically. Her hair turns straight and jet-black. "You took everything I offered. You took my bed, my food, and my honor. Do you not have anything in return? What kind of a man are you?"

Siegfried is silent with his head bowed. Then he looks up, "Why me?"

The Bead Lady is quick to answer. "Because you are the man of my dreams. I have no choice in this. You were destined to come along for me. I have no choice, and you have only one good choice. The choice is between me and your happiness. Your quest will be your ruin – it is in the cards.

This last bit confuses Siegfried, but he decides to stand his ground. "I do have a quest."

"I know. I can tell you that your quest does not matter. It is a big lie. All that matters is the two of us. You and I are all that matters."

Siegfried is in no mood for romance; he has never known fulfilled love. At least Digi Diva was a good sport when she let him be. Plus, he is not ready to break the ties to his mother.

The Bead Lady takes on a conciliatory tone. "I know it is not easy for you. It has not been easy for me, either; I have been very lonely. Together we would never be lonely again."

She brings him a tray of fruits and nuts as a peace offering. Siegfried grabs the fruits and nuts with both his hands and stuffs them greedily into his mouth. They are delicious, and he would like to savor them, but does not want to spend the time nor give the wrong signal to the smitten Bead Lady.

"I can see your hunger. You eat too fast. Maybe you cannot relax." She reaches out to touch his head. He withdraws quickly and continues to chew. The Bead Lady sighs.

"How do you know I will not let the Goths know that you are coming?" she threatens. "What are you going to do about that? She coos, thinking this joke would disarm him, but there are unintentional consequences.

"I must stop her before she stops me," Siegfried mutters to himself. "This world is not big enough for the both of us." The Bead Lady hears this and backs off. His last vestige of attraction to her is transformed into revulsion when he sees that she is afraid of him. He thinks she would divulge his quest if he rejected her.

"Maybe she is a D-train user with unauthorized privileges," he wonders. This would explain why she wants to get in his way. Siegfried suspects that she could be part of a much larger conspiracy to stop his quest.

Taking pride in his willingness to act decisively, he reverts to the hacker mission statement: *Allow them to do no harm to the general good*. He goes outside to pick out a large, heavy rock.

"You have come back with a large, heavy rock to liberate me, have you not?" the Bead Lady says with a mixture of resignation and sarcasm. "So, if it must be, rock on!"

"I have no choice."

Sitting in a lotus position, her eyes closed, the Bead Lady takes a deep yogic breath. Condor imagines her skeleton, the curve of the spine, and the position of her femurs.

"I am ready," she says quietly. "It was not meant to be."

Siegfried waits a while to allow the Bead Lady to

meditate. Looking at him before he has a chance to ready himself, she blurts out her final words.

"*The answer, my friend, is blowing' in the wind,*" she repeats in a singsong and extends her left hand toward him. "Take these beads. You are the child of the damned. Some day you will meet your fate, and I will not be there to help you. You will miss me when I am gone."

"What is your name again?" Siegfried asks. "I am not good with names," he tries to excuse himself.

"Beadina," she says.

Siegfried wastes no time. "So be it. Good bye, sweet Beadina." He smashes in her cranium and then takes the beads out of her limp hand and puts them around his neck victoriously. His nausea becomes unbearable when he looks at her face and her wide-open eyes staring at him. Her kaleidoscopic hair and face finally stop moving and become covered by a beautifully layered strawberry-blonde halo.

As he hurries to the doorway, dozens of house sparrows swoop down on him while the gentle bluebirds surround the Bead Lady's corpse mourning her death. Siegfried flees outside as the angry sparrows chase after him, pecking at the necklace that the Bead Lady relinquished as her parting gift. Siegfried fights off the little birds, killing a few with his bare hands. The necklace snaps, showering beads hither and yon as he runs away.

Alone again, he is dazed and dumbstruck by what he

has done; he struts about to bolster his self-confidence and to rid himself of doubt. He tells himself again that it is his destiny to have killed the Bead Lady and that this is what she wanted him to do, even when she told him that he was wrong. So it was her fault; she made him do it. Telling himself this story reduces his nausea; perhaps his nausea will go completely away if he conjures a chutzpah fantasy in which he kills Simon Girty to honor the Bead Lady's memory.

"One good turn deserves another," he says with a smile, patting himself on the back for thinking about the future demise of Simon Girty. He feels better and is now ready to hook up with the Goths.

CHAPTER 6
THE ANTHROPOLOGISTS

Siegfried sees smoke rising from the valley and thinks that down there he will be able to get something to eat. He heads down a ravine and then up a trail overgrown with brush and weeds. He sees the source of the smoke – a large mobile home on a meadow near the woods. Outside, a middle-aged couple, a man and a woman, sit at a picnic table stacked with books, taking notes from a tape recording, powered by a nearby generator that emits a steady hum.

As Siegfried approaches, the man hurries to clear the table. The woman gets up and moves towards Siegfried to greet him. Short and stout, she wears slacks and a side-buttoned shirt; a peace sign pendant dangles from her neck. Her graying hair is in a tight bun.

"Oh, we were not sure at first who you were. You might have been a Goth."

"No, I am Siegfried."

"With a name like that, you must be on a quest," she says with a friendly smile.

"I seek the hand of Tara, daughter of Olin," Siegfried declares.

"So we have been told. News travels quickly in these parts. Meet my husband, Gregory. I am Margaret." Gregory and Siegfried shake hands. Gregory is thin and tall, slightly stooped over, wears cotton trousers and a turtleneck sweater with holes in the elbows and front. The top of his balding head is flanked by shoulder-length hair.

Siegfried looks puzzled. "How did you know about it?"

"We are UCLA socio-anthropologists doing field work in The Valley, and our job is to know what is going on." Gregory is friendly and inclusive. "We know all about quests. In fact, we are doing a longitudinal study of quests like yours. Maybe we can help you."

"You have access to The Well?"

Gregory ignores the question and continues. "We are conducting *action research*. This means we are not just trying to learn something, but we are also trying to do something about it. We are pioneers in the field of post-cyber psycholinguistics. Our work is to understand the relationship between illiteracy and virility."

Siegfried looks puzzled.

"We are trying to understand how the Goths manage without books and writing, and why they detest grammar." Gregory picks up the books that he had tried to hide.

"Ours is dangerous work. If the Goths catch us reading, we could end up on a funeral pyre. They do not believe in research, and that makes field work difficult."

Siegfried asks, "Then how do you get your information?"

Margaret pipes in, "We use this old video recorder to collect interviews surreptitiously. The Goths do not mind that so long as we do not write things down. Of course, that complicates matters because we cannot jot down notes while we do the interviews."

"How many Goths have you interviewed?"

"Lots of them, especially the big shots."

"Have you met Olin and Tara?"

"You bet. We were particularly interested in them because of the Freudian angle. There is a bond between father and daughter that is...shall we say peculiar." Margaret's eyes roll as Gregory continues. "Not to mention that other sister. Gonorrhea. Hmmm, a real catchy name. She used to be called Goneril, but changed it when she left home. She was the apple of Olin's eye. But then someone took a bite out of her apple and so her father kicked her out. She had a motorcycle accident in which her leg was amputated below the knee, but she made out OK. She has a will of steel and has become...uh...quite an en-tre-pre-neur."

"I have of heard of her. She heads up the G-spot Femmes," Siegfried bellows out, pleased with himself for this bit of knowledge.

"You are *so* right, she and the other Uzi-packing sapphists. Oh, then there is Olin's son, Thor. A bright young man, but... what disappointment he has been to his dad. Olin would like Thor to succeed him, but his men would never allow that. The rest of the tribe wants a real he-man to be in charge."

"A real he-man?"

"Oh, do not get me wrong, but he is a bit..."

"Effeminate," Margaret supplies the word with a knowing look. "He only likes books and looks to the Greeks for inspiration. He thinks he will be kept safe because of his lock of purple hair."

"Kiss of death in the Goth leadership column," Gregory intones. "Thor is bright enough though, capable of learning and acting decisively. He does a damn good job making sure that the Goths do not get fleeced every time they make a bargain with the Greeks."

Gregory stops the recording and cannot resist giving his analysis of Goth society. He discusses how the Goths have developed a system of behavior that contributes to the growth and sustenance of their community. He offers his theory about Goths and their love for poetry.

"The Goths are good at remembering rhyming verse because their brains are primitive. Their brains are capable of remembering words in a sequence more easily than someone more sophisticated, like me, who thinks of so many things at once.

"Furthermore, the Goths have an inexplicable response to poetry. When they love a poem, they go out of their way to praise, but when they come across a poem they hate, all hell breaks loose. This is the way it goes with their oral poetry – it is all in the moment, and when that moment is betrayed by doggerel, there must be poetic justice."

"What do the Goths do with poetry that is written down?" Siegfried asks.

"Good question, young man. The rank-and-file Goths have no use for writing, period. The only thing that matters to them is the spoken word and action in real time. They communicate through restrictive codes. For them, there is no going back. They believe there is no future in history."

Margaret laughs at this old lame joke as Gregory continues, "But things are a-changin'. Some Goths are breaking ranks and are secretly learning how to read. Perhaps this is a good time to mention that Medea – the Greek who is well known for her encyclopedic knowledge of Greek culture – is tutoring Thor. She is probably the most important person you will meet because she is a kingpin who moves freely among the Greeks and Goths. She has a vision for their future."

"Yes, I have heard of her."

Gregory continues to talk, "The secret of her power is that she is an expert herbalist who has supplied Olin with Cialis for years; her bonafide curative abilities have made her a force to be reckoned with. She is very ambitious. She is planning to establish a new banking system based on sexual favors as the gold standard. She and Tara's sister, Gonorrhea, plan to expand sex work into a viable and respectable industry.

"But, can she be trusted?" Siegfried asks, remembering what the Bead Lady said about her.

"Some call her a sorceress because of her potions, but I think she can be trusted to do what she does well," Gregory says.

Siegfried looks puzzled.

Gregory explains, "Medea provides what a lot of people need, anything from D-train to virility and fertility. There has been virtually no health system since the Great Plague; health-wise, it is every man, woman and child for himself."

"D-train? What does Medea have to do with D-train?"

"She is the mastermind behind the D-train trade, and there is a fellow named Eric, who is the darling of the G-spot biker girls, who helps Medea out."

Siegfried is surprised that these anthropologists know about Eric and his connection with Medea. He would prefer to keep his relationship with Eric quiet because he does not want his cover blown.

"Is there anything between Eric and this...herbalist? Are they lovers?"

"I do not think so. I do know that he is quite taken by her. I suppose you want to know more about Tara."

"Yes. About Tara, my destiny is to marry her."

"Ah, the quest," Margaret says with a touch of sarcasm.

"Tara is a different story. She is just like her father," Gregory volunteers with a straight face.

Margaret interrupts, "Oh Tara." Margaret obviously does not like Tara. "You are not the first to seek her hand in marriage. What makes you think you will succeed with her when so many others have failed? To win her, you will have to convince both Olin and Tara's sister that you are worthy. Once you prove yourself to be a worthy suitor, you would then have to undergo a pre-marital inspection tour with Gonorrhea and the G-spot biker femmes.

Siegfried turns to Margaret. "My Mother, Julia, says I should try to woo her and that I *will* succeed."

"Julia? That makes all the difference. It is always good to have your mother on your side, especially when she is a voice in your head," she quips sarcastically, "Now what about the lucky girl?"

Gregory pushes the playback button on his machine.

"Here she is, the real GAP –

Gothic American Princess."

The screen flickers and Tara appears in an evening dress. Tara has a shrill little voice. She is all about consumerism and recites the list of the earthly possessions she has and the wish list of what she wants.

"I have a Honda, but I want Fat Boy and an Indian. I wish someone could find me an Alexander McQueen in black. I simply cannot have enough golden crucifixes; there must be more out there that Gonorrhea can find for me. And all the music I listen to sucks – it is all too popular, somebody find me some jazz. I just love Erroll Garner playing *Misty*," she squeaks.

"She would have been a great flapper in the Silent Era, but now that we have to listen to her." Gregory puts his arm around Siegfried's shoulder and continues, "I assume you know what you have to do. Are you up for the task?"

"I know what I have to do is not easy," Siegfried replies.

Gregory sighs, "This is very risky."

"Also very unbecoming," Margaret adds.

Gregory puts his other hand on Siegfried's shoulder. "You look like someone who is easily smitten. I wish you the best of luck, but personally you would be better off with..."

Margaret interrupts, "You mean *her*? You bring her

up just because you have a crush on her. I think she is boring; she has a one-track mind."

"Yes, I mean Beadina, the Bead Lady." Gregory looks at Siegfried. "She is the one for you. Have you met her?"

Siegfried gets a guilty look on his face and shakes his head. He wonders whether word has gotten out about her.

"I bet you are a real lady-killer," Margaret adds with a laugh. "You probably know all about the bluebird of happiness."

Siegfried's face turns white. After a long silence, Margaret gets up and brings a tray of food. "When in doubt, eat," she says.

Seeing Siegfried's sudden change, Margaret and Gregory become nervous and eat very fast. "The race is on. He who eats the fastest wins," Gregory calls out almost choking after taking a huge bite.

"Do not talk with your mouth full," Margaret blurts out at Gregory, propelling a drumstick of unknown origin at Siegfried that almost makes him fall off his stool as he dodges it. This time it is Margaret's turn to win, but the race is close. Both wipe their plates; Siegfried, meanwhile, has barely started his meal.

"Go ahead, chew your food. Do not mind us. We are anthropologists; we like to observe."

Siegfried feels uncomfortable and does not like the kind of attention he is getting. He thinks, "Maybe I ought to sunset these two and do everybody a favor." But, he is too hungry to kill anyone, and so he keeps on eating slowly, devouring about six kinds of meat while Margaret and Gregory watch. Margaret and Gregory keep on talking while Siegfried nods into his food and falls asleep at the table, oblivious to their chatter. When he wakes up, Gregory and Margaret are gone. He wonders if they drugged him as he rushes off to his next destination.

Siegfried continues his travels north to the Valley to the Goth headquarters. The crunching sounds of his steps on the gravel road punctuate the silence surrounding him. Behind him he hears rough voices singing a snippet of a German drinking song, "Wir wollen unseren alten Kaiser Wilhelm wieder haben," but this thrill gives way to disappointment at seeing two miserable Goths slowly making their way towards him on two battered Harley motorcycles held together by bailing wire. The motley singers bring their bikes to a sputtering halt. One Goth is tall and thin, and the other one is quite short and stout. "I am Nanna," the tall one says. "And I, Gunnarr, I am," the fat one identifies himself. The first thing Siegfried notices is the smell of their filthy, tattered clothes. Nanna wears a red headband; Gunnarr sports an LA

Dodger baseball cap. They both have rings through their noses and eyebrows as well as their ears and chin, and, God knows where else. It is plain that these two were scraped from the bottom of the barrel – "the dregs of Goth society.

Siegfried asks, "Which way to Olin's camp?" The answer does not come right away because Siegfried's correct usage marks him as an outsider. The taller of the two challenges him with WTF in French, "C'est quoi ce bordel! "Who beez you. Where in ze hell ye from." Siegfried is fully aware that many low-life Goths speak a fractured patois, occasionally peppered with French phrases introduced by Cajun bikers some years back.

Siegfried politely explains that he has escaped from the Bionicans and that he wants to start a new life with the Goths. "I have renounced them. I have never taken Daytrain – that is why I do not smell."

"*Merde a Dieu*, D-train shit just we sell, no take," Gunnarr says. Siegfried is not so sure whether to believe them because he knows that there is an upswing in the Daytrain use among the Goths.

"He man of utmost reasoning," Nanna says looking to Gunnarr, "He gives no smell that he do, but me smacks a Bionican. Long time a Bionican, forever of that breed."

The two Goths get off their bikes and start pushing Siegfried around. "We see what you made of." Gunnarr draws a knife. What they do not know is that Siegfried is a skilled fighter. A few quick moves and it is all over; both Goths are sprawled on the ground. "Sacre Bleu!" Nanna shouts. The two Goths do not know what hit them.

Nanna and Gunnarr fear that their fellow Goths will kill them if they find out that a Bionican bested them. Knowing that, Siegfried promises, "I will not tell anyone about your weakness in battle if you keep your mouths shut about my being a Bionican. Now tell me, where is Olin?"

Gunnarr says that Olin's compound is on a mountaintop so that he can see what's going on in The Valley. To this Nanna asks, "Why see him, pour quoi?"

Siegfried explains his mission and shows him the gold talisman. "I want to give this to Olin, Tara's father. I am told she is very beautiful."

Nanna agrees, "Vraimente, de beauty is known far and wide, but what is a person to say fer sure?"

Fat little Gunnarr chimes in, "Fer Olin no man's eyes, not even a peek see. The peekers must fight and many die." Siegfried understands that Olin is making it very difficult for those who seek Tara's hand if he sets a battle of life and death before them.

"Where can I get a ride to see Olin?" Gunnarr points towards a ravine and says a trucker is heading to Olin's compound thirty miles northwest in Simi Valley. Siegfried follows the bikers down the ravine to a gravel pit where the truck and its driver are standing. Gunnarr talks to the trucker. "Tis fellow wants see Olin. Maybe he good for heavy lifting."

The trucker, Otto, welcomes the help. Otto is a lean, older gentleman with a pockmarked face, a goatee, and an intermittent stutter. Siegfried and the two bikers help load up the truck with gravel and then join the trucker in hearty portions of roasted jackrabbits turned on a spit over a fire in an empty oil barrel. Otto provides the final burp that signals the end of the meal, and they all pile into the truck to drive north to meet up with several chain gangs that are filling holes with gravel and tar and stomping them down with iron tools.

The road winds upwards and reaches the summit to reveal The Valley – Simi Valley – the place that all Goths call home. Their truck passes through fields of cattle and sheep herded by Goths on horseback along with their dogs. On another field are young Goth boys practicing martial arts and weapons handling, much to the delight of a group of young Goth girls standing by, gossiping, giggling and cheering the young men on.

"Do not be fooled by those nice little girls. I heard that the G-spot Biker Femmes recruited them."

Siegfried nods knowingly, wondering how tough these ladies are. Siegfried sits next to Otto in front while Nanna and Gunnar are in the cargo area singing "valderi-valdera." They travel on for a while in silence. Toward the end of the journey, Otto slows down and points out a building on the side of the road.

The truck continues up the hill and turns to the right to reveal the Goth auto pit. Otto explains, "Here is where we fix our motorcycles, our c...cars and our tt...trucks. This is also a supply depot for the grain alcohol and the biofuel that we need to keep our fleet running." He points to several vehicles that are being refurbished by Goths using blowtorches to weld cannibalized parts. "There a...are a lot of trucks out there that w...we can still put to use."

As they pass the now defunct Bob Hope Airport, he explains, "we t...took over when it was abandoned." He points to a field with hundreds of aircraft. "We also have th...th...thousands of junked planes used for scrap and parts. Some day they w...will fly again." Otto waves to workers in the junkyard who are welding and pounding metal in the work area. Behind them, on the perimeter of the Goth compound, is an airplane hangar.

Otto drives his gravel truck past the hanger and into the main compound where Quonset huts are arranged in a grid pattern.

"Here is where m...m...most of us live. Over there is m...m...my place." Siegfried notices a motorcycle parked in front of Otto's place. "Yep, it is mine, a restored Indian," he says stutter free. He continues to drive a few miles.

"That is Medea's school of healing. Sh...sh...she grows

hundreds of herbs and teaches us about them. Th...th... th...that is where Medea took me in and taught me," Otto sputters. Unlike the Gothspeak of Nanna and Gunnarr, Otto's speech is grammatically correct.

In front of Medea's cottage is a garden gnome with an erect penis, representing Priapus, the Greek God of fertility.

"She teaches children?" Siegfried asks.

"N...no, she teaches only adults; you have to be an adult to study with her. Olin will not let her teach kids because he is afraid that she will corrupt them and turn them into cultured little Greeks. Otto stutters. "But, sh... sh...she can have anything she wants. Without her, Olin w...would have been dead a long time ago. She h...has powerful Greek connections."

Siegfried asks, "I heard she knows Eric."

Otto does not answer right away, and Siegfried suspects there is something behind his silence.

"E...Eric is her right-hand man. I...I cannot tell you m...much more."

Accompanied by two Goth women, Medea comes out of the school with gardening tools as the truck passes. She is a striking middle-aged woman dressed in a fashionable gray gardening outfit.

"Always dd...dressed nice, that lady," Otto says admiringly. "I do some odd jobs for her." Medea waves to them and yells out a cheerful greeting to Otto. Siegfried stares at her, knowing that their paths will cross.

"N...n...now I am going to show you where Olin and his daughter, Tara, live."

Otto's truck goes uphill and winds along a curve, ending with a full view of the mesa.

"This is it. Here is w...where you will find Olin." He looks up and points to the Sky House, a rambling Gothic-style structure that has undergone constant expansion.

"Over in that corner is where Mad Moxie and his men live. Last year we built another addition for Tara's collection of stuff she brought from the Pasadena Polis Mall run by Gonorrhea and the G-spot femmes. She likes to go shopping there with Medea."

The sounds of motors running catch Siegfried's attention. Below the mesa, he sees a steady stream of traffic. Everywhere trucks are being loaded and unloaded in front of a huge warehouse; heavily armed men supervise the activity.

"T...t...trade is what k...keeps us going." Siegfried notices a green truck that he has seen before. Otto explains, "That is the truck that we use to haul D...Daytrain from Bionica. We have to make sure there is enough biofuel available for them."

Otto takes Siegfried to the other side of the mesa, revealing a huge open-air meeting ground, enclosed by rows of cabanas made from scrap metal.

"These are used by Goth leaders and visiting dignitaries to w...w...witness our celebrations." Otto points out where a group of workers are setting up a large tent, using both cloth and animal skins for the covering. He waves to the artisans, construction workers, and truck drivers milling about, a few of them cooking food over open fires.

"In a couple days we are going to have a poetry s...s... slam followed by c...c.... combat. Attendance is mandatory for all."

Otto looks up to point out a wing of the Sky House that has an unobstructed view of the meeting grounds. "S...s...sometimes Olin and his daughter stay up there watching the poetry slam, but they eventually join in, especially during our c...c...combats. Olin likes to kill, and weaker opponents are often c...c...chosen for him for this reason. No one wants to fight Olin because of this."

The truck stops at the gate guarded by fierce-looking, heavily armed bikers dressed in black leather.

Their leader, Mad Moxie, steps forward, raises his AK47 in the air, and jingles the jewelry that pierces his ears, lips and eyebrows. His bushy red hair and beard stand out in the crowd. He is dressed all in studs-in-duds, motorcycle gang black. He wears a bandana when he is not wiping his nose with it.

"Whatcha got, mon vieuz?" Mad Moxie snarls.

Otto explains that he is bringing gravel for the washed-out road leading to the Sky House.

"Whatzis scumbag yonder doing here?" he points to Siegfried.

"I am Siegfried and I am here to see Olin." The smallest of the warriors, Tyko, looks him over. "Who in the hell you be, *abruti*? You funny talker." Tyko's long hair keeps getting into his eyes.

Siegfried makes up a story, a complete lie. "My parents came from the East and were ambushed by the Bionican hackers who killed my parents and took me hostage. The Bionicans thought I would make a good hacker and made me eat Daytrain. I never took to it and planned my escape from the very first day; I hated those smelly sons of bitches."

Mad Moxie rolls his eyes, spits on the ground, and looks him over. "Why you to see Olin?"

Siegfried pauses for a moment, "I have come on a mission. I seek the hand of his daughter, Tara." The bikers roar with laughter.

Little Tyko pipes up, "So you wanna man hand Tara?" knowing what lies ahead. "We have special place for you who wanna to impress Olin, you *imbécile*."

Suspicious, Mad Moxie kicks a rock and gestures obscenely. "What can be squeezed from his tits? Will that I trust this breathing heap funny story." He pulls out his knife, "Better your watching step or this is it." demonstrating the time-honored throat cutting technique, the Moxican slice, that has earned Mad Moxie his fierce name.

Tyko and the other warriors pull Mad Moxie back. "Let him trot stuff. We are in laughing for his chance. Die he will anyway. He who wants to man hand Tara."

Mad Moxie agrees, "Okay, lad. You on. Proving yourself as you do now that you are with us. Show this lad the works," he says, beckoning Otto to show Siegfried where the Goth King and his family work, live, and play.

CHAPTER 7
THE GOTHS

Otto brings Siegfried to the back of the Sky House that originally served as the officer's quarters before the Goths took over the army drone base there. The building is a pentagon with telephone poles serving as structural support for the wings. Double chain-link fencing is filled with plywood and other scraps that is salvaged from abandoned buildings to form security barriers.

Otto explains, "We wanted this b ... building to express our way of life, so we decided to build t...towers, topped with Gothic spires, at each of the corners of the p...pentagon. Our builders constructed exterior walls with sculptures of N...Norse gods like Odin, surrounded by ravens; and Thor, wielding a hammer; and F...Freyja, wearing a coat of feathers."

Inside the pentagon's courtyard is a ceremonial area covered with a huge canopy made from animal skins. "This is where our marriages are p ... performed. Olin also uses them for important meetings."

They climb the stairs up one of the five towers. Otto shows Siegfried several optical telescopes. "We use these to observe the s...sun, moon, and s...stars, but we also use them for security. Olin likes to keep t...tabs on what goes on in the village. Let me show you." Siegfried takes a look through the telescope and sees the iron works west of the Sky House where Goth workers melt metal in huge cauldrons and pounding metal over fire.

"They are now working on a new sword for Olin for his collection. There is also a gunsmith, but we do not like guns. We prefer to use s...swords and knives because we like to see blood spill out when we kill. O.K., it is true that blood gets spilled with guns too; we just like it when a lot of blood gets spilled, and this is something that swords and knives do better. Now I am going to show you where you will stay until you prove yourself to get your own place."

Otto brings Siegfried to one of the Quonset huts on the edge of the compound that is used to house itinerant workers. Inside, fat Einarr who is in charge acts as if he had been expecting them. He looks Siegfried over and then barks at him in Gothspeak, "You, top bunk. Eat when the sun is down. Never alone. Always in company. Otherwise it is...dead you," Einarr snarls as he makes a throat-slitting gesture and slaps Siegfried on his back.

"Otto takes Siegfried aside and advises him, "This will

be your home for the t… time being. Oh, by the way, t… try to learn Gothspeak. It will make life easier for you."

Later that day, Otto returns to escort Siegfried to the Mess Hall, where plump and rosy, smiley-faced bare-breasted Goth maidens serve food and drink. Two older women turn a pig roasting on a spit, sadly reminding Siegfried of his porker friends that he and Berk sacrificed.

There are about twenty warriors eating with their hands, gorging themselves. Mad Moxie sits in the middle of these lowlifes including Nanna, Gunnarr, and a dozen other Goth warriors.

They all tear the meat apart with their teeth and spit out the gristle. Siegfried joins right in, biting, tearing, and spitting with the best of them. Their common love of meat and mead is the bond that paves the way to acceptance for this new outsider who claims to be one of them.

"That boy's teeth be gnashing," one Goth warrior observes.

"Learned that I do from the best they are," Siegfried says with confidence, trying his hand at Gothspeak.

"What is yer pleasure with cut-cut," one brandishes a knife.

"I fight with the best I do."

"Like the weenie Thor?" The warriors laugh out loud. "Olin's bitch be with girls."

"Heard he drinker from breasts of the nursie hands," Mad Moxie says making a sly reference to Thor's connection to Medea.

"Ah, next time the sun down went, he be reading book."

"Hey, Siegfried, you read dem books, eh?" Moxie nudges him.

"Do not drink from that hand. I man of action." Siegfried grins in an effort to be one of the boys.

"Ah, but not a man of words?"

"Words?"

"Yes, words. We no read, but we like words, ah we like dem words."

Siegfried momentarily forgot about the Goth love of poetry. "Ah yes, I like words, too, especially beautiful words," Siegfried says, forgetting to mangle his syntax. He tries again, "Sticks and stones be break my bones, but words will never stabber the heart."

"We can fixie that for you," Moxie says, laughing out loud, and slapping Siegfried on his back.

"Now for that man after my own heart go. Let the words fly," he commands and on cue the Goths begin to exercise their oral tradition, ranting Libertarian tidbits from another era. Moxie gets things going by channeling Ayn Rand.

"A equals A."

"I am, I think, I will."

"Existence exists."

"Never think of pain or danger or enemies a moment longer than is necessary to fight them."

This last one gets only a mild shout-out from the crowd, and they bang their fists on the table in rapid succession as a clamor for more snappy stuff. Gunnarr and Nanna chime in, yelling out anything smacking of Libertarianism that comes into their heads.

"Live free or die!"

"Give me liberty or give me death!"

"Don't tread on me!"

"Drill, baby, drill!"

"We don't want no thought control!"

"Who is John Galt?"

This last one confuses the group and puts an end to the exclamation medley and sets the stage for what comes next. As is customary after dinner, the warriors sit around an open fire singing and reciting poems. Goths have a longing for the mythical days of the North Country where the summer's sun gives way to the winter's snow. They speak about long voyages and fierce battles against monsters. They are on their feet thrashing about as Mad Moxie takes his turn to recite. His fellow Goths push him up and their strong hands lift him above the pit. After being dumped on the stage, Mad Moxie, widely regarded as an accomplished poet, brushes off his clothes and begins to recite in the polished diction reserved for poetry, no fractured utterances now:

Across the silken seas to the North

To the winter lands of fierce Arctic winds and water flows

Our hearts are in the hardened earth

Our thoughts leap from the trees of desire

Our enemies grow older and more dangerous

They chill the world with their lies

And so we lift the banner of raw meat against the sun

And so we raise our goblets to the ice spirits

And so we slay the monsters that own the dark

Long ago our ships left for the land of no return

And now we are here to regain our honor

Our hearts no longer welcome strangers

Our eyes have seen too much

Our blood runs through the rivers that empty to the sea.

Otto pays his tribute to Mad Moxie by refilling his drink and yelling. "J...j...jolly wonderful, hip, hip, hurray." Those assembled raise their mugs in praise. Moxie sits down with a fat satisfied grin. Gunnarr and Nanna are guzzling mead from one mug that they pass back and forth.

Another Goth rises to recite his poem. This one Siegfried recognizes as his old friend, Eric, the trader who introduced him to the world outside of Bionica. Eric does not recognize Siegfried, now bearded and with long hair and leather clothes, as he addresses those assembled.

"I hope my words be sweet for truth," he prefaces to

acknowledge the purpose of the occasion with his simple verse.

Mornings, she rises to the sun and I must watch from afar
Midday, she walks among the flowers and I must not follow her
I hear her in the waning afternoon talk
The gracefulness and dignity of her walk
I am the slave to the sway of her derriere
A joy to behold, the more the merrier
And with the approach of night I dream the rest
The sweet smothering her bountiful breast
And the mystery of her smile I will never own
I long for the day when she will be mine, and mine alone.

"Jolly good." Otto exclaims persisting with his fake British accent and then continues in Gothspeak without a stutter, "But thinks we not that dear Eric not angle strange waters, *n'est pas*?"

"What is that he is talking?" Siegfried whispers to Otto, again trying to make out the strange local patois. Otto becomes formal again, "Rumor has it that Eric p… pines for Medea. He hopes to succeed if T…Thor should fail to win her hand in marriage."

"Thor?"

"People think that Thor could win Medea's hand if he wants her, s…simply because he is Olin's son."

"So what are Thor's real chances?"

"They say he has no backbone, no brawns, no s…sex appeal." He points out Thor who is staring into space, "People say he begs for her embrace, but he is s … smarter than he looks. He is uh…fishing in another p…pond."

"And what about Eric's chances?"

"N… not in the cards. He does not have the s…smarts. Medea has no desire to marry a common Goth. She w… wants to be free to do what she wants."

"What is that?"

"She has a vision for the f…future. She wants to bring back m…money."

Siegfried is intrigued. He looks forward to seeing Medea to see what all this talk about *money* is about.

The poetry slam finishes but the drinking and back-slapping go on as the assembled congratulate Eric for his performance. Siegfried waits for his turn to congratulate, inching towards Eric, who still does not recognize him.

"Remember me?"

Eric looks puzzled. "When youze gets old, everybody looks like you see 'em before."

Eric stares awhile at Siegfried and eventually recognizes him. "Condor?" he hesitates. "I heard that you might be joining us," he says switching to standard speech.

"Yes it is me; now I am one of you guys. Call me Siegfried, my new Goth name."

"Siegfried? What made you leave Bionica? I thought you were a lifer. Your old buddies will kill you if they ever catch up with you." He is delighted to have Siegfried come aboard, but there is something that bothers him. "What made you do it?"

Siegfried sighs, "Bionica is the blue screen of death. I will let you in on a secret; I want to marry Tara."

Eric looks dumbfounded. "Are you mad? Do you have any idea of what you are in for and what you are up against? Despite what he says, Olin does not want her to marry. You probably know that Gonorrhea, his oldest daughter, deserted him to form a biker gang. So Olin wants to keep his younger daughter for himself. Many have died seeking her hand."

"Were you ever interested in Tara?"

Eric laughs, "Not my type although she is very pretty. Besides, you have to be blind not to see that she is the apple of Olin's eye. I could never have her, but for you this is different. My problem is that I am in love with Medea. I have been devoted to her for years. She is one of the smartest ladies in these parts. She knew that you were coming, and I know she has taken an interest in you. Maybe, when you meet her, you can put in a good word for me."

"Think you have a shot?"

Eric pauses a while. "If things fall the right way, I am in."

Overhearing snatches of the conversation between Eric and Siegfried, Thor approaches them. Thor, whose alert eyes continuously scan the environment, has a sensitive face partially covered by a stringy beard. He has more than his share of lip and nose rings. He is too thin and too delicate to be a man's man.

Eric continues, "She will only marry the man with her vision."

Eager to know more about her role in the D-train trade, Siegfried asks, "What vision is this?"

"She is looking for that Mr. Right who combines Goth brawn and Greek beauty, someone with smarts, someone hard to find."

Thor butts in, "Eric is right. Medea has high hopes. I have had the privilege of working with her; I can barely catch up with her."

Eric introduces Siegfried to Thor, "Meet Thor. He has been working hard to bring civilization to the Goths."

"Even though we avoid becoming civilized," Thor jokes. "We Goths are a stubborn people – been that way ever since we got burned by all those god-damned intellectual Greeks and the Bionicans and their fucking computers."

"Do not be vulgar, Thor, people will talk. They may even think you have decided to go full he-man," Eric teases.

"Choice is a person's prerogative." Thor's lame pronouncement makes Eric laugh. Thor shrugs him off and goes away.

Siegfried and Eric are alone again. Eric wants to continue their conversation about Medea.

"Do you know Medea?"

Siegfried pauses and then whispers to Eric, "I do not know her. Does she want to see me?"

Eric blurts out, "I hope you won't have a thing for her, too."

"I doubt it, but I heard she is quite a woman, and very strong minded. I learned that somehow I am related to her but that I am destined to marry Tara."

"Are you sure? Maybe you can give me some advice. I want Medea very much, but she is brushing me off; she says that she will only marry the warrior who will bring freedom to the Goths."

"Freedom?"

"That is another word for taking power away from Olin. She wants to align herself with Olin's true heir."

"And who is that?"

"Tara. She is the apple of his eye. I have got a deal for you, Condor, uh...Siegfried. I will help you get Tara, and you help me win over Medea. Maybe we all can get what we want."

Siegfried puts his arm around his old friend. "Sounds like a plan to me, but what can you do to help me get Tara's hand?"

Eric tells Siegfried about himself, things that Siegfried had never known. "You see, I am the son of one of Olin's royal guards; so he considers me one of his most trust-worthy fighting men. They have put me in charge of the round robins for Tara's suitors.

"So how many times do these take place?"

"Many times," Eric explains. "For years, Olin has been seeking a husband for his daughter, but no one has ever been successful in becoming the right suitor. Olin always defeats the one that has battled his way through the others. I am not sure you want to do this."

"But this is the only way, right? This is a tradition for all Goths, correct?"

"Yes, if you want Tara, you to have to fight for her. You should certainly talk to Medea. She spends hours with Tara and advises her on all sorts of health and beauty matters. With me and her in your corner, you are sure to win. She will persuade Tara to want you and can make sure that her father will not challenge you if you are the victor."

Siegfried likes this arrangement. "I can win on my own but I value your friendship. Maybe this time Tara's prince has come."

Eric now shifts the topic to what he wants for himself. "Now for your part, please get to know Medea and tell her about me."

Siegfried visits Medea. As he approaches her schoolhouse, he notices a blackberry bush and samples the sweetest berries he has yet tasted. With each berry that he swallows, the more clearly he becomes aware of Media's presence. She beckons him to come closer.

Medea is standing by the door with her arms crossed. Wearing an earth-colored dress with a yellow daffodil in her hair, she smiles confidently, revealing the lines of a strong face. He enters the house and looks around. She asks him to sit down with her to have some tea.

"I like your house."

"It is Arts and Crafts à la Brothers Grimm. The Goths go for this kind of stuff."

Siegfried nods but is at a loss for words. After an awkward pause, Medea continues, "So you have finally come. As I expected, you are now Siegfried, but you were once Condor, son of Julia, who is my mother, too; she has always wanted us to find each other and to be together. I know because I can feel that it is true."

"My Mother's child? You are Julia's child? That is impossible." Siegfried says in astonishment.

Medea explains, "Like you, I am the child of bioengineering. I was born inheriting the legacy of Julia. She is throughout me; I feel her; sometimes I am she."

"You ... are my mother?"

"Well, not quite. I am more like your sister, although culturally we have no direct family connection; we are family. Biotechnology took care of that. The important thing is that we share a genetic heritage."

Siegfried feels instinctively drawn to Medea because of her connection to his mother. More and more she sounds like the voice of the woman in his head who has guided him to leave Bionica. She tells him all about his mother.

"Your Mother was loved by many men, especially the strong and powerful ones, but she had a weak spot for the sensitive types. Many of her eggs were fertilized, though she gave birth to none of them. They were all frozen instead. I must say that in vitro fertilization took the glamour out of fornication and replaced it with uncertainty."

While Siegfried is fascinated about the biology of his birth, he is not so interested in hearing about his mother's lovers and promiscuous egg donation. His dad could be anyone. Instead, he remembers his promise to Eric about telling Medea about him.

Medea seems to read his thoughts.

"I know about Eric. He wants you to put in a good word for him."

"He tells me he is in love with you."

"Oh, that is just like Eric. I am not interested in his love. Why do you care?"

"As a D-train trader, he worked closely with me and I trust him. He considers me a friend."

"But, *are* you his friend?"

Siegfried is slow to answer.

"What use is he to you now? He is a creature of the moment. He is without a portfolio. He has no future."

"But, I made him a promise."

"Forget your promise, dear brother. You have too much to do to worry about passing friendships such as his; Eric will mean nothing to you in the end.

"Eric said that he will help me win Tara's hand in marriage."

"Fine. So, let him help you. It will make him feel good. Do you not understand? As a Greek woman, I tell you that Goths serve one purpose, to help Greeks breed. We put up with them so long as they provide offspring. You know we Greeks have a low birth rate."

Siegfried does not quite understand what Medea is saying and how she fits in with the Goths.

"So you left the Polis for good, Medea?"

"Not exactly. I live in both places. I own Elysium, a large mansion in the Pasadena Polis. I run a finishing school that combines Greek culture and the practical arts. The Greeks make use of my Goth connections. The Goths make use of my Greek connections."

"Are you happy here?" Siegfried asks.

"Happiness is hard to come by. Like many Greek women, I took up with a sexy Goth out of desperation. This guy drank, and he would beat me while reciting beautiful poetry about me. At first this was exciting, but later I could not stand him. One day he simply did not wake up."

"So why did you not go Greek after that?"

"Not a chance. Greek men fail to understand that sometimes it is necessary to put one's book down. They do not know how to get down and dirty on the up and up." And she adds with a wink, "Mind you, I am not desperate; I would rather have a fling with a Goth than marry a Greek."

Siegfried looks around Medea's living room, and stares at a print of a Renaissance era Madonna and child tacked to the wall.

"What about children? Do you not want any?"

"I enjoy them, but you know how it is if they are not yours; you can leave when they are no longer amusing."

Siegfried thinks about this. When he was a hacker in Bionica he never had to deal with children although he fathered quite a few of them. Children just happened.

"Do you not miss living in your big house with the

Greeks, your Elysium?"

"I do love it there, but my work is here. I split my time between the Greeks and the Goths. The Goths want me here because of my knowledge of herbs. The Greeks want me here to promote book learning among the Goths. I am the universal *donna*."

"That must be a tough sell."

"Actually a tough buy *and* sell. I have taught Olin and Thor how to read. They love it."

"What do they like to read?"

"Best selling 20th Century romances like *The Bridges of Madison County* and anything by Danielle Steel. They do not like anything too heavy. I have had a devil of a time locating large print books for Olin as his eyesight is very poor."

"Are not most Goths suspicious of education?" Siegfried wonders.

"It is the intellectuals they cannot stand, but they want the things that Greek learning brings; so, they add a little respect to their contempt. You should see the way the Goths suck up to us when they visit Polis."

Siegfried is astonished to hear that the Goths liked to visit Polis; he had always thought that the Greeks and Goths live in completely segregated societies.

Medea goes on, "They come in groups on refurbished buses. Only the most influential and powerful Goths come; the rabble stays behind. The Goths prefer it that way; they do not want their riff-raff getting any ideas."

"What do the Goths like best?"

"They like our goodies, the finer things in life piled up in our shops. There was so much stuff available after the Great Plague. The Greeks carefully collected and cataloged it all. They know what things are worth."

"I came across luxurious things mentioned in The Well. I did not know that it was possible to get my hands on them."

"You were probably ruminating over the virtual collections that the Greeks created. The Well includes a repository for Greek metadata; everything you think about draws from Greek culture. Ideas just do not come out of thin air."

"So, you know a lot about The Well."

"Only enough to know that it is there and how it came to be. You well know that we Greeks don't have access to its inner workings. Of course, we are into the D-train part. We encourage our slaves to take D-train to keep them happy with music and pornography. Otherwise, The Well is pretty much useless to us, but that could change in the future. You are aware that The Well has run dry, are you not?"

"You mean it is worthless?"

"Not exactly, it is a useful repository, but it may not be all that valuable anymore because it is only a snapshot of the knowledge that existed in 2211 when Cybergeddon made further contribution of knowledge impossible. We have no way of recording and storing digital information through The Well. We do not have the neural networks implanted in us as babies. Maybe someday you can help us regain the ability to have a vibrant, working Well."

"I doubt it; I burned my bridges with the Bionicans when I deserted."

"We will see what develops. Perhaps you will still be able to access The Well."

Siegfried wonders how far they would go to gain full access. "So how can the Greeks continue without The Well since the Bionicans rebelled?"

"We have tried very hard. It would be handy to have direct access to The Well for technical information and online publications. For now, we have to depend on pre-electronic written sources, particularly books, for information, but that has its limits. We are particularly interested in developing a modern banking system, which was destroyed by the cyberterrorists. We need to have money to develop our economy. So, for the time being, all our energy goes into rediscovering things. We are in a renaissance.."

"Renaissance?" asks Siegfried betraying his ignorance.

"You do not know about the Renaissance that benefited from ancient learning and wisdom? Is that not included in the current version of The Well? Where else did you receive your education?"

"Berk, the dwarf, taught me to read and lectured me a lot, but aside from that, all I know is through The Well and what I picked up during my quest.

"Berk is a clever sort with a good book collection, but it appears that he did not tell you everything on purpose. We told him to allow you a chance to get your feet wet. There is a lot that you can learn from reading, and you can learn even more from experience. You need a liberal education. You need to learn more about how things work."

"What should I learn next?"

She puts her hand on his shoulders, "My dear brother, that is the whole point about education: discovering what you have to learn next. The Victorian Era philosopher John Dewey said, *"Education is not preparation for life; education is life itself."*

"So that means I am not well educated," Siegfried says, crestfallen.

"No, it only means that you have a lot more to learn. Even if you do not know what you want, knowing that you want something is enough. You must find a way to have knowledge that will go along with your libido. If you have trouble with your libido taking over, use me as your muse. With my help, you will know what to do."

"Why are you teaching Thor and Olin if the Goths are opposed to books and learning?"

"Nobody is supposed to know about that. I am teaching Thor specifically because I want him to deal with the Greeks when his foolish father is gone. And I am teaching Olin, so he does not suspect anything when I teach his son, Thor."

Siegfried is surprised to hear Medea talk so highly of Thor.

"The Goth warriors do not respect him; they think he is womanish because he speaks like an intellectual."

Medea replies, "I would not underestimate Thor. He is capable of more than book learning. He has a fighter's character, and he understands numbers well."

"Numbers?"

"Yes, numbers. I am working with him to develop plans to replace bartering with money. We have already established universal ledgers for the Daytrain trade. We are now working to do the same for trading slaves and sex."

"What kind of money?"

"Right now, all we have is Daytrain as the means of exchange. The plan is to replace Daytrain with money – you know printed paper and coins that were used before the cyber era. But to do that, we need to ramp up our mining and manufacturing. Right now, we depend too much on our slaves and agriculture and on salvaging technology from the past. We have to do more to move forward."

Siegfried looks dumb. Medea's talk about economics is beyond Siegfried and so he changes the topic. Siegfried is not interested in Thor or Eric and wants to focus on his next step of winning Tara's hand instead.

"Where do I fit in? What happens if I am able to marry Tara?"

"If you marry Tara, you will be in charge here. That is if you can keep the high-maintenance Tara in line. If you can do that, you will also enjoy prominence among the Greeks. You have quite a future if you can liberate your thoughts and become more flexible. Meanwhile, I think I will marry a Goth to help you move things along."

"You mean you would consider marrying Eric?"

"I am not so sure about that. Marrying Eric does not matter now. First, we need to get you married to Tara, and we need Eric to help you with making that happen. That is in the plan."

"Oh, there is a plan?"

"It is in the cards, in the beads – whatever you like; it is your destiny." Medea looks into Siegfried's eyes. "We have a lot ahead of us; I hope you are up to the challenge. Will you be my pupil?"

"To learn about herbs?"

"No, much better than that," she teases him. "What Berk taught you was just the beginning; your real education starts right here." She takes Siegfried to her study, which looks like a medical examination room – a hospital bed and a credenza full of medical equipment. She disappears for a moment and returns wearing a short-skirted nurse's uniform.

"Lucky man, you are going to get the full treatment. Please drop your trousers and put on this gown, dear, and lie down on your tummy." She approaches him with a strange hose."

"What is this?" Siegfried asks.

"Have you not heard of high colonics? I am going to make you pure with my finest herbs, and when this is finished, your *real* education begins. She removes her white medical gown and flings it to the floor, and now stark naked herself, begins the procedure that makes Siegfried grimace and roll his eyes. After removing the application tip from his posterior, Medea hands him a golden chalice.

"Drink this. This is the stuff that dreams are made of."

"This is not D-train?"

"Not on your life. A lot better – a stiff shot of courage. It will do you and me for the night." Moments after downing a drink, Siegfried feels like Wild Bill Hickok and takes Medea for the longest ride in his life. She, meanwhile, calmly takes everything in stride.

The following morning Medea cooks Siegfried a full English breakfast and hands him a package for Eric.

"Here are the potions that Eric will need." Medea kisses Siegfried's forehead. "Thank you for last night.

May Tara be yours," she says in a motherly tone.

Siegfried leaves to catch up with his new Goth buddies, Mad Moxie and Tyko. He finds out that there will be another feast and poetry slam at the pit tomorrow. He shows up for the festivities the next day. A comely Goth maiden greets him and offers him food and drink. As Siegfried enters the pit he senses trouble in the air. Tritus, a known alcoholic, who has had too much to drink, insists on having the floor even though it is not his turn.

"Sit down, lard bard. Yer rhyme has no reason. Words have their way with you. They finish you before the end."

Undeterred, Tritus declares, "It is time for me to upget because me moves the spirit," he says hiccupping. After a long pause, he begins with a preface, "There be no better way to understand a woman than to drive a truck," and then continues with his ill-advised doggerel.

Me Motor Mama
Ma truck is me only love
She never fails to start

Some people in the audience start to hiss. Siegfried also sneers and hisses. Tritus rants on.

Different with my lass
Much to ma chagrin
She always outa gas
Each time I get in

The audience tries to drown out the poem with catcalls. "Douche Dog." Still he continues. "No speak, Rat-boy, poem bad," the crowd yells, but Tritus presses on.

They say ma motor Mama the worst
Slower than a funeral hearse
But I love her bumpy ride
Make a me feel all good inside.
And when I grab the shifter
I hope she can go swifter
So I can unload
My precious fluids on the road.

The reaction to this poetic effort is not kind. "Fink-weed," yells Siegfried, adding to the calvacade of catcalls directed at Tritus. With his feelings finally getting hurt, Tritus pauses momentarily and looks around to see who is out to get him. As he tries to resume, stones begin to fly, and one hits his head.

Dazed momentarily, Tritus recovers to continue his ill-fated "rhapsody" with another couple of lines:

No matter what you say
My Mothertrucker is here to stay.

The audience throws more stones at Tritus, one landing squarely on his head, knocking him out before the crowd has a chance to beat him to death. With Tritus out of commission, Monkey Face, the oldest Goth warrior present, strikes the gong. It is all over; the spell of poetry is officially gone for the evening. Tritus is hauled off to prison to await his fate.

Monkey Face approaches Siegfried, "Next time you

be the one to poetize the mother board. Better be good. Better do what is right for the fair sex."

Siegfried pauses momentarily and then takes a deep breath, and mutters, "Good advice, but time this I pass."

The following afternoon, Siegfried is taken on a tour of the prison compound. An old fat throbbing Goth, Dick, escorts him to the dungeons. "Here de rule breakers." Among the prisoners is Tritus, who yells in their direction, "I take you fuckers on, especially you." He makes an obscene gesture in Siegfried's direction.

Dick explains to Siegfried that tomorrow at noon there will be a gathering and that Tritus will have a chance to win his freedom by fighting him.

Siegfried protests, "Why should I fight him?"

Dick responds curtly, "He is the one who has insulted your honor. If you do not fight him, you will never see Olin, you will never wed his daughter, and, we will have to kill you."

Next day after the noontime bells ring, Siegfried and Tritus are handed swords. Dick explains the ground rules. "This is a fight to the finish. Only the victor is allowed to leave; whoever tries to flee from the circle will be tortured and killed."

Dick strikes the gong and the whole Goth gang, which has come to watch the live fights, cheer and raise their clenched fists. The battle between Siegfried and Tritus begins slowly as the two men face off and circle each other warily like roosters in the barnyard. Tritus goes for a quick thrust that Siegfried readily deflects.. The swordplay begins and builds as each man deflects the other's blows; both become sweaty and agitated as the battle heats up.

Siegfried is cut on the arm but manages to sidestep a second blow, turns on his feet, and smashes his sword through Tritus's neck; Tritus reels and collapses as his severed head tumbles towards the crowd and comes to rest in front of them, confronting the onlookers with his eyes and mouth, which are still moving. Apparently, yesterday's poetry reading is still not quite finished as Tritus's head emits the following lines:

Whether you know it or not
I am the true poet lau-re-ate.

"Let us shut him up for good," yells a skinny young man, who retrieves Tritus' head and puts it down at Siegfried's feet. But, the head, eyes turned upward, continues to babble.

"Bring on the laurel wreath," Dick says, taking the wreath from one of his men and places it on Tritus crown. This does the trick. The head breaks into a smile and then freezes into oblivion. The Goths raise their swords in salute. Dick addresses Siegfried, "You have earned the right to be among us. Your sword has raised our poetic standards. Let free verse ring." There are resounding cheers.

Tritus' head and headless body are taken to the special burial ground for miscreants who spout rhyming doggerel; his head is kicked in front of the procession like a soccer ball to the defiled burial grounds used as a communal outhouse and garbage dump. The burial takes place in a flash. Siegfried wanders off with Dick and asks him, "When can I see Olin to seek the hand of his daughter?" Dick tells him that he will arrange an audience for him with Olin.

Siegfried prepares to meet Olin. He trims his beard and polishes the gold talisman of the pig, Gullibursti, which he will present to Olin. When Siegfried arrives, Olin makes him wait for hours outside his reception tent. Siegfried does everything he can to keep from fidgeting. After a while, one of Olin's underlings comes out of the tent to take him inside where Olin sits between two burning torches. Olin is wearing a long red robe tied by a golden sash, his gaunt face covered by a white beard. Siegfried presents the talisman.

"Where did you get this?" Olin barks at Siegfried, "I have been searching for this all my life. It was once in my family's possession."

Siegfried explains that the dwarf, Berk, gave it to him

and that Olin would understand what it means. Olin strokes his chin and remains silent. The gold talisman represents a message, but he never thought that this day would come. Siegfried is here to seek his daughter's hand. Now he is faced with the prospects of his daughter marrying a filthy Bionican.

"That damned dwarf is up to no good," Olin says to himself. He knows that someday he will have to give Siegfried a shot at his daughter.

"You are aware that you must undergo trials before you can compete for my daughter's hand. There are no guarantees. First you must prove that you are one of us by working for us. Though you try to hide it, I know that you are no Goth, and that you are a Bionican. And I also know that all Bionicans are scum."

"Just give me a chance and I will prove you wrong," Siegfried pleads his case.

"I guess I have no choice. This evil bargain of the golden pig was made a long time ago," Olin mutters under his breath.

CHAPTER 8
RISE TO POWER

Expecting Siegfried, Medea receives him in her study, where she is surrounded by her encyclopedic herbal.

"You have come for the herbs to heal your wounded arm?"

"Yes, but I also want to talk."

"About what ails you?"

"About Tara, Eric says I do not stand a chance. Her father is dead set against me."

"Siegfried," Medea sighs, "You have got to learn how to juggle your approach."

"What do you mean?"

"You should adjust your moods and words to suit the situation."

"But I want to be who I am. I want people to know who I am."

"Big mistake for someone who does not know who he is," says Medea letting loose an ironic giggle.

Offended, Siegfried bellows, "Do not play with me." Medea backs off and cowers in a mock huff. Then she gives Siegfried her perfect therapist smile.

"I just want you to learn to keep your inner thoughts to yourself. If you are to succeed, you must allow people to regard you in a way that makes them feel comfortable. You must learn how to listen and when to shut up."

"I *am* listening to you. Tell me what I should do."

"Let us talk about your relationship with Eric. You should work with him to smooth out the D-train trade. Just focus on that."

"But, what about Tara?"

"That will come in good time."

"Meanwhile, you should become friendly with Olin's son, Thor. I would also like you to coordinate the D-train trade with him. He will work the numbers."

Siegfried is a bit confused. "I thought that is what Eric does."

"Work with Eric to expand the delivery system, but keep me and Thor in the loop. I will handle Eric myself. I will arrange a get-together so that you can get to know Thor.

Several days later, Medea invites Siegfried to a small

dinner party given at her place. When Siegfried arrives, Thor is already there. Her servant, Thrall, seats him and quietly disappears.

"I have learned a lot from a very good teacher," Thor breaks the ice. Medea smiles to acknowledge the compliment and Siegfried nods in agreement.

"But what if they find out that you have been reading books?"

Thor laughs. "I am not worried. Then you will know the truth, and the truth will set you free."

Medea laughs as Thor continues, "But if I am caught red-handed, they will make me eat my words."

"Ah, blissful ignorance," Medea chimes in.

"We Goths say what we mean and mean what we say, but do not ask us to remember what it was," Thor says. They all laugh at his silly joke.

"Deep down we know that things will have to change if we are to move forward," Thor continues thoughtfully. "We have to modernize. We need a new order. It is only a matter of time." Thor does not come right out with it, but everyone knows he looks forward to a time when Olin will be gone.

While Thrall pours the drinks, Medea serves her boys a spicy meal of mutton and potatoes laced with elixirs for expediting affinity and cooperation

"If all goes well, Siegfried will marry Tara and you, Thor, will work with me to manage day-to-day operations regarding our trade with the Greeks. We will continue to build up the Daytrain trade and figure out a way to bring back money. You know what they say."

Thor laughs, knowing the answer that Medea gleefully provides, "Money makes the world go around."

She then turns to Siegfried. "I know you are not the money type. I will count on you to make sure that business is taken care of in another way, and you know what I mean. You and Eric will make sure that nothing stands in the way of getting the slaves and supplies we need."

"That includes Daytrain," Thor says giving Siegfried a knowing look.

Siegfried responds as expected, "I know all about that. Daytrain also makes the world go round." They all share an obligatory laugh as Medea continues, "Also, do not forget Gonorrhea and the valuable contribution that will be made by the G-Spot Femmes. Remember, they too make the world go round." Thor smiles at the mentioning of his badass sister who has been rocking the Goth boat ever since she left the Sky House.

Medea has one of her brown servants offer a tray of doctored food and spiked drinks to Thor and Siegfried. The three toast one another and keep downing drinks until both Siegfried and Thor fall asleep. When they wake up the following morning, Medea's chair is empty. Thrall informs them, "Medea has gone home to Elysium. She has things to do and will return in a fortnight. She said you both know what to do next."

Thor and Siegfried leave together, but go their separate ways upon approaching the Goth compound. They need to keep their pact with Medea secret; they know it will take quite some time for things to fall into place. They also do not want to be seen together because of Thor's reputation as a closet gay.

A year passes. Siegfried and Eric have expanded the Goth operations and join Otto in a run to Polis in Pasadena to catch up with their dealers, heading up a fleet of trucks loaded with D-train and slaves. They approach a group of young Greeks clustered in small groups on the steps of the Palace of Classic Culture. One of them, Pharmakia, steps forward, with a ledger sheet in hand.

"Got the stuff?" Eric nods but doesn't say anything. Clearly, he doesn't like Pharmakia, a Greek pusher who sells to Greeks youths. On first sight, Pharmakia looks and acts like many Greek young people, but there is something sinister about his looks and voice.

"A lot of my customers have been waiting. What took you so long?"

Eric answers perfunctorily, "We ran into road blocks, but thanks to Siegfried, the problem was handled."

Pharmakia laughs, "I know how you boys handle things." He is referring to the strong-arm tactics used by Siegfried and Eric as Medea's feared enforcers.

Eric and Siegfried follow Pharmakia into one of the Polis shops to cut a deal. Pharmakia supplies D-train in exchange for clothing, tools, furniture, and food that will be brought back to Olin for distribution to the Goth leadership.

The fleet of trucks then continues its final run to the Macedonian countryside to deliver the slaves huddled in the back of the truck. They pull up to the last of the plantations on their list, the one belonging to Medea.

"This is Elysium," Eric shouts out.

Siegfried is impressed by the grandeur of the plantation house hidden away northwest of Chatsworth, within a day's walk to the Goth Sky House. "So this is the place that Medea has talked about."

Eric nods. "Medea talks a lot about Elysium, but she has not invited me here. She likes to keep her life here separate. I have no idea of what goes on here, but there are rumors – a lot of fancy parties, Plato and Aristotle, with Greek boys."

Siegfried takes in the splendor of Elysium, a large white Greek revival mansion surrounded by well-manicured irrigated gardens engulfed in the smell of eucalyptus. In the distance, hundreds of brown-skinned slaves toil the fields, harvesting chard, collards, and tomatoes.

The trucks head out to the fields, where slave drivers come to greet the new bracero arrivals. The rear truck doors roll up, and dozens of slaves in chains emerge, pushed out by Goth warriors.

"Here they are," Eric says to the foreman of the plantation, accompanied by his men who have their whips ready for the new arrivals.

"Just keep them on D-train and they will stay happy," Eric says with a laugh, slapping the enslaved foreman, Thorax, on the back. Eric unshackles the slaves and Thorax orders them to get to work unloading bales of D-train and then loading up freshly harvested boxes of kale, turnips, and potatoes in exchange. After some brief small talk, Eric and Siegfried head home with the agricultural goods. On their way, they see lines of workers, who are laying irrigation pipes needed to bring more water to the parched earth. They are chanting:

Daytrain, Daytrain, Daytrain
On de brain
Whatta we gonna do
When there is no rain?
Daytrain, Daytrain, Daytrain
Please ease my pain.

Siegfried and Eric wave to the slaves as their trucks rumble on the barely impassable dirt road. Later, Eric sees something up ahead and shouts to his driver to watch out, pointing to the shadows of figures hiding behind the rocks. Siegfried quickly gets out of the truck with his men to confront them – four men dressed in rags, including their leader, Lars, a burly unkempt creature wielding a cudgel. They are about commit "Mundraub" – a face-feeding crime punishable by death under the Goth code.

"Just give us some of yer cargo, enough for us to eat, and we'll let you through." Lars confronts Siegfried, pretending that this is an official Goth Checkpoint.

"Step aside!" Siegfried orders Lars as Eric stands by, hiding his gun.

"Over my dead body," Lars sneers, wiping snot from his nose. "We are too hungry to care."

Siegfried draws his sword and lunges it into Lars' belly, goring his innards.

Frozen in place, Lars puts up no resistance as Siegfried lops off his head while Eric pulls out a gun to finish off the others.

"Members of the Pachuco gang," Eric explains, picking up Lars' cudgel to inspect it. "There are a lot of them out there – hungry and dangerous and we have to be ready for them."

The trucks arrive home for unloading at the warehouse where Medea is expecting them.

"Last stop was Elysium."

"How did things go?"

"Things went smoothly, except for this." Siegfried

grabs Lars' head and waves it in front of Medea.

"A present for Mad Moxie, I take it."

"No, a present for you."

Medea holds her nose and laughs, "Not this one. Next time I would like to see better grooming. Look at those nose hairs! But you are right; I could use a skeleton of my very own for my office. Maybe the next one you kill will be cleaner."

"And that you shall have," Siegfried takes note of Medea's request.

That night, Siegfried and Eric meet to celebrate the first anniversary of their partnership at a mead bash in the Mess Hall attended by Goth truckers and warriors. Eric backslaps his Goth colleagues and gives him a lot of the credit for increasing Daytrain imports and for building up the slave trade.

Eric and Siegfried then sit down to talk shop.

"You know what our biggest challenge is?" Eric asks his friend.

"Killing the bandits and hijackers?" Siegfried assumes, pointing to Lars' severed head resting on the exhibits table they brought to this special occasion.

"Nope, it is the Christians and their crusade against

D-train. They want to takeover our spiritual lives. Every day they are finding converts among our people; that's what's gonna kill us."

As Eric and Siegfried continue to rub shoulders in the Mess Hall, the obligatory bare-breasted Goth maidens serve up mead to their rambunctious clientele. Mad Moxie raises his tankard higher than the rest, as Eric and Siegfried approach him to receive recognition for their success.

Eric gives Siegfried a congratulatory pat on the shoulder. "We had a good year. The Daytrain trade is going well, thanks to your help." Eric makes sure that Moxie hears this.

"I see you broughts us company, *n'est pas*?" Moxie says laughing out loud as Siegfried holds up the decapitated head by the hairs and shows it around before putting it on the table for Moxie to see.

"Whoozad?" asks Moxie.

Eric steps back to explain, "Name is Lars. Killed dem all at high noon, thanks to Siegfried, my good man."

Eric puts his arm around Siegfried's shoulder as Moxie directs a Goth maiden at his side to pour them both drinks without spilling any on her boobs.

"Drink up boys. Drink cuz there be no tomorrow today," Moxie shouts out.

Several Goths approach the exhibits table to examine the decapitated head and body parts, and one of them says, "You natural born killer, huh?"

Siegfried smiles, "This is what I hafta do."

"Yes, and you think you now one of us," one of the Goths sneers.

Eric comes to Siegfried's defense, "We need him, and the Greeks like what he does."

"So, what job next for dat Greek woman?" Moxie asks Siegfried.

"We have gotten an assignment from the Greek Praetorian Guard," Siegfried says proudly.

"Oh?" Moxie is not impressed.

"A secret mission. I am not at liberty to say."

Moxie responds sarcastically, "A mission secret. He is at no liberty to say."

Eric and Siegfried leave the group and go for a walk to talk about their plans. Eric starts, "You know, with all our success in the past year, there is one problem that might spoil the future. Daytrain production has not run as smoothly since you left Bionica. The quality of the green is not up to the Greek standards. Medea says we need to do something about it. The Greeks only accept the best bud and are refusing to accept any new shipments until things change. We have to go to Bionica to straighten things out."

"Who is running things back there?" Siegfried wonders, having lost touch with his old colleagues.

"I hear that after you left, Digi Diva took charge. She is pissed that you left and wants your scalp. She has placed a price on it, but I think she has as much a thing *for* you as she has it *in* for you. There are even rumors that the Greeks might get Daytrain through another channel and that the Bionicans are selling us the worst of their harvest to flush you out. Olin believes that Simon Girty is behind this and that he has worked a deal with the Christians to undermine us."

"Simon Girty? He is wanted dead or alive. I cannot believe that the Bionicans would rather do business with him than with us."

"I believe that he has something on Digi Diva. Everyone knows that they were once lovers and that he left her for Gonorrhea, who quickly dumped him."

Eric suggests, "Perhaps it is time to get to the bottom of this. We definitely must go to Bionica together."

Siegfried agrees. "Digi and I were lovers once too. But, it would be dangerous for me to go back; they might recognize me."

"They will not if you keep quiet; you will be incognito. I will tell them that you are a mute Goth. With all your hair and your leather clothes, no one will recognize you if you do not speak."

"Another thing, Olin is mad because the Greeks have cut off the supply of the carnelian jewelry that Tara wants in protest over the low-grade D-train. He says we must do something about the supplier problem. So we have no choice. You must brave a return."

Eric arranges for a meeting with Olin. They both go to see him at the Sky House. Olin stares at Siegfried. "So you think you can help us with the lousy Daytrain that we are getting from the Bionicans?"

Eric answers for him, "Yes, and he can help us track down Simon Girty."

Olin looks at Eric. "Good. Make sure to bring me back his scalp and his nose. Now go!"

Eric and Siegfried head for Bionica. They follow the same route Siegfried took leaving Bionica, waving to Gregory and Margaret as they pass by their log cabin. They also pass by the abandoned house and withered gardens where the Bead Lady once lived. Out of the blue, a host of sparrows dive down and peck at Siegfried's skull.

"What is this all about?" Eric yells.

Siegfried does not say anything after warding off the birds. They walk a while longer, passing by the ruins of the Getty Museum and the Los Angeles California Temple.

"There it is, Bionica!" Siegfried says with excitement, pointing to a plume of smoke, wondering how Bionica has managed without him. He feels both dread and exhilaration at the prospects of seeing his old stomping grounds again.

When they finally arrive, Eric approaches Digi Diva, who is in the middle of supervising the cultivation of the new Daytrain crop. Things have changed since Siegfried left. All of the hackers have uniforms – white kaftan tops and identical black jeans. Digi's kaftan has red embroidery that gives a softer look to her serious face. Siegfried remains in the background, mute and incognito. Much to his surprise, he longs to speak because Digi stirs in him an unexpected longing for a simple Go-For-It, something now completely missing from his life.

"Cannot you see I am busy," she screams at Eric as he asks for an audience.

"Easy does it. We are here to understand what the problem is with the Daytrain harvest. Why have the quality and supply dropped off?"

"If you must know, Girty has been messing with our operations."

"How so? I do not get it. Would you guys not just kill him if he came here?"

"He does not come here. He does his damage from far away by sending bad vibes that prevent us from nurturing the Daytrain plants. We believe that he is in cahoots with the Christians who want to convert our users. He has cracked the security codes of the Daytrain firewall, and we cannot shut him out."

With a big hug, pulling her strong, tight body towards him, Eric comforts Digi Diva in a way that makes Siegfried envious, and then presents her with a packet of red meat. "Maybe tonight we can feast together. I want you to meet a dear friend, Siegfried, my partner; he is a mute and cannot speak, but he can be trusted." Digi gives Siegfried a routine nod while Siegfried squirms, afraid that Digi Diva will recognize him if he continues to feel anything for her.

That evening Eric and Siegfried arrive at the hacker hangout to feast and spy. Eric deftly sprinkles a potion supplied by Medea into the meat he serves to the Bionican hackers.

Digi stares at Siegfried, who averts his eyes, afraid that he might give himself away.

"He is the strong, silent type," Eric explains while Siegfried nods and smiles.

"A Man after my own heart. I love men who listen, since most do not."

Watching her, Siegfried suspects that Digi Diva is still working with Simon Girty and that they may still be secret lovers. He can feel his jealousy tickle the hairs on the back of his neck.

The hackers bring out their best manners as they eat. They trade stories and talk shop with their guests.

"I wonder whatever happened to Condor," Jimmie the Greek asks.

"I do not have the faintest idea," Digi Diva responds curtly, hoping to end this topic.

"Do you think he ever made it to the Goths to become one of them like he pledged?" Pengo asks Eric, knowing that he and Condor were friends.

"I do not know, but one thing is for sure, some say he made it as far as the Bead Lady. I have heard that he was with her."

"Lucky her," Digi Diva spits out. "May their beautiful children rot."

Siegfried starts to squirm.

"He does not have the stuff to be a Goth," offers Draper, who is eyeing Siegfried with suspicion.

"Yes, they will kill him if he ever tries to read a poem; Condor never did have any soul," Phiberoptik adds.

Hearing this makes Siegfried wince.

"They will see him for the phony he is, just like we finally did," Jimmie the Greek says quietly.

"What a loser," Pengo rolls his eyes. "I cannot imagine why he collected all those human bones. What a pervert!"

The hackers raise their goblets into the air.

"Who needs Condor? Not when it is one for all," Draper yells.

"And all for one," the rest reply.

As Medea's drugs begin to take effect, the hackers, except Digi, lose steam and start nodding out.

Digi, Eric, and Siegfried move away from the fire to continue their conversation without a chance of being overheard.

"We have no choice but to go after Simon Girty. Olin has ordered it. How do we find him?" Eric whispers to her.

Digi becomes nervous and says, "It is possible that I could communicate with him through The Well. Maybe I can trick him into revealing his whereabouts."

Digi closes her eyes. She goes into deep communion with Well. Siegfried looks at her intently to gain information from the mental spillover.

Eric presses, "Can you lead us to him?"

"Yes. I think I can ferret him out because he still has a thing for me, but I do not want to come face-to-face with Girty, that son of a bitch. Helping you will be my revenge."

"Why do you hate him now?" asks Eric with a puzzled look. "I thought maybe you two were still lovers."

Digi decides to confide in Eric. Medea's elixir had loosened her tongue. "I met with Girty, after he went AWOL to take up with Gonorrhea. When Gonorrhea got rid of him, he threatened to blackmail me. That bastard said that he would broadcast that I betrayed the Bionicans with him and that I am a spy for the Christians. So I had to pay him off, but he is still on my back. I know that once I am accused, the hackers would never take my side; they do not understand what a woman has to deal with, how lonely it can get. I have needs too! Now I do not want to end up in the boneyard because of my betrayal," she says as she starts to cry.

Digi says, "If you catch up with Gonorrhea, *she* would lead you to him. I heard that she left him. Tell her hello from me, we still are friends."

Siegfried squirms in silence. He does not want to know more about Girty's relationship with Gonorrhea and is surprised Digi knows and cares about him to the extent she does.

Digi continues, "I have heard that he is holed up in Chavez Ravine Arboretum. That is not far from Dodger Stadium where the Christians hold their revivals with The Others, mostly brown people from the LA basin.

He says that he has been saved by the Christians and wishes I could join him. But I know I cannot. My duty is right here."

"Where exactly can we find him? Are you zoning in on anything?" Eric asks.

"Here is where I think he is. I picked up these coordinates from The Well." Digi takes Eric's hand and draws a crude map on his palm.

"Will you come with us, Digi?"

She hesitates, "I cannot leave Bionica. If I leave, one of these guys will take over. I am in charge here, and I want to keep it that way. I hope you understand that."

This statement bothers Siegfried, but Eric throws him a bemused glance to quell his envious thoughts; he is surprised that Siegfried still cares about Bionica and still has a yen for Digi.

Holding her close, Eric keeps comforting Digi while Siegfried remains in the shadows scowling with his arms crossed.

"We will take care of old Simon Girty. Just keep the Daytrain flowing, and make sure that you get enough water and that you do not harvest it too early. We can only use the good stuff." Satisfied, Eric knows that he has won over the proud hacker femme.

Digi looks up to Eric and does her best Marilyn Monroe, puckering her lips and batting her eyelids at him, "Daytrain is a girl's best friend. See you later, big boy."

Siegfried does not like Eric's ready rapport with Digi and wonders whether he would have a Go-For-It if he had the chance. He knows that he has blown his.

Eric and Siegfried leave the Bionicans in the middle of the night to join up with Mad Moxie and his posse of twelve good Goths to track down the renowned and dastardly Simon Girty. Eric looks at his palm for Digi's directions. Magically they morph into a cartoon-like tattoo showing an illuminated red route, a black arrowhead points the way. Eric leads the posse on until they see Girty's encampment in Chavez Ravine.

Eric shoots a flare into the sky to announce their arrival. Simon Girty's men stick their heads out from the stone turrets of the compound.

"Come on out of there, Girty, you scumbag!" Siegfried calls out. "I want to fight you mano a mano – that means man to man, in case you do not know."

Simon Girty recognizes Siegfried's voice and replies in a fakey British accent.

"Ah, Condor, my former student. So, hombre, you have come for me to teach me a Spanish lesson." Girty emerges from the compound, flanked by his two trusties, Long John Silver and Big Dickie Doolittle, who are wearing enormous codpieces.

Siegfried calls out, "Whatever happened with you and that Gonorrhea babe?"

Girty does not answer. Siegfried is not aware of exactly what happened between the two. All he knows is that Girty left Digi Diva for Gonorrhea with the idea of teaming up with her to take over the Daytrain trade. He knows they broke up, but does not know the details. Girty does not want Siegfried to know that Gonorrhea discovered his collusion with the Christians to penetrate The Well and disrupt the Daytrain trade. Girty does not want anyone to know that Gonorrhea and the Biker Femmes, armed with Uzis, kidnapped him and Long John Silver and Big Dickie Doolittle, and took them to the Burning Man Festival in Black Rock where the rising flames of huge bonfires proclaimed the New Order brought on by Cybergeddon. Gonorrhea and the Biker Femmes paraded the three up to the altar. They were then seized by burly Goth warriors and ritually castrated by none other than Mad Moxie, who wanted their oysters for his keepsakes. Gonorrhea then forcibly returned the trio to their Christian base, knowing that the shame of being neutered would keep them quiet. Blessed with a new kind of freedom, Girty and his buddies had nothing else left to lose, and so decided to throw in their lot with the Christians to join their crusade against Daytrain.

"To think I once admired you," Siegfried speaks as if

it has been too long between dust-ups. "And look what has happened since then. I heard that the Christians converted you in a revival meeting at Dodger Stadium. You, of all people."

"Ah, you heard right," Girty sneers. "You realize, of course, they have God on their side. The Christians love and trust me because I said I would help them penetrate The Well and to boldly disrupt the evil Daytrain trade."

Siegfried winces at Girty's use of the split infinitive.

"And they believed you?"

"They did, right after I was saved."

"And then you are going to tell me that they forgave you for killing the Bead Lady's mother and father."

"Forgiveness is unconditional," Girty says with a smirk. "And I understand that you know the Bead Lady, too. I heard it through the grapevine."

"Heard what?

"I hear that you killed in her in cold blood, and for nothing. You are one hell of a patsy. You do not know what is going on, do you? You, a hero, hah! You and that greedy little tart, Tara, you covet. You will end up like the rest of them – the Bionicans, the Goths, and the Greeks. You shall all fall on your knees before us mighty Christians. We know the power of the Word."

"What do you know about Tara?"

"Everybody *knows* Tara. She is everybody's girl. Every Goth has had a chance to pluck her sweet berry, and her old man does not have a clue."

Siegfried tries to control his anger as Medea has taught him. He looks Simon Girty straight in the eyes, "That is enough of your talk. You have just signed your death warrant, teacher. Let the duel begin.

Girty's two seconds, Long John Silver and Big Dickie, stand by, confident that their man will emerge the victor. Likewise, Siegfried's seconds, Mad Moxie and Eric, also stand by. Then the duel begins. None of the ruffians on either side think anything should stand in the way, least of all the facts, of a good fight between two men who hate each other.

But this turns out to be anything but a formal duel. Siegfried draws his sword as Simon Girty grabs his pistol and shoots Siegfried in the arm. "Just a flesh wound," shouts Siegfried. Girty pulls the trigger again, but the gun jams, preventing a second shot, and Siegfried, with all his fury, lunges forward with his sword but misses.

As Siegfried pulls back, Simon throws his gun at him and misses, and then picks up his sword again, brandishing it while Siegfried holds his ground. The fighting is fierce. Both are expert swordsmen who know how to fight dirty. Siegfried has the tactical advantage because he knows Simon Girty's weak spot – he cannot manage his hair-trigger anger.

Siegfried taunts him. "You have no father, and your blind mother is a wandering wretch. And besides *your mother was a hamster and your father smelt of elderber-ries."*

Siegfried thinks that Monte Python crib will get Girty's goat, and then adds a more personal insult, "Digi hates your guts and it was she who told us where you were and sent us here to kill you. No other woman will have you. What are you going to do now, call on your ex-bitch, Gonorrhea? Where are your *cojones*, hombre?"

Not a word from Girty, who is now convinced that Siegfried knows about his castration. Now he has nothing left to hide and does not care what Siegfried thinks or knows. Sadly lacking his manhood, Girty relives his dark day at Black Rock. As far as he knows, he has been outed, and there is nowhere else to go. He has no desire to put up a real fight.

Siegfried sneers, "You will die childless. You are genetically at a dead end."

Girty lies to save face. "I have a chaste Christian wife," he protests as his anger starts to get the better of him. Girty loses his concentration as he seeks an equally stinging retort to insult his former protégé, but he is at a loss for words. This gives Siegfried ample opportunity to thrust his sword into Girty's throat, thereby keeping the promise of vengeance he made to the Bead Lady.

Mortally wounded, Girty tries to eke out the right phrase in the final seconds of his life, but all that gushes out is blood and the barely audible single word, "Rosebud," a term of endearment he used for Digi. His last word is punctuated by a diminishing series of gurgles. Siegfried then rips off the bloody crucifix from Girty's neck and stuffs it in his pocket as a souvenir.

"The slings and arrows of outrageous words got him again," Siegfried laughs as Girty collapses and dies. "So now you can manage your anger, rest in peace, sucker." He stoops down to take a close look at Girty's inert body and imagines what it would look like without flesh. He is flushed with the desire to possess his bones and wonders how Digi would feel if she could see him now. Girty is finally dead, and now Siegfried's feeling of guilt for having killed the Bead Lady can be put conveniently to rest by his having avenged the death of her parents. He smiles, convinced that he is free at last from his erstwhile mentor.

Simon Girty's coterie of thugs scatters. Siegfried slices off Girty's scalp and cuts his nose off. He gathers these body parts of his former teacher, as well as his crucifix and puts them in a box for presentation to Olin as evidence of this kill. He also orders his men to load Girty's corpse on the truck.

Escorted by Eric and Moxie on his return to The Valley, Siegfried heads for the Sky House to meet with Olin to present the lurid spoils of victory.

Olin opens up the box. "Is that really him?" Olin asks Moxie, who confirms this with a nod. Olin presses his hands together with sordid pleasure. "Girty is finally dead. Simon Girty – dead."

Olin calls out to his daughter, tiny Tara, who walks past her father to see Simon Girty's remains, and also to get close to Siegfried. Winking at him, she smiles, revealing an oval face with two dimples under the wimple that her father made her wear for the occasion.

Tara's tight long dress drags on the ground behind her, draping over her voluptuous torso. Strands of her long blonde hair, packed under her wimple, find their way to her bare shoulders, tickling the cleavage of two bumptious breasts that potentially could feed a nursery full of Siegfried's babies. Siegfried is not so taken with Tara's physique since he has had plenty of exposure to buxom babes during his hacker days in Bionica. It is her massive smile and dramatic make-up, especially around the eyes and Clara Bow lips, which intrigue him. Her pink fleshiness makes him forget the bones that lie underneath. Tara's dolled-up body, the eye make-up, and scads of jewelry – earrings, nose rings, lip rings and body piercings – gin up Siegfried's desire for the girl of his dreams soon to be his. She speaks in a baby voice, which is OK with him, because he does not want a real person with powers of persuasion, like Digi Diva or like Beadina, who wanted his heart and his soul without coming to grips with the hollowness gnawing inside him. Now there is no going back on his pursuit of Tara. There is nothing else in his imagination that he might want at present.

Tara's flirtation with Siegfried does not go unnoticed by Olin. Siegfried naively believes that Olin will let him woo Tara because he killed Simon Girty.

"Sir, you will remember that I came here to present you the gold talisman of the pig, Gullibursti. I killed Simon Girty and so I demand the opportunity to marry Tara, the woman of my dreams."

"Not so fast my boy," Olin bellows. "You are a Bionican, and now you want my precious flesh and blood. Nobody gets Tara unless they are willing to die for her. You must fight for her hand, like the others."

Tara lingers as Siegfried is shown the door. As he leaves, she throws him a kiss, which Siegfried acknowledges with a grin. He knows he has more than just a fighting chance.

Olin summons Eric and Mad Moxie to his private quarters to discuss his misgivings about Siegfried and his prospects.

"This cannot, this will not happen," Olin tells Eric and Moxie. "I want you two to make sure that this Siegfried is eliminated in the round-robin.

"We will make sure that he faces some of our toughest warriors who seek Tara's hand," Moxie replies and Eric nods in agreement.

"What about you, Moxie?" You could marry my daughter and become king of the Goths after I die. Olin does not know about Moxie's sexual predilections and his secret desire to marry Thor.

Moxie hesitates momentarily before answering, "As I have served you faithfully, I would like to remain as a single warrior to serve your chosen successor, the one who will marry Tara and thereby mingle his bloodline with yours."

Moxie knows that Olin's only son, Thor, is out of the running because he has shown no interest in marrying to produce the next heir. Eric, too, excuses himself because of his dream to possess Medea. Both swear to Olin that they will do everything in their power to prevent the ascendancy of Siegfried as King of the Goths.

Having promised Medea a clean skeleton for her office, Siegfried arranges to have Simon Girty's corpse cleaned and defleshed. Once this is accomplished, Siegfried and Eric deliver Simon Girty's skeleton to Medea's office.

"Here he is all assembled – 206 bones. It took fortnight to get him ready for you." Siegfried says proudly as he taps Girty's skull.

"My, how clean and handsome he looks. I see he has nothing to hide."

Olin announces that there will be a contest for Tara's suitors and that Siegfried will be among them. Since this has happened before, there is very little excitement at the prospect of another round robin. According to Goth tradition, the competing suitors, pressed into participation by Olin, must get to know each other and become friends; they have to be committed enough to kill friends to prove their ardor. Tara always retains the option to accept or reject the surviving suitor; Olin, too, can call the marriage off. After the previous year's competition among suitors, Olin annulled the marriage plans and had the victor killed, declaring the winner unworthy of his daughter's affections.

Olin puts Eric in charge to make sure that the deck is stacked against any real possibility of Olin giving his daughter's hand in marriage. But, this time things are different. What Olin doesn't know is that Eric is in Siegfried's corner. To ensure Siegfried's chances, he picks the five least-likely-to-succeed gladiators: Quintus, Sextus,

Auctus, Lugo, and Nasir. But there are other obstacles
that stand in the way. Even if Siegfried proves to be the
victor, Olin could still nullify the results; and only then
would Siegfried qualify for the pre-nuptial inspection by
the G-spot Femmes to endorse the purity of his intention.

Dick, who is in charge of all duels and pit executions,
tells Siegfried that he does not have a tinker's chance in
hell to win. This worries Siegfried although Eric assured
him that he would take care of things to ensure his victory.

"What if someone drops out?" Siegfried nervously
asks Dick, careful to avoid giving the impression that his
ardor has diminished.

Dick makes a throat-cutting gesture and tells Siegfried to join the other gladiators in the barracks. Here
they must eat and sleep as a team and prepare for the
day when they have to fight each other to the death. They
are fattened with food to die for, huge portions of sir-
loin rubbed with parsley, sage, rosemary and thyme in
Greek olive oil. Siegfried is still amazed that these louts
are willing to give up everything – their very lives – for
the privilege of contending for the hand of Olin's daughter. They know that Olin doesn't want to give her up, and
would marry her himself if he could. For some perverse
reason that Siegfried doesn't understand, these guys regard death as inexorably tied to their sense of occasion

with scant awareness of its absurdity. It turns out that none of the ill-suited suitors is particularly interested in Tara; they are being forced to fight for her to give the impression that there is widespread interest in Olin's daughter. They are paying liege homage to the King of the Goths.

Eric shows up at the barracks and gives Siegfried a knowing look to indicate that the fix is on. He addresses the group in a stentorian tone, "It is my duty to inform you that the day of reckoning is in a fortnight. I hope you have all had enough to eat."

One of the gladiators, Lugo, is still picking at the platter piled high with meat. After he burps, he says, "Food very good." They all know that it won't get any better than this. The men never had it so good as the day to die approaches.

Well aware of her father's opposition to her marrying, Tara asks Medea to visit her at the Sky House to discuss Siegfried's prospects.

"Of all the men that have sought my hand, I like Siegfried the best. I see the uncompromising lust in his eyes when he looks at me. I just know he would make me happy. I would very much like to marry him, but I am afraid my father will not allow it. He says that I am all he has left since Gonorrhea deserted him."

Medea takes her hand and assures her, "This will be arranged."

Medea visits the combat training grounds where Tara's suitors exercise on the hillside, guarded by Goths whose swords are drawn, and pistols cocked in case anyone tries to get away. This time the guys are chained to each other, so there is little chance to escape. Medea approaches the group and gives Eric a hug as well as tiny bags of potions to spike the food for Siegfried and his opponents.

She whispers, "Here are a few drops for Siegfried to make him strong, and here are the drops for his opponents that will make them weak. It will all be simple, Eric," she says softly, "Just make sure that Siegfried wins. He will take Tara's hand, kill Olin, and then he will become our Goth warlord. You and I can be free to marry and live in peace and harmony when this is accomplished."

Eric is surprised at the depth of her devotion to him and he is thrilled that he can also help his friend. It makes him feel proud to know that the powerful Medea is interested in him.

On the day of the combat, she meets with Eric again, sidling next to him with a package tied with a ribbon bow. "I made these organic, gluten-free muffins especially for you to see you through this ordeal." What Eric does not know is that she has spiked these with a debilitating time-release oleander-cannabinoid concoction that will take effect as the events of the day unfold.

The gladiatorial combat begins as the crowd gathers around the large pit, which is surrounded by an extensive, terraced overlook for spectators. Olin leads a procession that includes his lieutenants, including Eric, plus the combatants who stagger forward to face the crowd. Eric introduces each with a slap on the back. The crowd hisses when they hear the name of the Bionican interloper. After Olin introduces Tara, the spectators rattle their swords and knives in admiration of the fair daughter of their Goth leader.

Olin notices that Tara has eager eyes for Siegfried and clenches his fist in anger. He takes Eric aside and orders him to make sure Siegfried loses.

This is no longer possible since Eric has already fed Medea's potions to Siegfried's opponents; there is no way for them to win because they are now infected with a loser mentality. Siegfried, meanwhile, feels like a winner after ingesting Medea's non-gluten, dairy-free, GMO-free super mixture for winners, spiked with tiger's milk.

The initial fighting warms up the crowd — a clumsy sword thrust into the abdomen, a head split with a machete, an arm severed with the blow of an ax. Flesh, blood, and more blood, entrails on the ground – the crowd has seen all this perfunctory quarterfinal slaughter before. They are waiting for the final round of fighting that counts, one in which there will be an ultimate victor, who will dig his heel decisively into the body of the departed to bring closure to the event. They want to see and feel the power of blood flowing in full velocity in response to the crowd's roar for more. They thirst for the terror of the final thrust and the music of the final gasp. They want to numb the pain of their monotonous lives by cheering the victor and the idea of victory, no matter whose it is.

While watching the fight, Eric munches on Medea's muffins, and his enjoyment of the decapitation of the losers increases with each bite.

Siegfried easily becomes one of the finalists after dispatching two of his hapless opponents in a round robin involving cudgels and swords; the crowd boos, suspecting that the fights are fixed. They realize that Siegfried's victories have come too easily. What the crowd comes for – the authentic ferocity of ruthless combat between worthy opponents – is clearly absent. Siegfried coasted to victory, and the audience is unwilling to attribute it to bravery and skill.

Furious, Olin faces the crowd with a nefarious proposal. "Let Eric take care of this stranger in our midst," Olin shouts while pointing his finger at Siegfried. The crowd roars approval for this unorthodox proposal because they suspect that Eric must have something to do with the third-rate performance by the combatants. Olin hands Eric his mighty sword. Eric shudders at the thought of fighting his friend, but to refuse is to invite death. He knows better than to argue with Olin.

Olin steps out to referee the fight to the finish. Eric and Siegfried, standing in opposing corners, approach each other to receive their instruction from Olin. They go back to retrieve their swords.

"May the best man win," Olin proclaims.

After a fanfare played on a trumpet, the real title fight takes center stage. First Eric salutes the cheering crowd. He is clearly the favorite. He tries to make light of his predicament by jutting his jaw and sporting an exaggerated grin.

"Rip him to pieces!" The crowd shouts

"Long live Olin!"

Siegfried steps up. The crowd boos and whistles.

"Die, you scum!"

"You are not worthy of the hand of our princess."

Tara looks at Siegfried with her demure eyes and wipes her lips with a handkerchief. In Siegfried, she sees a tall man bound in muscles that would envelop her. She hopes that he may live for her to savor that union. But this is not the first time she has watched a fight that finished off an appealing suitor.

"Let the fight begin." Olin proclaims.

The onlookers raise their weapons and cheer loudly, expecting Eric to finish Siegfried off easily, but by this time Eric feels the effect of Medea's cannabis muffins. They circle each other warily.

"Why have you betrayed me?" Siegfried asks, "I thought you would clear my way to Tara."

"Helping you will only clear the way to my death. Olin has sold us out. This fight between you and me must proceed. This is the way of the Goths. Now win this fight fair and square or relinquish your claims and leave The Valley."

Eric stops the fight and calls out to Olin, "Can I let my friend go if he withdraws as a suitor and leaves?"

"Fine," Olin replies, "but, get him away fast, or I will cut his throat and yours, too."

Eric shouts to Siegfried, "If you leave The Valley, Olin will spare your life." But the crowd wants none of this. They scream louder for blood. They will not allow death to take a holiday.

"Not a chance, my friend. My fate is with Tara," Siegfried says raising his sword, taunting Eric to attack. Although the booing crowd is against him, he knows he has the upper hand.

Eric loses his balance as he prepares himself to attack Siegfried. Observing that her performance herbs are taking effect, Medea flashes her wicked smile. Eric looks up at her and cries out, "Why have you betrayed me?" Medea averts her steely eyes and says nothing.

The battle begins; it is no contest. Without compunction, Siegfried attacks his friend in a fury, hacking him mercilessly, and while catching his breath, proclaims, "This is my destiny."

The crowd boos and jeers as Siegfried is poised to finish Eric off with a *coup de grâce*.

"This fight is rigged," they scream.

"Eric, stand up like a man, you pussy."

Eric cowers as Siegfried deals the deathblow to his head, burying the blade of his sword into the back of Eric's skull, forcing him to stumble and collapse into a heap. After he puts his boot on Eric's body, he digs it into his bloody groin to proclaim victory. After a long silence, the onlookers boo and hiss, unwilling to accept this messy conclusion. They cannot believe that Eric failed to put up a real fight.

Numbed by his victory over his best friend, Siegfried puts his right foot on Eric's chest, forcing more blood to ooze from the gaping wound. After Eric takes his final breath, Siegfried bends down to close Eric's eyes and then gets up to raise his clenched fist as the victor. He recalls Medea's dismissive words regarding friendship and frees himself from all compunction in savoring this victory. And so on this day, Condor's beautiful friendship with Eric comes to an end. Another one bites the dust and another one down; the quest goes on.

While Siegfried savors his awkward victory clouded by intrigue and betrayal, the crowd shuffles uncertain of what will come next. Prodded by her sister, Gonorrhea, Tara steps forward and after a moment of hesitation embraces Siegfried, who is preoccupied with wiping Eric's blood off his boot. Tara stands by him as he re-arranges his garments and cleanses his hands in the victory bowl brought to him. By this time, Medea left the scene. Olin, instead of crowning Siegfried as the victor, pulls Tara away. Angrily, he kicks over the victory bowl, spilling the bloodied water, and thrusts his finger at Siegfried shouting, "You cannot have my daughter's hand, you Bionican scum." Warding off Olin, Siegfried taunts him. "You no longer have a say in the matter, old man. I won her fair and square."

Olin stands over Eric's body and then retrieves the sword from Eric's limp hand, which he flings away in disgust. Having counted on Eric to defeat Siegfried, Olin raises his sword in a fit of rage and addresses the crowd, "I will finish the job myself. Down with this Bionican scum." The crowd, unsure of the outcome, provides a reluctant, gasping shout of approval. Nothing gets in the way of a Goth sword fight, even between unequals.

Olin is barely able to raise his arm as they clash their

swords; his hesitant movements betray his age and so Siegfried defeats the old man easily with a single thrust into his soft abdomen. Olin staggers back, clutching the hilt of the sword that cuts right through his body with the tip sticking out of his back. In tears, Tara approaches her dying father, who is unable to utter any final words to his daughter. His impotent stammering lips spout hot blood and spittle.

As her father takes his final breath, Tara calls to him, "Why have you abandoned me? What will happen to me now?" She sobs loudly and dramatically so that everyone present can witness the distraught emotions of a grieving daughter. Unperturbed by her father's demise, Gonorrhea puts her arm around her sister to comfort her and tells her matter-of-factly, "It is all for the best. Tomorrow is another day, but now you will have to embrace your fate like a brave new woman."

"Olin is dead. Who will lead us now?" exclaims a voice in the crowd. All know the answer, but it is up to Tara to tell them; Tara looks down and then slowly raises her head back up to look at Siegfried with a wink. "Do your duty, Conqueror; it is your destiny. Tradition holds that I must accept you as my future husband and as our new leader."

Thor, never Olin's favorite, also comes to his sister's side. There are a few catcalls from the crowd by warriors who have no time for the unmanly Thor. Siegfried is too

preoccupied to pick up the cue right away, but then recovers to make an announcement in his deep voice, "I
will follow the tradition of your, uh, our people and I will
marry you, Tara, and make you my queen; I will become
the proud leader of the Goths."

Everyone knows that this is not yet a done deal. They
know that Siegfried will have to undergo the pre-nuptial
inspection and walk-through by the G-spot Femmes to
ensure that he will make a good husband, but everyone
is confident that things will move forward because of
Gonorrhea's implicit endorsement of the new regime.

"A toast, a toast," Thor prompts the reluctant crowd
to cheer. The crowd becomes quiet as Thor, raising his
goblet slowly, proclaims with authority, "This is happening now as it has happened before; the stronger man pre-
vailed. We have a new leader – Siegfried. May you find
happiness with Tara and may you lead us to greatness."

Siegfried's acceptance speech plays to the crowd. "I
am here to set things straight. We do not need those
Greeks and their fancy ideas and useless books. They
distrust our manliness, and they hate our freedoms."

The crowd responds favorably to Siegfried's
Greek-bashing; his plain talk is winning them over. A few
yell out, "Bravo, bravo!" They are glad to have a tough
leader who speaks openly of Goth resentment, someone
who is not intimidated by the Greek brainpower.

"I believe what you believe; I believe in the greatness

of the Goths and what we stand for. No one tells us what to do. We tell them what to do, and if the girly Greeks do not like it, we will sack their fancy homes, pillage their food and take their women."

A warrior shouts out from the crowd, "That be easy; we got their women already. Their men are AWOL in that department." Some laugh and others snicker.

"Yes, we deliver the goods and take care of business," another yells.

"They keep their noses in their books while their children get blotted on Daytrain. We are different because we say what we mean and mean what we say."

"I am walking the talk and talking the walk," Siegfried announces, waiting for cheers.

But instead there is a lull in the crowd. A warrior shouts, "How wez know you for us, and not fer yourself?"

Sensing the need to assume command, Siegfried makes his power play. "Is there anyone here who dares to challenge me? No one volunteers. "Then pledge your loyalty to me – your new King and War Lord and to Tara, my Queen." Thor and Gonorrhea yell out their support and the other Goths reluctantly follow their lead out of respect to Olin's daughter. After several hollow cheers, "Long live Siegfried," the crowd disperses.

CHAPTER 9
MARRIAGE

Medea advises Siegfried to move into the Sky House with Tara to establish their reign, but Thor reminds him of the last hurdle. He still has to be vetted before he can marry Tara.

The following day, Gonorrhea and the G-Spot Femmes arrive on their motorcycles to pick up Siegfried at the Sky House for the pre-nuptial inspection and walk-through. Gonorrhea is every bit the leader of the pack – tall, athletic, with long flowing unkempt hair. One thing that stands out is her platinum artificial lower peg leg, decorated with diamonds and rubies, used for stomping those who dare to challenge her.

After donning a helmet, Siegfried gets on the rear seat of Gonorrhea's motorbike and holds on to her breasts as she roars off to their destination – the defunct Universal Studios. The femmes lead him to a movie set decked with incense candles and jars of perfume to neutralize the lack of hygiene. They tell him to disrobe and to sit still and be quiet in the dark until further instruction. After a long period of waiting, the lights go on, and he is surrounded by the Biker Femmes, each directly lit with studio lights, squatting around him in a perfect circle. They are wearing only garter belts and stockings, whips in hand, exposing their pudenda in defiance.

"Clean as a whistle," Gonorrhea declares, tapping her platinum leg on the ground.

Siegfried is not sure what to do next and tries to hide his unwanted erection. Instinctively, he crawls towards Gonorrhea cowed with his head bowed, waiting for a cue.

"Cunnilingus is not the answer," Gonorrhea bellows out, cracking the whip. "You are here to listen. We are here to wean you from your male chauvinism. For starters, you must abide by Julia's 21 Marital Principles if you are to marry Tara."

Siegfried is surprised to hear his mother's name, but does not let on his relationship with her. Gonorrhea reads out each of the 21 Marital Principles that Siegfried is required to know by heart, starting with, *"Get her anything she wants. Do whatever she wants. Whisper sweet nothings in her ear and say, you are always right, dear."*

Siegfried recites each commandment verbatim as the Biker Femmes raise their clenched fists in affirmation. Gonorrhea then orders Siegfried to rise and man up by walking Homo erectus inside the circle formed by the Femmes. After Siegfried completes his short walking tour, the Femmes applaud politely. He passes the inspection.

Siegfried is escorted back to the Sky House by Gonorrhea, who tells Tara that Siegfried passed with flying colors. It is now up to her to make sure he fulfills the 21 Principles.

"You have to do something big and splashy so that you can be effective as king and queen of the Goths." So, on Medea's advice and with her help, Siegfried and Tara decide to give a big wedding, the largest in memory, to celebrate their union and thereby solidify Siegfried's ascendancy. Medea, her wedding planner role in full force, discusses the invitation list with Siegfried and Tara, as well as with her brother, Thor, over tea.

Tara blurts out, "Let us invite just the hoity-toity Greeks, you know, the ones who would bring the best gifts from the Polis shops."

Medea responds tactfully, "Gifts are important, dear, but you have to be careful not to offend the most refined, powerful and important class of Greeks. They may not come bearing glitzy gifts, but they will be mad if you exclude them from such a prestigious event."

Thor says in his lispy voice, "This event must be dignified. We have to show the Greeks that we are more than just Barbarians."

"It is my wedding," Tara says with a petulance that does not go unnoticed. Medea takes on a motherly role. Siegfried shows little interest.

"Tara, you are now the first lady of the Goths with real responsibilities. It is important to provide leadership, and you must help Siegfried to maintain the delicate balance between Greeks and Goths, just as your father did."

Upon hearing her dead father mentioned, Tara starts to cry; she is still her daddy's girl. "I miss him so much. He would let me have what I want. I wish my daddy were still here."

Medea tries to calm her. "He is here in spirit. Let us give you the best Goth wedding just like he would. Now back to planning your special day. Remember distinguished, powerful people take part in royal weddings; common people look on and take note."

Every bit a princess, Tara likes to dress up in fancy clothes and spends hours having her platinum blonde hairdo done up. Her two plump girlfriends, Alarica and Hattie, fuss over her appearance and play up to her as they do manicures and pedicures to while away their lazy hours. She expects a constant stream of compliments and habitually regales her audience with boring stories about her most recent, mundane experiences.

"Medea, you should have seen the look on Alarica's face when I asked her to get me my favorite cloth, you know the one with the nice flower pattern that Thor gave me to me."

Media cuts Tara short "Look Tara. We have to focus on what is important, like wedding invitations." Medea goes over the invitation list and rattles off some names.

"We will have to invite the old families." Medea then explains how they would seat families prominent in the arts and sciences. On the east side would sit the Newmans, the MacArthurs, the Knights, the Kochs, and the Prebyses; and on the west side, the families in science and technology – the Ciscos, the Windows, the Bluetooths, the Linnuxes, and the Ebays.

"What about sound and lighting?" Tara asks. She wants to make a lavish spectacle.

Thor volunteers, "I will handle that. I will ask for Aristotle's help. As head of the Greek Skunk Works, he is in charge of special effects for big events."

"Can he do it?" Tara asks, "Audio-visuals can be a nightmare. Last thing I need is for there to be no sound for the toasts. Sound engineering is critical."

Thor responds, "He can handle it. Back in the old days, Aristotle was the youngest fellow of the Triple E-I, The Electrical Engineering Enterprises Institution."

"What happened to that?"

"The EEEI consisted mainly of engineers until the computer people took it over. When computing and networks collapsed after Cybergeddon, the EEEI all but disappeared. Aristotle is head of its only remaining chapter; he still wears his EEEI pins and likes to remind people of his glorious technical achievements with implants that led to the total elimination of the stock exchange.

"But can he do weddings?" Tara asks.

Thor replies, "He is the only game in town, he will have to do."

The wedding day nears. Tara tries on the dresses she picked out in Polis, and settles on a black satin gown, decorated with jet beads; it has a finely stitched, skull and crossbones motif around the hem. Tara's make-up is almost ghoulish – a foundation of chalk-white base and powder, heavy black eyeliner and purple eye shadow in four shades. Her blood-red lipstick is visible through the spiderweb lace of her gossamer black veil and her onyx and diamond necklace is fashioned to echo the motif of sparkling metallic newts embroidered on the bodice of her dark dress.

The bridesmaids, wearing gray Victorian Lolita

Steampunk dresses, ooh and aah over Tara's gown. Thor claps his hands as Medea enters, wearing a modest, but almost transparent white dress with tiny flowers and ginkgo leaves embroidered on the sleeves, the dark of her nipples clearly visible. She announces the departure of the bridal party and calls out, "Where is Siegfried?"

Siegfried emerges, dressed in a black leather aristocrat tail tux, with a shiny bronze codpiece, and a faded vintage Harley-Davidson insignia on the lapel. His silk vest has chains hanging elegantly from the pockets. A high hat with a wide top and velvet band completes the bridegroom's outfit. Kissing him on the cheek, and wishing him the best, Medea helps him adjust his intricate, lace-up string tie as Tara stands by, watching jealously.

Otto picks up the bridal party in a truck decorated with flags showing skulls with top hats and veils; bones and tin cans drag behind; the truck is followed by a procession of motorcycles – first the G-spot Biker Girls, dressed in leather jumpsuits, twirling nunchucks as they go around a circle and park their wheels. Then, the male bikers in tuxes wield Emperor Katana swords in a show of support. The entire motorcycle entourage arrives at the slopes of the Goth compound and enters the courtyard of the sacred Sky House where the ceremony is to take place. Thor escorts the bride. Mad Moxie and his men surround Siegfried, who is struggling to loosen his tie.

The all-Goth men's choir sings in a falsetto, "Here

Comes the Bride," as the bride and groom approach the altar, fronted with an escutcheon of crossed sabers draped in black leaves. They stand under a canopy of thick vines decorated with animal fur as leaders from both the Goth and Greek communities await the ceremony. The Goth men sport leather and hats embroidered with bones or weapons; their women, all wearing bonnets, their round breasts mounding over their clothes, show off their hand-embroidered kirtles that are worn over dark, flowing smocks. The Greeks in contrast look sleekly clean and bright – the men in their white togas and the women, decked out in embroidered chitons, wrapped in deftly adjusted himations.

An old woman, wearing a lilac striped toga with a deep purple border, conducts the service. This is Athena, blind and deaf, who was selected by Medea as an officiator because of her deep knowledge of and respect for Goth wedding spells. Siegfried recalls that Athena was banished from Bionica many years ago and that she is Simon Girty's mother, who had lost touch with her son after he left Bionica. Siegfried has met her before.

Before the ceremony begins, Athena whispers to Siegfried, "I know who you are and what you have done. You are the killer of my only son – my one and only love. Now you must tell me who you will be and what you will become." He takes a deep breath before muttering, "I am Siegfried. I will lead the Goths to greatness."

She does not hear him, but seems to know what he said. "We will let the stars take care of that," she says cryptically. As part of the ring ceremony, she shouts out some mysterious babble about the sun, moon and stars and waves her wand to bless the marriage. "By the powers of the universe, you are now a Gothic man and wife," she declares laughing out loud, "This is a marriage made in Valhalla. Till death do you part."

The reception begins in the courtyard outside of the Sky House. Unmarried Goth men line up to recite short poems in honor of the wedding. Athena introduces them.

"Each of these young men will recite a poem that will be judged by our distinguished panel of Greek guests. We look for poems of sincerity and strength. The words must ring true. The winners will receive laurels and the losers must participate in combat."

The young men step up to the podium to recite in turn. After the judges rule either thumbs up or down, the winners are escorted to the right and the losers to the left. According to the Greek judges, there are many losers. After the readings, Athena returns to the podium.

"Now it is time for the second round. Bring them on."

The losers enter the combat arena and are paired off to fight. They begin with their swords raised high and engage when Athena shouts, "Begin." After several minutes of noisy combat, the young men flail their swords wildly, and on several occasion hit the adjacent participants who get in the way. Having placed wagers on their favorites, the old men in the crowd cheer them on and shout out directions as if they were overzealous drunken fans at a Greco-Roman wrestling match. Those still alive gasp for breath and beg for mercy from the crowd as the victors stand on their bodies waiting for the cue. But, this time it is thumbs down, and so the victors administer the *coup de grâce.*

The Greek onlookers snicker, making cracks about how the Goths handle the problem of youth unemployment while the old Goth men continue calling for blood.

"Finish them off."

"Cowards."

"Let us clear the air. All the losers must die."

Athena announces the names of the victors and losers. She recites a customized anti-heroic couplet, starting with the loser's first name:

George was by all accounts a terrible poet
But, because of his pride, he didn't know it
So he lived by the sword and held up his chin
As he had no more words to save his skin.

Now time for the post-combat ceremonial phase, Athena places crowns of laurel leaves on the heads of the Goth winners, those who recited the least offensive poems and those who had survived combat.

"It is with pride that I crown you. Your words and your fight will live forever in our hearts."

The crowd becomes restless hearing so many hollow words. They are ready for the next phase of the celebration: the feast.

Young, unmarried Goth maidens, their skin covered with body art depicting wild animals that have long been extinct, bring roasted meat and vegetables on huge platters; the feasting starts with medieval gusto. The Goth men grab whole piglets from the trays and baring their teeth, tear the tender flesh apart and lick their fingers clean. To insulting their Goth hosts, the Greeks reluctantly participate in the barbarian feast, fingering their food delicately before inserting it for consumption.

Among the Greek wedding guests are Medea's parents and their three beautiful daughters whose flowing gossamer Aegean blue gowns and long hair flutter in the wind. The golden embroidery that decorates the edges of their sleeves and necklines catch the light and give them a fairy-tale aura. Medea introduces them, "I would like you to meet Siegfried and Tara. These are my parents, Socrates and Xantippe, and my three beautiful stepsisters – Memory, Meditation, and Song."

Memory flirts with Tara's two friends, Alarica and Hallie, while Medea continues the introductions, Xantippe notices the flirtation by her lesbian daughter, and tries to cut things off with a friendly rebuke.

"Ah, let us now focus on the happy couple," she says to her daughters.

And so the second oldest sister, Memory, steps forward to say hello to the couple and the other two sisters follow suit, bowing lowly in front of them. Tara notices that Song, the youngest of the three sisters, has caught Siegfried's eye and smiled at him. Tara hastily grabs Siegfried's arm, prompting him to move along to greet the other guests.

With their wedding behind them, Siegfried and Tara scamper off to the Skyhouse for their first night as man and wife.

"You know, Siegfried, this is my first time. Please be gentle." Siegfried does not believe this, but goes along with it, thinking that is what brides are supposed to say. He does what Gonorrhea advised during the Prenuptial Inspection – whispering sweet nothings into her ear based on the 21 Marital Principles, but this only makes her cry. He then proceeds in his perfunctory best, rounding the bases for home, huffin' and puffin' until the house falls down. Afterward, both are stretched out with their eyes upward, lost in their own thoughts, neither sure what they gained or lost. He reaches out to take her right hand and places it over his heart, but does not tell her what is in his heart of hearts.

The next day, she wears her wimple and weeps, "You took everything away from me. How can I believe you will love me forever?"

"What can I ever do to win your heart? What do you want? What can I get for you?"

These are the words that Tara has been waiting for, but she is not sure whether they ring true. She looks directly into his eyes and says, "I have so much, and yet I want so much more." Siegfried does not respond, and wonders what it will take to please her. Perhaps he can discover the formula for pleasing this little bundle of wants.

Tara and Siegfried go about setting up their household in the Sky House. Tara's mood turns lovey-dovey again and they make their wishes and dreams known to each other as the sun goes down. They do share an interest in "things" and spend hours going through Tara's huge hope chest of treasures that her father had given her. Siegfried is interested in what the items are, who made them, and whether they are made from precious materials. Tara is more interested in how things look. Seated on the Sky House veranda, they can overlook a field where young Goths are practicing the martial arts. In the background, several Goth women are scrubbing the walls of the compound.

"I want to have fabrics that are blue and gold, all around here; I want colors everywhere. I want to get rid of all this black crap. I want my things to reflect the rays of the sun."

Siegfried nods mechanically as he surveys the piles of colorful fabric that Tara intends to integrate into their household. Since he is color blind, he is clueless when it comes to décor.

"We need to build a life for ourselves. I want to be engulfed by beautiful things." Then Tara sighs and clasps her hands together because she has something special to say.

"I want a baby of my own. A child will make things perfect for us. We need an heir."

Upon hearing about her wish to have a child, Siegfried plunges into a dark mood as he begins to have second thoughts about becoming a father again. God knows how many Bionican babies he brought into the world; he had nothing to do with any of them, and now things are supposed to be different. Tara wants a child, but the question is, does he?

A servant girl brings in a stack of new clothes for Tara to try on. She puts on various garments and asks Siegfried for his opinion.

"Siegfried, you must know which of these looks better. One always looks better than the other; I need some fashion advice. What use are you if you cannot help me make up my mind?"

"What possible difference could it make?"

"You are pathetic. You are depressing and depressed. People who cannot make up their minds are depressed. People who cannot bring themselves to say yes or no are sad sacks. What is wrong with you? Do you not want to be happy? Do you not want *me* to be happy?

Siegfried takes this as an invitation to make advances. "Of course, I want you to be happy." At first, she resists his clumsy groping and then gives in. He skips the tenderness of foreplay and proceeds to his goal. Tara is silent and feels empty after he is done with her. As she falls asleep, Siegfried is still awake, staring at the ceiling before he finally slips into slumber. He has a fleeting dream about Digi Diva, who wants to talk to him about his life. Her words flow acrobatically through her teeth and he tries grabbing at them to see what they have to say. Just then, Tara, who is apparently having a nightmare, awakens him,

"Daddy, daddy, why have you forsaken me? Please do not let him take me away." Siegfried is put off by Tara's daddy fixation. He wonders what life would have been like with Digi Diva, who simply wanted to be his soulmate.

Next morning, Tara wears a laced wimple again, to show up Siegfried's *peckerdillo*. Looking at him with furrowed brows, she says, "What have you done to me? You robbed me of my virginity." Siegfried responds with arrogance, ignoring the 21 Marital Principles that he swore to uphold when he was initiated by Gonorrhea.

"You are now my wife. You are supposed to please me."

"It is all about you and your happiness, is it not? What about the Principles you swore to uphold? I wonder what do you know about me and about what I need? Why did you marry me?" Tara demands an answer.

"I married you because it is my destiny."

"You mean you married me for some reason that has absolutely nothing to do with me and everything to do with what I have."

Siegfried does not say anything.

"Let me tell you, when I want something, I say so up front, I am not some coward who hides things. What is it that you are after? What are you hiding from me?" She has become petulant, something that does not appeal to her emotionally hollow husband.

"I cannot say," Siegfried replies.

"You mean you *will* not say."

"No, I just do not know what my true purpose is yet. It has to do with the Greeks."

"What do you want with them? No, you do not have to tell me... I know...you do not know... but, I... I do know what *I* want from them."

"I know what you want from them – more stuff, Thor told me."

"Yes, I want some of the golden threads embroidered

into the dresses of the three Greek maidens at my wedding – the ones I saw you desiring with your eyes. I want a lot of the things that they have. I want our lives to be beautiful. I am sick of seeing men slash each other and recite their stupid bad poetry."

"But *how* would you know what is beautiful?" Siegfried says, deliberately belittling her.

"When beauty speaks to me. When pretty things surround me. When people like me are by my side. Maybe someday you will like me, and then, who knows, maybe you will even love me for whom I am. I just want you to love me," Tara implores.

"What is the point? Things have to be useful before I bother with them. I am not one for pretty things. I just want to know where things fit in."

"Why not try to learn a little bit about the finer things in life? Could you do that for me?"

"I have more important things to do."

"You are *all* about killing people, like my father."

"He tried to do everything he could to kill me, and you pine for him. I fought hard to win your hand."

"Why then can you not be gentle with me?"

Siegfried does not say anything.

"You know, Medea is a good friend. She knows what I need. She understands a woman's heart." Tara hopes that this will make him jealous.

Siegfried ignores her; his mind is elsewhere. Siegfried and Tara start to avoid each other, and this sets other forces in motion, with Medea at the center.

Medea and Tara spend a lot of time together. In a weak moment, Tara confides in Medea, "Siegfried does not care about me. He never says he loves me."

Medea puts her hand on Tara's shoulder and then massages her back. "Just be patient and let things work out. You have to let Siegfried do what he does best."

"You mean killing people?"

"You have to admit, he does a good job doing that for us. We need Siegfried to enforce discipline."

"But what about me? I want him to share the good life with me."

"Killing is priority one. All good things come to those who wait."

Tara looks annoyed. "It is easy for you to say. You and Thor run the show."

"We have to. Siegfried wants Thor to do the books, and I have to keep Siegfried out of trouble and keep him busy with what he does best. You know he does not have good people skills."

Tara nods. "He never seems to be able to say the right things at the right time."

"But we need him. Right now, he is taking on evangelical Christians who want to destroy our Daytrain trade; that is very important for us. Without the Daytrain trade, our way of life would not be possible."

"But some of our relatives have become Christians," Tara says with reluctance. This is a taboo topic among the Goths. More and more of them are flocking to hear The Word.

"Do not worry. We will only make pinpoint strikes to avoid civilian casualties.

Medea takes Tara into her arms to comfort her, fondling her hair, thinking of the possibilities down the road as she brushes her hand against Tara's breast.

Kissing her on the cheek she adds, "Just be patient. Things will work out for you. I will make sure you get the beautiful things that your daddy promised you. I know what you need."

"What will we do if Siegfried finds out?"

"Do not worry, Tara; what we do is not important to him. He is focused on his duty. Just let him be."

Later that day, Siegfried shows up unannounced, unsettling Tara while Medea and Thor sit nearby looking amused.

"So how many Christians did you kill this week, my hero?" Tara's contempt for Siegfried shows as she makes the sign of the cross across her breast in a silly act of defiance.

"We must keep our society pure and safe," utters Siegfried, ignoring her while he defends his genocidal search-and-destroy missions with talking points. "The Christians are like a virus. They will destroy our way of life if we let them. They have no shame."

"But my daddy said they were harmless. He told me that we should just let them keep busy talking about the great hereafter," she says, turning to Thor. "What do you think, my dear brother?"

Thor looks the other way. He does not like what Siegfried is doing, but still buys into it so long as someone else does the dirty work.

"It is important for someone to act decisively. We will not survive in the long run if we let the Christians spread their word," Medea says impatiently. "Let them achieve what they want -- martyrdom. We cannot let them get in the way of the Daytrain trade. We cannot let them upset the delicate balance of power. Without Daytrain, we are nothing."

Put off and dejected, Tara wanders outside and encounters a raggedy pet goat that stares at her. Tara approaches the animal and starts to talk to it.

"I feel like nothing. I am nothing. I am all alone."

Meanwhile, Thor and Medea continue their chat as Siegfried stalks off.

"What is going to happen to her? I am afraid she is a stick-in-the-mud. She is going to bring all of us down."

"Do not worry, Siegfried will take care of that," Medea says cryptically.

"But maybe you can talk to her, woman to woman," Thor says in the high-pitched voice that he uses to convey his exasperation with his high-maintenance sister.

Medea sighs, "I have tried. I have also talked to Siegfried. He asked me to talk to Tara. He wants her to be less demanding and to understand him better and to accept what he now believes is his true destiny – to hunt and kill Christians."

"And what did Tara tell you?" Thor prods.

"She wants Siegfried to pay more attention to her and to forget about the Christians. But I tell her that for now he cannot do that because *that* is the work he does."

"Do you believe he is up to the challenge?"

"I am not sure. He needs to learn more about himself; his tunnel vision and passive aggression worry me, but it is useful to have him to do what is necessary."

Thor and Medea continue their worried conversation later, meeting secretly at Medea's house to discuss family politics. Over a cup of rooibos zinger tea, they gossip about the meteoric rise of Tara's sister, Gonorrhea.

"She has formed a partnership with that ugly Greek pusher, Pharmakia – they are now a real power couple," Thor says sarcastically what Medea already knows. "The Greek women love her because she supplies them men.

The Greek Gays also worship her because she supplies them with men. Gay or straight, they all react to the G-Spot Femmes Variety Show at the Hollywood Bowl – it is pure exhibitionism: lewd contortion, shrieking rap topped off by twerking and the lethal demonstration of martial arts. These women are shameful, immodest *and popular*," Thor says with envy.

Medea's assessment is more matter-of-fact. "She is disgusting but also useful to us. She is quite an asset, completely unlike her spoiled sister. She has simply worked fertility wonders in priming eligible Goth men for the Greek women desperately trying to get pregnant. She and the Biker Femmes do a great job preparing the men for duty, including weaning drunks from Mead and turning them into pliable studs through the aversion therapy protocols developed by Julia and the Xtreme Marketing Movement. This has done wonders for Greek-Goth relations and to maintain our way of life."

Medea and Thor affirm their decision that Pharmakia will handle D-train commerce with Bionica in addition to his work as a Greek pusher.

Medea says with a smile, "He will help us distribute Daytrain beyond the Polis to increase our slave supply. The Browns in the Basin will do almost anything to have it because the freedom we cherish means nothing to them. Daytrain and slavery, perfect together!"

Medea and Thor give each other knowing looks, cementing the growing understanding between them. And as they often do, they talk about Siegfried in hushed tones. Thor begins with his kitchen psychoanalysis. "You should understand that deep down he is very simple; for him everything is black or white. If you do something for him, he is your friend; if you get in his way, he is your enemy. I am not sure how useful he will be in the future."

Medea nods in agreement and sighs. "He has a long way to go in becoming subtle and sophisticated, but it is in our best interest to give him a chance. He holds the key to Bionica. It is in the script." Medea shrugs her shoulder, not sure she is backing the right horse in her fight to dominate the future. "By the way, did you know that Tara is pregnant?"

"No, that is a surprise. I thought her marriage to Siegfried was on the skids. He is no good as a husband; he is too doctrinaire to be an effective leader. This could lead to a disaster."

"Maybe the prospect of becoming a father will turn him around. At the very least, we will have a newborn."

"Good wishful thinking. I can always count on you to see all the angles," Thor says, looking for a glint of sisterly affection as he sees her smiling wanly.

"We have a lot in common, a marriage of minds," she says, leaning in to rub his knee.

Later that year, Tara gives birth to a boy and names him Pericles, as suggested by Medea. Medea is at her side in the absence of Siegfried, who is out on yet another Christian killing mission. Meanwhile, Tara devotes her energies to her newborn son.

Medea, now Pericles' godmother, is indispensable. Tara hoped that Pericles' birth would encourage Siegfried to take pride in his new family, but to her dismay he expresses only annoyance at hearing his newborn son cry.

"I do not know what I would do without you," says Tara, turning to Medea, who is tending the baby. Medea accepts the compliment with a smile and then looks straight at Tara.

"You know, Tara, it is now time to throw another banquet to celebrate the birth of your son."

Later that month, the banquet takes place on a beautiful sunny day in the courtyard outside the Sky House. Tara and Siegfried join the Goth elders at the head table, already being served food and drink. Medea announces the arrival of additional Greek guests, who are seated and served. Meanwhile, Tara and Siegfried's Goth subjects mill about on foot in a special area assigned to them where they can pick at huge trays piled high with roasted pork. While the baby's auntie, Gonorrhea, works the Greek women in the crowd, signing them up for Goth male assignations, Pharmakia hobnobs with the Greek men, promoting his D-train trade with the special favors he provides to his steady clientele.

"It does not get any better than this," a young Goth cries out. He is a participant in a free-for-all wrestling match, organized by Gonorrhea; he has just won his match and is ready to claim his prize. "I would like that one," he points to one of the Greek ladies, anxiously awaiting the outcome of the match, who runs towards him kicking up her heels, to join the strapping lad for a frolic in the grass.

And then there is the usual main event, the inevitable poetry slam. The readings begin with fanfare. Plato, the plump chief philosopher of the Greeks, struts before the assembly and introduces each contestant with large rhetorical gestures while summarizing their poetic aspirations. Skinny Aristotle, meanwhile, helps to line up the poets participating in the fest.

"Today each of these young poets will recite in the honor of baby Pericles. So now, ladies and gentlemen, here is our first poet – another man of the word, the spoken word, mind you." The phrase "spoken word" gets a few giggles from the Greeks who are bemused by the Goth aversion to written literature. The first of many aspiring poets comes forward.

"I have the extreme pleasure of introducing to you a man, who is a true believer in his meter and rhyme. He will touch your heart if you let him."

And so the introductions go as the poets wait for their chance for the big time, drinking pints of mead to give them courage and inspiration. The poets are judged on a scale from one to ten by the notables at the main tables who hold up cards to announce their score. The three lowest scoring Goths are relegated to the pit where they are given another chance to compete. Each gets up, completely drunk, and gives his best until it becomes clear which among them is the very worst.

"The death wish is at the root of Goth poetry," Plato whispers to Aristotle after the introductions are given. "There he goes," Aristotle replies, "I think we have ourselves a winner." The Very Worst Poet Award will go to this showstopper:

Pericles, baby boy Pericles
Testicles, full of joy
Wag a finger at his nose
And see the wiggle of his little hose
And when he makes his little pish
Let's grant him every wish.

Tara, holding baby Pericles tight, suddenly hands over the now dripping bundle of joy to Medea. The baby starts to cry, and Tara steps forward to nominate this hapless bard for the Very Worst Poet Award because of the impact of his poem on her precious baby boy.

"Off with his head! Off with this head!" Queen of Hearts Tara commands in her shrill, piercing voice.

"Your wish is my command," chuckles cardman Plato. Since this is Tara's baby shower, all of the carefully crafted protocol for selecting winners and losers goes out of the window. Plato embraces and fondles the winning drunken bard and then removes his arms from around the poor sot and shoves him in the direction of Mad Moxie, who draws his sword, whops off his head, and then holds it up to please the crowd.

"Life is not cheap here, but we do offer death at a discount," proclaims Tara, basking in the attention she is getting during her pisher power shower.

As always, bad-poet killings are real crowd pleasers. The Goths cheer wildly, and the Greek men clap politely and smirk while their women look bored, surveying the crowd for eligible men in exchange for the baby loot they bestowed on Tara's babe. Meanwhile, Gonorrhea's partner, Pharmakia, schmoozes with Plato and Aristotle and with their coterie of young men, give out samples of the latest crop of Daytrain as they chat.

After the festival is over, Tara takes stock of the baby gifts, including handcrafted tiny clothing, blankets and sweaters, luxury toys, and mood-enhancing drugs for tired moms.

As a diversion, Medea arranges a visit to the Polis in Pasadena for Tara and Siegfried and their entourage. It takes a full day to make the journey by truck from The Valley winding through the legendary Santa Monica Mountains to the center for fine antiques in Pasadena. Tara is looking forward to the shopping excursion. This is the first time she will go to visit Greek cultural institutions and shops without her father, and it is also the first time with Siegfried. Medea helps Tara and Siegfried prepare for the trip.

"You know, of course, Macedonia was named after a region in ancient Greece ruled by Alexander the Great, whom we greatly admire. We also refer to our towns as "Polis" to pay respect to the Greek ideals of democracy. Pasadena is the name that the old Angelinos used for this place," Medea explains.

Tara laughs. "I remember Daddy talking about your democratic ideals. How do you explain your complete dependence on slaves?"

Medea scowls. "We need slaves to support our way of life. You know slavery in ancient Greece and ancient Rome was commonplace, and so there is nothing wrong with it. We need slaves so that we can live green, which is *so* labor intensive. You know – reduce, recycle, reuse, and...recover. Slaves make the world go around much greener."

Tara does not buy Medea's idea of democracy. "But slavery is wrong, is it not? Deep down, we Goths believe that people have a right to be what they are, so long as they fight for it."

Media laughs. "You have a point. Willingness to fight is the essence of freedom. But you of all people should understand. You are involved in the slave trade. There was no other way to develop the finer things in life for the community of superior equals. Finery – is that not what entices you to visit the Greeks?"

"I suppose it is," Tara says with indifference. Siegfried looks on bored as the two talk and takes no notice when Tara tries on yet another outfit for the trip to buy yet more outfits.

"I refuse to wear black for this outing. How do you like this white top? Do the colors go together," Tara tests Siegfried.

"The colors do go together; you look very beautiful," he says mechanically. For the time being, this response will do. Tara is mentally ensconced in "the shoppes" of Polis located near the new "City on the Gravity Hill District."

"They say there are all kinds of interesting places there. I have never been there; have you?"

"I cannot say I have," Siegfried says in a whiny passive-aggressive put-down voice.

Later, Tara and Siegfried arrive at the Macedonian Visitors Center of Pasadena in a Goth truck driven by Otto, who is hauling building materials to the Greeks.

Otto is talkative despite his stutter. "Y...you...s... should see the exhibition of sick puppy art."

"Puppy art? Are we going to see some cute little puppies with big eyes?" Tara asks.

"No, I think that was 20th Century renaissance painter, Margaret Keane, whom we greatly admire today. These are the artists of the Sick Puppy Movement who tried to tell us w...what is wrong with the world."

Tara shrugs him off. She has had this conversation before and wants to end it. "You think I am superficial and that all I like are happy endings. That may be true, but I am not sick and I know what I like."

The group makes its way inside the Macedonian Visitor's Center, which has postings of all the Greek museums and other cultural institutions, including the most prestigious Palace of Classic Culture that regales visitors with the glories of the civilizations that preceded Cybergeddon.

The Greek visitor guides have been expecting them. A middle-aged woman in a toga approaches Tara and Siegfried and announces their visit in a condescending voice.

"We have some rather special visitors today, Tara and Siegfried, wife and warlord, who hail from The Valley, the land of the Goths.

Tara fusses with her clothes, straightening out her white top and her jewelry, while Siegfried wipes his brow and looks around. As they explore the Visitors Center, another woman, a docent, approaches them. "My name is Hygieia and I will be your guide during your visit to our beautiful Polis. You are now in our observatory and library looking over the City on Gravity Hill, which is dedicated to the perpetuation of wisdom of all the ages. This is our nexus of learning, libraries, and museums."

"Nexus? Ugh, those books again," Tara mutters to Siegfried. "When are they going to get to the good stuff, the stuff that I want?"

"Now be patient," the docent scolds her. "We will get out to shop The Hill in due time. But it is important that you get a complete picture of what we are about."

Tara mutters under her breath, "More about books and museums, I cannot wait."

The docent takes Tara and Siegfried up the hill to the Palace of Classic Culture, an impressive wood structure, painted with trompe l'oeil freezes and fronted by columns to make it look like the Parthenon. All around are advertising billboards with quotations from the great thinkers such as the ancient Socrates' "All I know is that I know nothing" and "The unexamined life is not worth living."

Tara and Siegfried are led to the entrance. "These are replicas of genuine Doric columns. Inside we have a current exhibit on technology of all the ages."

"You are in for a real treat today," Hygeia says beginning their tour. The exhibit begins with a diorama of the caveman and tools. There are other exhibits focusing on the Iron and Bronze Age, the Middle Ages, Ancient Greece and Ancient Rome, the Renaissance, the Industrial Revolution, the Post-Industrial Information Age, and the Cyber Age.

"We will take you on a tour of our history and culture. We will show you how we rebuilt Polis based on Ancient Greece and Rome, and what we are doing to develop our culture utilizing appropriate technology."

Tara rolls her eyes. Everything that the Greeks talk about is so boring.

"And I am pleased to announce that we have developed a system of electric lighting using human power."

Hygeia pulls a curtain to reveal a room full of slaves pedaling hard on stationary bicycles that are wired to a generator that powers the flickering lights in the room.

She continues laconically, "You will be pleased to learn that we have rediscovered electricity and its uses. Solar batteries and a wind-powered generator could power this museum, but we still rely on the conventional batteries that we have managed to salvage. Unfortunately, today there is little technology for capturing sunlight and wind to produce electricity. So we have to use our *bracero* slave laborers to convert human power to electricity. We have managed to find many kinds of old appliances that run on electricity. Thanks to our hard-working staff, we figured out the instructions for these things that had ceased to function and made them work again. The staff at our materials projects shop, run by Mr. Vulcan, deserves a lot of credit for fixing and making parts."

Mr. Vulcan peers out of the curtain and is greeted by scattered applause from several Greeks who have decided to tag along.

"Let us go to an exhibit on the computer revolution that occurred many years ago. This exhibit includes many early computers, including a TRS-80 and a Commodore, as well as the IBM 5150. These were called personal computers. Here is a much larger computer, the PDP-11/24, a fourth-generation PDP-11 system used by organizations."

Siegfried raises his hand to ask a question.

"Yes?"

"How did computers in the old days remember and communicate?"

"We are not entirely sure exactly how these early systems worked, but we have some of our scientists working on this in the Caltech Skunk Works run by our very own Aristotle, who is an expert on reverse engineering. Now that we have electricity, we can turn these machines on, but we are not sure how to use them."

Siegfried shouts another question, "Where did you get your information about the Digital Age?"

Hygeia is quick with her answer. "We got it from printed materials. It is all in the library upstairs.

Siegfried tries to show up the docent, "Your sources are obsolete; the real stuff is online. If only you could consult The Well directly you could get the record straight."

"Oh yes, the Bionican Well," Hygeia says, bored at the prospect of having another discussion about The Well. "We know all about it, but we are not sure how reliable it is. Some say it contains a lot of vaporware. The Bionicans in the South are the only ones who can get at that information, but they will not share it. What is the use of data if there is no way of capturing and analyzing them?"

Siegfried is a bit offended at this swipe; he still thinks that The Well is the true fount of human knowledge and wisdom. He gets in another dig.

"So what is the point of all these museums?"

"We need to have the real stuff we can see, feel and touch; that is what museums are all about. We want to preserve the past for future generations."

"What about the Cyber Age?"

Hygeia is slow to reply. "Our exhibits about that era only cover the things that we definitely know. It has to be written down, and there have to be relics. We have limited information and only some relics from the Cyber Age because it went south and disappeared into The Well. There is not very much left of the corporate memory of that era, except in the minds of the Bionicans who worship useless data that no one cares about today. But I would be happy to show you what we have from the earlier days of the Cyber Age."

The docent walks the group to a long hall and points to a group of skeletons crouched over laptops and peering into tablets and personal communication devices against a backdrop of 21st Century company logos – Apple, Google, Facebook, Twitter, Instagram and many others that dominated the virtual market of yesteryear.

"The skeletons you see here commemorate the first "Like War" when users were forced by their corporate masters to name their babies after their products. Some who refused appeared in snuff videos on YouTube. This helped that campaign along.

"What is that?" Siegfried says pointing at a poster that reads, *Net Neutrality: Empower the people, not giant corporations.*

"Oh, that was politics in the early days. Eventually, the protests became violent, and led to the destruction of the "master race" that came to dominate the Cyber Age with their brain implants," Hygeia explains while ushering the group to the next exhibit.

On the left, there is an installation protesting the

proliferation of electronic devices. Siegfried walks up to it and picks up a poster from behind the pile. It looks like a photo of someone's buttocks on it with these superimposed words – *I don't mean to brag, but I'm so fast with technology.* But, but before Siegfried can finish reading them out, Hygeia screams at him, "No, no – do not touch. That is a rare Yoko Nono." After he puts it back, the docent continues to lecture, explaining how implants became the next big thing ushering in the great Cyber Age.

"How did that happen?" Siegfried asks the docent.

"Implants – people thought that they could be more intelligent with implants."

"Implants?" Tara betrays her lack of education resulting from the Goth ban on books.

"Yes, implants. That ended Net Neutrality for good." She goes up to a model of a head and opens up the skull to retrieve a tiny device.

Tara is grossed out. "Ugh! I can't believe people would do such a thing."

Hygeia smiles and continues her talk. "First, they were surgically inserted into the brain; later they were made part of the genetic code so that knowledge could be handed down from one generation to the next genetically without surgery. But, they were arrogant; they thought they could get access to everything that is known. What they did not realize is that the important thing is to be selective and to verify the data so that useless stuff does not pile up. Less is more."

"And as you know, the foolishness of the Cyber Era continues to this day," Hygeia says disdainfully. "The Bionicans are the church of latter-day fools, who pray through their Teach-Ins for outdated knowledge and obsolete wisdom. What is the point of keeping disconnected data alive unless we can use it to produce more useful information?"

Siegfried probes further. "What do the Greeks want to do with the knowledge they have?" Hygeia is taken aback. She is not accustomed to being asked so many questions by a Goth.

"By understanding the past, we can better prepare for the future," she responds by repeating the museum's talking points.

Siegfried becomes petulant, "What do you Greeks want to do? Do you not need The Well's data to complete the picture? From what you say, it seems that the Greeks want to expand and control everything."

"Definitely not. We are for keeping our community small enough so that democracy can thrive here without tyranny, unlike you Goths who praise your tyrants. We are even fine with the idea that the world is flat if that is what it takes to maintain harmony. We know that the ancient Greeks believed in a flat earth for hundreds of years, even though we know that this is not true. All we want to do is to spread the word about truth and beauty. Small is beautiful. We believe in an appropriate technology, one that is harmonious with nature, and that will not upset the balance, no matter what shape the planet is."

Siegfried thinks that this sounds too good to be true; he recalls all the Bionican rallies warning about the dangers of bringing back technology; deep down he does not believe the Greek propaganda.

Hygeia takes a slow, determined breath and continues, "In the Cyber Age, people extended themselves beyond what was decent. There was the Xtreme Marketing Movement which later came to be known as Xtremus."

Siegfried's ears perk up. He wants to hear more. "What about the Xtreme Marketing Movement?"

She continues carefully, "This Xtremus movement went too far. In the beginning, it was a good thing because it tried to convince people not to consume natural resources, but as it got going, Xtremus proponents tried too hard to force their will on other people. It became another form of Communism."

"Communism?" Tara has never heard of this term.

"Yes, Communism. This was a 19th and 20th Century philosophy with many slogans, such as, "all for one and one for all." Xtremus, like Communism, failed because it did not understand human nature. Frank Zappa once said, *Communism doesn't work because people like to own stuff.* People like to own physical things; they like to hold and touch things, even hug them. People like to look forward to pleasure; they want to have good taste."

"I just *love* fine things," Tara giggles.

"Yes fine things are nice; you must be a Greek at heart," the docent says, meeting out a spoonful of woman-to-woman flattery. Seeing Tara smile and blush, the docent smiles back and continues, "A long time ago Xtremus tried to get people to act like consumers without consuming anything; this was inherently false. People soon caught on, and there was hell to pay."

Siegfried is uncomfortable hearing this. Although he has issues with his mother, he does not want anyone else to trash her achievements.

"Who founded this movement?"

Hygeia glares at him, "Julia was a piece of work, a real power hungry lady. She had fire in the belly but no warmth in her heart. She meant well at first, but you know what Lord Acton says about power?"

Siegfried tries to contain his murderous impulse and asks. "Now just what did this Lord Acton say about power?"

"Power tends to corrupts and absolute power corrupts absolutely."

"I had no idea. Is that what you Greeks are trying to do?"

Hygeia responds angrily, "We are not trying to corrupt anybody. We have no real power, except to influence. It is the Goths who have the power because they have the muscle, the machines and the weapons."

"You mean our boys can kick ass," says Tara showing off her crude side.

"Yes, it is important for you Goths to be strong; we need you to be strong."

"And free," Tara adds, wiping off several invisible tears of pride. Like many Goths, she is very susceptible to flattery.

She continues with mock seriousness, "Goths keep us on an even keel. They make us think hard about our cultural values. Since they reject us for what we stand for, we have to work harder to convince them that we are for real. We need you and I hope you need us."

This politically correct speech pleases Tara. "I am glad to hear you guys have something nice to say about us. All I hear is that the Greeks think we are a bunch of uneducated clowns and that we have no class."

Stifling a smirk, Hygeia continues her exercise in diplomacy. "Now you know we do not feel that way. Goths are the real thing; we need you. You guys are not corrupted by the past the way we are. You are the yin to our yang."

Tara gets annoyed. "What are you talking about? What is all the yin-yang stuff? When is it time to shop for goodies?"

Hygeia smiles, "You are right, Queen Tara. The good-ies are what count. What would civilization be without the goodies? But that all changed with the Cyber Age."

"So what were the goodies of the Cyber Age?"

"I will get to that, but first let me talk about com-puters. These devices could operate faster and faster and could produce things faster and faster. They made enough things to last for thousands of years and even today we rely on things manufactured many years ago. There was no way to stop what they called 'progress.' They had tiny machines that could store a thousand, even a million books. You could have conversations with perfect strangers all over the earth."

"Is that not confusing?" Siegfried asks, trying to imagine what it was like for so many people to be com-municating at once.

Tara is getting impatient. "Why should I care about all this cyber stuff? Goodies are what make the world go around," she groans.

Hygeia responds patiently, "Oh that is what got the world into trouble. There were not just one or two good-ies, or even a handful of goodies; there were billions and billions of goodies. More people were born wanting more goodies and Mother Earth just said: *I have had enough. I have no more to give. My resources are depleted.*"

Siegfried becomes oppositional. "Wait a minute, Tara has a point; it is all about entropy."

Hygeia, surprised to hear a Goth use this difficult word, says to him, "Entropy is a word to end all words. All we want to do here is have some intellectual stimulation." The docent's voice trails off.

Siegfried does not want to let go. "What is the point of that? Stimulation has to lead to something." Tara nods mechanically in agreement. Meanwhile, Hygeia, tired of arguing, ends the discussion.

"Why do we not go to the Xtremus Museum down the road? It has a lot of interesting stuff that will shed light on our discussion."

Another docent, Pasithea, a frumpy middle-aged woman wearing an old Xtremus button, leads Siegfried and Tara into the Xtreme Marketing Museum. When they arrive, Medea is there to greet them in a gothic black dress with red flowers in her hair, revealing her breasts and cleavage, much to the surprise of Siegfried and Tara, who had been used to see her dress with reserve and dignity. Berk, the dwarf, is bobbing at her side in a strenuous effort to catch a glimpse of her bosoms as Medea pivots to meet and greet her visitors. She has been expecting them.

Medea seizes the moment, upstaging Pasithea. "Welcome to the Xtremus Museum, Home of Xtreme Marketing, a one of a kind experience. This is Berk, the curator of this wonderful museum that is a tribute to Julia, who gave her life to cyber truth. She was a role model to women all over the world. She revolutionized our concept of consumerism, and she foresaw the problems that would face humans as they tried to develop an economic system that respected the environment. Julia is no longer with us, but her spirit lives on in our collection."

Medea leaves the group and the docent, Pasithea, takes over the tour. Siegfried notices that this museum has some of the same videos that Berk showed him before he left Bionica. The video now being shown shows his mother as a young woman, explaining the essence of Xtreme Marketing. She is talking about "footprints" on the environment and the need for sustainable "green" technology.

Suddenly, Siegfried hears his Mother's voice. At first he thinks it is in his head and then he realizes that the sounds are real because Tara also hears them. They are coming from another video screen.

"Finally, you are here my son; welcome to this exhibit that has been prepared especially for you; please sit down and listen to my instructions."

"Who is she," Siegfried asks, pretending not to know. He is apprehensive because of the presence of Berk and wonders whether he will blow his cover. He certainly does not want Tara to know anything about his Xtremus connections.

Berk steps in, going along with Siegfried's charade. "Oh, that is the voice of Julia that was recorded before she died."

Pasithea continues, "The story goes that she prepared this tape for some future son who would carry on the Xtremus Movement; there has been many a boy who thought he was that son."

Siegfried's mood darkens and he looks away.

Berk shrugs his shoulders and looks over to Medea, who is chatting with Pasithea.

Meanwhile, Berk takes over the docent's duties.

Berk continues his talk as he looks straight at Siegfried. Medea nods in agreement. "The tragedy of the Xtremus movement is that it promised too much to too many. Whenever a mass movement does this, the outcome at the very end is never beautiful. Xtremus is all about the gods that failed."

Berk places another Julia data module in the play unit and introduces it. "This newsreel was produced under the most difficult jungle conditions with outdated 21st Century technology. During the making of this program, genome data was taken from a willing donor, Winston, to create sperms to fertilize Julia's ovum. Winston was a 39-year old transsexual, who became a man to woo Julia. Even before becoming a physical man, Winston and Julia knew each other as lovers."

Berk pauses a moment and then continues to explain, "There was a real data exchange between these two people, which is best described by that venerable word, love. This four-letter word ceased to have much meaning once The Well was created to control any emotional forces that got in the way of the pragmatic and unselfish thought needed for a green and just planet. While Julia championed a love of living large, it was love embedded in jealousy that ultimately killed Winston when he tried to isolate Julia from the Xtremus movement. He was filled with great longings that could not be satisfied. He ended up jumping off a cliff with the suicide cry, "Control, alternate, delete! Control, alternate, delete!"

Berk takes a deep breath and gives Siegfried a knowing sideways glance before continuing. "Julia filled cyberspace with her laments, vowing revenge. She said the authorities eventually drove him to suicide to stall the rise of Xtremus. She failed to understand that it was her hubris and suicidal impulses that led to his demise. Let's take a look at a video that Julia produced with Winston to gain support and notoriety."

The video shows Julia and effeminate Winston, both young and naked, in what appears to be the Garden of Eden. Surrounded by ferns and flowers, they move through this "paradise" as snippets are read from Ovid's Metamorphoses:

Before the ocean was, or Earth, or heaven
Nature was all alike, shapelessness
Chaos, so-called, all rude and lumpy matter
Nothing but bulk, inert, in whose confusion
Discordant atoms warred.

As the camera moves in for a close-up of Julia's face, the audience is treated to a broad smile, a rare occasion for Julia watchers. "I am happy, and my dear Winston is happy. We are in love, happy and content. Join us. Join us with Xtreme love. Power to the People!" She raises her trademark clenched fist salute.

The narrator of the video continues, "Julia became an instant celebrity in Cyberland. Children collected virtual dolls in her likeness. There were thousands of online communities to discuss Julia and her cause."

Berk abruptly shuts off the video and inserts another one. "I want to show you yet another video, her last one, which will help you better understand Julia. This one was produced at the onset of the Great Plague that wiped out 95% of humanity."

Berk explains that this video deals directly with the Great Plague right after the cyberterrorists unleashed it. Julia, in a red sari, is interviewed by N2, a bald albino cyber guru in a loincloth.

Looking unwell, an emaciated Julia takes a deep breath, grimaces, and then barely smiles. "You know, N2, we are now a dying breed. We were the hopelessly romantic." N2 nods with a wan smile. Julia's voice is barely audible. "All I wanted to do was to stir things up a bit. To remind people of love, real love."

N2 gently nods his head and chants softly, guiding Julia into the spiritual domain.

"Julia, your hours are numbered. Perhaps someday the world will be ready for the kind of freedoms you are talking about." To which she answers, "I am ready."

N2 continued to chant, mostly numbers. Two orderlies come to take her away in a gurney. Julia musters enough strength to lift her head and cry out, "Long Live Xtremus. Makeitso!" The video fades to a screensaver of June bugs dancing to the sounds of Binary Stream.

Berk shuts down the video and sums things up.

"That was the last that we heard from her," Berk says solemnly. "She thought that Xtremus would save the world, but in the end she failed to realize her vision. People lost heart and so civilization declined. It was a mistake to centralize information and remove it from daily life."

Tara is getting tired hearing all the terrible things in the past. "It happened. So why bother with the past? There is not a thing we can do about it."

Berk gives Tara a superior look. "Do you not know that those who are ignorant of history are condemned to repeat it?"

Tara is not buying it. "I want to be around beautiful

things. I do not want to dwell on the bad and the ugly. I want to go shopping, and I want to see beautiful things."

"So the lady wants to see beautiful things. How about some house tours?" Pasithea, the docent, suggests. Tara and Siegfried join a group of ladies standing off to the side, and the docent gathers the group and tells them, "Today we have a special tour. We are going to see how some people lived years ago during the high and mighty days of Greater Los Angeles.

Pasithea leads the group to an empty apartment complex to join other tourists. "This place was once inhabited by Beatniks." She quickly corrects herself, "By Hippies, I meant to say. Do any of you know the difference between Beatniks and Hippies décor-wise?"

One lady in the group raises her hand. "Beatniks lived very simply, and they were sloppy, took drugs and drank a lot; they read poetry aloud and liked to put candles into empty bottles of wine and did dumb things like offering visitors a chance to sit in empty bathtubs instead of comfortable furniture."

Pasithea nods. "A very creative answer and perhaps true. The Beatniks wore a lot of dark turtleneck sweaters and did not like the way most respectable people live. Many of them were poets and artists. We do not know much more. What about the Hippies?" the docent asks another lady.

"The Hippies took a lot of drugs, painted colors on

their faces, and ran around naked like the Bionicans."

Pasithea nods again. "That is partially true. They liked to be surrounded by a lot of strange colorful things. Let us take a look at a typical hippie pad."

She leads them through the apartment that has mattresses on the floor, a no-longer functioning lava lamp, a mandala made out of colored string, and lots of drug paraphernalia, including a giant hookah.

"They thought of themselves as free spirits. Some died doing drugs and a few grew up to become the mothers and fathers of the Information Revolution."

"Were they anything like the Bionicans?"

"The Bionicans are a special case," the docent lady replies. "Let us not go there today. Let us go and see how normal people once lived."

Pasithea takes the group for a long walk up the hill to a large development house. "Here is how people lived when the world was rich in energy. Their daughters were called Valley Girls, destined to become employed in the studios of Happy Silicone Valley, the center of pornography in the Western World. This large home accommodated just one family. It was fully equipped, as you can see, with appliances, wall-sized 3-D movie screens, comfortable furnishings, and things made out of synthetics that gave people a lot of health problems. Look at the high ceilings and the huge kitchen. Today it would be inconceivable to build a house like this.

"I love it, love it, love it," Tara says, clasping her hands together, wishing she had been alive during that opulent era. "I am so sick of making do."

Pasithea looks at her askance. "We have better things to do today. We live more modestly today in the name of truth and beauty."

Tara becomes impatient. "What about all those beautiful things that we were promised? What about the artifacts left over from yesterday?"

"Ah yes, the hand-me-downs."

Pasithea takes them to another part of the Polis, on the flats that can be clearly seen from the top of the City on Gravity Hill. Close by are the shoppes named The Silent Spring, Hope Springs Eternal, and Fruit of the Loom.

"This is the last part of today's grand tour. Please feel free to shop on your own. Here you will find anything that you could possibly want. These stores offer pre-owned or surplus goods that were manufactured eons ago. There are so many pre-owned things available so that there is no need to manufacture additional goods today."

"Who were the most recent owners?" Tara asks excitedly.

"I think you know the answer. These goods were liberated from the finest homes of those who perished during the Great Plague," the docent replies.

Tara and Siegfried wander off to visit the stores. They

go into a store called Crowning Glory that has nothing but hats. Tara tries on several, as Siegfried looks on, bored. She comes out of the store with three hats that she hands to Siegfried to carry.

The next store, Face Time, carries thousands of toiletries such as combs, brushes, and make-up.

The store lady, an older woman, approaches Tara.

"I have just what is right for you. You have nice blonde hair. Here are some very fine brushes, all the way from France."

"Where is France?"

The shop lady is not surprised that her Goth customer does not know.

"France is very far away. We do not know if there is a France anymore. It is very sad. So many people died. *C'est la vie*," she sighs.

The old lady wipes her tears. Siegfried and Tara continue to poke around the store. Hesitantly, Tara picks up a brush to buy. The shop lady makes note of the purchase.

"Your name, please?"

"Queen Tara."

"Let me see. Yes, here you are. Your word is good. I see you have visited our store before. Did you bring your loyalty card?" Tara nods in obedience.

Tara and Siegfried leave the store with another bag of goodies and join up with the tour guide.

"There are so many things I want," Tara exclaims clasping her hands.

Inadvertently Siegfried and Tara enter a bookstore. Tara tugs at Siegfried trying to get him to leave, but his attention is drawn to a shelf containing some of the same books that he burned when he stayed in the house in the Alamo Estates. In the corner of the store is a seated skeleton, with a book on his lap. He appears to have been boning up on fuzzy logic.

The storeowner says, "Oh, this is the first owner of this store. A true bookworm, he collected some of the most important works of the 20th Century."

"Looks like the worms got the better of him," Siegfried laughs. Tara giggles.

"Maybe we should move on."

Tara tugs his shoulder. "Perhaps you can take us to a shop with nice stuff that shows how happy people once were."

They go to another meticulously arranged shop, Family Bliss, where a family dinner table is set with Herend fine bone china and silverware, a basket of fruit, and a bouquet of flowers. There is a beautiful wood crucifix on the wall. Paintings on the wall depict scenes of domesticity: a family at the dinner table, a woman combing her hair, children playing with toys, a steaming pot of coffee.

The shop girl explains, "You can buy anything you

see here. Today we have a special sale on princess outfits and accessories."

Tara squeals with delight because she has wanted to update her princess collection that her daddy had gotten for her since she was a little child.

Tara points to a princess outfit that she wants to buy – a replica of the Disney Snow White dress made out of 100% polyester, a yellow pullover gown dress, a stretchy blue velvet bodice with golden trims, a white stand up collar, satin and red shoes, a dark blue vest, satin short sleeves with tear drop accents, and a long yellow satin shirt with mesh layer, and a headband with attached bow. Tara sends Siegfried in the back to make a deal, taking for granted that this will go smoothly. She is aware that Medea and Thor, in cooperation with Aristotle at the Skunk Works, have paved the way for her shopping excursions by setting up a crude ledger banking system using Daytrain as collateral.

After Tara and Siegfried leave the shoppes, the docent shows up to announce their next stop. "The best is yet to come. We are going to take you to a genuine Greek musical event at the Palestra where we usually have our Greco Roman wrestling classes." Tara grimaces and yawns.

Tara has heard Greek music before. The Greeks have a chamber orchestra consisting of the fife, drum, and lyre; they often play pieces written on a pentatonic scale.

Bored, Siegfried and Tara yawn and then nod out on one of the wrestling mats. After the first movement, Tara gives the signal to her entourage that it is finally time to leave, and they all get up before the second movement has a chance to start. Pasithea shakes her head. She is accustomed to Goth rudeness.

It takes about five hours of arduous driving in fully loaded vans before they reach home in Simi Valley. The servants unload and unpack the coffers of Greek goods, and bring them into the Sky House, which Tara plans to redecorate. They add these to the stack of Greek goods – fine material, vases, dishes, and knickknacks – that she brought back from her previous visits. Soon there is barely enough room for the new arrivals.

"I want to show you my new dress," Tara says to Siegfried, hoping that it will please him. "I will put it on just for you." Tara disappears with her two servants, and then reappears as a fully dressed princess, wearing the Snow White outfit she bought in the Polis. She dances around the room, showing off her new red slippers, blowing kisses in Siegfried's direction. She tells him that this will be a dance especially for him. The swirling dress gets his attention, as she executes her ballet moves, culminating in a *grande pirouette.*

Tara finishes her dance, exhausted, hoping for kind words of appreciation, but all he wants to do is to remove the dress as fast as he can to execute a go-for-it, but she is in no mood for a quickie. She wants the real McCoy, but allows him to proceed with his manifest destiny, hoping for a word exchange, perhaps some endearments, Siegfried is mainly interested in talking about his Christian-killing missions and resents Tara's unwillingness to let him share his work during their most significant moments together.

As he tries to launch his favorite topic, Tara cuts him off. "I am not interested in discussing the fine points of taking a human life. If you are going to do it, make quick work of it. I want to live the good life."

Dead tired, Tara and Siegfried go straight to bed upon arrival. Tara, like a nesting doll, removes her many layers of clothing and snuggles close to him. She takes his right hand and encourages it to fondle her breasts.

"Please talk to me."

Siegfried, removing his hand, does not respond. Hurt and angry, Tara stares at him.

"Why do you not talk to me?"

"I have nothing to say."

"Why did you want me in the first place then?"

No response from Siegfried. She starts to cry. "I want us to be happy. We have a son."

After a long silence, Siegfried speaks, "Maybe what your father said was true. He was against me no matter what. I *had* to do what I did."

"Who are you? What do you want from me?" Tara asks angry and confused.

"I do not want to talk anymore. I have to leave early tomorrow for a mission." He proceeds to exercise what he considers his marital rights, and after a short struggle, she allows him to delivers the *coup de grâce* that puts the final nail into their marital coffin.

They turn their backs to each other and gradually sink into angry sleep. Next day, Tara overhears two servants talking about Siegfried.

"They say once a Bionican, always a Bionican. Soon he will show his true Bionican colors," she says, holding her nose.

"We will never be free from his Bionican stench."

"Some say that he and Tara must go."

"She is so needy and lazy and will not do anything for herself."

"Tara is too cozy with the Greeks."

"Look at all the Greek stuff she brought here. There is so much that the floor is caving in, and she keeps getting more crap that no one uses. What a pack rat! What can we throw out so that she does not notice?"

"How about the pink linen? They are piled to the ceiling. They are a health hazard."

"Good idea!"

Tara tells Medea about what she overheard, "The servants talk trash about Siegfried. They are calling him a Bionican. They also say that we are betraying the Goths." But what galls her is the conspiracy to throw out her stuff.

"It is like throwing away a part of me. They have no respect."

"We cannot have *any* of that," Medea says nonchalantly. "You better do something about it. Here, put this in their food."

Medea hands Tara ten vials of poison sumac flavored with sweet honey and cinnamon.

"Give it to them in the next few days. They will gradually get sick and die. After that happens, my men will get rid of them."

Several weeks later, Siegfried returns from his mission. Medea is waiting for him.

"Things are not going well. We have to talk."

Siegfried does not hear what she said and instead forges on with his report.

"The mission went well. We had some good kills. We found many Christians hiding in the forest. They are all dead now."

"That is not what I want to talk to you about. We have some real problems here at home. We had to get rid of the servants. Yesterday, I called my men to take their bodies away."

Siegfried looks surprised.

"They were spreading rumors about us. People are talking about you. You have to do something."

"I am too busy looking after our interests. You know that."

"Yes, I know. But, you should spend more time mixing with our warriors. To help out with damage control, you have got to cozy up. Maybe it is time for you to have a drink with the boys. You need to have moxie to do that, and having Moxie on your side wouldn't hurt.

Following Medea's advice, Siegfried joins the boys at the Mess Hall for the Happy Hour. He meets up with Mad Moxie, who whispers to him, "Your reputation is on the skids; you have got to find your words. The men are demanding that you speak out your poetry. They suspect that you don't have it in you. All of our leaders must be poets at heart. Now is your turn."

This is the last thing Siegfried wants to do. He is afraid the Goths will kill him if he improvises with verse, and so he tries to wiggle out of it.

"This is not a good time. I have too much on my mind."

Moxie looks at him with contempt. "You cannot expect us to make you one of us just because you chop off heads to show them off in front of the boys. It is time to for you to show off your words. You have got to inspire before you kill. Where is your poetry?

"I have license to kill. I am no poet. What about Thor? He is no poet."

"Thor the son of Olin and the brother of Tara. We know the words inside him."

"But, he is no he-man."

"Thor knows his numbers. He knows when to speak. He is every inch a man. Speaking of the man, there he is." Moxie sees Thor and invites him over for a drink. Siegfried notices that there is something special about the relationship between Thor and Moxie,

"Why do you not show Siegfried how poetry reveals what is inside you? You have got the stuff." Moxie puts his arm around Thor affectionately. This is the first time there has been an inkling of public affection between the two men, who have managed to keep their intimate liaison completely hidden. But since Moxie flaunts his masculinity with great gusto, none of his warrior buddies suspect the true nature of his sexual preferences. So moments like this between the two are accepted, even though their veil of secrecy dips slightly.

"I am a bit shy when it comes to poetry," Thor says bashfully.

"Nothing wrong with modesty, but do not hold out on us."

Mad Moxie gently escorts Thor to the stage and announces to the men.

"Thor iz goin' ta read ya'll a poem, straight from da heart. He beez de real man."

The men raise their goblets of mead in the air and cheer. Visibly uncomfortable, Thor recites:

I am the son of Olin
I am the brother of Tara
And the sister of Gonorrhea
I am the friend of Mad Moxie
And I want to be your friend
Because I can be what you want me to be
Because there is Goth blood in my veins.

Even though the verse is mediocre, the Goths are taken in by the veracity and sincerity of his words and they raise their goblets in Thor's honor. They shout out hurrahs, loud enough to obliterate the fact that power and influence trump poetic standards.

"Thor really one o' us."

"Man o' true words."

"A real-time he-man's he-man."

"Thor wails."

After the hurrahs subside, Mad Moxie whispers into Siegfried's ear, "Learn, practice, speak out. Your turn come very soon." Moxie and Thor then slip away.

Moxie escorts Thor to their secret hideaway, a large tree house in the woods guarded by three Uzi-toting G-Spot Biker Femmes, who are committed to the idea of sexual and marriage equality. They are very protective of the relationship between Moxie and Thor.

The tree house is surprisingly posh inside – a large canopy bed, a chaise lounge, a bombe chest of drawers and charming Country French chairs on which anatomically correct Stiff bears wearing lace caps are placed, and to top things off, a portrait of Queen Elizabeth by Andy Warhol, an artist who popped for 20th Century connoisseurs. Moxie carries Thor over the threshold.

"Welcome home, my dear boy, to my chi-chi lair."

Moxie proudly points to his gorgeous vintage wrought iron console, adorned with curly flourishes, on top of which he placed a garnished tray of tea sandwiches and a bottle of 21st Century French Beaujolais-Villages wine.

"No mead here in this neck of the woods," Moxie laughs, giving Thor a hearty slap on the back.

"Do not forget the sweet nothings," a female voice outside admonishes this romantic duo to proceed with due diligence.

Moxie whispers sweet nothings into Thor's ear.

Thor replies, "And so what is your dream for you and me?"

"I want to go with you up in the air in a hot air balloon."

Moxie grins as Thor giggles loud enough so that the guards outside can hear and sigh with approval. After a while, the giggles turn into thumps that rattle the tree-house rafters worse for wear.

Tara is home alone, waiting for Medea to come for a sit-down talk. Hours pass before Medea arrives.

"Where are the new servants?" Medea asks.

"I do not want anything I say spread around. I told them to take little Pericles for a walk." Tara replies.

"Are things better now with you and Siegfried?

"Same as always. He is never around."

"Away on his killer missions?"

"What else. He has no time for me."

Medea laughs inside because she encouraged Siegfried to carry out these missions.

"Do not worry, Tara, someday Pericles will rule both the Goths and the Greeks, no matter what happens."

"Where will that leave me?"

"You will be taken care of."

"And what about my brother? I have not seen him for a while."

"He has been working with Moxie to build support for Siegfried."

"I know that has to be done. What will happen to me and Pericles if things go wrong?" Tara begins to cry. Medea comforts her, cradling her head.

"Do not worry; you can stay in my house until things get better. There is plenty of room at my place where colorful flowers and fabrics will surround you. I have made arrangements for Siegfried. Perhaps someday, you and he and your son can have the kind of house you want, one with beautiful things and plenty of slaves."

Tara is intrigued. She had always wanted to live like a wealthy, stylish lady, now she has her chance even if that means joining the Greeks. Medea gets up and moves to the window to look outside.

"I will stay behind to help your brother take charge of things here. That is part of the deal that I made with Moxie, but I will be with you when I can."

Tara is aware of Thor's romantic ties to Moxie and the extent to which Thor is under his protection. She is not sure what this means for her future.

"Yes, Moxie is going to be directly in charge of the Daytrain trade. That will bring him and his men tremendous wealth and power. I will make sure of that. Good changes are coming."

"What about me and my son? What will happen to us right now?"

"You will have to wait until your husband returns."

"I do not want him anymore."

"Maybe you could divorce Siegfried and marry Moxie should Siegfried abdicate; he would at least protect you. And you know, he is AC/DC."

"I do not like that kind of music. I am not an AC/DC fan. I would have to share him with Thor; I am not sure I would like that. I do not like to share," she says, picking up a tie she bought for Siegfried, which he has steadfastly refused to wear.

"Do not worry about Moxie; there is an understanding, and being with you would make things so much easier. You would fit right in with the Greek ladies."

Tara sobs, "Oh, I wish Daddy were still alive. Life was so much simpler then." Why was not my marriage made in heaven?"

"I will be with you as much as I can and we will have our good times together, as we did before. There is no choice." Medea smiles and pauses awkwardly, thinking about what will come next. She then goes over to Tara and kisses her on the forehead.

"Come on now; come to my house where you can rest."

Medea and Tara depart, leaving Pericles in the care of the new servants at the Sky House.

"I like it here. You have so many beautiful things." Tara touches the white lace curtains that Medea had just drawn.

"You should come to visit Elysium, which is the most beautiful place in Macedonia. There are many things you would like."

"Wish I could, but that would not go over well with Siegfried."

"We can talk about that later," Medea says abruptly.

Tara stays at Medea's house for a few days, calmed by the herbs given to her by Medea. Their peaceful time together ends when Thor comes to the door.

"There is trouble. You must come."

Medea and Thor arrive at the combat pit where Siegfried killed Tara's father, and meet up with a large group of important warriors, including Moxie, who are about to hang Siegfried in effigy. Medea and Thor stand back as the warriors shout out in their best patois.

"He no friend."

"He Bionican scum."

"He no leader."

"He no poet."

"He no one of us." Their voices become louder and

more heated as they hoist a dummy corpse up a tree and torch it.

"Ye burn in hell."

As the flames shoot up, Moxie stays back and draws his sword, throwing his lot in with his disgruntled men. Medea, crossing her arms, pretends to look on with approval.

Medea and Thor arrive at Medea's house where they find Tara anxiously looking out of the window. Medea grabs her hand. "We have to get you back to Sky House before Siegfried returns. A lot is happening. The warriors are becoming restless." They escort Tara back to the Sky House, expecting Siegfried to be back before nightfall.

"We have a lot of mending to do," Medea tells her without going into details.

"I am afraid," Tara sobs. Medea gives her some valerian to calm her down.

"You have got to get a grip," Thor says impatiently, "We must go."

Medea and Thor leave, and Tara is left alone in the Sky House – full of her Greek things but empty otherwise, except for the servants. Later that night, Pericles wakes up crying. One of the servants comes to comfort him. Tara goes to bed and starts talking to herself.

"I cannot go on," she whimpers. "Where is Siegfried? He has no real feelings for me. I am all alone." She locks herself in her room and lets the servants attend to Pericles' needs without her.

Next morning, another servant tries to interest Tara in breakfast.

"I do not want to eat. Take it away."

"But you must eat. You have not had food for days."

"What difference does it make? It is all over for me."

Tara stays in bed for days and develops a fever. Medea comes to her bedside with a mysterious infusion to help her sweat out the fever.

Tara is delirious, moaning and groaning. "Where is my daddy? Where is my beautiful boy? Where is my mirror? I am so alone. Where did he go this time? Liar, liar, liar. He has stolen everything from me. I want my old life back."

Tara's face turns blue as she continues to moan. Medea feels her pulse as the servants look on.

"We are going to lose her," Medea says.

"Is there anything else you can do?" one of the servants asks.

"I am afraid I have done everything I can. Nature will take its course."

The moaning continues throughout the night and by

daybreak Tara is dead. Siegfried finally makes it to Tara's bedside too late as Medea and the servants stand by. He looks at her briefly, lifts her hand to make sure she is dead, and then turns away with nothing to say.

"She died because you neglected her," Medea reproaches him in a cold monotone.

Dumfounded, Siegfried mutters after a long silence, "She seemed perfectly all right when I left."

"You neglected your duty to your wife and son," Medea responds tartly.

"But, I did my duty to protect the Goths from the Christians. You wanted me to go on the missions."

"She died not because of what you did, but because of who you are and what you say. You have no poetic bone in your body. I am afraid your days are numbered." Siegfried turns away from Medea, afraid of what will come next.

Thor enters the room and kisses the forehead of his dead sister. "We must prepare her for the funeral. That is all that is left for us to do."

The servants carry off Tara's body as Medea and Thor continue to talk in private. Thor whispers to her, "We have to be careful with what we say from this point on. There are rumors going around that you gave her hemlock."

Medea gives out a disingenuous sigh. "I *did* try to help her. There was no way to satisfy what she wanted.

What happened was inevitable even if I helped it along."

"She was always daddy's girl," Thor says derisively. "She died with him."

Lying in a casket, Tara looks serene and at peace in the Disney Snow White dress that she had just gotten from her latest shopping trip. After the nightlong wake of heavy drinking, Moxie and several Goth warriors carry the casket outside and are joined by a procession of Goth warriors brandishing their swords. The pallbearers bring Tara's body to the Sky House and place it on a funeral pyre in the courtyard. Moxie throws a rose as the flames consume Tara and her casket. Thor wipes his tears and throws a kiss while Siegfried, following Medea's advice, stands back and says nothing with his head bowed.

The mourners, rounded up by Medea, continue to drink mead while they watch their queen turn to ashes. Moxie, by now quite drunk, gives Siegfried a dirty look. A little ragamuffin girl among the mourners says, "Mommy, why does she look so sad?"

"He not our kind," Moxie yells as he brandishes his sword. "He broke Tara's heart. He no lover. He no poet. He Bionican scum." Moxie melts into the crowd to conspire with his close comrades. "We make Siegfried be poet tonight. He gives toast after Tara's ashes are scattered to the winds." Moxie makes a throat-cutting gesture.

Moxie announces that Siegfried will recite this evening in honor of his queen Tara. There is no way for Siegfried to avoid this.

"I am afraid you will have to say something at the final benediction led by Moxie that will be held this evening in the courtyard," Medea whispers to him. "If you do not, they will kill you on the spot, and if you do not deliver the words that they need to hear, they will kill you later."

"I do not have it in me."

"You are going to have to dig down deep to find your words."

Standing behind a podium in the courtyard, Moxie officiates the benediction. He orders everyone to sit down after they pay their respects to a pile of Tara's belongings, including the wedding dress she wore when she married Siegfried. The servants bring the urn of ashes, which they place under Siegfried's nose.

"Why not you recite a poem about your dead wife," Moxie says loudly so that everyone can hear. Unable to back out, Siegfried rises slowly, steps up to the podium, and begins his poem.

I fought for her and won
I fought for Daytrain and we all won
I loved her and we had a son
When I came home she was gone
What is done cannot be undone.

Moxie grabs Siegfried and pulls him off the podium,

clenching his fist, shouting, "This stinks. This iz no poetry. There iz no feeling." While he does this, he accidentally topples the urn, which breaks and scatters the ashes that are picked up by a gust of wind. There is a long silence and no action; then Thor half-heartedly intercedes on Siegfried's behalf. "You cannot force him to make up poetry. Poetry is about inspiration. This goes against everything that we Goths stand for. Besides, Siegfried is only human; he has just lost his beloved."

"Bullshit!" someone in the crowd cries out. The warriors stamp their feet demanding poetic justice.

Moxie relents and addresses Thor with mock officiousness in proper English, "We respect your loyalty to Siegfried, but we want leaders whose words are true. Now that Tara is gone let us get rid of this Bionican scumbag."

As Thor distracts the warriors by bringing out vats of Mead, Siegfried slips away and makes his way to Medea's house where she later joins him."

"Your poem was terrible and they want your head. Your time has run out, and you must go into hiding. I will talk to Moxie to see what he can do. I am sure he will play ball."

Medea shows Siegfried to a secret chamber in her house. She has already stocked it with books that she wants him to read to prepare for what comes next.

"You can use this as your man-cave to prepare for the

next phase."

"My quest is still on?" he says staring at her in surprise.

"You bet. Your quest now is to educate Pericles, our son."

"Our son?"

"He is now. I made a promise to Tara that I would be his godmother and educate him, and you have the most important role to play as his father."

Siegfried shows discomfort, not sure that he has it in him to be a father. Medea notices this.

"Yes, your quest calls, loud and clear, for you to be a good father. Are you up to it?"

"I will do my best."

"With Tara out of the way, I hope you will make a great father. It was meant to be. You still have much work to do, and you have a lot to learn."

"Where do I begin? I no longer have a kingdom. I am a wanted man. The Goths have sentries everywhere, and I am well known in these parts."

"Do not worry, I have arranged your escape from The Valley. No one will recognize you. I am good at disguises and will give you a makeover." Medea invites him to a special room where she stores her magical makeup and medicinal herbs.

"Let us turn you into a fashionable Greek. You will have to cut your hair short and curl it. Then you will shave your beard. I will get you some togas and sandals. The body piercings definitely have to be removed. Most important, to be convincing, you must study these books as if your life depends on it since it does."

She points to the bookcase. "These are the books that all the Greeks are reading now. If you know them well, I guarantee that you can make it through a Greek conversation." Here's Plato's *The Republic*, Aristotle's *Metaphysics*, Herodotus' *The Histories* and Thucydides' *The Peloponnesian War*.

"You should know that every Greek child's complete education includes the study of works in the original as well as in translation. Those who are truly educated can read and recite these in ancient Greek. Children must also study Latin, which is not too popular. There is still another thing you need to do." Medea puts her hands on his shoulder in a motherly way. "You need to control your nausea."

"I know. Whenever I feel it creeping up, I want to kill."

"Is that what happened when you were with the Bead Lady?"

Siegfried does not say anything, pretending not to have heard. Medea also pretends that she did not say anything. "Here, for your journey, is some valerian root. Take these capsules before bedtime. If you feel the nausea creep up, this is an emergency fix – drink some Passionflower tea and sniff this lavender oil – just a drop or three on a bit of cloth. There are many situations in Macedonia that will confuse you and having a few helpers handy is not the worst thing in the world."

"What do I do next?"

"Educate yourself. Get started. Here is a short one to start with; it is a favorite of mine, *The Prince* by Machiavelli. This book will help you navigate what lies ahead. Later, we can discuss what you have read."

Days pass as Siegfried immerses himself into his reading, hiding in Medea's man-cave. Every day Medea pops in with snacks to check up on her pupil's progress.

"How is it going?"

"I like what *The Prince* has to say here: *The lion cannot protect himself from traps, and the fox cannot defend himself from wolves. One must, therefore, be a fox to recognize traps, and a lion to frighten wolves.*"

"I like that one, too," Medea says with enthusiasm. "How about this: *Never attempt to win by force what can be won by deception.*"

Medea scratches her nose. "That will do. Let us role play to help you conquer your tendency to stink like a skunk when provoked."

They both sit on chairs facing each other. Medea looks him in the eye and begins the session by pretending to be a Christian trying to convert him.

"I think you should give up your heathen ways and

become a good Christian. Remember what the good book says: *Enter through the narrow gate. For wide is the gate and broad is the road that leads to destruction, and many enter through it. But small is the gate and narrow the road that leads to life and only a few find it."*

Siegfried turns pale and starts to sweat. Medea sniffs.

"You are starting to smell. I know that smell."

"I cannot help it. It is the Bionican defense against religion."

"We cannot have that smell in your new home. Eat this rosemary peppermint candy quick. And do not forget to use the deodorant that I will leave out for you."

Siegfried chews and swallows the tasty lozenges and waits for the effect to kick in.

"Do you feel better now?

"Much better."

"The smell is gone, too."

"You are almost ready for Macedonia. Ah, but you have got to change your name. Siegfried will not do with the Greeks. How about Jason?"

Siegfried doesn't answer. He recalls that Berk suggested this name a long time ago, and wonders how Medea came up with it, but he is no position to quibble.

"The name will do." Siegfried proceeds to change his name as he did before. "Jason, Jason, Jason." Nothing happens because he still has to repeat his old name once and then repeat his new name three times. He says

"My old name is Siegfried. My new name is Jason, Jason, Jason." He gets it right.

"Now it is time for your makeover."

"Oh, yes." He says as he touches his hair and feels his beard and tugs at his leather trousers.

"Only members of the Hellenic Council are allowed to wear beards. Our young men must be clean-shaven. So, off it goes."

Medea clips Jason's hair and shaves off his beard and makes him take off his pants. Shaven, he looks so much younger. Medea cannot help but brush her hands over the skin of his exposed legs. He lets her hands linger for a moment before she hands him a white toga to put on.

"We will have you looking like a young philosopher in no time; that is the easy part."

Then momentarily Jason's face darkens with the knowledge that he has forgotten something.

"But what about my, uh, our son? Does he *have* to come with us?"

"We must bring him along. I have already discussed that with Thor. That is part of the deal. I will marry Thor, but I will encourage him and Mad Moxie to fulfill their partnership desire. The Goths will accept Thor as their leader, and the coast will be clear for our future work. For you, there will be no more uncouth Goths. You can now become a refined and learned man. You will have a hand in educating your son, Pericles. I will be a frequent visitor because there is still so much I have to teach you," she says as she puts her hand back on the inside of his thigh. As he rises to the occasion, she takes his hand and leads him away to her private chamber for their second tryst. Jason again conveniently forgets that Medea could be his sister, or at the very least, his mother's daughter.

"We are going to have to catch up on more than reading tonight. To be a true Greek, I have to teach you the art of seduction. But, we need to be discrete, at least for a while, since I will be officially married to Thor, who is fine with our sisterly arrangement. You will be my toy boy, and you will keep me satisfied and, if necessary, I will supply you with booster herbs to make sure you are up for it."

Jason, a.k.a. Siegfried, does not like the terms that Medea offers; he wishes to be no one's plaything, but under the circumstances, he has no choice but to accept them without questioning.

"What about Mad Moxie?

"Do not worry about him; Moxie understands what it takes to get power, and he is coming around to our way of thinking. We will need his help to make things change. Thor can deliver him for us if I become his beard."

The moon is full on the day of Thor and Medea's wedding. The ceremony takes place early in the morning at the sacred Sky House, where the Goths pay homage to the sun, the moon, and the stars. Outside the compound, thousands of Goths, who have flocked to the area during the night, believe that this union will lead to Goth strength and prosperity. Even the G-spot Femmes, who purposefully did not attend the Tara-Siegfried wedding, show up in full regalia on their roaring motorcycles. They do wheelies while the men juggle their swords and knives to the delight of the onlookers.

After things quiet down, the entire entourage sits in a semi-circle on logs in the courtyard in the twilight, looking east to witness the yellow-red sunrise beginning to flood through the distant mountains. Among the notables are Thor, Gonorrhea, and Moxie, who will conduct the wedding ceremony about to begin.

The Goth all-male kazoo band strikes up the tune, "Here comes the Bride." Thor and Medea, completely nude, approach the stage where two separate vintage bathtubs are waiting for them – a touching moment in their society where personal hygiene is only an afterthought.

Several slaves have already filled the tubs with barrels of warm water and bubble bath powder, and now check the water for temperature. The audience cheers the couple as they approach the tubs, ushered by a squadron of

the G-Spot Femmes. After Moxie gives the high-five signal, Medea enters the tub on the left and Thor lowers
himself into the one on the right. Moxie signals again,
and the couple reach to join their hands so that the actual ceremony can begin.

The timing for the ceremony is perfect. Shortly before sunrise, Moxie begins the torch-lit ceremony attended by the Goth elite dressed in their 20th Century
punk outfits designed Vivienne Westwood and Jean Paul
Gaultier. The ceremony takes place in a flash.

"In the name of the sun and moon, I hereby pronounce Thor and Medea man and wife. Moxie then instructs the couple to rise so that everyone can see the
identical tattoos over their hearts – the Venus and Mars
symbol merged as one. Moxie laughs inside because he
knows that Thor belongs to him.

After the I-do's, Thor and Medea get out of the bathtubs to show off the tattoos of the joined sun and moon
that they will share for the rest of their lives. The guests
cheer as the couple flashes their union tattoos before
donning the monogrammed black bathrobes Moxie
hands to them.

Moxie announces the wedding feast that night. "This
be the big wedding everyone wants. This be the new beginning for all of us."

The wedding feast is attended by every Goth man,
woman, and child as well as their animals gathered un-

der a full moon. Since this is a private Goth event, there are no Greeks in the audience.

Thor and Medea, still in their bathrobes, link their pinkies while the guests gather around several pigs on roasting spits. Before the feast begins, a carnival of jugglers, contortionists, fire-eaters, and acrobatic young girls do handstands and flips while the young boys throw knives at chalk outlines of toga-clad figures.

After the feast, Mad Moxie gives the toast, "I see you have enjoyed your meal and mead. Now I drink to Thor and Medea. And in their honor, here are the can-can guys. Let the music begin."

As the music erupts, the can-can dancers, the most bloodthirsty warriors under Moxie's command, kick up their heels to the delight of the cheering crowd. After the music subsides, the burly dancers disappear into the crowd,

Moxie gets up to speak again. "Thank you, thank you for your bravery, men. Now, I proudly present to you our very own – the G-spot Biker Femmes, led by the no other than the indomitable femme fatale, Gonorrhea."

Gonorrhea roars on the proscenium on her pearl-studded pink Harley, waving to the cheering crowd and then takes over as mistress of ceremonies.

Addressing the crowd, she bellows, "I am here to honor the bride, who will bring us strength through joy. Bring on our twelve angry young men!" The young men are crowd-surfed to the stage by the dozens of Biker Femmes in the audience.

Gonorrhea proclaims, "We have trained these young men to be perfect lovers. They will recite for you little love poems of sweet nothings."

The poetry recitations begin, but it is nearly impossible to catch the words because of the loud cheering and cursing by the male warriors in the crowd. When the twelfth young man finishes, the warriors continue to yell and brandish their knives. Looking like Liberty Leads the People, Gonorrhea bares her breast to quell the crowd. She leads the young men to the proscenium where the twelve Biker Femmes are waiting on their idling Harleys to take the boys away to their appointed destination.

Gonorrhea proclaims, "There they go to spread their seeds." Medea and Thor scamper off to Moxie's lair.

"Thor, things went rather well today, do you not think?" Medea says to him coyly.

"I am happy with the way things turned out. I hope Moxie is; he promised me he would catch up with me later." Thor breathes heavily in anticipation.

There is a tap on Thor's window. It is Moxie, with a huge grin, lugging up a bouquet of flowers so that he and Thor can celebrate their nuptials.

"I wish we could marry for real as they used to do," Thor whispers into Moxie's ear. Moxie responds, giggling in the special voice that he reserves for his Liebling,

Media smiles. "Boys, you know there is a fat chance of that happening, especially now when everybody thinks procreation is a priority."

Thor playfully touches Moxie's body piercings and tells him, "Maybe we could get us a couple of dogs, maybe a couple of black labs. Then our family would be complete."

Thor and Moxie cuddle up in their tree house hideout, which is under constant guard by the Biker Femmes. "Let's celebrate this union – the three of us, united," Medea exclaims. They drink to that and then transition to a polymorphous threesome that seals the deal on their triumvirate.

CHAPTER 10
LIFE AMONG THE GREEKS

Jason passes days hiding in Medea's house, preparing for his getaway to his new Greeks life. Medea finally arrives to tell him the news about her wedding, but none of the details. Jason has no idea that he is the *fourth* wheel in the arrangement, but that should be no surprise since Medea has never been forthcoming.

"It is done. Thor and I have tied the knot; so this is a good time for you and me to leave. I have made the arrangements for you and little Pericles to live at Elysium in Macedonia at Chatsworth. Remember, you are Jason. Siegfried is dead and must remain so."

Medea and Jason wait in silence for Otto to arrive. An old Ford with Otto at the wheel pulls up to take Jason, baby Pericles, and Medea to Macedonia. Jason comes out of the house carrying sacks of his belongings. Medea puts the basket containing Pericles in the back compartment. Because of her prominence in the Goth world, Medea is disguised as a servant.

"W...we have a rr...rocky road ahead," stutters Otto. Medea tells stories as the truck clatters down the road. Pericles is sound asleep in his basket.

Medea asks Siegfried, "Do you know the story about Jason and Medea? It is a long and complicated story." She pauses for a moment and then begins.

"Jason was too young to succeed his father, King Aeson, who was tired of governing. So, he gave the crown to his brother, Pelias, on the condition that Jason would become king when he grows up. Pelias sent Jason on a quest for the Golden Fleece. Just like you, do you not agree?" she pokes Jason and continues, "Jason took fifty men with him in a boat called the Argo, so they were called the Argonauts. After surviving a perilous voyage through crashing rocks, Jason and his men landed in the kingdom of Colchis where King Aetes said he would give up the Golden Fleece if Jason could perform certain tasks. First, he would have to harness two fire-breathing bulls and sow the teeth of the dragon. These would then turn into armed men whom he would then have to kill. Jason made a deal with Aetes' daughter, Medea, a powerful sorceress, not unlike me, who could help him slay the men and put the dragon to sleep with herbs. Jason succeeded in bringing the Golden Fleece back to his father, thanks to Medea's help."

After a long moment of silence, Medea laughs and

then says, "You can learn a lot from Greek mythology, but you cannot take it literally. You have to keep an open mind. The sky is the limit."

Mystified, Jason remembers the old Indian, Red Cloud, who told him while pointing to the sky, "There will always be that moment of silence when you will forget why you are here. Meditation is very important."

Jason looks up to the sky to see if the clouds have anything to say to him. He meditates on the clouds that take on the shapes of ancient philosophers in the agora in Athens, and hears a discourse in Greek. He assumes that they are talking about wisdom and the pursuit of truth.

The truck jolts Jason out of his reverie as it hits a huge pothole. "Watch out!" Medea cries out to alert Otto that there is a slab of concrete in the middle of the road.

Otto spots a Goth checkpoint ahead and warns Jason to hide under the pile of soft goods to avoid being discovered. Medea swaddles little Pericles to keep him quiet as they approach a Goth checkpoint.

Medea, her face partially hidden by her headscarf, explains to the Goth sentry, "We are bringing cloth from the weavers." He lets them pass.

Medea and Jason arrive at a safe house in the country for an overnight stay. There are clean clothes as well as food to tide them over. After spending the night there, they leave that morning to complete their trip. The truck passes by a faux Greek revival house; outside, a group of men wearing togas and sandals read from Plato's *The Republic*.

Medea explains, "They do this once a week – they read from original Greek while they get fresh air. Let us stop by and say hello."

Medea and Jason get out of the truck and approach the group that is struggling with a passage from Plato. Medea approaches Alexander and several young men, "Do not let us interrupt you; we just want to say hello. Meet my long-lost, half-brother Jason and his young son, Pericles."

After the round of introductions, Alexander offers Medea a turn to translate the next passage. She does this without missing a beat.

"When a man thinks himself to be near death, fears and cares enter into his mind which he never had before; the tales of a world below and the punishment which is exacted there of deeds done here were once a laughing matter to him, but now he is tormented with the thought that they may be true: either from the weakness of age, or because he is now drawing nearer to that other place, he has a clearer view of these things; suspicions and alarms crowd thickly upon him, and he begins to reflect and consider what wrongs he has done to others."

After Medea completes the translation, she explains that her brother's young wife died and that Jason, the widower, is joining the Elysium household to raise his son. Alexander and the young men come up to Jason and comfort him and shake hands. Two of the younger Greeks, Herodotus, and Thucydides, take special notice of Jason, admiring his strong muscular chest and his tall and handsome good looks.

Medea asks the group, "What is the good book this time?"

"We are going over *The Republic*. Our goal this summer is to memorize the entire work by heart."

"Do not let us stop you; we will catch up with you later."

After the leave, Medea explains, "These are dear friends of the family. The father of the house, Alexander, is a member of the Hellenic Council. You have just met two of his sons, Thucydides and Herodotus, who are members of the Praetorian Guard. You will see them again in due time."

Jason changes the topic, staring at the house. "Do all the houses here have columns?"

"Yes, the goal is to have all buildings in the Greek Polis designed in the Greek style. Before we arrive at my family's house, I will show you the site for the new Parthenon that will be built entirely out of granite. This will be the first of many replicas of ancient Greek architectural wonders that will attract visitors from everywhere."

They continue for a few miles and arrive at a noisy

construction site on top of a hill. Hundreds of brown workers, all of them slaves, are cutting stones. The workers, covered in dust, struggle to position stones for the foundation.

Medea explains, "The Parthenon will serve as a beacon for a renaissance of Greek culture here in Chatsworth; it will house marble busts of members of the Hellenic Council and other VIPs.

They travel for a few more miles. "I can smell the eucalyptus," Medea cries out. "We are almost there." They pull up to Elysium, Medea's fine antebellum Greek revival house. Eliza, a dark-skinned servant girl with a slim body and olive eyes, recognizes Medea right away, greeting her with a big hug. Not far away, brown-skinned slaves work the fields that are planted according to the Golden Mean.

Medea explains, "We grow olives, lemons, cotton, grapes, and vegetables; we also have cattle, sheep, and llamas."

"Hello, Miss Medea," the slaves cry out with joy from the fields and wave to her. She waves back with the regality and imperiousness of the old Queens of England.

"Looks like the braceros are content," Medea reassures herself haughtily. "Last year they took to cursing us in Spanish and we had to bring in a Goths militia to enforce the law and crush their insubordination. The few instigators were easily found and killed. Now everyone appears to be happy, about as happy as they can be."

As Medea enters her house, Eliza runs towards her gushing, "Oh my sweet lady Medea, how nice it is to see you. I – we – have missed you so."

"Oh, has it been that long? Still, I missed you, too."

With her nose in the air, Medea hands Eliza the smelly bundle containing Pericles. "Ah, is he not the cutest; he looks just like his mother." Medea smiles as Jason stares at her in disbelief. Medea's condescending treatment of Eliza visibly repulses him. Medea takes Jason aside and scolds him, "Do not give me that superior look. You Bionicans are all slaves to your almighty Well. Ours is a better system. It is not slavery, but rather a form of voluntary servitude or involuntary freedom, whichever way you look at it. The bottom line is that they are better off; we take good care of the ones that agree to the terms of our freedoms."

Jason does not respond, but murmurs to himself, "Live free or die. I'd rather be dead." Medea ignores this Goth-inspired Libertarian outburst and takes Jason for a walk in the garden surrounding the house. It is a well-kept formal garden full of shrubbery, flowers, and herbs. Several gardeners are at work maintaining it. Aqueducts distribute water throughout the property.

Jason kicks a stone in his path and persists in being holier than thou. "I do not understand how you justify slavery when all Greeks talk about is freedom and equality." Medea does not rise to the bait. Realizing that Jason is always grumpy when faced with ambiguity, she backpedals to improve his mood. "The *truth* is our thing. We have a lot of patience for philosophy, but when it comes to getting things done, they talk about this or that truth, or talk about truth with a capital T. Ultimately, it boils down to the truth of the way things are." Jason appreciates Medea's candid comments but is not sure what she is driving at, and so she tries to explain again.

"Thanks to your time with the Goths, Jason, you are now a man of action, not just words. I know that, but you are going to have to get used to words as a form of play, theater, intrigue and aggression. Everything the Greeks do to each other, we do with words. We believe that words are deeds. You are going to hear a lot of words used for entertainment, and many of them will be actual Greek words. Here is my advice, *When in Greece, do as the Greeks do*. Oh, and if you have a fear of sex between men, you had better lose it. I encourage you to ease up and go the AC/DC route. Whatever it takes to fit in."

Jason's petulance continues, "All my early life, I have had words invading my head. I am sick of them. I want my own words."

"You are coming along well with your gift of gab. Do not blame everything on your Bionican childhood. That is all you knew then. If you are going to succeed, you have to grow up and get with the program – the Greek program!"

Jason whines, "I agree with the Goths that words have to mean something. Words should be tied to real actions and real feelings. Words should not be just for words' sake."

"I thought you were interested in power. Our words create power. What could be more real than that?" Medea chides him for failing to understand the efficacy of the well-turned phrase, lowering her voice for emphasis. "Do you not understand that words can be used as weapons and that the written word can be more powerful than anything in the world?"

Jason, "Yes, yes, I have heard that the pen is mightier than the sword; however, I have seen men killed by my sword, and no man has been killed by my words."

"At least you know part of the truth." Medea laughs and continues, "The Goths are a primitive people. No matter how many muscles they flex and no matter how hard they fight, the Goths do not understand real power. So long as the Goths insist on being illiterates, the Greeks will be in charge. We base our power on words and slavery."

Jason starts to tune out, but Medea continues her

spiel. "Because of words, we can say that our slaves are volunteers because they have nothing else better to do. We house them, feed them, and have sex with them. They are happy here. Someday money will eliminate slavery as we now know it, but we are still a long way from developing the banking system that is needed to organize wage-based employment. Sure, people question the institution of slavery, but deep down they understand that slavery is for their own good. Abolition is only a form of neglect. The bedrock of our civilization is slavery. How else would there be the leisure time to do the things that we need to do?"

"I see your point," Jason says mechanically.

Medea is satisfied that Jason is sufficiently prepared to meet her family. After Jason and Medea complete their walk in the garden, she tells Eliza to prepare their meal and beckons another servant to spread the word to the entire household that they have arrived.

"Come meet my adoptive parents, Socrates and Xantippe, and their three daughters, Memory, Meditation, and Song. You have seen them briefly before, but now you will get to know them better. Later, I will show you our school and our students."

They enter the house through the front door where the family is gathered to greet them. House servants surround Medea's mother. Old and hunched over, Socrates shuffles back and forth cursing under his breath. Xantippe, weighed down with costume jewelry, is considerably younger than Socrates, who is in the early stages of dementia.

"Look who has come." Xantippe points to Jason. "Must have something to do with Project Pygmalion." Medea ignores this remark while Jason is distracted by Pericles' crying. Medea motions to one of the servants to attend to the little boy.

Medea says to Xantippe, "Next time I go to The Valley, I will bring back two Goth girls, Alarica and Hallie, to help out with Pericles. They are very good with young children. They need a livelihood, and I think they will blend in very nicely here." Medea knows that Xantippe wants to find suitable maids for her two bisexual daughters, and she thinks Alarica and Hallie are perfect as maidservants willing to go that extra mile.

Jason does not like the idea of importing these two women who were Tara's friends. He thinks they blame him for Tara's death. But, Medea assures him that the girls will exercise discretion and will not want to cause any trouble, since they know what is good for them.

Medea is about to proceed with the introductions, as Xantippe whispers to her, "So whom have you dragged in this time? Is he one of your next projects? He looks familiar."

Medea gives her adoptive mother a dirty look. Xantippe, who is rather outspoken, has not learned to stifle criticism even though Medea is their sole source of support and runs the show. Medea answers wearily, "No, I do not think you have met him. He is not a Goth, nor is he a new slave. He is a prince. His name is Jason. He will help me with the school."

"Me help?" Jason expresses surprise.

"Yes, you will help with the school. More about that later," Medea says.

Jason introduces himself to Medea's adoptive elderly father, Socrates, who has a long white beard that curls out on both sides.

"Do I know you? Are you one of my disciples?"

Xantippe whispers in Jason's ear, "He thinks people are trying to poison him with hemlock. They think he is too far gone, but they are wrong."

"Know thyself," Socrates says in an inappropriately loud voice.

Xantippe, a fussy plump woman with a dowager's hump, has spent a lifetime complaining about people and criticizing them. She directs her remarks at Medea. "What is happening to you, dear? You do not look healthy. Are you letting yourself go?"

"Mother, we've been on a long trip," she says without hiding her irritation. "How are you doing, Socrates?" she says, knowing the response she will get. He gives her a broad smile and says again, "Know thyself," which is his favorite phrase among several that are at the core of his repertoire.

Medea looks into Socrates' eyes and tries to learn something new from them.

"Even now he has so much to give," Medea says, recalling the days when she and the other acolytes from the Praetorian Guard used to sit at his feet participating in a discourse. "Deep down, he has a lot more to tell us. You have to listen to how he says *know thyself*."

"Philosophy is what made me the woman I am today," Medea exclaims with pride. "I owe a lot to Socrates." She is referring to the fact that Socrates got Medea into the Praetorian Guard, which had never admitted any female members before her. Socrates also paved the way for her position with the Hellenic Council.

Xantippe complains, "I have spent a lifetime tending to the needs of philosophy. Even today, young people come to the house wanting to meet Socrates, and my job, as it has always been, is feeding them. Where is the appreciation of my philosophy – eat good food?"

"Oh Mom," Medea whines, readying herself for a prolonged family argument. Fortunately, the argument is quelled when the servants put food on the table. The group dines together amicably and soon retires for the night.

CHAPTER 11
MEDITATION, MEMORY, AND SONG

"So what do you do?" Xantippe asks Jason, as if she were interviewing a future son-in-law.

"I am on a..."

Medea interrupts him. "Do not worry, Mother, Jason is a colleague. He will stay with us and help out with the school, and concentrate on increasing his knowledge of Greek philosophy and literature. Afterward, he will work with the Hellenic Council to do some Goth work."

This explanation seems to satisfy Xantippe, who knows about Project Pygmalion that extends educational and mating opportunities to promising Goths. She is not aware of Jason's Bionican past.

"I hope that Jason will like it here and that he will be able to help us."

Medea asks, "Where did the girls get to?"

"They are teaching the children. Soon they will be here to practice their instruments."

The three girls – Memory, Meditation, and Song – are much younger than Medea. Rumor has it that Medea is a natural child of Socrates since she calls the girls "stepsisters." No one questions Medea regarding the circumstances of her artificial birth.

Jason remembers seeing the three girls at his wedding, especially Song. He wonders whether they will recognize him this time, but they don't because of his successful makeover, especially the loss of his beard that transformed Siegfried into Jason. Still Jason is nervous, afraid he will be found out and killed by the G-spot Femmes.

Jason mentions to Medea in private that he thinks that the girls may still recognize his voice from their first encounter at his wedding.

"Don't worry, I told them a little about your background, but I did not go into any details. I will leave that up to you. They are looking forward to meeting you."

So life is about to begin for Jason at Elysium. Jason knows that he must adapt to Medea's comings and goings. Every other week, her trusty driver Otto takes her to the Sky House where Medea, Thor and Moxie have set up their operations. Everyone has a routine, with Medea at the center of things. Medea, with a clipboard in hand, tells Jason more about the three sisters and their schedules.

Today, after school hours in the morning, a leisurely lunch is followed by studies and cultural activities. She brings Jason to the drawing room where her three step-sisters are tuning up their instruments, looking out to the veranda. Meditation is at the piano. Memory is plucking strings of her violin, and Song is alternatively tuning her lyre and fingering her flute.

"I would like to introduce you to Jason," Medea says in a formal tone of voice. After a short awkward period of silence, Memory breaks the ice.

"We have heard a lot about you," she says flatly.

"A lot of good things. I heard you want to learn about our culture," Mediation says, putting aside her instrument.

"It is great to have you here. The children would benefit from having a man around," Song blurts out as the faint voices of children become noticeable in the background. A servant closes the door to shut out the sounds, and then the girls pick up their instruments to play a few tunes for Jason.

One of the older children, Doula, barges into the drawing room blurting out, "Pericles is crying. He will not stop, and we cannot study," Medea takes the girl by the hand and says to the group, "Continue without me.

I will help Alarica and Hallie calm down Pericles. The child needs some time to get used to things."

The three sisters calmly resume tuning their instruments as Jason watches them intently. Meditation, the tallest of the three, has a long neck and an angular face, framed with long black hair and punctuated with a prominent nose and luminescent eyes. She moves her athletic body with precision and uses grand gestures that draw attention to her large graceful hands. Her white linen toga shuffles across her broad shoulders, revealing parts of her compact breasts that move decisively against her garment as she opens the cover of the piano and neatens up the sheet music. As the most serious of the three, she takes deep breaths before speaking, talking slowly to get attention so that she can make her points.

Memory is shorter than her older sister, Mediation. Her face is also softer, and her body is rounder and fairer. Her unruly light brown hair barely reveals her bold eyebrows and penetrating hazel eyes that dart back and forth with her clipped speech. Her chest is disproportionately large for her short body; she seems to regard her bosom as an onerous burden she is forced to carry. She is very impatient and tends to hold grudges.

Young Song is petite and delicate, with a beautiful child-like visage and lovely lidded eyes set in a web of auburn hair with long, gently curling tresses. Although not athletic, she has a fine posture and speaks with a small but precise voice that conveys a moral imperative without commanding authority. Jason, still obsessed with the relationship between garments and female breasts, notices that Song's toga tugs on her delicate bulbs as her slender shoulders rise and fall between breaths. He is transfixed by mentally enumerating her delicate finger bones as she gently strums her lyre: *Pollex, Digitus Secundus Manus, Digitus Medius, Digitus Annularis*, and *Digitus Minimus Manus*. Staring at her delicate frame, Jason tries to determine whether Song's pelvis is broader than her rib cage, and whether her tiny body is capable of childbirth. But these mechanical musings quickly give way to thoughts about Song's garden of delights and the possibilities of exploring with all three sisters the finer points of the Kama Sutra in a bacchanalian romp.

Demure Song is aware of the attention given to her by Jason. She holds her lyre tight between her knees as if imagining a lover who would leave her should she weaken her grasp.

After they chat for a while, the girls play their special welcome song to honor Jason. Song lifts her lovely voice to sing the beginning verse:

You have come a long way my friend
You have ruled the hackers in Bionica
You have crossed swords with the mighty warriors of Olin
You have had a difficult marriage that ended in tragedy

Your journey has been long and hard
Please let me bathe your tired feet
And nourish your aching body
For my caress will feed you
And when I hold you, tell me what you have seen
And when you lie with me, tell me what you have heard.

Song's voice has a hypnotic effect on Jason so that he is almost asleep when the tune reaches the end. The segue to conversation stirs him back to wakefulness.

The girls chatter about what they are studying and the progress they have made with the children. Jason is amazed to learn how many books they have read. Determined to catch up, he vows to go to the library every day to read books that are part of the curriculum devised by Medea.

Jason quickly adapts to the household routine, looking forward to the hours with Memory, Meditation, and Song.

"Jason, would you mind helping us with the children's lessons?" Song asks suggestively. Mesmerized, Jason agrees.

Since it is a sunny day, the servants open up the exterior doors of the library so that Jason and the three girls can tutor the children in the garden under a cypress tree. Song gently strums the lyre as Jason reads with the children. Pericles is off in a corner hammering on a toy xylophone. He is growing up fast, reaching the age when formal instruction can begin.

In the following year, Jason teaches the young students what he has learned, paying special attention to his son. During the day, he assists the three sisters in the garden or a classroom located in a separate building on the grounds. Surrounded by a small group of boys and girls, he has them read and recite Socrates' sayings in ancient Greek. The lessons include mathematics, science, rhetoric, and music. In contrast to the three sisters, Jason is stiff and strict with the children. From time to time, the girls ask Jason to ease up, to be as indulgent and flexible with the children as they are with him.

One day, Medea sits down with Jason to discuss his education about Greek culture, using the procedures established for Project Pygmalion.

"Jason, it seems like you have come a long way. How do you feel?"

"I am a changed man. Everything seems clear to me."

Medea is proud of his accomplishments. "I knew you could do it. Perhaps soon, you will be ready for society."

Jason is pleased and walks into the garden, taking special note of the yellow and orange poppies blooming all around him. He contemplates this graceful life in Elysium and wishes it would never change. This is a far cry from the days when he had to watch over Bionican users and bash in the heads those who strayed. He remembers how unhappy he had been then, despite the privileges and powers he enjoyed as a Bionican hacker.

Jason is full of novel ideas that are inspired by the pleasant surroundings in Elysium. Sunbeams bounce off the elegant mirrors, the furniture, paintings, and sculpture; golden rays punctuate the rooms creating an aura of magnificence.

The newly cultivated man even takes pleasure in learning the names of the flowers and herbs meticulously tended by Elysium's gardeners who go about their work unnoticed. He smiles at the thought that when he first came here, he scorned the use of slaves to support the life of luxury; now he understands why slavery is necessary to pursue knowledge and the good life.

Jason delights in the company of the three sisters who, when not running the school, attend studiously to his education. Today's topic is philosophy and feminism. Meditation starts the discussion.

"I love philosophy, but you have to be a man to be a philosopher. It would be silly to have a woman strutting about making pronouncement and engaging others in debate."

"But you forget Sappho, the great woman poet of Ancient Greece," Memory, the family historian, corrects her sister. "Sappho was a great poet respected by both men and women in her time, and she was a friend of philosophers. She was born in the island of Lesbos, and you know what that means," she says winking.

Memory and Meditation consider themselves bisexual, or allsexual, as they would like to call it. They enjoy sex not only with Greek men and women, but also with Goth men and women who are considered by other Greeks to be sub-human. Medea loves to accommodate the girls. That's why she brought Alarica and Hallie to provide her sisters with overnight amusement.

Song, the exception, is a shy, dyed-in-the-wool heterosexual, which greatly reduces her amorous opportunities. She once had her eye on Herodotus and Thucydides, but gave up when she saw them cavorting with other members of the Praetorian Guard. She cannot forget what happened a year ago. Medea arranged through the Goth procuress, Gonorrhea, to fix Song up with a Goth young man, Moritz, who trained to provide gentle romance, but that did not work out. He was brutish in his advances and painfully abrupt in his withdrawal. In the middle of the night, Medea arranged to have Moritz abducted by the G-spot Femmes. Gonorrhea's girl gang took him far away to the Burning Man Festival in Black Rock, Nevada, where he was ritually Bobbitted and then buried in the sand.

While Song wallows in her unpleasant and guilt-ridden memory, the other two sisters carry on with their feminist banter. "The men today will not acknowledge the intellectual power of women in public. That is because they want to be totally in charge, and they are afraid that women will take away their manliness, whatever is left of it."

Meditation has hit on the code word. Greek manliness is a perilous concept. The more men want to become philosophers rather than warriors, the more their manliness is in question.

"I do not have a problem with women being philosophers," Jason pipes in wanting to impress the girls. "Look at Medea and what she has accomplished." Jason notices that the expression on Memory's face sours. She cannot hide her jealousy, even though she is not particularly interested in him. She knows about Medea's life with the Goths. She is convinced that Jason is the latest of her many boy lovers, but she accepts the importance of her work among the Goths and respects her intelligence and fears her cunning.

"Medea is a special case. She can think and act like a man, and when it suits her, she can apply her feminine charms; she is more of a trickster than a philosopher. Who knows what she is up to now? She is a hit with the Goths

"They sure love her cures," Meditation says sarcastically.

"She was very helpful to me," Jason says with a smile.

"I bet she was," Memory says, rolling her eyes teasingly. Meditation smirks while Song sighs.

Jason knows he has to play it cool with the three sisters so as not to let on that he is very close to Medea.

"She'll eat you half alive," Memory says with a laugh.

"Just ask Berk, he'll tell you," Meditation adds, mentioning the dwarf because of the significant role he played in Jason's education and his reputation as a Medea sycophant.

"Medea has to do what she has to do," Jason says lamely.

"That is a tautology. You are going to have us in a tizzy," Song laughs.

Memory continues her provocations. "Men are such simple-minded creatures. They do not remember anything, and that is why they are always devising ways to keep track of things. Men fixate on what they want, but they often overlook what is important."

"I know what I want and I know what I like."

"I wish I could be that sure of myself," quips Memory.

"Maybe Jason has a point. He knows on which side his bread is buttered. That is important," Song says, deepening her little voice.

"If only I had a key to The Well, I would unlock all of its secrets." Song sighs. Jason's ears perk up; it has been a while since anyone has mentioned The Well to him.

Memory laughs sarcastically. "Pandora once tried to unlock secrets and look what happened to her."

"Pandora?" Jason asks.

The girls laugh. Memory says, "There are gaps in your education."

"The problem with The Well is that there is no way of getting to the information you need. It is stuck in a lot of empty heads," Jason interjects, trying to get his two cents in. He thinks his anti-Bionican statement will impress the girls.

"I hear it is quite a zoo in Bionica – all those users who spend their time hallucinating stuff from The Well," Memory teases him.

The girls giggle, but relent when they notice Jason's discomfort with all this talk about Bionica.

Memory uses another tack. "You mean to say that The Well is... obsolete?" Memory says, thinking she has hit the nail on the head.

Jason jumps in trying to make points with the girls and ends up sounding a bit defensive. "I am not sure. The Well is based on the Golden Age of Information. Maybe it is a case of backward instead of forward obsolescence."

Pleased, Jason realizes that he has mastered formidable jargon that he can eagerly trot out whenever he wants.

"The Well certainly has some secrets I would like to know." Song says, persisting to state her dream for the future. "Perhaps in time we can transform the information from Bionica into some useful knowledge."

"Knowledge is power," Meditation reminds the group. They all agree. Meditation changes the topic.

"The problem is that we do not read the classics in the original and a lot gets lost in translation. It is good that we are trying to change that with our school."

Jason does not appear to be interested in discussing the school.

Memory picks up on Jason's growing disinterest and tries to lighten things up. "Do not get us wrong, we can be a lot of fun. We better let Jason enjoy his life here in Elysium as a new man and give his past a rest. Let us forget the Bionicans and the Goths for the time being."

Meditation puts her hand on Jason's knee and proclaims sarcastically, "Wanna beat drums with a stick-in-the-mud?" She wants him to feel like a woman while she plays the aggressive man, but does not expect anything to come from this.

Jason ignores her proposal and fixes his eyes on Song, whom he considers the most charming of the three sisters, though not necessarily the brightest. Memory shrugs her shoulders as Jason's attention wanders to Song, who is a fabulous lyre player and singer. She poses no threat and is less trouble than the other two sisters.

And so things come to pass. Jason continues to spend many happy evenings with the three girls in stimulating discussions, sometimes individually, and sometimes as a group, sometimes with their clothes on, and sometimes without. As devotees of the *Frei Körper Kultur Movement*, the three sisters believe that skin-deep beauty is something lovely to behold. Although they enjoy philosophical discourse, they avoid contentious "deep" discussions that lead to jealousy and conflict.

During these many evenings, they make extensive use of the library to pull quotes in support or rejection of points made in their discussions. These books support a wonderful liberal education for Jason, who has not known the pleasures of intellectual pursuits before.

One evening, as he hears the three sisters bantering from a distance, a female voice he has not heard for a while comes into his head. It is Julia, "Jason, do not judge too hastily. Nor should you agree too quickly either. There are many things you must learn; you must learn humility before you can know anything."

He is taken aback by the intrusiveness of his mother's voice. He is afraid she will erode his confidence; he knows better than to go against her. Julia's voice fades away when he tries to ask it for clarification. It is only a matter of time before his real purpose becomes clear to him.

He wracks his brain with the same nagging questions. "When will that day of fulfillment come? When will I finally be free?"

Jason imagines himself among the gods in ancient Greece. He likes playing the role of Jason in search of the Golden Fleece. He sees himself with Medea and pictures himself as another Alexander the Great, the great king of Macedonia, with Medea as his Roxana.

Everyday Jason works his way through piles of books, finding fodder for his next discussion with the three sisters that evening.

"Tonight, we celebrate," Song announces.

"We have studied enough," Meditation declares.

"Eat, drink and be merry." Memory laughs out loud.

The house servants bring in food and drink, and the music begins. The girls provide their own accompaniment. Memory plays the flute; Meditation is on the drums; and Song strokes her lyre. After the performance finishes, they dig into the Greek victuals, a sumptuous assortment of goat meat, olives, dates, and wine. The slaves look on with contemptuous amusement as all three daughters vie for Jason's attention.

That evening Song retires to bed early. Jason remains in the company of Memory and Meditation, who entice Jason to join them in the inner chambers for an evening repast. It starts innocently enough with the recitation of poetry but ends up in the consumption of high-octane nectar that the slaves bring by the bucketful.

"Why not stay with us for a *ménage de trios*? But, you must understand, we are political lesbians, like Julia.

That keeps us on an even keel. Never mind that. Our purpose is to school you in the fine points of real love, and for that reason we think that before you join in, you should first watch and to listen to the sweet nothings that are shared between two committed women. But, listen carefully. There is to be *no* penetration. Remember, if it moves, we will fondle it, but if it disappears, all bets are off."

And so begins the polymorphous perverse rolling romp of Memory and Meditation, with Jason eagerly following the trajectory of their breasts and limbs. They place a garland around Jason's neck and grab at his extended member to force him to submit. This sexual merry-go-round goes on until the three crumple in exhaustion.

Later, Jason tells Medea about the attention he is getting. "All three of the sisters are falling for me in one way or another. What do you suggest?"

"That is fine with me. You can have your pick. Who knows, perhaps one of them will wind up being your wife. You have to let things play out, but keep your feelings to yourself. Do not let them know what is happening between us. You must become sophisticated if you are to survive here."

Jason is used to the routine. Medea travels to and fro Elysium and the Sky House, dividing her time equally between her Greek and Goth worlds. When in Elysium, she usually meets Jason in private to discuss the Daytrain trade. This time she mentions Pharmakia, the Greek pusher she had hired to replace Eric, extolling his success in expanding Daytrain usage outside of the Polis. Jason remembers meeting him through Eric and does not like him very much.

Jason is happy to be removed from the world of Daytrain pushers. After all, he has become a gentleman. He has learned to speak with a more refined accent. He has become more meticulous in his habits and dress. His years with the Goths seem far away.

But for all his recently acquired gentility, Jason's former skills and habits as a hacker become increasingly useful in overseeing the day-to-day operations of Elysium. He makes his daily rounds on the fields to make sure that the preparation for the crops is on schedule and that tractors and trucks, as well as tilling and harvesting equipment, are in good repair. His tall stature and silent stare are effective in keeping the slaves in line. Copious quantities of Daytrain continue to ensure their harmony and compliance with the order of the household. Following Medea's advice, he exercises droit du seigneur with the female slaves to ensure future population growth.

His current libidinous approach differs from his Bionican days when persuasion was enough. In these more
civilized circumstances, his brutality is visited upon the
lowly field women who sometimes refuse to comply. All
too often, the sobs of the women he has raped puncture
the still of the night untempered by the gaiety inside the
stately Elysium.

Every time Medea returns, she and Jason go over and
over the details of household matters and the running
of the plantation. Jason rarely mentions his son. Medea
knows that Jason has stopped going out of his way to
spend quality time with his son, although he continues
the morning routine of teaching children at the school.
She notices that Pericles is barely aware of his father and
expects little from him. Jason stares at her blankly every
time she prods him to spend more time with the growing boy.

One fine day, Jason sees Medea after leaving the
school, where the three sisters continue with the lessons.

"How are things going with your three admirers?"

"We have had some very useful conversations," Jason
tries to make it sound like all business. Medea rolls her
eyes.

"*Conversations?* Is that what you kids are calling it these days? So, I see you are coming along quite nicely; soon you will be the darling of the Greek world. You already have all the tongues of Polis wagging with your entrapment of their three most coveted daughters," Medea tells him with a nudge-nudge, wink-wink. But she is only joking as she settles in to retire for the night with her boy lover.

That following morning Medea jabs Jason in the chest. "The three daughters have taught you well. You have become quite the lady's man, and your mastery of sweet nothings is phenomenal. You no longer make love like a Goth, but that is not what I want to talk to you about. There is an upcoming opportunity at the Macedonian Society for you to give a talk. I have told them that you will speak for them. And so now we need to work on that."

Medea helps Jason develop a speech that she calls, "The Ontology of Knowledge" that integrates Jason's knowledge of Bionica with his experiences among the Goths and Greeks.

A day later is the dry run with Medea taking notes. Jason clears his throat and begins, "Dear Colleagues. There is so much to know, but a human being can only focus on knowledge incrementally. Humans aggregate experience as fragile memories over a lifetime, but they can only understand what they know by translating ideas into action."

"The ancient Greeks," Jason says with emphasis, "understood that human beings like to pursue knowledge for its own sake. They thought that this made sense. They talked about truth and beauty; they celebrated the human form. They underscored the importance of balance and proportion, but in the end they also understood the downside of pursuing knowledge *only* for its own sake."

"Socrates gave up his life in the pursuit of knowledge," Jason says with emphasis.

Medea interrupts. "I would not talk too much about Socrates - we know too much already about his pursuit of young boys. There are still those who believe children should be off limits and those who believe that taking young lovers is for the greater social good. To be safe, you had better stick to the Stoics."

Jason sticks to the Stoics, emphasizing duty more than beauty. He contrasts the wise and temperate Stoics to the Bionicans and their preoccupation with useless data and the Goths with their love of unbridled force.

Fully prepped by Medea, Jason gives his talk at the Macedonian Society where it is well received. Medea applauds him. People want to know him.

"Like I told you, you are getting to be quite the man about the Polis," Medea teases him.

The Greek idea of beauty and form appeals to Jason. In his mind's eye, he sees white alabaster Greek statues whose revolving hands reach out to the deep blue sky. As the statues revolve, the blinding flash of the sun reveals new gestures and expressions trying to tell him something. As he tires of these reveries, the heroic Greek statutes turn into naked Bionicans dancing in a wild frenzy.

Jason is taken aback, horrified by the Bionican images. He does not understand the connection between Apollo and Dionysus. He wants to forget his association with Bionica.

Medea brings him back to the moment. "You are becoming a bit too concerned with your lecture and its impression. Do not become too boring, or you will force me to find myself a real Goth as my lover."

On their day off from teaching school, the three sisters take Jason along on field trips to local museums in the Polis.

Meditation brags, "We are justifiably proud of our local libraries and museums. What great exhibits and special collections! Where shall we go first?"

"We have *so* much stuff from every culture and from every time," Memory says with a laugh. "There are collections of art and anti-art. We have exhibits on holistic health, world religions, insects, architecture, psychology, early computing machines, gadgets, marketing…"

"I once went to the exhibit on Xtreme Marketing," Jason blurts out.

Memory gives a knowing nod. "Xtreme Marketing, ah yes, Xtremus, that is an important one because it helps us understand the waning of civilization. But you know we have to look ahead, and we must not be distracted by the past."

"Keep your eyes on the prize," Song laughs.

"There is an eternal wellspring of inspiration in our Greek civilization. Meditation intones seriously, "First, study the original sages to keep things clean and simple."

"But does that not make us very unoriginal?" Song points out.

Memory disagrees, "Originality is not the point. It is truth and beauty. Much that came after Ancient Greece was corrupted by religion and sentimentality."

"Originality is habit forming whereas truth and beauty are eternal," Meditation chuckles. "Why do we not go the current exhibit on 20th Century art?"

Memory and Song agree, and so they head off to the Palace of Culture where an exhibit on 20th Century art just opened. Jason and the three sisters proceed through the massive Corinthian pillars to enter the impressive museum. As they walk through the galleries, Meditation and Memory engage in a running critique of the art on display while Song keeps her gaze on Jason to see how he reacts.

"Art got out of hand," Meditation says as she starts things off.

"A lot of 20th Century culture was drug-inspired," Memory adds.

"You mean money-inspired." Meditation replies.

Meditation and Memory continue with their banter. Memory looks up and says emphatically, "And then they threw the baby out with the bathwater."

"Figuratively or literally?" Meditation asks. No one answers her and so she offers up her perennial explanation, "It began when the modernists ignored the grand masters."

Memory bites her lips. "After the grand masters, artists tried to save us with movements and fads – the 'isms' – Impressionism, Fauvism, Expressionism. Then they mucked about with form – Futurism, Cubism, Abstract Expressionism."

"Yes, they even had something called Minimalism. Boy was that original!" snarls Meditation.

Meditation lowers her voice with authority. "Less is more. It was all about getting down to basics."

"That is true, more or less," Memory adds.

"Then came Post-modernism," says Meditation

"Conceptual art!" shrieks Song in delight.

"And Post-post modernism that the artists then turned into Neo-modernism." They all laugh.

Meditation lowers her voice inviting Memory's response. "And before anyone knew it, the artist had made everything art."

"Those that resisted protested. *Art must become anti-art*, they yelled," Memory responds.

"Together at last, art and commerce, finally inseparable. Viva Warhol!" warbles Song.

"Art and technology," they say in unison.

"Art and commerce."

Meditation takes a deep breath and says as if knowing something profound, "And when it was all over, and when art was truly dead, the computers took over."

"Digital art got out of hand. So much became too much," Memory adds.

"Yin-yang," sings Song,

"So that is why, in a nutshell, we were thrown back to ancient Greece and Rome, back to where Western civilization began." Meditation says, clapping her hands together in glee.

She suggests, "Why do we not look at some religious art. And so they walk to a gallery that contains paintings depicting Madonna and Baby Jesus and the crucifixion. Song notices that Jason has become restless looking at these. She suggests that they go to the museum café for a bite to eat, providing an opportunity for the sisters to continue their conversation about art.

Song wants to draw Jason in. "Jason, what did you

think of the art in the exhibit?"

Jason says hesitantly, "I am not sure what I should think about what you girls talked about in the galleries," he says looking at Medea and Meditation. "I liked looking at the colors of the abstract stuff, but quite honestly, I prefer to look at the earlier paintings where you can recognize the images people, cities, landscapes. But some of the religious works are quite nasty."

"Nasty? In what way?" Song wonders.

"All that Christian art, I do not think that it should be exhibited publicly. I think it is dangerous."

Song is taken aback by Jason's statement. "You have to keep an open mind, even for things that you do not like and that you think are dangerous."

Jason's seriousness greatly amuses the girls. Memory looks at Jason and smiles with a wink.

"It looks like we still have some work to do."

CHAPTER 12
CIVILIZATION AND
ITS CONTENTS

Jason and the three sisters continue to explore the polis on foot.

"I wonder how many people come here each year to visit the shops and museums?" Jason asks.

Meditation responds, "Thousands. Our existence depends on people coming here to buy the stuff we sell in our shops, but we cannot let them know that our supply is practically limitless."

Memory adds, "They bring us what we need – foods, spices, livestock, slaves and raw materials. We trade them retro-technology items and antiques – lots of antiques. We give them healthcare, medical herbs, education, and designs. A win for us and a win, win, win for our customers."

The three sisters show Jason a huge outdoor area reserved for laundry. Here hundreds of unclothed female slaves, with rivulets of sweat running down their bodies, are washing and bleaching togas in huge steaming tubs of water heated over open fires.

"I cannot stand the bleach," says Song holding her nose.

"Let us go somewhere else," says Meditation with a smile as she sees Jason display a salacious interest in the laundresses. They head to the Agora, a marketplace where intense haggling is the norm – a noisy place overrun by chickens and goats as well as people looking to barter for all kinds of things.

"Here is where we exercise our free speech," Memory says pointing to the old man speaking to a group of acolytes who are busy jotting down what he has to say.

"What he says better be good," Song says with a laugh, "because paper is scarce around here."

Mediation looks impatient. "I have had enough of this hustle. How about the Etruscan baths? Jason, I believe this is your first time. So let's go. Tomorrow is a good day for a bath. Let us bring some slaves to rub us down."

They return to Elysium to fetch slaves to carry the soap, brushes, togas and sandals needed for going to the baths.

As they arrive at the church building, Mediation explains, "This was once a Roman Catholic Church that was repurposed as a public bath. It was named after St Johns Eudes, a member of the French Oratorians, who tended to those sick with the plague in the Seventeenth Century. He slept in a casket in the middle of a field to avoid infecting the rest of his community."

When they go inside, she continues to explain, "The Baths are fed via an aqueduct from huge cisterns. The baths are divided into several rooms, including the Frigidarium, Tepidarium, and Caldarium – for baths taken in stages, from cold, to warm, to hot."

They take a full tour of the building. Jason notices that there are a dozen slaves stoking the furnace with wood.

"Are they always here?"

Memory replies, "Yes, these baths are open twenty-four hours a day. It takes a lot of wood to keep them going. The Bionicans say that all this continuous wood burning is harming the environment, but what they say does not matter because they are unwashed."

"Cleanliness is next to godliness, right Jason?" Meditation insinuates with a smirk.

The three sisters and Jason prepare for the baths in a large vestibule equipped with refurbished stationary bicycles and Stairmasters. The routine starts with the time-tested Royal Canadian Air Force Exercises. This old-school exercise plan is from the 1950s. A doctor designed it as a series of five exercises for men and ten exercises for women. The group enters the baths where they disrobe and enter the Frigidarium completely in the nude. Song does not like this part and skips to the Tepidarium as the others laugh at her unwillingness to be like a polar bear. The group completes the cycle that includes a healthy plunge into the Caldarium and ends at a relaxation station stocked with books.

Jason feels like the odd man out among the three women who have successfully divorced nudity from sexuality, unaware or unconcerned with the sneaky stares from the fully clothed slave attendants. He does not like to be naked when he is not in charge.

Jason asks, "Do the slaves get a turn in the baths?"

Meditation says with indifference, "Well...only when no one else is coming that day. After the slaves bathe, they have to change the water. The Greeks would never want to bathe in the same waters as the slaves."

When they are finished, they wave to the slaves, signaling them to come.

"You can use the waters now," Memory tells the slaves, who snicker stealthily in their native language that the Greeks do not hear or want to hear.

The slaves enter the bath area without establishing eye contact. Meanwhile, Jason and the three sisters continue their conversation while getting dressed.

Memory quips, "They should be happy that we allow them to bathe at all. In ancient times, slaves were not even allowed a splash."

Meditation interjects, "Those were the good old days, before Christianity confused things by saying things like the meek shall inherit the earth?" What we do know is that Christianity can get in the way of truth and beauty by linking morality to sacrifice,"

Memory agrees, "Christianity got lost in its doctrine."

Song disagrees, "Over the years, there has been a lot of beautiful art because of Christianity. What about all these wonderful cathedrals and the wonderful Madonnas that we saw painted in the museums?"

Jason wants to change the topic and offers his conversation stopper, a nonsequitur. "There is only one thing you can do with a religious fanatic, and that is to give him what he wants."

"And what *might* that be?" Song asks.

"Death, sweet death. They all secretly want to be martyred so that they can inspire religious art and go to heaven," Jason says.

"Do you mean that?" Song wonders.

Jason looks into Song's eyes. "We have to keep the slate clean. Mankind cannot afford a false future." He can tell from Song's look that she does not agree with his views.

"Yes, heaven is right here on earth, not in some far

away unimaginable place," Memory says offhandedly.

"Amen," says Meditation, ending the conversation.

And so ends the day spent at the baths.

The three girls and Jason continue their routine of teaching the children at the school in the morning. This time it is Pericles' turn in a show-and-tell.

Little Pericles begins, "Once upon a time, Jason lived with Medea as her husband, and they had children. But they never married. Jason then said he was going to marry the king's daughter, but that did not go well, and Medea ended up killing her children."

The children clap as the next child gets up to take the stage to share what she has learned.

Song looks at Jason, wondering what prompted Pericles to focus on this particular story. But, Jason is characteristically silent. He has no idea who put these words into his son's mouth.

Jason and the three sisters leave the classroom so that they can get ready to plan upcoming events in comfort while the house slaves remain to mind the children for the remaining day.

"Song," Xantippe's high-pitched voice cuts into her daughter's afternoon of serenity, "You have to give some thought to your dress; you must dress to make an impression. You should be getting ready instead of making music.

Song reluctantly leaves her music to join a lively group of women in the parlor who are discussing the upcoming event with Jason, but as is often the case, the conversation veers away from the practical.

Memory teases Song, "Now it is time for you to engage in this silly coming out. This year, you will be a debutante at the upcoming Annual Hellenic Ball."

Song tries to be matter-of-fact. "OK, I guess it is perfectly logical for human society to devise a public occasion for its eligible females. At least I do not have to be a virgin to participate," she says smiling at Jason.

Mediation makes a goose-mating call. "It is the survival of the prettiest."

Memory makes quacking sounds. "So much for Charles Darwin, the Victorian philosopher who said that man descended from the apes. He was wrong. We descended from geese. I get goose bumps thinking about it."

Humor is not on Jason's playlist. He wants to talk about evolution. "What an odd idea. I guess there must be something to the ape theory. They have arms and fingers like we do. Are there any apes left?" Jason wonders.

"I do not know for sure. They say all the big wild creatures are extinct. At any rate, apes used to stand up on their hind legs and have prehensile thumbs," Song adds. "But they did not have much speech and they could not do science."

"We no longer do that either. All we ever study is poetry, music, philosophy, and a little math for good measure," Jason grumbles.

"They say we are scientific illiterates, and proud of it." Meditation says.

Everyone laughs.

"For a long time it was believed that science was a dirty business that takes away from what is important – the art of living well," Meditation says with gravity. "Poor Aristotle, he has been trying to shove that science stuff down young minds for years."

"That is not the only thing he was trying to stuff down the young," Memory says giggling.

"Lo and behold, speaking of the man of science." Song points to the puff of black smoke signaling the arrival of skinny Aristotle, his dirty blonde beard and long hair fluttering in the wind. "Now there is a man of action," she giggles.

Aristotle pulls up, tries to calm his sputtering vehicle, gets out and greets the girls. Jason moves up to take a closer look at Aristotle's machine. Aristotle is a "mad

scientist" type who is now very much the talk of the Polis. As the head of the Greek Skunk Works in Pasadena,
he heads up research and development for the Greeks.

Jason sidles up to the car to introduce himself to Aristotle. Aristotle looks to the girls who are still giggling.
Song makes the formal introduction.

"This is Jason. He has lived among both the Goths
and... the Bionicans," says Song, inadvertently revealing
Jason's deep secrets.

"A man of the world, eh? I suppose we have a lot to
learn from you. I am Aristotle, the local nerd."

Song laughs, "We know why you are here."

"Yep, I am here to promote science. I know that it is
lost on you, girls."

"Oh, you are so right. You are here to promote something that is lost on us girls. You do not have to be sexist,"
says Meditation wryly because of Aristotle's constant
flirtation.

"Is there another way?" Aristotle jokes. "No, is there
anyone here I can kiss up to?"

"Since you mentioned kissing, you might start with
Jason here. Medea brought him to us. He is here to learn,
and I am sure that you will have a *lot* that you can teach
him," Memory says.

"I am sure he has learned quite a bit about himself
in your good hands. Plato and I have heard all about you
three and him from Medea." The girls ignore Aristotle's

innuendo as Jason looks the other way. They walk to the gardens where the servants have laid out a buffet. They want to look at the fruits and feel them to make sure they are fresh.

"Is there enough food?" Mediation asks one of the servants who nods in the affirmative. "You never know if someone else will drop by. Last week we did not have enough fruit when Plato and his followers stopped in."

The group sits in a circle, and the conversation picks up from a previous topic — the future of science and technology.

"How much science do we need? Is not what we learn from everyday experience and what we already know enough?" Memory wonders. Meditation takes on a thoughtful pose. "Aristotle, you were named after the ancient philosopher who wrote about science and was one of the world's early scientists."

"Yes, the pre-Socratics also thought hard about the essence of life," Aristotle adds.

"Yes, but very little of what they wrote survived," says Meditation, waving a book.

Song, not to be outdone, interrupts, "And then there was Archimedes. Where would we be if we did not have his principles? I think about him, imagining the old man every time I bathe," Song says as she mock-scrubs her breasts. "I am all for epicurean delights and against suffering," she adds.

"Our suffering is putting up with the good life. It is not easy being well off. They used to call it the white man's burden," Meditation says with a smile.

Today there is also the white woman's burden," Memory adds with mock solemnity.

The omnipresent Medea, who has overheard the girls' chatter, joins the group and exchanges glances with Aristotle.

"OK, girls, enough. I think your discussion of philosophy is getting topsy-turvy. I agree with Aristotle that you should take more interest in science and technology."

Song whines, "What is the use? I am OK with science, but I am not so sure about technology. Why do we need it? We have our slaves."

Medea admonishes the group, "We are like spoiled children. If we do not embrace science and technology, the Goths will eat our lunch."

Aristotle explains that the Greeks have a duty to understand science if only out of self-preservation. "Someday the Goths will wake up and they will discover science, and then what will happen to us? Right now, they are technicians at best. They are only interested in making things work, not in understanding why."

"So long as the Goths avoid education, they will not get anywhere," Meditation intones.

Medea observes, "Do not be so sure. It is only a matter of time. Every time a Greek maiden takes up with a Goth, we are closer to a Goth take-over, and the Humanities will disappear into thin air."

Aristotle disagrees, "We should not be afraid of sharing knowledge with the Goths. We have a superior philosophy and can manage their expectations," he says adding old corporate-speak to his argument.

Medea gets down to business and asks Aristotle point blank, "Why are you here?"

Aristotle smiles while stroking his bearded chin. His eyes dart nervously around the room.

"I am here to discuss the upcoming Hellenic Ball."

Medea expands, "Ah yes, the Hellenic Ball, a blast held each year at the New Science Institute – established by *my* father and *run* by Aristotle."

"I want to talk to Xantippe about providing servants and provisions." He doesn't want to deal directly with Medea even though he knows she controls the purse strings.

Xantippe, who has been waiting in the back, steps forward. The servants follow carrying pitchers of fresh ambrosia, which Medea had spiked with a sprinkling of hashish. Seeing that the evening is about to devolve into the logistics of the upcoming Ball, Medea and Jason go for a walk. As they leave, they can hear the faint trailing conversation about plans for the upcoming great event.

The day of the Hellenic Ball is at hand. Togas and sandals must be coordinated. The right perfumes have to be chosen. Jewelry has to be polished and donned, and the importance of the most fashionable hairstyles cannot be overstated.

There is an incredible fuss over what Song will wear for her coming out. The fitters put the final touches on her white chiffon peplos, the type that was all the rage in 500 BCE, a graceful garment, open on one side to expose the sides of her diminutive breasts. Memory and Meditation are picking out pleated chiton dresses made from linen. Jason, his hair curled and his chest glistening with oil, picks out his khlaina outfit, secured in front with a golden buckle.

Medea's dress took months to make. She decided on a pale pink and silver art deco flapper dress with hand beading and tastefully applied rhinestones. The intricate geometry of the gown's design shimmers over her soft curves and suits this maven of complex maneuvers; her tiara does not seem out of place.

On the big night of the ball, Medea, Jason, and the three girls are part of an entourage that includes Socrates and Xantippe. Their slaves accompany them. Aristotle is at the gala entrance greeting the arrivals wearing his new toga decorated with Greek mathematical symbols.

"I like your Delta, Pi, Sigma," Medea laughs.

"You look fabulous, and your girls, too."

Aristotle walks up to Song, inspecting her gown.

"Song, your gown is wonderful – a triumph. You look simply marvelous!" he says with lust in his eyes. It is the first time that Song has received a compliment from Aristotle. Even though he is an old codger, it makes her feel good to be noticed by him.

While Aristotle is in full flattery gear, Jason takes a look around. He sees an old Piper aircraft hanging from the ceiling in the corner. Aristotle notices Jason's interest in the airplane.

"When this hangar was repurposed, we couldn't resist keeping that little plane to decorate the dance hall."

Jason walks around the hall and tries one of the seats in the audience area, and then walks up to the stage, with Aristotle following him.

Aristotle and Jason join up with Medea, who is inspecting the buffet feast. There are bowls with perfectly ripe fruit and platters full of Mediterranean delights, including figs, dates, couscous, and a huge platter of lamb. The luscious, honey-dripping desserts have poetic names like baklava, galaktoboureko, and revani; many look like presents wrapped in phyllo dough, with pistachio bits on top. Jason does not stand on ceremony or pay attention to what the food is called; instead he pops a piece of baklava into his mouth in passing. It is delicious. He likes that it is honey dripped. Honey is as rare as the honeybee that has become nearly extinct. It is more precious than cocaine.

Medea whispers to Jason, "I would like you to meet the right people. They can help you get a commission with the Praetorian Guard. It's about time!"

"Why the name?" Jason asks.

"We took the name from Ancient Rome. The Praetorian Guard kept their emperors safe."

She takes Jason to the chambers where the Praetorian Guard meets. In a large ornately frescoed alcove, Aristotle is talking to Plato, one of the most powerful men in Polis. Plato is older than Aristotle. Plump and bald on top, his thick curly white beard hides much of his face except for his prominent nose and piercing eyes that he uses to command his acolytes. All of the Guards assembled around the two men wear identical white togas with a thin purple border. They wave Medea and Jason in; two of the Guards, Thucydides and Herodotus, whom they met before, come forward to greet them

Looking at them from a distance, Aristotle whispers to Plato, "Here she comes, the dragoness with her protégé."

"And to think she also has that dwarf under her thumb," Aristotle says cattily.

"Size matters," Plato chimes in, "You cannot judge a book by its cover."

Plato coughs and mutters, "We should not give so much power to a woman."

"I am not thrilled about her influence, but you have got to admit, she is effective in dealing with the Goths. And, like it or not, she is one of us," Aristotle replies.

"I worry about her allegiances. That fellow that she is with, Jason, he seems to have done wonders to clear out the trouble makers among the slaves."

"But there is something unsavory about him. He is a killer. From what Medea tells me, his pedigree is questionable," Aristotle adds.

"That isn't too unusual these days. A lot of people have come here to Polis to reinvent themselves. You should know, as I do that our history is not what we present it to be. We live in strange times," Plato concludes.

After Medea and Jason finish talking to the Praetorian Guards, they approach Aristotle and Plato again and bow slightly to them. Both men smile and wave back in acknowledgment before attending to the business at hand.

Even on this night of debutantes and dancing, the Hellenic Council leadership has decided to conduct business. Seated in a semi-circle, Plato is at the center with Aristotle at his right. Medea introduces Jason to rest of the Council members, including Alexander, whom he met when he first arrived in Macedonia as a refugee. The members of the Praetorian Guard remain standing a few steps removed from their seated elders.

This group of old men is responsible for all Greek economic and military activities. The younger men serve in the Praetorian Guard, which is a stepping-stone to the Hellenic Council. Jason is acutely conscious of the fact that his reputation has preceded him to the Council, thanks to Medea. Medea told Jason that as a member of the Hellenic Council, she is required to provide regular updates about his progress under her tutelage. Jason is aware that Aristotle and Plato know about his past identities as a Bionican hacker and Goth warlord and king, but he is not sure how much she told them about his private life with the sisters.

Plato stands and puts his hand on Jason's shoulder as if to accept him and asks, "So, how is my old friend, Berk?" Stunned, Jason hesitates not knowing how to answer, and so Plato jolts Jason's memory by spitting out, "You know, Berk the Dwarf. I understand that he is one of your teachers. He is well endowed."

Jason is taken aback. He wonders what Berk has told Plato and Aristotle about him, about Julia, and about Xtremus. He decides to play dumb.

"I have not seen him for ages - ever since I studied with him at the temple after I left Bionica," Jason lies. "Have you heard from him?"

"He will be visiting us very soon, and you will have a chance to catch up with him," Plato grins knowing that he caught Jason lying, which provides him with ammo for future use.

"I understand that you have come a long way with your education," Plato continues.

Jason is surprised that Plato is speaking to him this undignified way in front of the whole Hellenic Council. He now understands that know a lot about him. With humility and caution, he replies, "I have learned a lot, and I am looking for an opportunity to apply what I know."

"I bet you are," Aristotle cracks and gets a few laughs.

"Not so fast, young man, it takes a while to develop good judgment to go with all that learning, not just bravery and raw talent. Do you have any idea how hard it is to keep the peace?" To drive home this point, Plato quotes his namesake, *"To conquer oneself is the best and noblest victory; to be vanquished by one's own nature is the worst and most ignoble defeat."*

"I understand that well," Jason nods, eager to please and unwilling to admit that he understands very little.

"So you claim. We shall see. Tonight we are going to hear a lecture by my esteemed colleague, Aristotle, who runs our New Science Institute, which includes the Skunk Works dedicated to technological re-invention. You will find his lecture interesting in this regard."

"I have great respect for Aristotle," Jason says as he

looks over at Aristotle and says tactfully, "He is certainly a man comfortable with *many* machines."

Plato looks at Aristotle, adding, "He *is* a good man with systems, to be sure, but he still needs to focus on the big picture. Oftentimes he gets caught up in the small things."

Jason hears this as a backhanded criticism of Aristotle.

"Tonight we will hear what our man of machine systems has to say about the state of science. He will talk about the Great Past and reveal some things that many in the audience will hear for the first time."

Jason prods, "What will that be?"

"The rise and fall of technology," answers Plato.

Medea is tired of being quiet. "You men are at it again. I thought that this evening would belong to the women. This is all about the debutantes, and Song is one of the debutantes. It is Song's night."

"Ah yes, and so it is," Plato says. "It is Song's night to find a true man for her heart, supposedly her first love," he says staring quizzically at Jason.

Medea and Jason walk back to the Great Hall where the debutantes' young suitors gather. Slaves circulate with huge serving plates full of food and drink. Jason grabs a fistful of lamb to munch on while Medea takes a chunk out of a celery stalk. The mistress of ceremonies, a former debutante queen, announces each current debutante as the young women enter from an anteroom. There are appreciative sighs of delight from the young suitors and squeals of encouragement from their sisters. Each debutante, including Song, is expected to display her special talent in the next phase of this grand coming out. Some play a musical instrument and sing. Others show off their needlecraft or pottery. Song plays the lyre, firmly locked between her legs, with passion and intimacy. Each gets a polite round of applause, but Song's applause is both firmer and longer. She certainly is the belle of the ball.

And then the dancing begins. The first dance belongs to the debutantes and their fathers or some older, dignified partners. Much to her surprise, Aristotle asks for Song's first dance. She reluctantly agrees, thinking of all his leering glances to her sister in the past. This first dance more than makes up for it. Jason looks on sheepishly as Memory and Meditation are part of a musical group that plays as their sister takes a turn on the floor with her partner to exemplify the grace and refinement that this night salutes. After the first dances, the evening becomes less formal as the older men and their accompanying debutantes retreat. Tonight will be a night when many of these girls get their first true education in the art of love. The remaining young people eagerly cross the emptying dance floor and cluster near the dessert table, filling their faces with honey-dripped sweets of all kinds.

Aristotle does not stay with Song, for he knows that her education is more than complete. Instead, he moves toward the auditorium, avidly anticipating the evening's finale – his yearly state-of-the-Polis speech that sums up current accomplishments and challenges for the Greeks. By this time, most of the guests, even the Praetorian Guards, are tired and ready to go home. Some are yawning in anticipation of a long speech. As is customary, women and men sit separately on either side of the center aisle, the women on the left and the men on the right.

Jason has just taken his seat when to his surprise Berk suddenly appears on stage to introduce Aristotle. The dwarf struggles with the microphone and after a few embarrassing moments of unwanted feedback, begins his introductory remarks.

"Tonight it is my pleasure to introduce Aristotle, who has kept the flame of science and technology alive in our world. Before introducing our esteemed speaker, let me first take a moment to acknowledge Jason, a relative newcomer to your community. Let us recognize him for sharing with us what he has learned from his experiences with the Bionicans and the Goths."

Jason stands up hesitantly, and there is a bit of silence

before the obligatory, yet overly restrained, applause. Everyone in the room seems a bit befuddled by Berk's praise of Jason. They wonder why any attention is being paid to this former Bionican and Goth.

Aristotle comes forward to speak and looks around the Great Hall to get his bearings. His approach to the podium seems anti-climactic. "Friends, Greeks, and Countrymen," he begins with a joke. "Lend me your fears, for I have come to bury them."

Since most people do not get the joke, the Great Hall quickly quiets down with scattered laughs. He continues.

"As you know we have labored hard to revitalize civilization after the crippling catastrophes of Cybergeddon, but do we have the courage to learn from our mistakes and quell our fear of the future? All around us is the evidence of a great civilization – thousands of roads and buildings from huge automated factories. How can we recover a workable banking system that will promote growth and trade?"

People in the audience have heard this before. They become restless and disgruntled as they realize that he is, once again, restating the obvious concerning the predicament in which the Greeks find themselves.

"Wake up and smell the coffee!" someone shouts out. This gets a few laughs since coffee is no longer available because of the collapse of foreign trade. Many Greeks think Aristotle just cannot accept that the past is over and that it, along with its banking system, will not come back.

Never tired of hearing himself talk, Aristotle continues, "Some say we should leave things well enough alone. I say we should not be afraid of new knowledge." And then Aristotle quotes ancient Aristotle: *"It is the mark of an educated mind to be able to entertain a thought without accepting it."*

There is some scattered applause from those who hope to end the talk by clapping hard. Undeterred, Aristotle continues, "You say we have a good thing going with our enemies, the Goths, or should I say, our competitors. For many of us, life is good, and so why ruin a good thing? You say if we push too hard for science and research, the Goths will get nervous and finally take over with brawn instead of brains. Trust me, you do not want that."

"But, there is a problem. Look at our young people today. They are experimenting with Daytrain. They are spoiled; especially the young men who just want to play games and lurk at the Agora. If we continue like this, someday the Goths are going to wake up and take over anyway. So I ask you, is it possible to turn the clock back and to move it forward again? I say, yes. Pursue science and technology or we will lose our competitive edge."

There is polite applause from the exhausted audience

and a period for questions.

One young man, Laius, the shortest member of the Praetorian Guard, says, "We do not have the means to build what we need to bring back advanced science. The infrastructure is hopelessly broken down."

Aristotle jumps in to answer, "Wrong! The knowledge to build again still exists, but it is in the wrong hands. Our problem is with the Bionicans. They created a cult around The Well and have lost sight of why it was created in the first place. They believe they are saving the earth by trapping knowledge so it cannot be used in creating dangerous technologies."

Having heard this all before, many in the audience walk out of the room. They think that Aristotle is chiefly interested in promoting himself and that he will destroy the cushy Greek way of life by messing with the Bionicans.

The hall quickly empties, but Aristotle keeps on talking to the hearty few who remain – Medea, Jason, Berk, and leading members of the Hellenic Council, including Alexander, as well as Alexander's two sons, Thucydides and Herodotus. Meanwhile, Memory, Meditation, and Song have wandered into the lecture room to sit with their stepsister, Medea.

Up to this point, Jason has paid close attention to Aristotle's lecture, but now his attention is elsewhere. He is gazing at Song, who is visibly bored, playing with her long beautiful auburn hair fluttering in the slight breeze in the room, as if she were waiting for him to make the next move.

After Aristotle finishes his long, boring speech, he enjoys the vigorous applause of the few remaining listeners. Jason claps very hard; Song yawns. More questions arise. Herodotus asks, "What will happen to Bionica?"

Aristotle answers briefly, "I predict that in two generations, Bionica will be dead. Daytrain cannot sustain them forever; memories will fail and bodies will age. No one knows how to insert new implants. Our only hope is to learn directly from the Bionicans and see whether we can train our people to work with them."

Herodotus' brother, Thucydides, stands up to ask, "Are we sure The Well data is not just garbage data in, and garbage data out? How can we be sure that the Cyberterrorists did not infect it?"

Aristotle responds, "We have to keep an open mind. Everything has its risks. It is a fair bet that we will learn more from The Well than we will in our woefully incomplete libraries. We do not even have enough people to mine all the books we have for the knowledge we need. The Goths have the highest birthrate, but they are staunchly and purposefully illiterate so they will be useless in saving our civilization. We have no choice but to take our chances with this Bionican database."

After giving his speech, Berk comes out of the dark

and puts his arms around Jason's shoulder. "So you are finally going to lead us. They say you have a good head on your shoulders. The Greeks tell me that you will lead them on an expedition to Bionica to access The Well."

Jason nods in agreement while trying to avoid eye contact with Berk, visibly embarrassed to be seen with him because it brings back memories of humbler days when he knew so little.   Medea comes to the rescue, grabbing Jason by the arm. "Let us go back to Elysium," Medea tells him and then admonishes Berk,   "You have to be more careful in what you say." Without saying a word, Berk throws a kiss at Medea and Jason as they leave.

"What was that all about?   How does all this affect my quest?"

"I think you better put your quest on hold. You still have a lot to learn."

CHAPTER 13
THE FEAST

When there is uncertainty, it is time for diversions at Elysium. Medea uses these occasions to solidify her political contacts and to mend fences whenever necessary. This time, a garden party will also give Xantippe and her family the opportunity to show off their prize-winning plants and vegetables. Memory, Meditation, and Song striving to look exceptionally beautiful, wear garlands of tea roses and marigolds.

The guests are greeted first by the servants who help them out of their carriages. Aristotle and Plato arrive in Aristotle's sputtering car. A few minutes later, a carriage lets off a group of old Hellenic Council members and neighing horses announce the arrival of the young men of the Praetorian Guard. A few more relatives of the family arrive, but because they are inconsequential, they draw little attention from the servants.

Meditation, Memory, and Song sit in a corner with

their instruments, ready to provide soothing sounds for the occasion. Although heaps of flowers are everywhere, there are no flower smells. Bird sounds echo through the house and gardens, but there are no birds in sight.

Xantippe and her family are famous for their sumptuous feasts. Xantippe, the mistress of ceremonies, introduces Meditation, Memory, and Song, who stand up to take their bows. The outdoor festive atmosphere muffles the sound of the music as well as the appreciative applause for the threesome. Ice cream parfait is the treat du jour.

"Today we are going to have our regular hootenanny, but with one difference. Aristotle's star pupil, Dylan Roberts will give us a song on his electric lute. I am proud to proclaim that amplification is back."

The audience gasps, "Treason!"

Dylan, dressed in a white suit and boater hat, starts to sings the opening lines from his tune, "Where have all the Flowers Been, Señor," only to be drowned out by the electronic screeches of his lute. After he rambles through a few stanzas, the talented bard wanders off.

"How about the girl singer, I mean woman singer?" someone shouts out. Aristotle takes the stage again.

"I am pleased to announce another star pupil, Bias Jones, our newest badass singer-songwriter. She exemplifies what Aristotle once said, *"Musical training is a more potent instrument than any other, because rhythm and harmony find their way into the inward places of the soul."*

Bias begins her signature song. "Your Diamonds and my Trust" that has become a feminist anthem that satirizes the Greek marry-go-round.

She begins the song in her clarion voice with the cribbed line, *"Well I be damned, here comes your ghost again,"* and in the middle of her song the sound system acts up again, but she manages to complete her set to the adulation of her doe-eyed fans.

To move things along, Xantippe asks Aristotle to give a toast. Aristotle begins, "I want to raise my glass in honor of Socrates."

Socrates, hunched in a corner of the room, is oblivious to what is going on. "Know thyself," he mutters in his slobber.

Although some have said that he should be put to death, Xantippe does not want to euthanize Socrates. She has always said that as long as he can say, "Know thyself," Socrates deserves to live.

Aristotle continues his toast, "And I drink to Xantippe, Socrates' lifelong partner, and their wise and beautiful daughters – Memory, Meditation, and Song – who regaled us with their music and their beauty."

He then raises his glass one more time. "And one more toast to our dear Medea for bringing Jason here, the man of the hour. Jason, please stand up."

Song plunks a sour note on the lyre and looks away. She had first assumed that Medea was just a point on Jason's learning curve. Now she is jealous, realizing that Jason and Medea are closer than she thought. She may never have Jason all for herself as she had hoped when she and her sisters used to play with him – a time that seems so long ago.

Jason stands up and raises his hand waving to all in a dignified manner as the occasion demands. Medea regards him approvingly.

Aristotle continues, "Jason, we are very interested in what you think. Many here still know very little about you, except that you are a fine man and that you are being chosen to become a member of the Praetorian Guard."

There is a hush. Even Medea is surprised; she thought that more time would be needed for Jason's induction. She is not pleased to see the handsome Guards, Herodotus and Thucydides, vying for his attention with big congratulatory hugs.

Song continues to strum her lyre and sighs while Meditation and Memory put down their instruments and perform a dance with fancy footsteps in which they hold hands and go spreading flowers among the guests.

After the hubbub created by Aristotle's announcement subsides, Jason sits down among the members of the Hellenic Council, mentally preparing himself to respond to questions about his background and beliefs.

"So what makes you tick?" Aristophanes, a member of the Hellenic Council, asks him sarcastically.

Jason answers mechanically, "I am a man of my word. If I want something, I get it. If I promise something, I do it. If I tell you something, it is the truth."

Aristotle says with mock approval, "As I have said before, *those who know, do. Those who understand, teach.*"

"Very impressive," Aristophanes says as he puts his hand on Jason's shoulder with a squeeze. "I wish your credo were true for the rest of us," he says with a laugh.

Meanwhile, Herodotus, interested in finally get some time alone with the recruit, tries to chat up Jason, who tactfully extricates himself from this unwanted attention. Jason is well aware of the sexual proclivities of the Praetorian Guard. Jason knows that he is going to have to swing both ways.

The time for chatting is over, and the deal making begins. Those seated in this little klatch know that the real decisions are made when the powerful few get together. Democracy can get in the way of action. The Hellenic Council heavyweights weigh in on today's real topic, Daytrain.

With the increased use of Daytrain by the children of the alpha classes, several influential Greeks favor the abolition of the Daytrain trade even though that means the loss of profits and power.

The first is Achilles, who intones in his deep voice,

"The Daytrain trade is getting out of hand. The kids think they can get access to the Bionican database, but they are being duped. The Bionicans give them access to useless trashy data, and they think they have it made. But it is nothing but recycled celebrity gossip, video memes and mind numbing games. Daytrain is evil and needs to be stamped out."

There is a long silence. Achilles' position is not popular with most members of the Hellenic Council, who are convinced that the Daytrain trade is needed to keep the balance of power with the Goths and to keep the Bionican "experiment" going.

Xenophon, another member who is also actively involved in the Praetorian Guard, supports the continuation of Daytrain use.

"We need the Daytrain trade to continue our way of life. Daytrain is the lesser of the evils that could befall us if we do not master our little universe. We also have to lay off the Bionicans so they will keep us supplied."

"Maybe all we need is a 'just say no' campaign for our youth," Aristophanes suggests tongue in cheek.

"No, what we need is military education. Our youths are getting soft," Xenophon says, raising his finger.

"We still need Daytrain to preserve our way of life. We should make more Daytrain available to the slaves. It may slow them down, but it keeps them less uppity," Xenophon continues to hammer his point.

"*The opiate of the people* they called it," says Aristophanes, visibly pleased with this comment.

"Regale us with info on the Bionicans for Jason's benefit. Let us see if your intelligence jibes with his." Achilles prods Plato.

This is a poke because the Hellenic Council wants to know how Jason might be useful to them.

Plato, the Knowledge Harvester, starts to talk while the onlookers stare at Jason to gauge his reaction. He speaks about the conditions that led to Cybergeddon and the role that The Well might play in his vision for a more civilized future. Meanwhile, several members of the Hellenic Council go to the back of the room to retrieve snacks that the slaves have placed on a banquet table. They especially like the pecan caramel nut clusters.

Aristotle speaks up after listening carefully to Plato's discussion of Bionica and turns to Jason, "Is there anything you can tell us about the Bionican vision for the future? Is there anything we can learn from The Well?"

Jason hesitates, trying to decide what to tell and what to keep private. Now whenever he thinks about his experience as a Bionican hacker, he does not remember all that much. He has shut a lot of things out. There is no longer a context for him to discuss these experiences fully. It is like waking up from a dream, barely remembering the details. He begins to talk cautiously.

"I will tell you what I know. I was a hacker in Bionica.

My job was to help the people manage their involvement in The Well through the proper cultivation and use of Daytrain. As hackers, we trained users to cultivate and maintain areas of The Well held in the neurons of their brains through Daytrain. Most of the time, we traded virtual experiences. The only way to keep order was to have people fantasize about the things from the past that exist in the database. All we had to do was to focus our minds on The Well, and then events and people from the past would come in images and sounds."

Plato asks, "How could you remember the things you accessed?"

"There was no need to remember anything. Whatever one did on a day-to-day basis was routine and instinctive. If you wanted to reprise something, you would dip into The Well, which would anticipate what you wanted to revisit, and it would replay it for you. No one needed to remember anything. Everything was available through The Well.

"What are the most important things in the database?"

Jason answers, "Who knows. No one knows the extent of The Well. I believed that it was infinitely deep and that no one person could fathom it. We were left without a key to understanding how things relate, without a way to judge the validity of what The Well contains. Our single most important duty was to keep the database out of the hands of people who would misuse it.

"What do they mean by *misuse*?" Plato asks.

"The Bionicans distrust our motives. They believe that the revival of technology by us Greeks will destroy the Earth,"

Aristotle stands up and looks Jason straight in the eyes. "You now know that isn't true; we believe in the Golden Mean. We are committed to wisdom and sustainability. We need your help to convince the Bionicans that we can develop a future that will be good for the Earth as well as for mankind. You hold the key that will let us spread our way of life. We need the Bionican database to maintain our competitive edge."

Jason tries to explain, "But you must understand that we, I mean the Bionicans, believe that the now dormant *Makeitso* virus would come back if we Greeks tamper with The Well. They know that they will be the first to die if that happens."

Aristotle continues to grill Jason, "But why can't we make the knowledge work for us? I understand your concern, but perhaps we can all work together to make progress. We cannot be afraid of the future. Trust me, without technology, there will be no future."

Jason responds meekly "I will try to give you what you want, if I can." Jason feels uneasy about his split loyalties, but he does not want to budge from his quest.

Medea steps in to conclude the discussion that she

feels has veered off course.

"Jason has proven himself to be a valuable asset. He has come a long way from the dark days. Give him a chance to sort things through before we ask this from him."

Aristotle agrees, "Medea is right. Jason has the right stuff. His experience with the Goths and Bionicans is invaluable to us. We need more time to develop an effective strategy."

Facing Jason, he says, "Your time can wait, but it is coming, and you must prepare yourself for it."

CHAPTER 14
JASON'S INDUCTION

In a dim candle-lit cave, surrounded by the powerful bodies of his new brothers, Jason repeats sacred words of allegiance in the secret ceremony that marks his real initiation into the Praetorian Guard. "I pledge allegiance to the Guard," says Jason as he stands up, one arm raised in salute.

On behalf of the Hellenic Council, Plato presents Jason with his scutum that is decorated with the image of a scorpion poised to strike. Herodotus and Thucydides present his pilum and helmet. Aristotle presents Jason with fancy cingulum to girdle his loins, and Medea appears as if from nowhere to present a bejeweled dagger to fit in the sacred belt. Jason looks like a hero in this new outfit.

Plato raises a silver flask covered with a repousse depiction of Bacchus. "Welcome to the Guard," he says to Jason.

Following Plato's lead, Jason drinks from a special glass goblet while the others gulp wine from their own flasks. As instructed, Jason places this goblet on the ground and the other Guards cover it with a red cloth. Then Plato asks Jason to stomp on his goblet. He relishes the crushing sound of his initiation.

"This symbolizes that all of your previous attachments are over. You are now, in body and in mind, one of us, a member of the Praetorian Guard," Plato decrees. Everyone cheers as Jason smashes his foot down onto the cloth-covered goblet.

At the end of the ceremony, Medea takes Jason by the hand and whispers to him, "This is your special day. You are now one of the Guards."

Medea and Jason follow the others out of the cave and return to Elysium where Memory, Meditation, and Song are waiting surrounded by the house slaves.

"It is official," Medea proudly announces to all, "Take care of this Guard; I have to run."

Medea is off to join Thor to take care of Goth business. This leaves Jason the opportunity to spend unimpeded time with Memory, Meditation, and Song. He gravitates as ever to Song, taken by her intelligence and well-shaped lips that speak of her innocence. He imagines being with her, all alone, by the wonderful sea.

"Would you play for me?"

Song is eager but shy and not sure how to respond

to Jason's intense flirtation. Envisioning a future with him, she smiles shyly as she joins her sisters who are in the music room to play her harp solo, Bach's *"Jesu, Joy of Man's Desiring"* to celebrate Jason's success.

After the musical evening is over, Jason takes Song's hand and leads her out for an evening walk in the garden where he tells her about his dreams of becoming an enlightened leader.

"I want to be a philosopher king and I love to be beside your side." He sidles up to her and finds her sweet spot and proceeds to win her as she receives him in complete silence bathed in the moonlight. There are no words as they embrace under a lavender tree. Song hums as Jason lies exhausted, wondering what the next day will bring.

Left out of the arena of romantic love, Meditation and Memory feel a tinge of jealousy, but hide this unseemly emotion in a household that takes pride in tolerating elective affinities. To keep themselves busy, they keep company with Alarica and Hallie.

But their enlightenment only goes so far; they cannot resist a few barbs behind Song's back.

"She is the apple of his eye because he is rotten to the core when it comes to love," Meditation snickers.

"He loves her because she is not very well versed," Memory continues the catty exchange. "I do not think she will get very far with him. He has base motives, and all he cares about is getting past third base, I am sure of it."

"She probably dreams of converting him through her goodness."

"She may be able to hold a tune, but...can she hold a man?"

Jason's romantic dalliance with Song paves the way for her to give music lessons to Pericles. She spends hours with Jason's son schooling him in the music she loves. She revels in teaching him songs that she composed.

We feel sadness for the child
Happiness is but brief among mortals
Sorrow and anguish make it cold
Like the wind coming from the mountain
Sinking into the deep sea.

Pericles cries after she finishes her sad little ditty. He has become quite attached to Song and clings to her as if she were his mother. She cradles the little boy in her arms and sings a gentle Greek lullaby in a minor key to help him sleep.

Softly, Pericles my child, to sleep.
Come Hypnos, with poppy dreams

Seal the door and dowse all light
 Lull this child to sleep tonight
Carry my child from the hands of fright.

After singing Pericles into slumber, Song spends time alone with Jason, burning rosemary scented beeswax candles late into the night hoping that the rosemary would work its charms of love and remembrance.

"This is our candle, our very own candle," she says in a singsong voice.

Jason takes Song's hand and says to her, "I like to see your face like this, barely visible above the candle flame. Tell me about yourself, your truest self." This is an unusual request from Jason, who is deeply immersed in creating his own story. Song is too shy and self-conscious to reveal her true longing for the interested young man.

"All I am is what I can sing," Song says modestly. She sings many sad ballads for Jason about unrequited love and abandoned maidens. For a while, Jason is enchanted but as she drones on, his mind wanders. Song is starting to remind him of the Bead Lady because her goodness makes him feel nauseous. Luckily she stops singing and presses her head against his shoulder. Jason is experiencing a glimmer of hope that there might be a happy future for him through Song.

"You are hiding something. I can feel it," Song says quietly. She does not know about all the others in Jason's life. Medea had told her sisters about Tara and Beadina, but Song was deliberately kept out of the loop.

"Please tell me, I will understand." Jason tells her about Beadina and Tara, and even about Digi Diva. He is convinced that she already knows and hopes that she will forgive him now that he has shared his precious secrets.

Song tells Jason that she forgives him and makes him swear that he will be true to her and that he will always be gentle to her and to everyone. Jason, eager to make a deal, word sprays Song with all of the sweet nothings that he has been taught to say by Gonorrhea. He clasps her hand like a vise and smothers her with a kiss as if they were Errol Flynn and Olivia de Havilland in *Captain Blood.*

For a while, the force of their passion provides momentum for their courtship. But that changes when the topic shifts from *inner child* to *inner parent.* "You must be very proud of Pericles. Your son has a great talent for music."

"I do not know where he got that from, certainly not from me."

"But it is important that you encourage him."

"I think you spend too much time with him. He needs to learn to be on his own," Jason says firmly.

"Alone, like you?" Song has struck a nerve. Jason becomes defensive, "What do you mean?"

"You will always be alone unless you tell me *every-*

thing. I need to know so that I can feel safe. How else can I give myself completely to you? I need to know everything."

"Everything?" Jason is perplexed. He does not know where to begin, and he would have to start blabbering to make sure that there is nothing left out. He is not sure how much in his head is from The Well and what is truly his own. The more he thinks about what she is asking from him, the more he wants to scream and get out.

He turns away from her and leaves without saying a word, and decides to spend more time with Memory and Mediation. At least with them it never gets boring, and they do not seem to expect anything since they have each other.

"I have to spend more time on my own education," he tells Song. "I have a long way to go with my Greek studies."

"I can help you with that," she says, knowing that this offer would be rejected.

"No, your time is better spent with Pericles."

"Why are you treating me this way? I gave you *everything.*" Jason winces as Song pushes back. He is convinced she ruined things between them and feels justified in letting her go.

Memory and Meditation are glad to spend hours tutoring Jason, who becomes more responsive to them after his interest in Song declines. He likes the personal attention, and they find his naiveté amusing.

After some time he asks, "Am I getting any better?" He thinks he is ready for some effusive praise from his teachers.

"You are making progress. By the way, do you know why Song has locked herself in her room?" Mediation says, staring at him.

Jason looks blank. "All I know is that she has stopped tutoring Pericles."

"Did something happen, or not happen between the two of you," Memory asks slyly while he thumbs through a book. She knows, but wants to hear what Jason has to say.

"No, I just need more space. She should not stop teaching Pericles on my account."

Looking up and changing the subject, Jason says, "So many books, so many words. How does one know where to begin and end?"

"Any time is a good time to start but you will not find the end. You can only remember so much, though," Memory replies with a laugh. "I should know."

"I am overwhelmed. Years ago all this was done through effortless osmosis," Jason whines.

"Jason, those days are gone. Putting everything into memory misses the point. You have to choose what to internalize, and you only have a limited amount of time to make a choice," Memory explains.

"So who comes up with the reasons to make sure we are choosing the right books?" Jason asks naively.

"That is never easy. It takes real strength and perhaps arrogance to focus on what is important. You have to look inside for guidance," Meditation offers.

"Inside?"

"Yes, search your mind and your heart. You have to depend on yourself. Once you understand the arbitrary nature of knowledge and the number of choices to be made, you will want to pick and choose," Meditation continues.

Jason protests, "But I need to be right."

Memory laughs, "You and everyone else. Your education should guide you toward what you need to know."

Jason still sounds defeatist. "But how?"

Memory is bothered. Jason is not getting it. Her inner voice tells her that she is barking up the wrong tree. Against her better judgment she says, "Maybe Plato can help."

She advises him that he should become friendlier with Plato because he is the sage who guides knowledge mining, harvesting, and preservation. Plato has a staff of five young men who, aside from being his personal companions, assist in the collection of contemporary as well as ancient knowledge and wisdom. They strive to be familiar with as many resources as possible to facilitate the rebuilding of Greek culture.

"I shall take you to see him," she says.

Memory takes Jason to visit the former shopping mall where Plato's library is located. Jason sighs when he sees thousands of dusty books piled high on gray metal shelves. Plato's assistants shuttle up and down the corridors with carts full of books frantically organizing and cataloging the collection as if there were no tomorrow. A dozen Greek patrons peruse texts on a mezzanine that once was a food court.

"Glad to see you again. I have been expecting you," Plato says in his deep voice. "Coming to the library is not popular among fellows your age, Jason. It would appear that they would rather dally than read. Why do we not go into my private office where we can talk?"

They walk up an escalator that has long ceased to escalate and turn right into a shop that had once been a furniture store. Jason is afraid he is going to bring up The Well again.

"Have a seat." Plato jokes. "There are about twenty

casting couches to choose from. I warn you that they are a bit dusty and moldy, but nonetheless I guarantee that each one is comfy," Plato says with a wink while Memory frowns. "Or your money back."

Plato loves his own jokes and is now testing their limits with Jason.

A cloud of dust billows when Jason plops himself down. Memory, in contrast, sits down gently, liberating a single feather that gently rises to reflect the sunlight coming from a nearby window.

"Ah, so ladylike," Plato adds with a sexist edge, ogling Memory as he has since she was just a teen when he thought she would make quite a boy. As usual she steadfastly ignores him.

"So how may we enlighten your search for truth and beauty?"

"What is the purpose of your library?" Jason says bluntly.

"Ah, you get right to the point. I thought we might first chat a bit about the kind of books that intrigue you; Jason, what have you read lately?"

"The girls have been introducing me to Greek philosophers like Plato and Aristotle, and to poets like Euripides and Aeschylus."

Memory chimes in, "The Ancients said it all. Classic writings are the foundation of wisdom."

"Maybe so, but you have to build something truly

useful on the foundation that the wise Greeks laid," Plato says with a grand gesture. "Remember, *Knowledge becomes evil if the aim be not virtuous.*"

Jason is intrigued by this learned chat and sees an opportunity to score some points with the older man. "In my travels I read some 20th Century stuff in English – authors like Orwell, Bradbury, and Huxley – all about the future in the past."

"Ah, Aldus Huxley. Will we never escape our fascination with the 20th Century when things were edgy but somehow still coherent? That was before technology broke free from all human control. And you know the rest – environmental destruction, wars, and finally Cybergeddon."

"Why do you think things went so terribly wrong?" asks Jason. "Were not people grateful for having technology that produced so much stuff? Did they not want to remain vigilant to protect what they had?"

Plato looks down, "Jason, I think it has something to do with the fatal flaw in humanity, which the Ancient Greeks understood all too well."

"What is Hubris?" Memory blurts out the answer hurriedly as if she were a contestant on a vintage televised quiz show.

"How right you are, Memory," Plato says with a nod. "Arrogance and pride begat the fall. People exaggerated their own ability to have everything and more without incurring any debt of money or duty. They felt entitled to be free to pursue nothing but pleasure and they eschewed the freedom to exercise good stewardship of Planet Earth."

Plato furrows his brow. "We are trying to make sense out of the past, but in many respects that is an impossible task, like the one forced on poor Sisyphus."

"Sisyphus?"

"Yes, according to the myth, Sisyphus was punished for his trickery and deceitfulness by being forced to push a boulder up a hill. Each time he got to the top, the boulder would break loose and roll down the hill, and so Sisyphus had to start pushing the boulder up the hill all over again, only to have it roll down again. Perhaps the same goes for building our library. Every time we add to our collection and try to make sense out of it, we realize that we are no closer to the truth than before, and yet we keep on pushing that boulder up the hill by piling in more books. We have a definite purpose in mind, and it does not matter how absurd it is. We know that every traveler needs a compass as well as a destination, and books make it possible to travel where we cannot go. They are our only key to understanding the past. If the past has a future that was lost, our future may be in the past.

Jason looks perplexed, and his mind goes blank. Plato lost him when Sisyphus went up the hill.

Plato, seeing Jason blink dumbly, changes the subject. "Jason and Memory, I have a treat for you. Would you like to see my collection on Bionica?" Memory is very excited; she wants to know more about Bionica so that she can understand Jason better. Jason is less sure; he has become ashamed of his Bionican past.

Plato takes Jason to the bottom floor of the mall, the bargain basement area, to view the exhibition on Bionica. He takes them to a room with panels that are full of hand scribbles.

Plato explains, "These are the original designs for The Well database that were executed by a think-tank at Cal Tech. The purpose was to capture all kinds of knowledge for use by future generations."

"Did they foresee Cybergeddon?" Jason asks,

"There was always the fear that the entire system could collapse. People wanted redundancy. The Well was probably not the only giant database in the world, but today it is the only one we know about. The Well survived Cybergeddon because the data was transferred from hardware to Bionican peopleware."

"So who decided what went in and what went out?" Jason asks.

"Good question young man. There were gatekeepers who decided what was part of the canon. Some people talked about tension between 'two cultures' in which technology was the center of one culture, and literature and the arts the center of another culture. Of course, technology won and culture became canon fodder. People were more concerned about how fast and efficiently they could share information, and they forgot about the essence of content. All they wanted was fast, mobile access to superficial information with plenty of exciting graphics and sound. Everything else became secondary. It was so hard to keep up with a multiplicity of communication vehicles that no one thought deeply about what was important to communicate."

Plato takes Jason back to the library stacks where there is an ongoing Bionica exhibit.

Jason notices still photographs of his mother from the video images that Berk had shown him at the Mormon Temple. There are also glamorous photos of the Bead Lady. Upon seeing the Bead Lady, Jason turns white. He thinks that since these guys know everything about him, they must know about his crime. He failed to grasp her significance when he murdered her, and she is now part of his permanent history. Jason's personas, the killer and the learner, are at war within him. He starts to sweat and fidget, and is afraid that someone will call him out and seek revenge.

Plato notices Jason's preoccupation with the Bead Lady. "So you know Beadina, I take it. We have not heard from her for quite some time," he says pausing for a long time. "Although she was a bit odd, she had a reputation for her wisdom and kindness. Would you like to learn more about her?"

Reluctantly Jason nods, hoping that this would allay any suspicion of her disappearance, and Plato pops in a cartridge into the play unit. The Bead Lady appears in her garden explaining her philosophy of biodiversity - maintaining the world's variation in flora and fauna. She talks of the wisdom she has gained stringing beads.

Memory pipes in, "She was quite a lady, but not part of this world. Some call her a saint."

Jason keeps quiet. There is a long silence. Attention is riveted on what the Bead Lady has to say. The Bead Lady is in the middle of one of her lectures when a few phrases capture Jason's attention.

"Beware of those who are interested in power over others. Beware of those who speak for the entire human race. Beware of those who are incapable of laughter. Beware of those who are incapable of love. Beware of those..." Plato becomes impatient and shuts off the play unit.

"Do not worry about her. She is an idealist. The real world calls for resolving the affairs among men, not among women who believe in what beads tell her. Having been interested in what the Bead Lady was talking about, Memory knows when she is not wanted and leaves in a huff.

"Jason, now let us take our manly walk into the manly woods. Afterward, we can catch up with Aristotle who I know wants to talk to you about a project."

Plato puts his hand on Jason's shoulder, giving it a gentle squeeze, as they leave the library and follow the path for their walk in the woods, where he would like to continue to explore some possibilities.

"We are living during difficult times. Only years ago, we thought that everything was lost, but now we have a chance to rebuild."

"What is so different now?"

Plato looks away and then turns to face Jason, flushed with excitement.

"We need you to help us mine The Well so that we can fill the gaps of what we do not know. If you do, things will be different in a big way. We want you to download information from The Well so that we can develop electric energy. Technology is the key to our future, especially in the development of wealth banking and trade."

Jason recalls the Bionican tirades against greed that led to war and environmental destruction, and how those things eventually led to Cybergeddon.

"It is not that simple. I cannot just download from The Well. You have to understand I lost my access and privileges as a hacker when I left Bionica. And I cannot go to Bionica because I would be put to death. They would batter my skull in with a special hammer and then throw my dying body over a wall where I would be eaten alive by birds."

"I can see your difficulties. We certainly would not want that to happen to you. Why on earth, then, would Medea bring you here? I thought you would help us to access The Well, once you understood what is required. We still hope that you will."

Jason smiles and says, "I guess there has been a lot of mission creep. Or perhaps there were too many creeps on the mission," Jason jokes.

Plato responds in kind, "You know, all we Greeks care about is your nocturnal e-mission. So what is so special about your precious database that should exclude us?"

Jason continues in all seriousness, "When I was a hacker, I was absolutely sure that there was a possibility that The Well could be used by you, I mean us, to bring back weapons of mass destruction. Now I know otherwise, and I understand that you only need access to The Well to bring back conveniences such as electricity and banking. But, I still believe that bad things could happen despite all the good intentions. What am I supposed to believe?"

Plato responds, "I can see your dilemma. It is hard to prove that a possible danger does not exist. But, as you would expect, since I am a Greek, I happen to believe that the probability of misuse is small. I suppose there is always a possibility that someone could misuse The Well to build weapons of mass destruction, but I think you need to have faith in our institutions. We are not the Goths. We have good civilized values and we are sensible; together, with you, we can control our destiny for the greater good."

Jason is not too sure. What Plato says goes against everything that he learned when he was a hacker. Jason says in frustration, "What you do not understand is that no one person can mine The Well. It would require the cooperation of all the hackers, but they would not be willing to do this. You have to understand that they are not slaves. Furthermore, you would have to train hundreds of new people to hack The Well."

Uninterested in his objections, Plato does not listen to what Jason is saying and instead continues to press him.

"You have got to find a way to help us out. Maybe you and the other hackers could train others to mine The Well. With our slaves, we already have an army of Daytrain users, who might easily be trained to access and retrieve all the information that we need."

Jason replies, "But Daytrain alone does not make for qualified users, who must be bred to do what they do. There is no way for the Bionican hackers to train them to access The Well properly. And, frankly, this would not happen since the hackers have been taught since birth to distrust outsiders – especially the Greeks."

Plato scratches his head. "Together we have come this far, and I still think you can help us because you are well on your way to becoming one of us. For some time now, you have enjoyed the good life with us. You have eaten our foods, harvested and cooked by our slaves. You have philandered with our women, even going so far to have Song fall in love with you, and you dumped her, you cad! For all this I would think you would show your appreciation to step up to the plate to help us in any way you can. Maybe we can find a way for you to help us negotiate with Bionica for their support; maybe you can enlist the help of the G-Sport Biker Femmes. I know the Bionicans are willing because lead hacker, Digi Diva, is willing to deal with us. You know, she is friendly with Gonorrhea, but in her heart of hearts, she probably still loves you. I heard she misses you, and she likes the way we live. You could go back to her and help us."

Jason is troubled by what Plato knows and his willingness to use what he knows against him. He is shocked to learn of the re-emergence of Digi Diva as someone with connections and influence. He never trusted her. He knows that he should avoid contact her and with the Bionicans at all costs. He suspects that the Greeks are pulling a deal behind his back. Perhaps they are going to sell him out to her in exchange for access to The Well. Then the Bionicans will have revenge on his treachery, and the Greeks will have access to the Well. If only Jason had read the book Medea gave him, *The Prince*, more carefully. The problem is that even with all the time he spent with Medea, he never spent much time absorbing and applying what he read.

Plato and Jason finish their walk and return to the library where Aristotle meets them. The three go to Aristotle's lab that is part of the nearby Skunk Works located on the old Caltech campus that was ransacked by anti-technology mobs who left tons of ruined laboratory equipment piled high. Today, they remain as a painful reminder of those sad days.

The Skunk Works, on top of a steep hill, are surrounded by several rings of barbed-wire fences to prevent an attack from Greek "purists" who believe that Aristotle is up to no good. As they approach the building where Aristotle's lab is located, Jason is surprised to find several Goths thugs, hired as security guards, there to greet them.

"I see that you have noticed my Goth guards," Aristotle remarks. "I am afraid that some influential members of the Greek community do not trust me. As you know, they believe that technology is against the Greek way of life."

"What fools," Plato replies sarcastically as he and Jason follow Aristotle through a long corridor leading to Aristotle's labs.

Seated outside of Aristotle's office, Meditation looks up from her work. She greets the three men and takes them to the rear of the area where Aristotle's staff is working on a mock-up of a stand-alone power grid.

"Our vision is to develop one of these, but we need additional information about power technology, especially solar energy and batteries. Our written materials fall short of what we need."

Aristotle adds, "We are also working on radio communication that would be able to send powerful radio signals out. But, first we need some answers. Is there anyone out there to receive them? Are there others who have access to electric power? It used to be that people would send signals to outer space hoping to reach some alien beings. Today we are using similar methods to locate other groups of people on our own devastated planet."

"Power to the people," Meditation jokes.

Aristotle responds seriously. "It takes power to empower people. If you solve the power problem, you solve the people problem. First we need to focus on developing better hardware."

Jason interrupts the conversation between Plato and Aristotle. "Berk is your hardware guy. What does he have to say?"

Aristotle replies, "He is too enamored with useless equipment. Since you have already seen his outpost in Bionica, know that he has got every piece of old hardware imaginable. He is *not* a forward thinker; he is merely a collector, a hobbyist without an overall strategy." Plato groans while Aristotle blows his nose. Jason is not sure whether he wants to add to the criticism or to defend Berk.

Aristotle continues, "He just wants attention; he wants a place in history."

"What a joke," Plato laughs. "History depends on libraries. Without a system for storage and access, there is no legacy. Berk has his private collection of unordered bits of knowledge and techie stuff, but that is not worth a hill of beans."

"Ah, that is where you come in dear Plato, and you can leave the rest of us plebes to worry about the infrastructure," Aristotle says half-jokingly. Meditation has all but disappeared from the conversation. She scribbles down a few notes here and there and looks distracted.

It is no surprise that Aristotle is more favorably disposed to the man of action than the man of words. But he and Plato share one thing in common. They are both surrounded by bevies of young men, with names that are sometimes used interchangeably with their genitalia – the common Dick, the hard Peter, the willing Willie, the dodging Roger, and the enduring Jonathan. They would love to acquire Jason and to rework his name to fit in.

Jason looks around to see these men at work. "What about Berk?" Jason asks slyly.

Aristotle laughs. "Berk, the Jerk. He is a loner, not a team player. He is mainly a hardware nut who does not appreciate the importance of social systems the way I do. I admit that Berk is valuable because of his under-standing of equipment for storage and retrieval. Most of the recorded knowledge that survived Cybergeddon is only available through him. We need this Lilliputian for playback," Aristotle adds with contempt as Plato nods in agreement.

Aristotle turns his head to Jason. "We are also very interested in storing our most important current infor-mation electronically. We need something that will out-last people and paper. People die, and books can be lost or ruined."

Plato gets on his high horse. "I do not agree with you, Aristotle. Paper is not bad. Books have survived since the ancient scrolls. All that remains of electronic infor-mation is the buzz in Bionican brains and radio signals floating through space that left the planet forever ago. Storage in the cloud – bah, humbug!"

While Aristotle is talking, Jason sees in his mind's eye a strangely familiar condor circling in a brilliant blue sky. A large cloud moves to obscure the blinding white sun and the condor slips from view. Jason knows this vision and fears that his future is slipping away as well.

Jason gets defensive. "If what you are saying is true, the Bionicans are far more advanced than anyone in the world because they do not need equipment to support advanced communications. All we have to do is to keep them alive and..."

"Keep feeding them Daytrain," Aristotle completes his sentence for him. "That manna from heaven," he adds sarcastically. "You have to man up. Everybody has to serve somebody."

Jason is put off by Aristotle's cynicism. He does not want to service Aristotle.

Sensing Jason's discomfort, Plato comes to his defense. "Jason may have a point, but it is only a conceit. The Bionicans believe in knowledge for its own sake. Some of the Greeks even say they are the world's true intellectuals," Plato ventures with a devilish grin.

Aristotle, not to be outdone, inveighs, "Idiot savants may know a lot, too. But they do not know what to do with what they know or with what they have! That goes for you, too, Jason."

"Know thyself," Plato laughs out.

Jason is nervous. He believes that all this discussion – idiot savant and knowledge for the sake of knowl-edge – are simply veiled attacks on him to convince him to help the two old men get access to The Well. What he does not understand is that they want full access to something else."

"Just what do you want from me?" Jason asks.

Plato grins again, "Depends on what you have."

Jason becomes defensive. "Stop playing around. What gives?"

Plato keeps on grinning, "Show us what you can do. Then, if you can do what we need, we will let you in on *everything*."

Jason did not expect to be the butt of a joke, and does not realize that his butt is the joke. He is furious because Plato does not take him seriously.

Aristotle tries to soften things a bit, "Plato is toying with you. We would like your help because you have a lot to offer."

By now, with all this teasing, Jason is mentally off track, thinking the unthinkable. He wonders whether he should just kill both of them and thereby prevent their scheme to mine The Well and to undermine him as well. But if he were to kill the two old men, this would not be the right time because he still has to think of the future of his son, Pericles. So, he decides that the best defense is a good offense. He decides that he will control his anger and use the element of surprise to his advantage.

And so he says plainly, "You can count on me. I will help you get access to The Well." Reassured, Plato and Aristotle arrange for Jason to meet with the Praetorian Guard to finalize his induction.

CHAPTER 15
SEARCH AND DESTROY

"On behalf of the Praetorian guard, I would like to lead a preemptive strike against Bionica," Jason says, startling both Plato and Aristotle. His intention is to throw them off guard, allowing him to learn more about what their real intentions are. Jason slowly repeats the word, preemptive. Plato and Aristotle are surprised. They had expected Jason to be more protective of Bionica.

Plato sighs, "*Preemptive* is a powerful word that can lead to mischief."

Aristotle throws up his hands. "The Great Plague was preemptive, was it not?"

Plato strokes his chin casually. "The Great Plague was the endgame of technology." They are not taking Jason seriously.

Plato and Aristotle continue their effete conversation as Jason's mind roams. Did the Greeks have something to do with the Great Plague? Was it a giant reboot of civilization that got out of control? Confused, Jason says good-bye and walks back to Elysium. Upon returning to Elysium, he sees Medea, who is sitting in the garden sipping a cool drink. She invites him to join her.

Jason pauses for a moment and then says, "I cannot do it."

"What is it that you cannot do?" Medea asks with the laconic diction of a therapist.

"I do not want to be involved in what they want me to do, this technology transfer stuff. Deep down, despite what anyone says to the contrary, I still believe that there is a possibility of using The Well to develop weapons of mass destruction. I cannot rid myself of this belief."

Medea is annoyed. "I would have thought that by now you would see things for what they are and you would adjust your beliefs. Anything is possible, but I am telling you we do not have the power or the will to create weapons of mass destruction. Our population is too small. We do not need weapons of mass destruction to kill. We have our methods. As you have done with the Goths, we can do that just fine with the low technology that we have."

Jason misses the point. "Yes, but if we do a brain dump from Bionica, it is possible that people would use Bionican knowledge for evil purposes?"

Medea becomes impatient. "Do not be dense. We have our hands full already with the Goths. They have a much larger population, and they are the ones that have the potential to do some real evil. They have a lot of power already. They control the roads, and we cannot go anywhere without them. And while the Goths hate us, deep down they want what we have. We need to have some countervailing power to keep our culture, and our knowledge viable. I had hoped you would jump at the opportunity for a better life and do what sensible people do – like Plato and Aristotle; they see things for what they are."

"So what is it that *you* want from me?"

Media replies emphatically, "Forget weapons of mass destruction and work with us. We need your help to safeguard the Daytrain trade. We need to expand so that someday we will have a cadre of knowledge workers that will help us build up a new infrastructure based on what we could learn from The Well. We would like you to help us build up the Kurzweil Institute that will be devoted to managing virtual knowledge currently stored in The Well."

Jason still is not too sure what his assignment entails. He is mortally afraid of tangling with the Bionicans. He knows that they are out to kill him, and he is afraid they are already in cahoots with the G-spot Biker Femmes

Stroking his back, Medea entreats her apprehensive lover to be patient and to trust her.

"Hold on until tomorrow. You have been summoned to meet with the Hellenic Council. Wait and see what assignment they have for you. I think you are going to like it. They have crafted it especially for you."

Next day Jason appears before the Hellenic Council. Medea gives the nod to Plato, who then addresses Jason.

"Jason, Medea has informed us about your crusades against the Christians when you led the Goths, and we want you to lead an expedition, not against the Bionicans, but against the Christians. These bible thumpers have successfully infiltrated the Goths since your departure. These homophobic Christian terrorists are gaining influence among the Goths. They are distributing old Bibles that were found in an abandoned warehouse. Their ministers are teaching the Goths how to read the Bible and to hate us because of our so-called heathen lifestyle.

Jason is flattered. They are taking his ideas seriously and have deferred their plan to penetrate the firewall of The Well. Perhaps he can trust them after all. In the meantime, he can breathe easier now. And he will not have to kill the old men, at least not yet.

"What is so dangerous about these particular bible thumpers? Do they have weapons? When I led the Goths, it was easy to kill them as they all yearn to become martyrs."

Plato steps forward and says with his deep voice, "They may say they are peaceful. But, you of all people should know. Because they are true believers, they would want to see the return of weapons of mass destruction to bring on what they call the Second Coming. They are the ones who caused Cybergeddon because they did not believe in the future of technology without their God and their Savior. Remember Little Eddie? You bashed his head in because he was causing trouble for you Bionicans by preaching the gospel of *Genesis*. As a Bionican you were right to fear the Christians, because they are the ones who would use weapons of mass destruction."

Jason is shocked that Plato knows about Little Eddie and wonders if there is anything he does not know. One of the hackers must have been a spy for the Greeks. Maybe Jimmy the Greek, or perhaps, after what he has heard about Digi Diva, it is she. He starts to sweat and uses Medea's calming herbs as a balm to his mounting anxiety. Plato puts his hand on Jason's shoulder and then moves it to his thigh, with the customary squeeze that the old Greek men use with pliable young men. He speaks to him like the father he never had, "Praetorian son, these Christians are out to kill our Daytrain trade. Your job is to neutralize them. No one must find out that it is we doing the killing." A tear of joy falls from Jason's eye. He has never before been called son.

Aristotle quotes his namesake, *"We make war that we may live in peace."*

The Council authorizes the mission and assigns a

deaf-mute warrior, Tasman, to help Jason carry out the slaughter of the Christian proselytizers. The two desperados take off with a string of pack mules burdened with provisions and plenty of Daytrain to trade for whatever they can get that will advance their nefarious Christian killing purpose.

This mission is right up Jason's alley and returns him to a level of comfort that he can live with. In his heart, he is proud of being a paladin for a just cause; he is a born killer who relishes this chance to make his mark. He sets aside his earlier thoughts and fears of the Greeks and leaves all the scheming to his handlers – Medea, Plato, and Aristotle. For now, he will do as ordered.

Tasman prepares a hot bath and cuts off branches of a birch sapling to prepare Jason to kill the Christians. After Jason emerges from a hot bath, Tasman hands Jason a clump of branches for self-flagellation that will steel him for his mission.

"It is good to feel like a real man again," Jason says to himself after his round of self-flagellation. "All those nights with the sisters made me soft."

Going on this mission requires yet another name change, back to his Goth moniker. Jason knows the drill;

he says to himself three times, "I am not Jason. I am Siegfried, I am Siegfried, I am Siegfried." In a trice, he feels like his old Siegfried self again, able to take advantage of his Siegfried thoughts and feelings. Things are simple again. No more head-troubling discussions, no more playing with words. He is away from lofty thoughts and back in action at last. Already he can feel his muscles swell and the stubble on his chin start to roughen.

Siegfried and Tasman depart for The Valley. It does not take long to find the Christians. The praying and the ringing bells are a dead giveaway. Siegfried and Tasman approach the Christian encampment where several cabins encircle a small Quonset hut with a wooden cross on top. As they approach the make-do church, they hear male voices singing, "Amazing grace, how sweet the sound."

The singing stops and a man comes out to greet them. "Hello, I am Simon. What brings you here, stranger?" Simon is a short old man with a long matted beard, his clothing in tatters.

"We are searching for something," Siegfried says, looking at Tasman, who smirks back. "My friend here cannot speak or hear, but he obeys very well."

"You have come to the right place. Obedience is a virtue. May peace be with you." Paul, Simon's co-religionist, joins the group. "Welcome brothers; as ye shall seek, so ye shall find." Paul is taller than Simon and better dressed in his black cassock and ruff.

"We have something for you," Simon says. They go inside where Bibles are stacked to the ceiling.

 "God led us to a warehouse not far from here where we found bibles containing his Word waiting to be spread to all who seek peace."

"Straight from heaven, the Good Book," Paul exclaims, "Please take two as our gift." Smiling with ill intent, Siegfried and Tasman take the books from Paul.

"We have much to do in the name of the Lord," says Simon, "We are on a mission to bring Jesus to the Barbarian heart. We will summon their guardian angels to help them give up Daytrain and alcohol. The weakest among them is welcome to come to Jesus and join the brotherhood of the apostles."

"And sisterhood," Paul adds.

"Yes … to be sure, the sisterhood – all are worthy to greet the coming of the Lord."

Siegfried lies, "We too are in need of spiritual guidance. I know how to read so I can be of service."

Paul is very excited to recruit co-religionists who know how to read. "Come right in and be one with us."

Paul and Simon prepare a meal, and the four men break bread.

Paul explains, "As you can see, we have thousands of copies of the Good Book. Our sacred duty is to teach the Goths to read so that they can know the Word. We want to rid the world of Daytrain and spread the good news of

Christ instead."

Jason and Tasman follow Paul and Simon to the warehouse where there are still thousands of brand-new, never-used Bibles enmeshed in cobwebs.

"This is only one of the warehouses left behind by the Good Shepherd Movement. The mobs slaughtered our people. They accused them of spreading the virus that caused the Great Plague. There have been many Christian martyrs since."

Looking around suspiciously, Siegfried slyly asks, "Where are the people that you have converted so far?"

Paul and Simon beckon Siegfried and Tasman to follow them. After hiking for fifteen minutes, they come upon an encampment by a river. There are several hundred men, women, and children in the middle of a prayer meeting reading aloud from their Bibles. *"Yea, though I walk through the valley of the shadow of death."*

To Siegfried this is the height of subversion. When he was a hacker, it was his duty to annihilate anyone aiding and abetting Christianity. And on his crusades as a Goth he would have ordered all his men to kill these people. Oblivious to what Siegfried is thinking, Paul and Simon want to show off their flock to their distinguished visitors.

"They are good people, getting ready for a better world. Feel free to mingle and get to know them. You, too, may find a deep and lasting peace here," Paul says.

One of the starry-eyed male religionists approaches

Siegfried.

"When you see all things, you will know that He is near." The man's face is transfixed in a vacant but rapturous expression of awe.

Siegfried suddenly starts to hear voices from all directions. He feels every eye in the camp looking at him. A nasty twang catches his ear.

"We know who you are. You are going nowhere. Your place is with us, Praise the Lord," says an elderly man with an eye patch.

"It is not too late to save your soul," says a toothless woman.

"May the Lord forgive your sins," the crowd calls together at him.

Siegfried has heard such ejaculations before, especially the latter, usually right before cutting the person in half with his sword, but never with such intensity. The crowd slowly approaches him with hands extended to express friendship.

"We welcome you to our new community of the faithful," they chant.

Then they raise their voices in joyous song. The more Siegfried listens, the greater is his pain and revulsion. Hacker flashbacks take him to the times he used the hacker hammer to smash in the heads of Jesus freaks to restore order and harmony to The Well.

Hearing the crowd chant, Siegfried sees his duty in

a clear light. No longer obsessed with weapons of mass destruction, he now sinks his teeth into another mission – eliminating the religious contagion that he believes threatens the world again. Contrary to what he might have heard from the Greek elders, it was religious fanaticism that was the cause of the Great Plague, and his duty, as he now understands it, is to make the world safe for rationality. As a killer, his only destiny, his quest, is to kill the Christians again and again when called upon.

"Are you ready to accept Christ?" Paul asks Siegfried. Siegfried puts on a smile and says, "We have seen the way, the truth and the light. We will return with offerings to celebrate our rebirth," Siegfried says, confident in the newly learned powers of deceit that he got from the Greeks.

Simon looks the other way. He realizes what is in store for him.

"I know what is in your heart."

Thinking of his black heart, Siegfried says nothing.

Siegfried and Tasman then leave the encampment and return two days later with Charlie Company, a group of handpicked Goth mercenaries, to complete this search and destroy mission.

"I am going ahead to scout out the situation. Wait for me here until I return."

Siegfried climbs up the slope, looks back and then continues towards a wooded area of Eucalyptus trees where he hears trickles of water. Siegfried recognizes Simon standing by a stream praying. His lips barely move as his eyes turn upward.

As Siegfried approaches him, Simon abruptly stops his prayers and turns around to face Siegfried, stooping under the weight of a large metal cross strapped to his back.

"Are you looking for martyrdom?" Siegfried asks, recalling martyrs he met in his old hacker job. He is happy to be back facilitating Christian sacrifice.

"No, I just want to keep The Word alive." Simon looks up. "You have come back. I know why you are here, but it is too late."

"Too late for what?" Siegfried asks impatiently.

"Too late to save you."

"To save me? Save me from what? Maybe you are the one who needs to be saved," Siegfried responds angrily as his nausea index rises.

"You are on the path of wickedness. Your unrelenting thoughts will lead to your destruction. Your evil actions will doom you forever."

"I am on a noble crusade," Siegfried protests.

"Have you no shame? You are a sinner unaware of his guilt."

"What have I done?" Siegfried asks.

"You have killed. You will suffer everlasting shame unless…"

"And unless I do what?"

"Unless you let Him absolve you from your sins."

Simon's words pierce him with fear and loathing, and shame, especially the capital "H" with which Simon refers to his savior.

"There is only one way, young man," the old man says gently. "All you need to do is follow *Him*. He is the path to truth and light."

Simon moves towards Siegfried and touches his back. Siegfried wants to slash the old man down with his sword, but instead he stiffens. The unexpected warmth of the old man's hand penetrates his body, but his gentle touch only makes him feel sicker as his murderous nausea floods him.

All Siegfried can do is squirm. Simon's gentle words have a corrosive effect on him. The more the old man speaks, the more agitated Siegfried feels. "I am warning you. Stop spamming me... I promise I will kill you if you do not stop," Siegfried pleads.

Siegfried knows that he has to stop this zealot and all proselytizing zealots like him that have ravaged the earth with their righteous bigotry.

Siegfried's nausea creeps up from his stomach to his throat and he starts to heave as the old man recites from the First Epistle of Peter, 1:24: *"All flesh is grass, and all the glory of man as the flower of grass. The grass withered, and the flower thereof falleth away."*

A murderous impulse rushes from Siegfried's stomach to his brain. He recalls killing Little Eddie when he refused to stop quoting Old Testament scripture. Now he has to deal with the New Testament.

"Shut up! Shut up!" Siegfried yells at the old man who continues to preach the Gospel.

Siegfried recalls all the evil wiles of evangelistic religion. The evangelists are the ones who longed for Armageddon. They are the ones who preached salvation in the afterlife while despoiling the environment, destroying the forests and poisoning the waters. They are the ones who preached about heaven when they should have talked about salvation for the earth. They are the ones who developed weapons of mass destruction and rained death down from the sky on anyone who did not believe in their *Him*. They are the one who brought on the Great Plague. They are the ones who crashed the system, sending fundamentalist hordes to wreak havoc by sabotaging technology.

"What can I do to save you, young man?" Simon looks up with a pained smile as he continues to quote scripture. Siegfried's hacker instincts take over, and with a renewed sense of purpose, he does what he has to do. Moving swiftly, he channels his former self, Condor. He grabs Simon's beard and pulls him down on his knees. With the old man in his grip, he tears the cross from his neck, rips off his clothing and empties his pack, tossing out the contents on the ground – a shroud, a loaf of bread, and a bottle of wine. The dazed old preacher man is on his knees and looks to heaven one last time as Siegfried forces him to the ground and cruelly hacks him to death with the metal cross.

The martyred minion of Jesus speaks his barely audible parting words. "Father, forgive him; for he knows not what he does." Siegfried drags the old man's body into a nearby ditch, tidies himself up from his murdering and walks down the stream to wash off the old man's blood. As he rinses his hands in the stream, he sees the reflection of his face distorted in the red eddies.

As he looks at himself in the water, Siegfried eats the old man's bread and takes a swig from the bottle, spilling the blood red wine across the Lacryma Christi label; and then, without thinking why, he makes the sign of the cross across his chest and steps into the waters. He submerges himself until he feels sufficiently absolved to go on. He returns to his men, who have been waiting for him to execute the next phase of the operation.

After setting up a machine gun nest on a promontory overlooking the campgrounds, Siegfried gives Tasman the high-five sign – the order to kill. Charlie Company sets the camp on fire early in the morning just as people are rising from their sleep. Tasman leads Charlie Company into the campgrounds to "pacify" the Christian followers while Siegfried remains back to mow down those trying to escape.

"Take this, you righteous bastards," he cries out in

pangs of pleasure that comes with the rattling of a successful machine-gun killing that is so easy because of his physical removal from the actual violence. He so impressed with the results that he kisses the barrel of the machine gun, which is so hot that it burns his puckered lips in one of the most passionate acts of affection he has ever experienced. That night, exhausted from ending so many lives, he dreams about his victims, dancing and singing for more, happy that finally someone has put them out of their misery.

Next day, Siegfried inspects the carnage and coldly calculates the body count. The bodies include many women and children. Among them he finds the corpse of Paul, clutching a crucifix with both hands.

"Semper Fi," mumbles Siegfried, "Nothing worth having comes without sacrifice." Siegfried is anxious to return to the Greeks, expecting to be rewarded for his mission accomplished, but he has to take a long circuitous route to avoid being spotted by the Goth sentries that patrol the border regions. As he approaches the edge of Macedonia, he repeats his Greek name three times as he had done before, "I am not Siegfried. I am Jason, I am Jason, I am Jason." Tasman makes funny noises as if he too were changing his password. The password change makes Jason hunger for the Greek way of life.

Jason and Tasman stop by Elysium to see Medea before appearing before the Hellenic Council to give a report of the mission. Medea is not at Elysium. "She is with the Goths," Xantippe explains.

Memory, Meditation, and Song are off in a corner of the parlor room, very quiet. There is a wall of silence. Jason wants to resume things where he left off. He had been looking forward to further "explorations" with them. He is eager to justify his actions through philosophy. But instead, they confront him.

"Is it true about your mission? We have heard terrible things." Jason did not expect Meditation to know.

"It is true that I have been on a mission to the Goths authorized by the Hellenic Council. I have done my duty; I cannot say anything more. This mission is secret."

"We already know about it. You killed innocent people, and that is wrong," Song blurts out.

"How did you find out about my mission? Who told you?"

"I overheard Aristotle at the Skunk Works, talking about it to Plato," Meditation says.

"And what did they say?"

Meditation responds, "They said they were not sure it was a good idea."

Song is upset and starts to cry as Jason defends himself.

"I did my duty as I was told. It was *their* idea. We cannot let the contagion of religiosity spread. Medea will back me up on this."

Xantippe enters the parlor room and glares at Jason, "If you must know, Medea is off to the Goths to see if she can straighten out the mess you have created. Thor is very angry and wants you dead."

Song approaches him in tears. "Is there anything we tried to teach you that sank in?" she says with a mixture of anger and hurt. "You are nothing but a wanton, cold-blooded killer, and to think that I fell in love with you and believed that you would one day become a self-actualized person."

"All I can say is that I have been true to my duty. I stuck to my guns. I did it to defend your way of life."

"Not in my name!" cries Song.

Meditation gives Jason a look of reproach. "What *are* you talking about? Education was wasted on you. The hope was that you would learn to think for yourself and help us salvage what is needed from Bionica. Education is what allows you to act on principle and to disobey orders that are morally wrong."

Memory also confronts Jason with harsh words, "What made you believe we would go along with you and your killing?"

Jason responds angrily, "You are the beneficiaries of the system. What right do you have to question the very foundation of what sustains you? Look around you, all this wealth, all this privilege. Did it ever occur to you that the good things in your life come at a price?"

Meditation pauses before responding. "Do not think that we are that naïve. Of course, we know our good fortune is related to the misfortune of others," she says waving at her slaves. "It is our burden to be reminded of this every day."

One of the house slaves brings in a bowl of fruit and offers it to Jason as Meditation looks on.

"What would this bowl of fruit have to do with killing Christians?" Mediation asks sarcastically.

"Terrorists," Jason corrects her. "From now on we will call them terrorists."

"Why have you chosen such a violent path?" Song pleads.

"I had no choice. I did not choose my path. I was ordered to do this by the Hellenic Council," Jason responds.

"You did not have to follow the order; you did not have to take your assignment. They were just testing you. They wanted you to do what you did to prove you wanted it. They took advantage of you. You should have rejected the order. You failed their test."

After a long silence, Jason says in his defense, "I did my duty. If the religionists are allowed to preach what they want, it will end the Greek way of life."

Memory takes a deep breath and stares Jason down. "How do you presume to know what will happen to *our* way of life? Are you psychic? Do the beads tell you the future?

Song comes forward wiping her tears and says, "People who kill other people without remorse are monsters. You are a monster."

"I *did* feel bad when I killed the old man by the river, especially after I ate his only bread and wine. What was his name? Oh yes, Simon, I almost forgot. But a man has to do what he has to do. Do not condemn me for being honest."

"We are not condemning you for being honest. We are condemning you for killing innocent people. I am so ashamed of having been with you. I am ashamed of having exposed myself to you. I am ashamed of having a killer inside me in the name of pleasure. What kind of pleasure is this? I cannot go on," Song wails in despair.

Memory and Meditation comfort their sister. "We both slept with him as well. You are not alone in that. We all share your shame."

Jason storms out of the house with Tasman in tow on his way to the Hellenic Council to give his report. Regardless of what the sisters have said, Jason still expects the Council to look favorably upon what he has accomplished during his recent mission.

Plato opens up the proceedings. "I understand that you have created quite a mess."

Jason steps forward. "Sir, I followed instructions; my mission was to root out religionists."

Plato looks out of the window. "We wanted you to find a conspiracy, but not to commit willy-nilly genocide. You went too far by entrapping potential religionists. You killed women and children, and how could you, *a father!*"

Jason is close to shouting. "This was a necessary pre-emptive strike to prevent the spread of religions, anti-rationalist contagion, Sir."

Aristotle sighs, "And now the Goths suspect that we are behind this. You of all people should know that the Goths believe that summary executions are unsporting."

Jason responds with sarcasm, "Except when it comes to bad poetry. Goth life is cheap. Do not pretend to care about the Goths or pretend you did not set me up."

Medea rushes in to give her report, just back from her shuttle diplomacy with the Goths. "The Goths are very angry. Jason killed the relatives of some of the tribal chiefs in the leadership. I denied our involvement and instead blamed the Bionicans who are dead set against organized religion. I explained to them that the Greeks would never kill those who advocate reading. I think they bought this explanation."

Aristotle asks, "So they do not suspect that Jason is behind the killings?"

"Jason's name never came up. But, they said that one of the killers looked like Siegfried. Thor and Mad Moxie know, of course, about Jason and his former self as Siegfried, but they will not let on because they were in on Jason's coming here. Plus some of the deaths are beneficial to Thor."

Aristotle pauses and then says, "Still, this is a messy situation, but we cannot allow Thor's power to weaken."

"I will work with Thor to handle this," Medea says confidently.

She then wipes her face and looks at Jason. "I am afraid there is a price to pay, even if you think what you did was right."

"But I did what you wanted me to do," Jason protests.

"We are going to have to stop your missions. It is better that you lay low. I promised Thor that you would."

"Are we better off with religionists dead?" Aristotle asks Medea.

Medea shrugs her shoulder. "There is no real way of stopping people who want to spread the Word. Jason just slowed them down and created more martyrs in the process."

"Then what should we do next?" Plato asks.

Aristotle says quietly, "I will arrange for a large shipment of goods to buy them off."

Just as the group warms up to Aristotle's idea, a courier brings the news of Song's suicide.

Jason acts as if he is devastated by the news. "Why did she do it? Am I to blame?"

Medea puts her hand on Jason's shoulder – a perfunctory gesture to comfort him. "Suicide is a sign of weakness. Song should have understood what you were all about. Education was wasted on her as well. She remained too emotional."

Jason does not like this mean assessment and takes cold comfort in what Medea has to say. Who knows? Had he married Song, he might have made her happy, or maybe he might have killed her for being too intrusive. He leaves the house for an all-night walk in the fields. The voices in his head intensify.

At first he hears his mother's voice. "I created you from my last ovum and you will be forever mine. Be prepared for your destiny," she whispers.

Then all he can hear is a woman's sobbing, first one, then several, and then hundreds of sobbing voices. He lies down to sleep under a tree to drown out what he hears and returns to his reoccurring nightmare about Cybergeddon in which this time the three young women – Memory, Mediation, and Song – look at his naked form with scorn.

CHAPTER 16
PERICLES

Medea urges Jason to stay with her at Elysium to allow the fallout from his ill-fated mission to blow over.

"This is a great opportunity for you to immerse yourself in studies again, to become a true man of letters. You can no longer be involved in covert actions. You are safe so long as you stay here."

"But I was not wrong. I did what had to be done."

"Don't worry, things will blow over. You can be of real help to us, but not as a warrior. You must become a scholar. You must immerse yourself in studies again. Also, you need to attend to the education of your son. Do you even remember his name? Now that the sisters have abandoned you, Xantippe will help you with him. Meanwhile, I have to go back to Thor and continue my work with him and his disgusting Goths."

Again Jason immerses himself in the vast library at Elysium. He reads further into the tomes of the ancients, memorizing passages that Medea thinks will be useful later on, though none of her previous suggestions were helpful in any way. Thus far, all he has to show for his studies is a dead Song. Still Medea said that his skills would help her work with Thor to bring formal education to the Goths. Perhaps she plans for him to be a teacher to the Goths. She also told him that his mastery of Greek culture would rebuild his trust with the Greek leadership; they still want his help to harvest information from The Well.

As Jason studies away, Medea is gone from Elysium much of the time, spending most of her time at the Sky House as Thor's wife – the true power behind his throne. While away, she attends many functions with Thor as his beard, thereby giving continuous cover for his clandestine homosexual relationship with Mad Moxie. She is also indispensable as a strategist in handling the Daytrain trade. Medea's popularity with all of the Goths increases as the Goth standard of living rises thanks to her solid connections with the Greeks. Medea delivers very good trading terms to her subjects.

"I missed you, Jason," Medea says upon her return with mock affection. Her life with Thor has been largely all work and no play.

"You should see the other side of Mad Moxie. Thor is penetrating him on the education front."

"I know. I know. With you, education is everything."

"Well, not *everything*." She says as she entices Jason to the boudoir where Medea does what she likes to do best, cavorting while polishing up Jason on the finer points of rhetoric. As they make love, Medea commands Jason with Greek words, like piyeno (go), ne (yes), ohi (no), as well as with an established set of coos and grunts to provide positive and negative reinforcement. This time she utters exi (six) and enea (nine) – her favorite numbers, ending with a definite erhome (come); Jason executes with precision but without finesses, unable to savor the moment. Medea likes it best when Jason is stoking like a locomotive with her at the helm, but despite all his aggressiveness as a killer, he has settled into lovemaking with silent passivity rooted in obedience to Medea. Medea thinks she should feel lucky to have this arrangement, but the perfunctory nature of it leaves a lot to be desired.

"Jason, do you not know that getting there is half the fun? Why do you not stop and smell the roses?" Jason brushes off Medea's question by saying nothing. He is perfectly content to be free from Gonorrhea's 21 Marital Principles.

Next morning, Xantippe, leading the ten-year-old Pericles by the hand, joins Medea and Jason for breakfast. Pericles sits opposite to his father, who is unable to engage the boy in small talk since he is too embarrassed to reveal that he has momentarily forgotten the boy's name. "Ah, here is Pericles," Medea says coming to the rescue. She then fills the silence at the table by talking about her work with the Goths and how she believes her marriage of convenience to Thor will lead to everlasting peace and prosperity for both people.

After breakfast, Xantippe talks to Medea in confidence about Pericles. Medea already knows that Xantippe is struggling with Pericles' education and that Jason has been largely unavailable. Although he is no longer away on killer missions, Jason now spends his available time immersed in books and has left the education of his son to others. Song's death and the departure of Memory and Meditation left a gaping hole in the school program. With much regret, Medea closes the school and focuses on Pericles and his education.

"He still misses Song and asks for her," Xantippe explains, "I do not think the boy is quite right."

Pericles' mind wanders a lot. All he wants to do is to hear the slaves sing the latest selections from the D-train hit parade while they pamper him without wallowing in the sadness of their servitude. They know that Pericles witnessed Jason's rape of women slaves at Elysium. When in their presence, he averts his eyes ashamed of his father's brutality.

As expected, Medea has the answer. "It is time for a change. We need to find another school for Pericles now that the girls are no longer here to take care of him. He needs extra attention, and we need to find him a place where he can learn to study with students his own age."

Xantippe and Medea catch up with Jason, who is in the library thumbing through books.

Medea announces, "It is time for Pericles to go to school."

"Pericles to school?" Jason is not sure at first what to think, but then he likes the idea; that means even more time away from his son to lose himself in the Elysium library in pursuit of knowledge without distractions.

After the servants fetch Pericles, Jason scrutinizes him and says, "Pericles, I think it is time for you to become a man." Hiding his tears at the thought of being sent away, Pericles turns away and rushes out of the room to go outside and play with the slave children, leaving the adults to talk about Pericles' schooling.

Jason and Medea enroll Pericles in The Acropolis, a macho, rough and tumble, military-style boarding school in Polis. Girls were only recently accepted to this traditionally all-boys school to expose the fine young Greek specimens to the opposite sex. Medea was responsible for the change, insisting that a coed environment might cut down on homosexuality and the declining birthrate among the Greek elite. It had become clear that many of the young scholars decided never to leave their beloved school partners. They never graduated to hetero relations with women as their elders had hoped. Like

Medea, everyone in Polis is open to gay love as part of a person's life, but most agreed that the Greeks need to encourage heterosexuality early on to promote marriage and procreation.

Medea and Jason visit Pericles at The Acropolis during the short periods she is back at Elysium. They take the boy for walks to show him the new construction at the Polis. The dark workers in the chain gang fascinate Pericles.

Pericles says to Medea, "I like the music the slaves sing. I wish I could study them at my school."

Medea's face becomes stern.

"It is better for you to concentrate on your real education. But if you are already doing that, maybe you could use their songs as your poetry muse. It will come in handy when your time comes to be with the Goths. They love good poetry, and they kill for bad poetry."

Jason sneers inaudibly, "Yes, they love poetry. It is to die for."

Pericles shows off what he is learning, citing from memory in Greek the opening passage from Plato's dialogue, Apology, which presents the defense of Socrates against the charges of "corrupting" the young,

"Very good," Jason says, wondering why Pericles has chosen this particular text. Maybe it will turn out that his son is a homosexual as well.

"Perhaps you might take a close look at *The Clouds* by Aristophanes to learn more about the other side of the ancient Socrates. By the way, you should not neglect athletics. Remember, the Greeks were fierce warriors." Jason counsels his lad.

"But, force has to be tempered by wisdom. You are better off cultivating your metis than your *macho*," Medea says with irony. This comment is not lost on Jason, who is fully aware that Medea disapproved of his thoughtless *macho* handling of his killing mission. It exhausts him to think about how else he could have completed the mission. Sometimes these Greeks are insufferable, Jason thinks to himself.

For a while, Pericles conforms to the school's routine, excelling in Greek studies and the arts. Although he continues to develop a keen interest in music, his mastery of music performance lags behind the other children. Soon. Pericles has become a teenager – quiet and secretive.

Medea again returns to Elysium to spend time with Jason and to visit Pericles at school. But this time there are problems. Xantippe, who has continued to take care of Pericles' upbringing, confronts Jason and Medea. "Pericles is no longer doing well with his studies. He refuses to comply with school rules. He is not mixing in with the other children."

Jason, ever the absent father, never took much of an interest in his young son before he reached the age when he could become a soldier of sorts. Now with Pericles at boarding school, no one can keep an eye on his education.

Medea counsels Jason, "You have to become more involved in your son's education. I tried to fill in, but I am so taken up with secretly running the Goths from behind their King. I hate to be pushy, but I have told you time and time again, Pericles needs his father. He needs a man to teach him how to be a man. He is *your* son, remember that."

"All right, all right, I will teach him. Let me see what is going on with him and then I will have a father-son talk with him."

Jason sets out on a visit to The Acropolis. Upon his arrival, an older woman greets him. She is Aedesia, a striking person who retains the bearing and dignity of one who has been respected and admired all her life. Two younger men, Ammonius and Heliodorus, assist Aedesia. They bear a strong resemblance to Aedesia but seem overshadowed by her, perhaps they are her sons, Jason wonders.

"Your son Pericles is a very bright fellow, but he has been distracted lately, as if he is in a fog. Is there anything happening in his life that we should know about?"

Jason pauses and then says to Aedesia, "Song was Pericles' favorite teacher. As you know, she killed herself, and Pericles has never quite been the same again. I think that perhaps she was prematurely teaching him about the art of love, and without her he has been adrift all these years."

Ammonius and Heliodorus weigh in on this joint teacher-parent confab to add a lighter note.

"Your son seems to love music, but I am afraid he cannot carry a tune," Ammonius says smiling. Heliodorus quickly adds, "He often dances even when there is no music. Following the beat of a different drummer, I guess."

Jason next gets to observe the interactions among the students in Pericles' classes and notices that his son never plays rough games with the other boys. Instead of physical sparring, he prefers playing Dungeons and Dragons with Sergio and Julio, who are the brightest and most talented kids in class. From behind a secret hole in the wall, Jason keeps on watching and listening in as the boys play. Julio mentions D-train a lot, which elicits giggles from Sergio and Pericles.

Jason suspects that his son and the other two boys are experimenting with Daytrain and decides to investigate. He confronts Ammonius and Heliodorus, who are somehow taken aback by Jason's aggressive tone of voice.

"Are any of your students involved in Daytrain?"

"Not to our knowledge," Ammonius answers defensively.

Jason takes Pericles aside, engaging him in small talk. He notices that he is sporting a new nose ring. When he pulls the boy by his collar, an animated tattoo is revealed right above his clavicle, very much like Jason's tattoo from his Condor days as a Bionican. The tattoo is a revolving list of sayings from Socrates, such as, *Know thyself, All I know is that I know nothing,* and, *The unexamined life is not worth living.* Apparently, Pericles' tattoos are on a familiar Greek frequency.

Jason is shocked to see how much his son has inherited from him and wonders what he may have inherited from his long-dead airhead wife, Tara. One thing for sure is that Pericles has been a clothes horse, who had been driving the staff at Elysium crazy with his demand for freshly-pressed clothing several times a day when he was at home. He might have learned this from Song, who also insisted having freshly-pressed clothing all day long. Now that he is at boarding school, Pericles does not get to be a wardrobe hound. "I wonder what he is into now," Jason mumbles to himself.

Jason puts his arm around the boy and lectures him about the importance of becoming a man so that someday he can become a leader whom people will admire and respect. "Like father, like son," Jason smiles to himself as he leaves.

A week after his visit to the hallowed Acropolis School, Jason goes to the polis to meet with Medea at the Palace of Classic Culture regarding plans to restore his standing in the community. But before arriving there, he notices a group of seven boys loitering in an ally, including Julio, Sergio, and Pericles. They are meeting with Medea's pusher, Pharmakia, whose customers now appears to include Greek youths along with the slaveholders, who need a constant supply of Daytrain to pacify their slaves. Jason wonders if Queen Medea knows about this, or worst still, whether it is another part of her grand and devious scheme to unify the Goths and the Greeks by sacrificing Pericles to the great cause. Still, he passes by and thinks more about his ties to Pharmakia that could come to haunt him.

Jason is afraid that Pharmakia will let Gonorrhea and the Biker Femmes know his whereabouts, now that his cover is blown because of his Christian killer expedition. He knows there is a price on his head and so when he gets a moment alone with his son he urges Pericles to stay away from Pharmakia. Pericles just stares at him in response.

Jason considers killing Pharmakia to avoid the possibility of having his identity and location compromised, but decides against it because that would torpedo his standing among the Greeks. After all, Daytrain is the lifeline of Polis; without D-train the slaves would certainly revolt, and he also knows from Medea that Pharmakia is related to Aristotle. That should cover him.

Although he worries about his son's Daytrain use, he is mostly preoccupied with his problems caused by his ill-conceived eradication of the Goth Christians. Medea said she was working on a plan to enable Jason to recover from this bloody blunder. He knows that the plan will involve another huge social event to bring together the Greeks and the Goths because the only thing these groups ever do to solve things is to party.

Sure enough, Medea goes ahead with the party plans. In this year of strife, the party location will be the very lovely Galleria of Glendale, near the border between the Goth lands and the two Polis centers in Pasadena and Chatsworth. Jason is not in a party mood. The nagging feeling that he was set up to fail in the much-reviled Christian Containment Caper is hard for Jason to put aside. He even looks at Medea with a jaundiced eye though he knows that he is not done with her yet, nor is she done with him.

CHAPTER 17
XTREME DIVERSIONS

Time quickly closes in on the Greeks-Goths Agon – a fete to divert attention from their differences. Medea speaks to the Hellenic Council with a sense of urgency.

Medea tells Jason, "The Goths are still very upset because of our covert operations, and they still distrust us. Thor tells me that he is unable to contain the anger of his warriors. We need to do something dramatic at this shindig to get things back on track; otherwise, there could be an all-out war that will destroy us and them, too. First, we will hold the festival at our expense. Second, we will stage a rousing joust to clear the air between the Goths and the Greeks."

Aristotle checks the old sound system at the Glendale at Galleria. Slave crews build a seating area for dignitaries around a raised platform for the main events that will include juggling acts, acrobatic, and a rousing performance by Gonorrhea and the G=Spot Biker Femmes.

And so the games begin. After the customary fanfare, each side, Goth and Greek, enter in a separate procession. Plato and Aristotle, followed by the Hellenic Council and the Praetorian Guard, lead the Greek contingent. Jason is among the Guards, standing tall, waves to the women, both Goth and Greek, on the sidelines. Every time the Guards move, the women clap vigorously in appreciation. Medea throws him a kiss. Jason likes all the attention.

Thor and Mad Moxie, accompanied by their two black labs, lead the Goths warriors whose rough-hewn bodies are swathed in spiked leather, rangy fur, and puffs of wool. Each carries a spear that is adorned with feathers and odd favors and trinkets given to them by their women. Some have wild boars painted on their cloaks; some carry likenesses of the great, bearded forest deity – the Green Man. The sweet, pungent smell of burned Daytrain hangs heavy in the air.

Gonorrhea and the G-Spot Biker Femmes roar in on motorcycles, bringing young scrubbed male passengers, destined for the arms of Greek women eagerly awaiting them. The young men smile like prom queens and recede into the background, holding torches to illuminate the Biker Femmes as they settle into position to begin their act. The Femmes start with the routine nunchuck twirling and then proceeds with a rousing can-can while Gonorrhea stands in front of them, bursting into a rapid-fire rap as the crowd, besotted with mead, cheers them on.

We twirl our curls

We hurl our pearls

We are the G-spot girls

We pomp

We stomp

We chomp .

Get back, get back

We are the leader of the pack

We are the G-Spot Biker Femmes.

Gonorrhea finishes her rap and catches her breath to introduce the next signature act – the Goth destruction derby that ends when only one car of the original many remains running. The Greeks follow up with a decorous demonstration of archery to the sounds of bugles, followed by a line-up of "Greek Gods" armed with the *xiphos* – double-edged swords that they brandish with a safe sort of gusto. The Greek men finish their act with a javelin contest judged by Gonorrhea, who puts on quite a show strutting about on her shiny peg leg as she taps the shoulders of the winners. She yells out to the audience, "Let's have a big whoop for these tomboys." And everyone laughs as thoughts turn to food.

The mead and wine break comes on the heels of the first two events. The young women and men in the crowd vie for attention and notoriety through preening, drinking, and raucous behavior. Plato and Aristotle meet up with Mad Moxie and Thor at a wine tasting table where their two black labs eagerly await for the steady supply of morsels that come their way.

"Here is to all of us," says Moxie as he and Thor raise their goblets in a toast to the old Greek men.

"Cheers!" exclaim Plato and Aristotle, as they raise their fine wine glasses, "Here is to all of us. May we all prosper!"

"Here is to diversification," Moxie shouts out.

"Diversity," Plato quietly corrects him.

"Perversity," Gonorrhea corrects Plato. "We Goths fight to the finish while you guys eat our spinach."

"May our differences result in common strength," Thor adds wisely.

In a surprise move, Moxie steps forward, "That is all well and good, but this year brought things that need to be put right. There is blood on the tracks."

Thor adds, "Moxie is right. We have to resolve a serious breach."

Mad Moxie frowns, "You call it a breach to slaughter innocents? It is more than that. We Goths do not kill women and children."

Aristotle scratches his head. "There must be a mistake here, a misunderstanding perhaps."

Plato becomes defensive. "We never authorized any killing of Christians, men, women, or children. The terrorists have conspired to divide us."

Moxie responds testily, "So, how you know they Christians? We think you know the killer. And we think that you guys put him up to it."

All this surprises Plato. He thought that Medea had straightened things out with Thor beforehand and that Moxie was on board since he took part in killing Simon Girty.

"We were told that Siegfried is dead," Plato says disingenuously.

"We hear something else. We hear Siegfried is one of you. We want his head. If you are with us, we demand that you turn him over to us."

Aristotle steps forward, "We do not know Siegfried. But we will put forth a champion to restore the peace between our peoples. His name is Jason."

Mad Moxie sneers in disgust, knowing full well that Jason and Siegfried are one and the same person. However, after a long pause, during which he spits on the ground, Moxie agrees to this face-saving proposal. "Okay, so it will be Jason – if that is what you want to call him. Where is your champion? I will kill *Jason* myself." Unbeknownst to Plato and Aristotle, this is all for show because earlier Moxie and Thor had made a deal with Medea to fix the fight's outcome.

Thor and Moxie shake hands with Plato and Aristotle to seal the portentous match-up and then walk away to face the crowd of Goths.

"Let there be a fight to the death to settle the Christian question!" Thor shouts to the crowd. "We will have poetic justice." The word, *poetic*, rouses the Goths, whose craving for poetry is a blood lust.

"First, let us party; then, let us prevail!" Mad Moxie shouts out, raising his left arm in a clenched fist.

The crowd gathers around juggling acts and magic tricks. A Goth juggles three chainsaws. That goes over big. Then a Greek juggles volumes I-IV of the large-type Great Books. That receives polite applause.

Plato and Aristotle go in search of Jason and Medea.

"We have a deal that will put things back to where they were with us and these pea brains," Aristotle says with a sneer. Plato approaches Jason and says, "Jason, you must fight Mad Moxie as our champion."

"*I* have to fight Mad Moxie?" Jason responds reluctantly.

Medea turns to Jason. "You have to. We believe that they know that you are Siegfried. If you do not fight, the Goth people will rise against us. They want satisfaction."

"I am afraid, my son, you have to pay for going too far," Plato adds. "There is little else we can do. You must do your duty."

Medea slaps Jason on the back. "Go, bring us glory. Feel the power; die like a man."

Jason is sure that Thor has known all along that he

was Siegfried and is convinced he is being set up. He just cannot understand why he is now the sacrificial lamb in a secret deal.

When the party wanes, Plato and Aristotle lead a disturbed Jason to the ring where they meet up with Mad Moxie. "We bring to you our worthy champion. It is Jason, a member of the Praetorian Guard."

"You look familiar, buddy. Do I know you?" Moxie jokes.

Moxie's confidence is like a white, hot sword about to be forged for vengeance. He gives Medea a knowing look and a wink that she ignores while Jason stands by feeling abandoned. There is just too much scheming to keep up with.

"I will die defending my honor if I do not kill to protect it," Jason blurts out fighting for his battle legs.

Jason and Mad Moxie are set to fight. They are surrounded by the crowd of mostly Goths, led in cheering by the G-spot Biker Femmes, who have come to see Mad Moxie seek revenge in honor of the women and children slain during Jason's "unholy war" against the Christians. Thor high-fives his lover and joins the Goth crowd in cheering him on.

"Kill the dirty baby-killer," the crowd screams, holding up crucifixes.

"Scalp him and cut off his nose and ears!"

Jason feels physically vulnerable and hopeless. He

looks up to see the outline of a vulture sitting motionless in a tree still waiting for him. Then he notices Medea, also motionless, looking the other way.

Jason and Mad Moxie wear blades around their arms and feet. "WWX – World Wrestling Xtreme" they call it. The two participants grab and punch each other, making cuts with the blades attached to their bodies as the audience makes rooster sounds. They circle, then jab. Mad Moxie leers at Jason, calling him Bionican scum. Jason spits back at him and misses.

"You Illiterate, you bugger," Jason screams hoping to enrage Moxie's "manhood" so that he will slip up.

As expected, the insult enrages Moxie but does not debilitate him. Instead, Moxie replies, "Me? A Bugger? What about you, you baby killer!" His perfectly placed insult increases his speed and stamina; as a result, Jason is severely wounded, sprawled on the ground. Outmatched, he is declared the loser.

Moxie holds his sword to Jason's throat with contempt even though he has no intention of killing him. Looking up desperate and confused, Jason pleads for his life. Medea gives Thor the nod and he gives Moxie the thumbs up to spare Jason. The Goths in the crowd groan in dismay, but the Greek cheers drown them out. Mad Moxie is happy to spare him, as part of the deal that would give him free reign with Thor. As Mad Moxie is declared the winner, Jason, the humiliated loser, is cart-ed off from the field barely alive. Medea says to him as he is carried away, "Trust me. It is all for the best."

Medea brings Jason back to Elysium to recover. He whispers to her, "Why did you first abandon me and then decide to save me? What is your game, Medea? Did you do it just for me?"

Medea gives Jason a dismissive look. "It is not in my karma to get soft over any man. I saved you because your work is far from completed; the council has a lot invested in you. Now with your life saved, you owe us, and you owe me big."

"What will happen next?"

"We have plans for you," she says cryptically, "but meanwhile you must lay low. Perhaps you will even choose to *lay* low with me, now," Medea whispers into Jason's ear. "I know the biker girls want to get their Bobbitt revenge. I do not want that to happen to my boy's toy."

A smile of relief creeps across Jason's face.

With Song dead, Meditation and Memory move out of Elysium to work as full-time residents for Aristotle and Plato at the Skunk Works despite initial misgivings. The two of them are no longer on speaking terms with Medea and Jason, and have no desire to become embroiled in their affairs.

Healing from his wounds, Jason convalesces slowly at Elysium. Medea visits him during his recuperation period, bringing him her medicinal herbs and constant attention to speed his recovery. She does this at night, wearing the same nurse's uniform that she wore when she gave him his first colonic. "It is all over for me," Jason moans as her "treatment" begins.

"Stop feeling sorry for yourself, Jason." Medea barks at him, "This is not going to hurt." Jason is totally passive as she gives him her special makeover, from tip to toe. But this time, Jason feels uneasy as the recipient of ready-to-wear pleasure.

"I am beginning to feel doubts I have never had before. Nothing seems normal because all I think about is telling right from wrong. Now I know when things are right because I can feel it. I have never felt this moral sense so clearly before."

"What kind of killer are you? What makes you think you can change, just like that?" She snaps her fingers as she gets dressed. "Maybe you have had a change of heart to get yourself off the hook? But remember, you are still responsible for what you did. No matter how much you change and divorce yourself from the past, you are what you did. Your track record indicates a dark need to kill. And for that ineluctable compulsion, I will always desire you."

Medea leaves the room. Jason has a vision of individual Christians he killed in the raid. The old man from the river, Simon, looks at him and says, "The Bible says that man shall not live by bread alone, but by every word of God. Where are you now son?"

Jason responds to the vision. "I did my duty. I did what was expected of me."

"When will you see the light? When will you repent your wicked ways? The Lord is waiting for you."

"Which Lord?" Jason asks blindly expecting illumination.

When Medea returns, her voice dissolves Jason's vision, and she continues to berate him in a rapid-fire voice. "You were always so preoccupied with what others wanted you to do. When it came to choosing happiness, you turned your back, but when you had the option to kill, you did. You are a sincere killer at heart, and that makes me want you all the more. I desire your body even though you have no backbone, but you still have the lean muscular body of a killer. Who cares if you have failed to become a self-actualized person? You still want a mother figure to replace that ersatz mother of yours. Even to this day I know you hear Julia's voice. What about me?"

"I do not hear her voice. Now I only hear yours instead. I need you."

"That could be a problem. Need does not equal love. For me to love you in addition to wanting you, you need to give me something freely in return. What have you got to offer me?"

Jason is tempted to say that he could help the Greeks mine The Well for the information they need, but decides against this. He is afraid that by letting the Greeks tamper with The Well, all hell will break loose.

Medea wonders whether Jason can still be useful given his moral vulnerabilities. She promised Thor and Moxie that Jason would no longer participate in any more covert military actions.

Medea and Jason are sitting alone in the garden, surrounded by flowers. A hummingbird darts back and forth and settles down for its sip of nectar. While Medea discusses his future, a slave brings a pitcher of ambrosia and some victuals artfully assembled on a serving dish, which Medea spiked with a concoction of cocaine and heroin for speedballing fun.

Medea plays her next card, which surprises Jason.

"Your propensity for violence will come in useful in education, but you must learn to control it if you are to succeed. My goal is to bring formal education to the Goths without giving them the tools to take over. Mad Moxie is now the Über Minister of Education to make sure that education does not interfere with manly Goth virtues or our Greek way of life."

"How will I fit in?"

"You can be useful by helping us spread education to the Goths while at the same time making sure that the Greeks do not become over-educated."

"Over-educated?"

"Yes, the problem is that once we teach young people to read, they will end up reading what they want. The kids start to read subversive writers whose ideas challenge the very foundation of Greek civilization. We can be open-minded in the name of democracy but only for so long. For one, we cannot have our kids questioning slavery – like you did when you first arrived here."

"Who are in the top ten upstarts?"

Medea hesitates for a moment, realizing that there are holes also in her education. "You know – the thinkers who turned civilization on its head. They include the once "modern" political philosophers like Marx, Freud, Mao Tse Tung, Kropotkin, Hitler, uh, Susan Sontag, Ayn Rand; and, uh, writers and poets like Shakespeare, Goethe, Cervantes. That is your next challenge, coming up with a list of the thinkers who captivate the imagination of young Greek rebels. Your job will be to search and destroy subversive works of literature."

Jason cheers up, stretching out his arms. He is psyched. He likes the prospects for more bonfires. He will be a killer of forbidden books.

Medea smirks and mutters under her breath, "A little knowledge is a dangerous thing. Censorship will be the last refuge of this scoundrel."

Jason is excited with his new mission and makes his first proposal as an educator. "Let us find every subversive book and burn every copy," he says with enthusiasm, clapping his hands.

Medea puts a dampener on this approach. "You will only create more converts that way. It is better to start from the ground up. Books that corrupt our youth should only be burned as a last resort. There are more important things to do, like setting standards."

"How?"

"Censorship and bans. A common core. People love lists and rules and tests. Just remember what you did when you were in charge in Bionica."

"Yes, we had quite a job making sure that our users were kept on the path so that they would not stray into unauthorized information on The Well."

"Keeping people on the path is a good thing," Medea says with the authority of a supervisor. "What I want you to do is to take charge of setting and later enforcing standards for the education of the young, both Greeks and

Goths. There shall be one system of education, except in special cases. We shall institute testing to make sure that education meets the standards. We do not want any child left behind to read unsupervised. We will call it, *No Child Is Left Isolated.*"

"And my job is to set and keep standards?"

"Yes, we need someone like you with a sense of mission and commitment. You have the kind of resume that is perfect for the job – a sense of dedication and honor, no matter what the task."

Jason stiffens at attention like a military officer in uniform. Medea walks around him doing the inspection. She comes to a halt and faces him and addresses him in a serious and official voice. Jason eats this up.

"Yes, we have been given a job to do – to bring back civilization. It is your duty to move us forward. You cannot do that when people are pulling in different directions. With your lead, we must pull in the same direction."

"What about Moxie?"

"He is very important to us. You will have to suck it up and reach out to him. Your fighting days are over. Now is your time to lead by sucking up."

"And what about Plato and Aristotle?"

"I would listen to what they have to say, but do not be too influenced by them. Humor them. Use them. Service them, if necessary. Pay lip service to the sayings of

Socrates that Plato likes to trot out. But your real job is to make lists, set goals, and find ways to assure obedience."

"How will I do this?"

"Follow orders. I will talk to the Hellenic Council to have them appoint you to a new post, Director of the Institute of Character Correction for the Young. The first thing you must do is to develop a common core mission statement, goals, and a plan. Then, you will recruit members of the Institute who will work with you, and you will report directly to me. And by report, I mean in more ways than one."

Yes, Jason likes this idea very much.

Medea persuades the leaders of the Hellenic Council to make Jason director of the newly formed Institute for Character Correction in the Young, or ICKY. Plato and Aristotle object, warning that this kind of institute will impede creativity and progress. They also argue that Jason is too rigid and violent for the job.

"His time would be better spent helping us gain access to The Well," Aristotle objects.

"That will come later after we launch the Kurzweil Institute. To get the Bionicans on board, we will need an insider."

"It does not look like Jason will fill the bill."

"All in good time," Medea quips. The men respect Medea's talent for developing long-term strategies, and so they give in.

Plato laughs, "Now we are getting this killer to take charge of the education of our youth. What is the world coming to?"

Medea does not back down. "Jason is perfect for the job. Except for me, he is the only one among us who has had real-life experience among the Goths. I need him to spread our education as an alternative to Christianity."

Plato objects, "But, what use is a cold-blooded killer?"

"He is violently passionate about his work and experienced in the way of the world."

"But will this loose cannon kill again?"

Medea assures them that Jason has gone full cycle in his killing spree. "Jason has retired from his enforcement duties and is striving to become a philosopher. You can count on him; he loves following orders. Just tell him not to kill, and he will not kill. I promise you, this will work out. When the time is right, he will help you crack The Well."

So despite misgivings, the Hellenic Council goes along with Medea's plan. Jason gets space for ICKY in Plato's library. Once installed there, he recruits several young men to assist him in his tasks of reforming education. Meanwhile, Medea consolidates power among the Greeks and Goths by spending more time with Thor, who is an ex-officio member of the Hellenic Council – the first non-Greek to be so honored.

Jason, too, has joined the Hellenic Council as their chief educator. As an elder, he is entitled to grow a full beard.

Jason throws himself into his work establishing ICKY and develops its mission statement: "To promote education through character correction for the growth of the nation." His job includes setting goals and developing a database of approved knowledge and the training of teachers to carry out the ICKY philosophy. To bring teeth and muscle to the educational process, Jason asks Mad Moxie to recruit the toughest Goth warriors to serve on the Goth Reading Council. This group includes a token woman, Gonorrhea, who is put in charge of developing standards for sexuality and sexual conduct.

Jason meets with his staff to implement ICKY in a meeting at the Skunk Works. Plato, Aristotle, and Medea are in the background to make sure that things remain on track.

Jason says emphatically, "Our job is to make sure that every citizen can read and that they read the right stuff. Our motto is, *Read the right stuff or else*."

Jason commissions the development of a billboard

campaign depicting a book supported by an iron-clenched fist. *Read what is good if you know what is good for you.*

Medea takes Jason aside and whispers to him, "Another thing, it is high time we stem the rampant homosexuality among our Greek youth. Make sure that when you campaign for heterosexuality, you avoid homophobia. We don't want to give the Goths any ideas."

So, Jason and his colleagues think up another campaign, *On the Straight and Narrow*, designed to discourage homosexuality among Greek youth. Though at first the campaign confuses people since it is the young men who are mostly of the narrow build, and the young women are curvy. So later the campaign is changed to: "On the Straight and Curvy." However, this campaign is not implemented. Jason quickly realizes that a campaign against homosexuality will meet stiff opposition because Plato and Aristotle want to continue Athenian-style pederasty.

"You better focus on Daytrain instead," advises Medea. "But, do not forget that our future wealth is based on Daytrain. We should not discourage Daytrain, but instead encourage young people to put it to good use. We need to find ways to develop Daytrain protocols that encourages procreation. But, let us worry about this later."

Medea arranges for Jason to meet with Moxie and his Reading Corps at the Sky House, to get their buy-in.

He feels a chill recalling the days when he lived there with Tara when he was a Goth kingpin. Now with Tara long dead, it is a new ballgame.

Medea assures Jason that Moxie bears no grudges and looks forward to working with him on educational programs for the Goths.

"The best way to destroy an enemy is to make him a friend," Medea quotes the American President, Abraham Lincoln.

Jason meets up with Mad Moxie. Like Jason, Moxie, has also changed. He dresses in conservative Goth attire, very much like a 19th Century gentleman with dapper Thor at his side.

"So we meet again – same battlefield but different war."

"We both fight against ignorance, right?"

Moxie chuckles, "Jason, you have hit the nail right on the head. We Goths have always wanted to be more educated, but we never trusted the Greek version of education. But, now that we have manly education for real men, we like it."

The Goth Reading Corps gives a faint cheer, not sure where this is going. Moxie continues, "We can get the

Goths behind this movement. They know they will have to work with us if they want a better life."

After the program launches, Medea and Jason attend an education event at the Great Hall in the Polis to gain support for the newly formed ICKY.

"You have succeeded in removing the wimp image from education," Medea congratulates Jason.

"Absolutely! I will require all educators to learn martial arts so that they can enhance the teaching-learning process through targeted reinforcement. Today I am going to announce curriculum reform," Jason adds.

Medea joins Jason, who is addressing a group of Greek educators. Also in the audience are Thor and Moxie in their first visit to the Great Hall. After Plato introduces him, Jason steps up to the podium and begins his talk with a description of the new curriculum.

"We will continue to emphasize skills, such as counting, figuring, correct spelling and grammar. Each student is required to remember the 1,000 most important facts, and they must know passages of seminal Greek writings by heart. I have instituted ICKY, the Character Correction Institute for the Young, to isolate subversive ideas from the mainstream. Our job is to develop a database of dangerous ideas unwittingly promoted by philosophers, poets, and novelists. We cannot allow the subversive flow of information. We must stamp out pluralism and relativism to maintain our way of life. All ideas must be singular and objective instead, and they must contribute to the building of our nation."

Jason increases the pace of his talk, catching his breath.

"We cannot afford to squander our intellectual resources on ideas and thoughts that do not help us build our nation. Every irrelevant idea is a lost opportunity to think about something useful, and so a big part of our job is to sift through archives to eradicate intellectual weeds and to allow no one to have access to sensitive information without permission. When it comes to the education of the sons and daughters of slaves, we will make sure they appreciate the work of their betters. These children should only read manuals, and they should avoid books that encourage isolated thinking. We want education to provide a sense of place and comfort and to encourage all students to do their duty. A Greek child may be able to recite what Socrates said, but he or she must not allow knowledge to get in the way of doing useful work. Young people must understand that the reward for deviant behavior is the hemlock."

Jason finishes his talk by drawing from his experience.

"I want you to understand what it means to learn through joy. I do not want young people to make unnecessary choices that lead to nowhere – the way I did when I grew up. It is important to know one's place in an educated world."

Thor and Moxie join Medea in the applause, but it is obvious from the crowd's mixed reaction that more work needs to be done to get popular support. And so Jason quickly finishes up.

"I realize that there are some of you who are not with me. But, you should know by now that I mean what I say. I will not tolerate any deviants or any subversion."

Medea and Jason hurry out to avoid hostile questions, catching up with Thor and. Moxie for their planned get-together to discuss the next steps.

"We have a lot of work to do," Medea says to her team.

CHAPTER 18
THE LAST REFUGE OF A SCOUNDREL

Jason meets with Medea on a regular basis to learn about his progress as the director of the Institute of Character Correction for the Young. Medea places her hand on Jason's lap as he proceeds with his report.

"We are getting things under control; the Goths will learn only what we want them to learn. Daytrain use is on the rise, but so is compliance with our regulations."

Medea lifts her hand from Jason's lap and gets up to pat Jason on the back.

"Good report! We are proud of you. It has taken humanity thousands of years to get to this point. Now we are no longer burdened by the past. The Age of Information Overload is over. By eliminating useless and dangerous information, we will become liberated."

After discussing ICKY, Medea brings up a touchy topic. "Have you heard how Pericles is doing? I hear that there have been more problems."

Jason tells Medea about the lack of progress in Pericles' education. "I cannot seem to motivate him. The teachers at the Acropolis have given up on him."

"But you are an educator now. It is your job to motivate learning. Motivate him!"

"It does not work with your own. Pericles just will not listen to me."

"That is too bad. I will ask Plato and Aristotle to see what more they can do to mentor Pericles."

Medea brokers an internship for Pericles, who spends the next few years absorbing "useful" knowledge in Plato's library and Aristotle's Skunk Works. Much to the delight and satisfaction of Plato and Aristotle, Pericles thrives. Jason, however, is again out of the picture, losing touch with his son, unable to take joy in his achievements.

With time, Pericles, the intractable boy, turns into a tall, athletic, curly blonde-haired young man with a strong chin and penetrating blue eyes. On a regular basis, he competes in the junior decathlon and earns distinctions and honors as an actor in community theatrical productions, including plays by Euripides and Sophocles.

In violation of the policies that Jason is imposing on education, Plato and Aristotle place no barriers on what Pericles can learn.

Jason continues to live at Elysium, isolating himself with his books in an unused wing that includes Socrates' old office. Pericles avoids spending much time at Elysium to avoid seeing his father. Memory and Meditation no longer speak to Jason because they still hold him responsible for their sister's death. Likewise, Xantippe has little to do with him because of her prejudice against Bionicans. Jason's only regular contact is with the servants and with the demented Socrates, who occasionally wanders into his old office, muttering, *"Wonder is the beginning of wisdom."*

Despite misgivings, Jason still misses Medea, who now spends most all of her time with her Goth King and his lover Moxie in the Valley. Jason looks forward to her next visit as eagerly as he did when he was younger, so that he can once again "report" on his activities with ICKY, but he hopes to avoid the on-going discussion of his son's ascent into adulthood, especially since Medea's interest in the young man sheds light on Jason's deficits as a father.

Jason feels left out. He regrets not being involved in his son's educational accomplishments and lays awake at night imagining what he could have done differently. He wants to remove Pericles from Plato and Aristotle's influence, but knows he cannot. To Pericles, Plato and Aristotle are the father figures that Jason is not.

As in the past, Jason wanders about in the gardens of Elysium, obsessing about Pericles. He comes across Xantippe, unable to avoid her.

"Heard from your son lately?" Xantippe asks Jason in a flippant tone.

Jason gives her a dirty look.

"I understand that he is happy endlessly studying with Aristotle and Plato, but spending all his time with those dirty old men is no way for a boy to become a man. He needs to learn how to fight, how to kill." Jason says.

"If becoming a man is like being you, no thank you. I am glad that Pericles has a gentle side." Xantippe reminds Jason of all the benefits of education he received under the tutelage of Memory, Meditation, and Song.

"You have done well for yourself, following in the footsteps of Aristotle, Plato, and also Medea, who has you wrapped around her little finger. So you have become a man of words – words, words, words." Her sarcasm does not go unnoticed. "I would think you would want something better for your son."

"I have made a lot of sacrifices," Jason says bitterly.

"And so have the many others who have known you."

"But mine has been for a purpose."

"Purpose! You will just have to stew in your own juice."

Jason wants to smash her face in. Xantippe reads his thoughts and stares at him with contempt.

"There is very little more that you can do to me; I am already an old woman."

Medea has been Pericles' constant champion. In one of her regular chats with him, she sings his praises.

"When you finally finish your studies with Plato and Aristotle, you will be a great leader who will bring back the glories of the past without forgetting its lessons. You will   become a star at the Kurzweil Institute. You can do this. All you need is healthy-mindedness and optimism tempered by intelligence and a sense of proportion."

"What if people do not want to follow my wise leadership?" Pericles asks.

"Do not worry. There are strategies to manage reluctant followers. You might want to read some Machiavelli – something your father failed to do in any meaningful way."

Plato and Aristotle enjoy "opening" Pericles to all he can learn from them and others. Memory and Meditation spend time with Pericles discussing Great Ideas as they once did with his father, during those halcyon days in Elysium. Now they have another opportunity to introduce Jason's son to the ferment of a culture that vanished more than two thousand years ago.

During one of their many conversations, Meditation turns to Pericles.

"Word is getting around about you. There is a group of wealthy ladies interested in meeting you. They want to you to lead a discussion of the Great Books in light of the issues of the day."

Pericles is invited to a Great Books discussion in Aristotle's mansion, a residence that rivals Elysium in size and elegance. Aristotle's wife, Pythias, introduces him to the guests, starting with Gonorrhea, who is being honored by the group for her work in promoting Greek fertility through her procurement program. This time Gonorrhea does not wear black, and instead wears a white tunic to blend in with the group. The tattoo jungle of her true colors gently bleeds through her diaphanous garb. Although still striking, Gonorrhea's age shows in the severity of her finely lined face. But she seems perfectly at home with the ladies, who give her the encouragement she needs to smile a lot. She has seen them many times before. Pericles joins the group of animated women discussing the issues of the day. Pythias, a full-figured lady with graying hair, wants to stir things up and confronts Pericles in a breathy voice.

"Daytrain will destroy the Greek way of life unless we do something about it. What would you do to stop it?" Pythias has no idea that Pericles has become a regular user.

Pericles looks at her crossly. "You are right. We must do something about our dependence on Daytrain, but there has to be something to replace it. We should not sever our Daytrain trade with Bionica until the time is right. We need them as much as they need us."

Standing in the background, Gonorrhea approaches her nephew and says, "A very wise young man." She puts her hand on her nephew's knee and offers him the last morsel on the snack tray. Pythias gives a nod to one of the young ladies to make sure the slaves replenish the snacks, many of them honey-dipped, and refill the ladies' wine glasses. Gonorrhea whispers to Pericles, "We have a new shipment. Pharmakia has some great stuff for you." Pericles is pleased that his connection is intact and knows that his father can do nothing about it now that his formidable aunt is in his corner.

Pythias objects to giving Daytrain a pass, "The social

costs are too high. When our youths take Daytrain, they become hooked for life. They no longer want to read; the classics mean nothing to them. And what's worse, they become useless in bed."

Pericles strokes his chin, which appears to grow larger with each stroke. He pretends to agree with Pythias by nodding, and as a result, his nose appears to grow. Another much younger lady, closer in age to himself, Diana, steps in and delivers a jab with her question. "Now we have your father's *No Child Is Left Isolated Program.* I wonder if it is working."

Pericles does not answer the question and strokes his chin again. It appears to grow some more, catching up with his nose. Then, another mature bosomed lady, Persephone, enters the conversation. "They are learning the basics about Greek culture, the rock bottom basics, but still they are not educated. What about reasoning skills, ethics, and leadership?"

Diana wiggles her way up to sit next to Pericles. Grabbing his inner thigh, she asks, "What do you think education should be, Pericles?"

No longer feeling like stroking his chin, Pericles takes a deep breath, sighs, and clears his throat. A pregnant pause lends solemnity to his message before he speaks in a lowered voice. He is getting used to being put in the position of having to justify his father's programs.

The old woman, Persephone, listens intently to what

Pericles has to say, but Pericles addresses the young interlocutor directly.

"Diana, time and brainpower are limited; you have to choose what is important. Right now, the kids are interested in Daytrain because it helps them liven things up without much work. Maybe the secret is to get them involved in doing and building things, like sewer systems and other water drainage systems. Idle hands, idle minds," Pericles says, pleased with himself.

"Are you suggesting that the youth of today can take Daytrain and still be productive?" Persephone asks knowing full well that the answer is no.

Pericles forgets his chin momentarily but soon begins stroking it again. "We have to work with what we have; we must motivate kids to walk the straight and narrow, or the straight and curvy, I forget. Remember, learning will not work unless we grab the interest of our youth. Daytrain is interesting and it must be part of our curriculum."

After the Discussion group breaks up, the ladies keep on talking to Pericles, who gives Gonorrhea a little wave with his left hand as she mounts her Harley and roars off. She blows him a kiss.

Jason is aware of his son's popularity and is dismayed to realize that he no longer exercises much influence over the young man if in fact he ever did. If he interferes with Pericles' education, he knows that his son's followers will undermine his "No Child Is Left Isolated" program. He decides to meet with his son to see what he can do to channel Pericles in the right direction. Medea encourages Pericles to reconnect with his father. She arranges for Jason to meet Pericles in the garden at Elysium.

Knowing that he has been a poor father all his life, Jason begins on a hostile note. "What have you been up to now? I hear that you are no longer satisfied by the teachings of Plato and Aristotle and that you have taken to pleasing the ladies." Jason is referring to the popular round of Great Books garden parties that grew out of the one organized by Medea and since then was promoted by all of her distinguished lady friends.

Pericles answers laconically, "The women of Polis are very wise. I enjoy talking to them. They have open minds when it comes to the things that interest me."

"What might those things be?" Jason asks, feigning genuine interest.

"A lot of things – art, history, technology, education, and..."

Jason becomes impatient. "And what?"

"Music."

"You do not have a musical bone in your body."

Pericles' replies sadly, "I know. Thank you for reminding me."

"What kind of music do you listen to, and how do you get it? Are you on Daytrain?"

Pericles gives his father an odd look of bemusement and annoyance as Jason continues his attack. He wants his son to admit that he is addicted to Daytrain because that would explain a lot. "An awful lot of what interests you is a waste of time. You ought to focus on developing leadership skills. Also, you know, of course, I do not touch Daytrain. I never did, I never will."

"Whatever. I've got to go."

Pericles leaves the room and returns to his lair where he flops down to rest. He tries to cheer himself up by humming words of an old folk tune:

Irene goodnight, Irene goodnight
Goodnight Irene, goodnight Irene
I will see you in my dreams
Sometimes I live in the country
Sometimes I live in town
Sometimes I have a great notion
To jump into the river and drown.

His rendition is dismally off key, "I will never have an ear for music. I wish my father had encouraged me to study music when I was young. Song tried, but now she is dead. I think she listens to me from somewhere where my voice sounds great," he chuckles to himself. "I am doomed to sing while the shower is running. Maybe if someone had guided me after Song died, I could have become a cherished singer-song writer like Dylan Roberts and Bias Jones. I would have created wonderful music for Song. Instead, I was cursed with a father who did not care about music or songs, mine or hers."

Because of the tragic way his musical training ended, Pericles continues to nourish his secret obsession for music and for learning songs of the past. Little does Jason know that Pericles uses his animated tattoos to get into The Well to mine the data for songs that tell stories of how people lived before the great Plague. As a user, he is now getting a lot of help from Digi Diva and the other hackers in locating rare musical finds. Pericles has no intention of letting his father know that this is happening.

"How is your father doing?" Digi asks Pericles via his tattoos. "I heard from Pharmakia that he has done well for himself with Greeks. He filled me in on your father's past and about your mother, Tara, the queen of the Goths. What is life like at Medea's Elysium? I heard your father lives there with you. I heard it is very posh."

Pericles responds to Digi, "It is very nice. We both like it. But I want something else."

Digi Diva volunteers, "If it is music, we can help. We will provide you with full access so that you can explore The Well's musical database without interruption."

Pericles is delighted. Now he can listen to all his

tunes – classical, pop, rock, swing, blues, new age, and hip-hop. He wonders what Digi will want in return.

Pericles ponders his future. "I long to be surrounded by live music and live musicians, and I wish I could share my favorite music with others, but there is no one around. I wish I could sing in tune so that everyone would hear what I am trying to convey. I am surrounded by others but am so alone."

Pericles takes stock of his growing collection of world music from The Well that is pumped directly into his brain. Whenever he listens to his playlist, he locks himself in his room in Elysium to make sure no one discovers him or his tattoos. He stays in contact with the Bionican hackers who send him messages of encouragement. Digi Diva is intrigued by Pericles' level of commitment to music and one day sends him a special invitation.

"We love your enthusiasm. Please come to Bionica. We could use someone like you to keep on top of our music database."

Pericles does not respond right away because he does not want to cross his father so outwardly, but he continues to spend hours listening to music downloaded from The Well. When listening to pearls from the database,

Pericles is dead to the world. The Bionican hackers tell him online that they have accorded him special status. He is the Big Kahuna of tune surfing. He's not sure what that means, but he likes the sound of that.

Over time, Pericles and Medea end up walking in the gardens of Elysium a lot together. Medea has been counseling him on a regular basis to make up for Jason's lack of fathering and to deepen her influence with him.

"What have you been doing lately?" Medea asks.

Pericles is tempted to tell her about his contact with Digi Diva, but thinks better of it. He is afraid this would get back to his father.

"I have been trying to develop my musical side. I love music, though the whole world knows I am no good at it."

"It is fine to appreciate music, but do not get hooked on any of that hippity-hop. Just as anti-artists destroyed art, hippity-hop ended music long before the Great Plague, and it forced us to reconsider the beauties of melodies of the ionic scale in our rebirth of music."

"Yikes, the ionic scale is boring." Pericles protests.

"What do you want? What about four minutes and thirty-three seconds of silence?" Medea says.

Pericles rubs his eyes. "That is too long. I need wall-to-wall, ceiling-to-floor music in my life, real live music, and not just imaginary stuff. No matter how much I go into The Well and listen, I still cannot hum a tune or remember a lyric when I am offline. I want to feel the music, not just think about it."

"Whoa! Hold on! Are you using The Well? How did you get in?"

"I do not know, I think I was born with the connections," Pericles shows Medea his tattoos, explaining how the tattoos provide him with access to The Well.

"Who is helping you navigate the database?"

Pericles hesitates before divulging his secret. "Digi Diva. Pharmakia put me in touch with her."

Medea does not approve of Pericles' use of Daytrain and is only minimally sympathetic to his mooning over music. She knows all about Digi Diva and has put out feelers to her through Pharmakia to see if she would like to establish direct relations with the Greeks. She has little time for Pericles' shenanigans.

"Musical talent has to be developed early. You are going to have to learn to appreciate what other talents you have and move on," Medea says.

Pericles remains stubbornly silent.

Medea looks at him crossly. "You are getting off the deep end with music and mathematics. Maybe you better focus on real things, like politics and economics – the things that people think, say and do."

Ignoring her, Pericles wonders, "Perhaps we can grow civilization through the musical spheres. All we have to do is understand the musical essence of things."

Although a bit put off by Pericles' arrogance, Medea recognizes that there may be an opportunity to use Pericles to establish a foothold with the Bionicans. If Pericles were to be successful in penetrating Bionican society, he could extend Greek influence and solidify control over the Daytrain trade, and perhaps even enable the Greeks to access classified parts of The Well.

"Pericles, since you are so interested in the Bionicans, we can arrange to have you join up with them, that is, when the time is right. But, do not mention this to your father. You must also promise me that once you finish your mission as our inside man, you will return to work with our team to put The Well to good use. This could be a real growth opportunity for you. I know Digi Diva would work with you."

Pericles is interested in Medea's proposal, which he hopes will give his life more meaning. Perhaps he could undo some of the damage that his father has done to him and the people he loved.

"When do I start?" he asks.

"You must bide your time. Perhaps you should meet a nice, intelligent, and practical girl who is musical. That would solve a couple problems at once."

Pericles wonders if there is a truly musical girl for him. He fondly remembers Song and wishes he could have a girl like her with her tender caress.

"Maybe I could meet a girl like Song," he wonders.

Medea does not answer. She wants to let sleeping dogs lie, but Pericles presses her.

"Why did Song kill herself?"

"She was meant to die; she was not of this world," Medea responds coldly with contempt.

"I heard that she loved my father and that she killed herself over him."

"She was weak. I would not bother your father about this. He too has been trying to forget. And do not mention to him our conversation about your mission to Bionica. That is our little secret, Okay?"

Pericles nods in agreement.

Contrary to what Medea instructed him to do, Pericles becomes obsessed with what happened to Song and decides to confront his father. They meet in a library ostensibly to talk about Pericles' future.

"My education is not complete. I need to know more about music."

Jason throws up his hands. "Oh no, not this again;

you already spend too many hours lolling around The Well on Daytrain. What more can you possibly listen to? What more can you possibly learn about musically?"

Pericles answers surprised that his father knew about his access to The Well, "I need more musical education in my life. I want to make music."

"For what? Most of us cannot sing or play worth a damn."

Pericles throws Jason an abrupt curve. "Why did Song have to die? I heard she loved you. Did you not love her in return?"

Jason is thrown off by this question, not sure how much Pericles knows about Song and him, and is defensive in setting the record straight.

"I was taken by her ability to simplify the world through music, but I had too many things on my mind to meet her on that simple plane. She should have known that I could not give her what I did not have to give. She was, after all, an adult. I am not responsible for her death. She died of terminal naïveté."

"They say that your first and only love is your mysterious quest."

"What they say is true. My quest is always on my mind. A man has got to do what he has been told to do."

"Who has been telling you that?" Asks Pericles his curiosity aroused.

"My mother."

"Your mother?"

"Yes, your grandmother."

"I have a grandmother? Who is she?" Pericles is surprised that his father never talked about her before.

"She is…uh…was Julia - she was very important. She spoke to me through The Well when I was in Bionica and put me on a quest."

"When did you last see her?"

"I never saw her, except in virtual apparitions. She died before I was born."

"A virtual grandmother, really?"

"In those days that was normal."

"So what they say is true – you are a Bionican," Pericles feigns ignorance.

"Yes, but very few know my complete history; it is not much talked about."

"Who is Digi Diva," Pericles asks, not letting on that he has been in touch with her. Jason is taken aback and wonders how much his son knows.

"How did you learn about her?"

"Pharmakia told me. He said she is still in love with you."

"That was a long time ago. Digi Diva did not want me to leave Bionica, but I had to leave because of my quest, which first brought me to the Goths and then to the Greeks. I have traveled far and have done many things to get here. I have tried to do what is right. I just followed orders."

"You did the right thing because you were following orders?"

"It was right for me to follow orders, yes."

"Is it always right to follow orders?"

Jason draws a deep breath. "It all depends on who you are. I knew I had a destiny to fulfill because of my special tattoos. Unlike the tattoos of all the other hackers in Bionica, mine like yours were constantly changing and moving. They helped me navigate more efficiently through The Well. They signified that I was chosen to achieve something great."

"You had tattoos too?" Pericles asks, hoping to understand the connection between his tattoos and those of his father.

"Yes, the tattoos were invaluable in searching for information on The Well, but then there were the voices."

"Voices?"

"Only one voice, my mother's voice. She told me what I had to do."

Pericles is dumbstruck. "But was there not a point when you just thought for yourself?"

Jason ignores the question. Clasping his hands, Jason explains, "Eventually, my mother's voice went away when I learned that there was nothing special about my connection to her. Her DNA was not exactly an exclusive commodity, but I still believe to this day that my connection to her was real."

Pericles is suspicious. "What is it about you that people whisper about? There are rumors."

Jason interrupts, "I did some things years ago that I now regret, but I prefer to forget those days."

"They say you killed a lot of people."

"Yes, this is true. I killed many bad people, and there was also collateral damage. There were fanatic terrorists threatening our way of life. I had no choice."

"Terrorists?"

"Yes, they were also terrorists – like the ones who destroyed everything during the Great Plague. My motto was *Never Again.* We had to take pre-emptive action to stop the terrorists. I did my duty. There are times when the ends justify the means. It is OK to kill a few flowers if you get rid of all the weeds."

"But what about your feelings? Did not Socrates say, "To thy own self be true?"

"I did some shameful things, but I am still proud of the fact that I did them as a service in good faith."

Pericles does not respond to his father's assertion, but he is not through with his questions. He knows there is more. He heard through The Well that Jason killed the beautiful Beadina.

"Ok then, Father, tell me about what you did to the Bead Lady?"

Jason's face turns red and then white, the blood draining from his skin. He is not about to confess the wanton killing of a woman who could have been his only true love. He had hoped that the Bead Lady business would be forgotten.

"How did you find out about her?" Jason asks, his voice trembling.

"I heard a ballad sung by the Bead Lady herself. She mentioned that there was a man who would kill her, a man whom she loved with all her heart, a man with three names – Condor, Siegfried, and yours."

Jason is in shock to learn that his darkest secret is out. He wonders how the Bead Lady would know the name he goes by today. She died long before he changed his name to Jason. But he suspects that his name changes were somewhere on The Well; perhaps someone, maybe even Berk, mixed them into the Bead Lady's songs to implicate him in her murder.

Jason suddenly hears Beadina's voice. "I still live though my body is gone. I still love you, but *you took my joy; I want it back.* I will lie in wait until the time comes, and I will take it back."

Pericles' tattoos flare up and he finds he is able to eavesdrop on this exchange between the Bead Lady and his father.

The Bead Lady nags, "Why are you hiding so much? Why did you kill all those other innocent people?"

Jason grimaces, shuts his eyes and clenches his upheld fist, bellowing out with the deepest voice he can muster. "I had my destiny to fulfill. You were going to betray me. This conversation is over."

Pericles watches his father embroiled in his inner conversation, speaking into the void.

"What did you do to her? How did you kill her?" Pericles asks rhetorically echoing the Bead lady's goading. Instead of answering, Jason suddenly goes for Pericles' throat. Pericles easily fends him off and strikes him in the face. After Jason stumbles and regains his balance, the younger man stares at him and says, "I am ashamed to be your son."

For a long time, Jason and Pericles are estranged. Medea steps in to mediate.

"I cannot forgive him. No son should strike his father."

"Jason, I understand that you attacked him first. So, why do you not reach out to him? Why not support a project of common interest to heal your inner wounds?"

"Pericles, I am sorry I lost control. You struck a nerve.

There are a lot of things about me that I cannot explain. Perhaps this is something we share. I know that you, too, have a quest that burns in your soul."

Pericles pauses and strokes his elastic chin, which has become something of a trademark of his. He decides to humor his father by not mentioning his music obsession and instead suggests the project undertaken by his friends, Sergio and Julio.

"Yes, I want to reclaim the information legacy of the past. It can be done. Content is king. We have the power of the universe at our fingertips. We can bring back the glory of the past," Pericles asserts with seeming conviction. Jason smiles and says under his breath, "This boy is Greek to me."

Jason lets on that he is open to Pericles' youthful rant and feigns attention as his son describes an optimistic vision for the future. Pericles goes on, "We can reinvent the past, building up technology without making the mistakes of the past. We have it in our power to develop sustainable technology that does not pollute the environment, so long as we do not stray far from the Greek sense of proportion."

"Do not be so sure," Jason mumbles. "Let me be the devil's advocate. Why would you and your friends succeed where others have failed?"

"We have the past as prologue. We can start again, learn from the blueprint of the past, and learn what not to do. Maybe you can help us unlock the secrets of The Well. You were once the greatest hacker. I know I could learn from you, if only you were willing to teach me,"

Jason's mood darkens. Even his own son is in on the conspiracy to take over The Well. He sees the influence of Aristotle, who has been itching to get his hands on the Bionican treasure trove.

Pericles asks, "Then why your quest? What is it about?"

"I was sent here by Berk the Dwarf to determine whether the Greeks could access The Well from outside; and if they could gain the knowledge to develop weapons of mass destruction."

"Weapons of mass destruction?" Pericles says, perplexed. "What do you mean?"

Jason tries to simplify things for Pericles who still seems ignorant about the past.

"You must be aware that millions of people died when the cyberterrorists unleashed the Great Plague that destroyed the world's computer infrastructure. My job with the Bionicans was to safeguard the data that survived, including data that could lead to the redevelopment of terrible weapons. We diverted The Well users by giving them access to only approved information; that way, no miscreant could use the dangerous historical data left on The Well to decimate what was left of civilization on this sorry planet."

"I don't get it. If the stuff in The Well is so dangerous, why not just get rid of it?"

"Getting rid of The Well would mean death for the Bionicans and Daytrain. Sending me out on a quest was the only option."

"Whose idea was this?"

"I was told about my quest by Berk."

"You mean to tell me you went on your quest on account of Berk...the dwarf? He was probably just pulling your leg. He probably just made a lot of things up. People say that he just wants people to take an interest in his vintage equipment. A lot of which is irrelevant given the situation today," says Pericles who got his take on Berk from Plato and Aristotle.

Jason does not tell Pericles the full story. He fails to mention Berk's attempt to get him to be more flexible in interpreting his quest, and he does not let on that Berk warned him about the reliability and relevance of Jason's virtual mother and the failure of Xtremus. Instead, Jason simply tries to gauge what Pericles knows. "Berk told me about my mother and her work in the Xtreme Marketing Movement. You know about that, do you not?"

"What I know is from some outdated museum exhibit. It does not make much sense to me."

Jason realizes that there is a lot that his son does not understand. He tries to explain, "My mother, your grandmother, wanted technology and consumption to remain virtual so that the planet would come to no further harm. There was no way of denying the terrible things that happened in the past. The evidence is still with us."

Pericles rolls his eyes. "I hear about the war again and again, but today things are different. Why not just forget the past and move on with new knowledge?"

Jason is surprised that his son appears to be a Cybergeddon denier. "Have you not seen the extensive exhibit on our history in the Palace of Culture?" Jason asks.

"I found it boring, a lot of propaganda. My head was into music. I just do not understand why you make such a big deal out of things that are dead and gone," Pericles whines.

"If you do not believe me about the gravity of our tenuous hold on life on this crippled earth, why do you not ask Medea? You seem to respect what she has to say."

Pericles nods. He is very interested to know why Medea has played such a key role in his father's life and in his. She has been more than a mother to him, nurturing him while Jason was aloof.

Jason continues to explain his past. "Medea arranged my escape from the Goths after your mother died. That is another death they blamed on me – your mother's. But, I assure you that I did not kill your mother. Medea helped me get established here with the Greeks so that I could continue my quest."

"Medea told me that my mother did not understand

you and what you needed to do. Is that why she died?"

"I did not give her what she wanted, but I was not responsible for her death."

Pericles interrupts, "Yes, but I still do not get it. Why did you have to kill so many other people?"

"Killing flowed from the logic of the quest. It was imperative to protect The Well, the culture of the Goths, the rational knowledge of the Greeks, and the earth itself."

Pericles is dumbfounded. "Why are you making such elaborate excuses? Should you not take responsibility for taking lives? At least have the guts to admit that you enjoyed killing. Why else would you do it so easily?"

Jason scarcely hides his anger. "You just do not understand. In my own way, by telling you I am taking responsibility for what I did."

"In your *own* way? I do not get it."

Jason pauses to converse with his own mind. "He will never understand. I wish I could make him see how sincere I was in taking on my quest in the beginning. Clearly, things have gone wrong. I cannot expect my son to understand what I, myself, have begun to doubt."

"Look Pericles, you ought to be more grateful. I have kept you out of it and made sure that you have gotten what you need," Jason says.

"You have no idea what I need. Without a mother's unconditional love and a father's guidance, and without

Song and without her music, I feel empty inside. There are so many questions I cannot answer. It is useless to talk."

After a long silence, Pericles makes a move to leave. Jason quickly seizes upon the cue and gets up first, slams his fist on the table in frustration and rage, and then quickly walks away from his still-seated son.

Days pass. Jason pays a visit to Medea to talk to her about his parental difficulties. "I am not sure I can support what Pericles wants to do. As I understand it, he wants to put information into the hands of those who are ignorant of the lessons of the past. We are on a collision course. Our relationship is fraught with futility."

"Do not be so angry with your son," Medea counsels. "Like you, he has to find his way and that means making some mistakes. Our job is to stand back and try to guide him without getting in his way."

Jason half-heartedly agrees with Medea's wise words, but he keeps on clenching his fist as if he were preparing to strike someone in the face.

"You have no idea how much Pericles reminds me of you – he has that same fire in the belly that you do. Once he gets an idea in his head, there is no dissuading him."

"Maybe you can help him temper his passion."

"That is what I am trying to do."

"You are too preoccupied with your troubles," Medea scolds. "Perhaps now is the time for you to focus on his troubles. He still has his destiny to fulfill. You have fulfilled yours," Medea lectures Jason, all the while keeping mum about her intention to have Pericles go on a mission to Bionica.

"But he has no appreciation," Jason replies.

Medea says wisely, "You must have patience with young people. They have no idea of how it feels to be defeated. It is only a matter of time before Pericles loses. The day will come when he no longer has the heart to believe that life's games can be won. Then his real work will begin, the way yours has."

Pericles and Jason do not see each other for months. Pericles spends long hours with his two friends, Sergio and Julio, in Aristotle's Skunk Works repairing and retrofitting remnants of old technologies. They refigure all kinds of early electronic devices, motors, and components, using tools developed more than a century ago.

Pericles is soldering together a broken antenna while his two friends are spot welding wire mesh onto metal bars. Pericles turns to Sergio, who looks up and says, "We are getting close to fixing the equipment needed for transmission and reception."

"Maybe next year we can send a message from Elysium to the Skunk Works. We will still have to string some wire to make it," Pericles adds.

"In the old days you could send a picture, just like that," Julio says as he claps his hands. "Like magic – through the air."

Sergio chimes in. "Today sending a voice over wire is a big deal."

"We have to start somewhere," Pericles proclaims. "So, let us learn the venerable Morse Code for point-to-point communications."

"Starting with S.O.S. Maybe someone is listening," Sergio laughs.

"Voice will be next," Pericles assures them.

"And then images, video, data, all kinds of files."

"Someday we will be all connected."

Pericles smiles, "We certainly have enough found poles and wire for the job. A lot of electronic hardware survived Cybergeddon, too, but getting a reliable power source is our big challenge. We have to scavenge for good rechargeable batteries. Medea tells me that my father might help, but that is a long shot."

Medea encourages Jason to talk up his project with his father. At her suggestion, Pericles visits his father to discuss his communications work.

"We are going to make history," Pericles brags to his father. "For the first time in many years, we will have a functioning physical means of electronic communications."

Jason's reply is curt, "Been there, done that. The future has already happened. They went about as far as they could go when they developed The Well."

Pericles begs to differ. "You mean ESP communications – without wires, without electromagnetic airwaves, without technology? That was a fraud, a mere simulation of real communications. You had to be on Daytrain to make full use of it. There was never any real accountability. The Well system is obsolete, censored, and has limited reach. It is undemocratic. What we are building is the new future – one that never happened."

"Wrong! The Well is as good as it will ever get." Jason shouts to make his point.

Pericles replies, "Aristotle says it cannot be freely used, and so it is not worth anything to anybody." And with sarcasm, he adds, "Those who control The Well believe in Nyet Neutrality."

"If he feels that way, why does he persist in asking me to help him be the one in control over it?" Jason says sarcastically.

"Look Father, we want to strike out anew on our own, and if we could figure out how to use The Well, all the better. If there were a way to get the Bionican hackers and users to cooperate, we could manually transcribe what they know to fill the gaps in what we know. I think I know how we can do this through the Kurzweil Institute."

Jason thinks the Hellenic Council has bought his son and that there is nothing he can do about it. So, he proceeds to give his son some lame advice to slow him down.

"You do not have enough time or manpower for that. You are better off concentrating on the classics and the wisdom of the ancients, our only hope of transforming the mores and standards of society. Get these straight before you put bomb-making instructions in the hands of morons. "

Pericles throws down the gauntlet. "Father, you are out of touch. We can safely develop good technology because we are applying what we have learned from the Ancient Greeks. I have faith in our institutions because they are based on philosophy."

"Philosophy only gets you so far. Have you ever learned what the world is like?"

"What is it like?" Pericles asks.

"It is not for the faint hearted. It is a dog-eat-dog-world." Jason hesitates.

Pericles interrupts, "Yes, I know, and the first bite counts."

"Wise guy, eh?"

"I know those things, too; I believe that they must be imbedded in me from birth. They are part of our shared genetic code, Father. Is that not what you are thinking?"

"Oh, so now you know what I am thinking?"

"Yes, sometimes. I just know that your thoughts are driven by the need to control things. It is all about your quest, your damned quest."

"Yes, but now I do not know anymore. I am losing faith in my quest. I have been for some time," Jason says, looking away, trying to throw a monkey wrench into the conversation.

"Better you buried in doubt than me. I want a fresh start. Reinventing stuff is fine with me," Pericles says with finality.

Jason will not let go. "The party is over. You must make the best of things. You must let the earth recuperate, and this means saving it from technology."

Pericles scrunches his face and laughs. "I want to be set free. I do not want your kind of education. I want freedom to think my way. I do not want any part of what you have to offer."

Jason looks up and winces, "You are going down the wrong path. Ever since you were born, you have been condemned to repeat the mistakes of the past," he says bitterly. "Perhaps we all are."

CHAPTER 19
THE SKUNK WORKS

Sergio and Julio are going over the inventory of vintage equipment piled ceiling- high in huge storage area of the Skunk Works as they revisit their quest for power sources.

"Here are computers that we can rehabilitate," Sergio says as he points out the individual devices. "These are first Apple computers. We also have a collection of TRS 80s, IBM PC's and Commodore 80's. All of them come with printed manuals."

"If only we had more juice! All we have are these old nickel cads and solar panels that we got out of storage."

"Yes, that is a tall order." Sergio laughs. "You need to burn something to get power."

"Or use solar panels." Julio raises his finger. "But that is not the answer because when the sun goes down, we have too little storage capacity."

"There is always slave power, but the problem is that

you need a slave for each light bulb. " Julio keeps up the banter. They both laugh. Pericles is not amused to hear Julio and Sergio joking about serious business.

Julio continues, "It is constantly frustrating to imagine how before Cybergeddon, our bodies provided all the power for networking."

"Ah yes, inner resources."

"Technology went south."

"Yep! Crazy cyberpunks finished it off."

There is a long silence since it is considered bad taste to bring up Cybergeddon. Sergio breaks the ice by changing the topic. "So, what is going on in your genteel existence in Elysium, Pericles? We heard that you have become another Alan Lomax."

"Yes, I am still collecting vintage songs and I wish I could find a way to record and store them all. Right now, The Well is the only game in town. I want a real music career; I am bored out of my mind. I really am."

"What is going on with your father?"

Pericles' answers mechanically, "He and his cronies want to bury their heads in the sand and pretend they are building a just civilization based on reconstituted Greek culture and values."

"*Just* add slaves," Sergio says.

Julio laughs. "Do not worry about your father and the other old folks on the Council; we have a job to do. We have to get down to the basics."

"The basics?" Pericles is unsure what he means.

"Connecting people again, connecting them like in the old days," Julio replies.

"Telegraphy is just a start," Sergio adds.

Pericles looks in Julio's eyes, "I am not sure that everyone wants technology to work again. They are afraid."

Julio becomes angry. "I do not give a shit about their agrarian ideals based on slavery. We must revive technology. Otherwise, we will all be bored out of our minds in perpetuity."

"Yes, we will die of boredom," Sergio agrees.

Pericles is having some second thoughts about Julio's unbridled enthusiasm for what may be a lost cause. He turns to Julio and says quietly, "We need to proceed cautiously. We have to get support for what we do."

Sergio teases him, "You sound just like your father."

"I hope not. I am not like him. He is much too rigid, and there are too many ghosts in his life," Pericles shoots back.

"There sure are too many ghosts. Medea has told me a lot about them. She loves to gossip."

"Then I guess you know what drives him?"

"Yes, I know he thinks he was sent here to investigate whether we Greeks are up to no good, some nonsense about weapons of mass destruction," Sergio says.

Pericles nods. "Yes. That turned out to be a wild goose chase. I think he finally understands that he does not have the power to do anything. I think he realizes that killing people who get in the way does not work."

"Has your father found his new calling?" Julio wonders.

"He says he now believes in education, but I think he is into slow death."

"Would you ever work with him?" Sergio asks.

Pericles frowns. "No way. We do not get along."

"Perhaps then you can help us full-time with what we are doing here. We can do our thing for quite a while without The Well. At least as long as we all are having fun," Sergio says softly with a smile.

"I want to, but I doubt that we have materials enough to build what we need."

Julio looks up at the mountain of old computers and waves his finger in a circle at it. "You have to be an optimist. Otherwise, nothing ever happens."

Pericles does not answer. Sergio puts his arm on his friend's shoulder and pulls him close. "Maybe you should take some time off to work things through. Julio and I can continue the work on our own, or with you. Whatever you decide, we will still be here for you, my friend."

Pericles follows the advice of his friends and continues to spend most of his time downloading music from The Well, thinking that perhaps he should team up with Berk because of his expertise with recording devices. He thinks a lot about music and its power to uplift the spirit. Perhaps he could also join up with Julio and Sergio and build something wonderful. But, his ennui and his obsession with music overwhelm him. As he listens to the amazing world of music that he discovers on The Well, he loses his passion for the revival of technology and the advancement of his technical career.

"I wish could absorb music into me. If I could just get far enough into the music, nothing else would matter anymore. All my pain would go away."

Pericles closes his eyes, tunes into The Well, and selects the music from the brothers Nelson and the young Boy George from his playlist. For a while, he is at peace.

CHAPTER 20
BREAKING THROUGH TO THE OTHER SIDE

Pericles is downloading music while sitting at a table in the gardens at Elysium, surrounded by blue hyacinths that are in full bloom. Sergio and Julio come for a visit to check up on him. Pericles does not notice them as they approach.

"Hey, Pericles, how are things going?"

Pericles does not answer. He is in a trance, high on Daytrain.

"Come on, wake up." Julio gently shakes him.

Pericles comes to.

"Please leave me alone. I have a real cool band called Creed on. I am getting into faith."

Julio rolls his eyes. "We miss you. Come back to work with us."

"I want to, but I cannot."

Julio looks at Pericles straight in the eyes.

"It looks like what you are grooving on is Daytrain,

my friend. You know what that can do to you."

"I do not care. The magic is in the music, and the music is in me. Music rocks. Creed rules."

"What about your dreams and ambitions?" Sergio asks.

"Can you not see that I am riding the wave? The wave of awesome?"

Rejected, Sergio and Julio leave. Alone, Pericles goes into a new state of isolation and refuses to talk to anyone. The servants bring him food, but he refuses even that. Days pass. Medea comes to Elysium to look for Pericles, but he is not there.

"He told us he is going on a journey and that he will not be back until he completes it," a servant girl explains to Medea.

Medea rushes off to find Jason. "Your son has gone off the deep end. I am worried about him. He is constantly high on Daytrain."

Never one to be a worrier, Jason dismisses Medea's fears with sarcasm. "He is just growing up like you said he would. He is very independent. Just does not want to have anything to do with me," he says spitefully.

Medea tries to shake Jason out of his complaisance. "He is spending too much time downloading music from The Well; this could put an end to his future and endanger everything that I, I mean we are trying to accomplish. You must do something about it."

"He will find his way. Kids always do."

"But this time the pied piper has gotten him. No one has seen him for days."

"Then it must be Digi Diva?"

Medea nods gravely. It begins to dawn on Jason that there may be a real problem. Jason's tattoos tell him to see Pharmakia, the Daytrain drug dealer, concerning Pericles' whereabouts.

Jason and Medea go to Polis to find Pharmakia sitting among several youths plying his trade.

"I have been expecting you. Pericles asked me to tell you that he has gone over to them," Pharmakia says without emotion.

"Over to whom?" Jason asks.

"Bionica. He has decided to join up with them and asked me to take him there. When we got there, Digi Diva took him in hand, and he quickly fell into place among the users. The second day we were there, I saw him dancing naked among the Bionicans in a Teach-in. Digi Diva said he was deeply in the groove."

"What else did she say?" Jason asks.

"She said he was perfect," Pharmakia replied.

"Why did she say that?"

"She said that Pericles is the perfect user; he does not cause any of the hackers any trouble and he gives himself freely to those who want him. Also, she said to say hello to you, Jason, and that she misses you. I understand it has been years since you last saw her."

The idea of his son becoming a Bionican user does not go over well with Jason. He becomes enraged and reaches for his knife to kill Pharmakia. Medea moves to restrain him and says coldly, "Do not kill the messenger, unless I tell you to."

Seeing Jason's rage, Pharmakia beats a hasty departure. Medea says to Jason, "I think it is time for us to go to Plan B. Why do you not make a pitch to the Hellenic Council?"

Jason presents the situation to the Hellenic Council.

"My son, Pericles, has gone over to the Bionicans."

"Like father, like son – always going over from one place to another," Plato whispers quietly to Aristotle.

"He has gone on a music pilgrimage," Jason responds trying to put a good face on a bad situation.

"Maybe Gonorrhea is behind this. She has been around a lot mentoring the kid," Aristotle whispers to Plato.

Medea looks at Jason. "There is no use kidding our-selves," she says, taking charge of the presentation. "This is a serious situation. We do not want to lose Pericles to the Bionicans. But let's look at the bright side. This may be our last hope to access The Well. Maybe there is a way out."

Plato looks to Aristotle. "This would be a good time for us to clean out The Well cesspool once and for all. And with Pericles' help on the inside, perhaps it is finally possible to do something that we could never do before," he says, staring at Jason.

Aristotle agrees, "Pericles could help us understand whether The Well has anything to offer us. He would be a perfect insider to help us transition the users to help us. He has the perfect personality to do that. Everyone likes him," Aristotle says, looking directly in Jason's di-rection, implying with his stare that this is not the case with Pericles' father. Jason is numbed with repressed an-ger and indifference.

Plato adds enthusiastically, "Yes, he can help us get data to round out our library."

Aristotle interjects, "Never mind your library. We must have him focus on technology."

Jason does not say anything. He realizes that his son is being used as a pawn to betray him. He is dismayed that no one is upset that his son has gone over to the oth-er side; no one is worried about the young man himself.

All these old Greeks can think about is how this situation will benefit them.

Off in a corner, as if he has been hiding there for an eternity, Berk suddenly pops up again. He thinks that he alone has the expertise in dealing with The Well, and with Bionican defectors. He slowly moves to the group and waits for the gaping mouths to close and an opening to say his piece. "I can be of great help as you know." Berk smiles slyly. He has been passed over one too many times – not this time.

Medea says with a sigh, "*Finally*, we have been waiting for years for you to step forward."

"Yes, I know how," Berk confesses. "But, I also know how to get Pericles back. It will require Jason's cooperation," he says, turning to look at Jason.

Jason hesitates and looks away from the old dwarf while Medea tries to get his attention.

"Remember, he is your son," Medea says emphatically to Jason. "You owe it to him to help. And you also owe it to us to help."

Jason stares into space.

"Do not worry, I will be there to help you, Condor... uh, Siegfried ... I mean Jason, " Berk stumbles, repeating his offer to help. Jason could care less. He does not trust Berk; he has never liked him.

"What have we got to lose," Medea says encouraging Berk to say what he has to offer.

Berk gleefully announces to the group, "I have a deal. Digi Diva says that Pericles can come back to Polis if we bring Jason to Bionica as a goodwill gesture. What she wants is Condor – I mean Jason. If we arrange to have Digi reunited with Jason, whom she still claims to love. Digi will cooperate with us through Pericles. She might even allow us to access The Well through him. I am pretty sure we can work with her and the other hackers."

"She will kill me if I go to Bionica. That is for sure," Jason says emphatically.

"No, she said that there is no such plan. Whether you live or die is up to you. Digi says she is no longer angry at you. And besides, we have already made a deal. She only wants to see you, to hold you like when you were lovers, and to talk to you. She wants to understand why you left her and why you left Bionica, and whether there is anything left between the two of you. She understands that what you did was to protect The Well from us Greeks, whom you believed were bent on getting data on weapons of mass destruction. She also said to tell you that your son, Pericles, is finally happy."

"But what is it that is she after?" Jason wonders.

"She wants another way of life," Medea says, pretending to show her cards. Jason picks up that Medea is hiding something. He suspects that Medea wants Digi to take over the operations of the Daytrain trade. Everyone appears to be talking with Digi Diva about him. He has been traded like a horse. Jason feels that he is about to be checkmated.

"I do not believe you," Jason says.

Medea shrugs her shoulders and throws up her hands. "Does that really matter? You know the drill. You are in charge of your destiny. It looks like your life has gone full circle. It is time for you to return to Bionica and to face your history as Condor. You have to own up publicly for what you did. That is also part of the truth and reconciliation deal that we have with the Goths. As it stands, you are no longer of any value to us Greeks."

Suddenly, he hears a voice in his head again. It is trying to tell Jason something. It is the shrill and now even more phony-sounding voice of his mother, Julia.

"It is true. You must go back to Bionica to fulfill your quest. You must preserve my legacy. Xtremus is dead. Long live Xtremus!"

Jason fears everyone is setting him up and that the voices in his head have been hacked. He stares Berk down while Medea watches him with her cold, calculating eyes.

"I will travel to Bionica to rescue my son," he says with resignation and disgust. "But I will do so alone. I don't want any help," he says, glancing at Berk.

Jason leaves Elysium, taking one look back to what has become of his home for nearly twenty years. He passes by the fields where the slaves are harvesting beans. As he waves to them, they look up and just stare at him. No one waves back. He smiles, but no one smiles back.

Going South, Jason retraces his steps, taking the same path that took him from Bionica. He stops by the house of the Bead Lady, whom he murdered so many years ago. How might his life have been different if he had stayed with her, he wonders. The old blind lady, who has been appearing in his dreams, now inhabits the Bead Lady's house that has become an empty shell littered with dead monarch butterflies. The birds disappeared, and the Bead Lady's gardens are overgrown with weeds.

"Have you fulfilled your destiny, yet?" The old blind lady asks, offering Jason a bowl of rotten fruit crawling with worms. Jason recoils in disgust; he flings the bowl at her head, and she runs off weeping.

He continues to keep to his old path as if clinging to the only thing that he knows for sure. He finds the same abandoned house in the Alamo Estates that once provided him temporary shelter. As before, he is greeted by a skeleton in the easy chair with the hand-painted sign around his neck, "I am a pseudo-intellectual." He looks around the room filled with books. This time he is drawn to the self-help section, including the once popular, *The*

Fifty Minute Hour, written in the 1950s. He lies on a sofa adjacent to the skeleton and starts talking out loud about his life.

"I tried so hard to do my duty, but nothing has worked out. I had to kill for what I believed in. Jason re-imagines killing the Bead Lady and executing the Christians.

He turns to the skeleton whose empty eye sockets stare at him.

"You looking at me?" Jason asks. "You looking at me? You looking at me? Then who the hell else are you looking at? You are looking at me. I am the only one here. Who do you think you are looking at?" he asks again, looking the skeleton straight in the eye socket.

"I know, you are probably thinking that it was wrong for me to do all the things that I did, to kill all the people that I did, to have all the mindless sex that I had. To neglect my only son as I did – is that what you are thinking?"

The skeleton, which has been inert for all this time, starts to nod. Jason hears a woman's voice as the jaw of the skeleton opens and closes to mouth the words.

"Having doubts, now? If so, it is too late."

Jason recognizes his mother's voice and proceeds to talk about himself.

"I wanted to experience the world and to enjoy its pleasures."

"You are an unreconstructed petit bourgeois hedonist," the skeleton says in his mother's voice. "You fell in love with the trappings of the good life without understanding the responsibilities that it entails. You are no longer a young man. You are just a shell, without real purpose and passion. We expected more from you."

Jason looks at himself in the mirror, wondering who the "we" is that she is talking about. He has grown older. His hair has turned gray. He has become fat. He has learned about as much as he can learn. No wonder Julia and Medea and the rest are through with him.

There is a knock on the door. Jason is surprised because he thought that this area had been totally abandoned. It is Gregory and Margaret, the anthropologists.

"Hello, can we come in?" Gregory says as he pops his head in through the door.

"OK, with me. Welcome to the haunted house. Have you been following me?"

"Sort of," he says. "Your movements are easy to track."

"How so?" Jason wonders.

"Because you are the star of the show," Margaret says.

"Star of the show? What show?" Jason asks.

"The only show there is," Gregory says cryptically.

"What do you mean? I do not feel like a star."

"That is because you are a falling star. You have become a nobody."

Jason is puzzled.

Gregory explains, "We have been tracking your life

like an old TV reality show – a longitudinal case study of identity, dedication, and..."

"Moral confusion," Margaret pipes in.

"What do you mean by moral confusion?" Jason asks.

"To put it bluntly, since your childhood you have had a penchant for murder and mayhem, and through your life you have confused the means with the ends. Now, ultimately, you are the one confused."

"But I had to do what I did; it was my duty."

Margaret sighs, "Something sure went wrong with your moral education. You are so outer-directed. That is what we have learned."

"Duty is not enough," Gregory agrees.

Jason objects, "What about the possibility of weapons of mass destruction? I was asked by Berk to investigate whether the Greeks have the knowledge to build them."

"The possibilities of weapons of mass destruction are endless. You should have figured things out sooner. It is not rocket science." Margaret says dryly. "Besides, Berk encouraged you to keep an open mind. The problem is that you DID NOT listen."

Gregory looks Jason straight in the eye and says, "Berk's job was to give you a challenge, but he never told you to kill anyone. You did that on your own."

"But I was led to believe that I had the discretion to kill people. He and the others all knew about my hacker training. They knew about me killing the users."

"And you chose to kill other humans just to resolve your, uh, cognitive dissonance?" Margaret responds disdainfully.

"Cognitive dissonance?" Jason wonders.

"That is just a fancy phrase in psychology. Maybe a better word describing your frame of mind is *moral turpitude*," Margaret clarifies.

"I like that one, Margaret."

Jason's face gets progressively redder. He looks around the room.

"Looking for a weapon, I presume?" Gregory laughs nervously.

Margaret mutters, "I told you, Gregory, we should never have undertaken this study. It is not replicable. He is a one-of–a kind deviant."

"I resent your intrusion in my private life."

"You never had a private life. You had a shot at private life, but you made your choices in public," Gregory replies.

"You are a creature of free will, are you not?" Margaret taunts him.

"What do *you* want from me? What does *everyone* want from me?" Jason blurts out, desperation seeping into his cry.

"We do not want anything from you. We are researchers, and this is *action research* and you should know that we have always had your interest at heart and that our study adheres to the highest ethical standards."

Gregory pulls out a paper, "It is stated right here, our professional code of ethics. We are informing you of your rights to know..."

"thyself," Margaret says finishing Gregory's sentence.

"Know thyself," she repeats with a pause and then finishing her thought she adds, "And that is very important, the most precious gift of God."

"Be a sport." Gregory pats Jason on the back. "As a hacker you were privy to everyone's thoughts. You had a license to kill. Only now, the tables are turned because you yearned to be free. With freedom comes opportunity and responsibility. You could have made better choices."

Margaret looks downright cross. "Maybe it was all about sublimation. Maybe you were too caught up in material things or sexual desires."

Gregory laughs, "Margaret, you are getting positively psychological. Remember, we are anthropologists."

Margaret backs off mockingly. "Oh, pardon me, sir, for transgressing the discipline boundary."

"What do I do now?" Jason asks as he looks to the floor.

"Oh, buck up. You know what you have to do," Margaret says.

"I have to go to Bionica to free my son, and..."

"And what?" Margaret asks.

"Set the record straight."

"You do that."

Gregory adds with emphasis, *"And remember, the truth shall set you free."*

Gregory and Margaret suddenly evaporate into thin air.

"Just another crappy vision," Jason mutters to himself. "First I meet a talking skeleton, and now I am lectured by imaginary anthropologists who claim that I am a longitudinal study about deviancy. I must be going insane."

He gathers his belongings, leaves the house, says good-bye to his host, the skeleton, and leaves the gated community.

He walks for several hours and comes across two Goth motorcyclists who zoom by him and wave, as if they knew him. It is Nanna and Gunnarr showing off doing wheelies. He keeps on walking and comes across the old Indian, Red Cloud, sitting down, smoking a peace pipe. It has been years since their paths crossed.

"Did you follow the clouds?" the Indian asks. Jason shakes his head.

"Why not sit with me for a pow-wow."

"Can't. I am going to Bionica to rescue my son."

"Then I can't help you. You already know what you are looking for."

Red Cloud continues to puff on his pipe as Jason resumes his trek, kicking stones to scare the rabbits that cross his pass. Then another distant roar – motorcycles again – only this time a cavalcade led by no other than the notorious Gonorrhea and the G-spot Biker Femmes, dressed in identical black leather jumpsuits. The encircle him and Gonorrhea gets off her bike, and he notices that she has exposed herself in the same way she did during the pre-nuptial inspection and walkthrough that preceded his marriage to Tara.

She pulls out a switchblade and, whammo, out comes a razor-sharp blade that appears to have his name on it. "Drop your trousers!"

Jason obeys and is not sure what Gonorrhea wants from him, or what she intends to do to him. He knows that his former sister-in-law has had it in for him for driving her sister to suicide.

Gonorrhea shakes her head in disgust as the other bikers nod in agreement.

"Yours falls short of our expectation. You have passed your prime." Gonorrhea and her bikers mount their bikes, and without uttering another word, they roar off so that Jason can bite their dust.

Jason pulls up his pants, and realizes that everyone knows everything about him and that everyone has his number, which when last he looked was 33 – a magic number according to the Freemasons and other occultists.

Jason continues to walk south, looking for that elusive stairway to heaven. He stubbornly retraces each step he took when he left Bionica, footprint by footprint. When he reaches the point on the Santa Monica Mountains where he can see the LA basin, it is time for the final name change – back to his original name, Condor. He says, "I am Jason no more. I am Condor. I am Condor. *I am Condor*." Suddenly, in the back of his mind he gets an error message stating that he cannot connect to The Well with a banned name. So he tries Condor Junior, but that appears to be taken or possibly banned as well. He tries Condor33, Condor4U, and "Condor1976. None of them work. Finally, he tries "The Real Condor" and that works fine. His sentient tattoos return, but he is unable to read some of them since they appear to require an update. There is one smudgy tattoo that is barely legible; it reads, "Always listen to your mother." He suspects that this message is a virus that his old hacker buddies have entered into the system to prevent his use of The Well. They probably know that he's trying to gain access again.

Condor arrives at the huge Mormon Temple topped by the angel Moroni looking out towards Bionica. As he enters he has a vision of his favorite pig, Google, following him down the alley and through an opening in the fence leading up Santa Monica Boulevard to the Mormon Temple. As before, workers in uniform are tending the vast manicured lawn surrounding the Temple while others are cleaning out the reflecting pool. Several are posted at the entrance and inside the building. Again Condor is asked for his identification, and as he once did before, he shows them his one permanent tattoo, Xtremus, and the guard stamps his hand and lets him pass.

"Berk is back in town and expecting you," the guard says.

Condor enters through the front door that leads to a huge empty hall, where he sees Berk's head bobbing among piles of computer hardware as he did when he was a young man.

"Welcome home, Jason. Oh, I mean Condor, right?

Condor corrects him, "Now it is The Real Condor."

Berk says dismissively, "Let us try this again – short time no see, The Real Condor. Let us just stick to Condor. It would make life easier for those of us who remember you. Now let me show you my collection. Your son loves it."

"He comes here?"

"All the time. I have the best physical jazz collection in the world. I have long play vinyl records, VHS tapes, CD's, DVD's, memory sticks, external hard drives, and more recent stuff – you name it, I have it. Your son cannot get enough of it. This is not virtual stuff; it is the real McCoy. I prefer the vintage formats myself, none of that file-sharing crap. My collection is legit and copyright cleared for the most part. Your son is looking at my collection to evaluate what he can download to The Well, not *from* The Well, but from me *to* The Well. As you can imagine, there are serious gaps in the available jazz music on The Well."

"Does he want to come back with me to live with the Greeks?"

"Not really. He loves Bionica and the Bionicans. He says that with Digi Diva he has found his groove. Or, might I say, her groove," Berk teases.

Seeing his joke fall flat, Berk begins to explain how Pericles became a Bionican.

"He was content to start at the bottom, a humble user. He gave up his Greek clothes – an act of humility that was appreciated by everyone. They say he has the potential to become a good hacker, like you, his old man." Berk laughs with a heavy dose of irony that Condor ignores.

Condor stays on track, "What can I do?"

"It is time for you to settle your accounts. The chickens have come home to roost. The game is up. The fat lady has sung. It is time for you to come clean."

"To come clean? How am I dirty?"

"It is time for your homecoming."

"What do you mean?"

"You still do not get it? It is time for us to focus our attention on *you*, Condor. It is time for us to recognize *you* for the person that *you* are. It is all about your truth and reconciliation. It is all about *you*."

"It is all about *me*?"

"Yes, *you* are going to get the kind of attention that no one in recent history has ever received."

"Why am *I* going to get that? Why should *I* be so lucky?"

"That is what you are going to find out through this hearing. We want you to review for us what you have done, when you have done it and why. This is going to be your special day. Who knows, you may even receive something special."

Condor pretends to like that idea. He has always felt that his work has not been sufficiently appreciated.

Berk then continues to elaborate, "Or, maybe you will have to make amends, but that takes time. Time is a very precious commodity, perhaps the most precious commodity."

Condor ignores this phrase meant to foreshadow what is to come. Instead, he blurts out, "I want to see my son."

"But the question is, does he wants to see *you*?"

"Can I see him?"

Like the younger Pericles, Berk strokes his chin. "I

think that this can be arranged." But instead of his chin, Berk's nose enlarges.

Berk whistles and two guards enter the room.

"Take him to see Pericles. But, first shave his head and cut off his beard so that the Bionicans will recognize him." The guards quickly seize Condor before he can protest, and they forcibly shave his head and cut off his beard. This means that all his ties to the Hellenic Council have been severed. Still Condor is unsure that the Bionicans will recognize him, considering how old and fat he has gotten lolling around Elysium and eating their honey-dipped treats.

Following Berk's lead, the guards forcibly escort Condor to Bionica, to his old stomping grounds at the beachfront Palisades where under the palms a group of young Bionican users dance naked to a drumbeat, their bodies covered in grime. And there Condor sees her – Digi Diva, sitting in Condor's beloved old throne-like chair made from carved wood, supervising the users.

Condor scans the group, makes out Pericles' naked body moving among the dancers, and then catches the eye of Digi Diva, who rises from the chair to greet him.

"Hello Condor, long times no see. My, you have changed. You are fatter than I remember," she giggles flaunting her slim figure. "Regardless, I have a deal for you." She bares her buckteeth.

Condor replies, "There will be no deal, unless I get

my son back."

Condor covers his face in dismay seeing his naked, filthy son gyrating to the drumbeat, and as he tries to approach Pericles, the guards move quickly to restrain him.

Outraged, Condor screams at Digi, "What have you done to him?"

Digi coolly explains, "We have done nothing to him that he hasn't done himself. He came here of his free will. And today, your son, your only son, is preparing for your big event tonight. You will, of course, have a chance to talk to him then." Pericles continues to dance, swaying blindly to the beat, paying no heed to the exchange between Digi and Condor.

Berk whispers to Condor, who bends over to hear him better.

"I think you should accept the deal. It would be better for you and all of us," he says, waving his hands towards the dirty naked dancers.

"What deal is she talking about?" Condor asks.

"You are to work with Digi. Together you would make a great team."

Condor does not reply.

"I do not think you are going to like the alternative," Berk says and then explains what is in store for him. "We have organized an old-fashioned reunion for you, a sort of *This Is Your Life* show at the Temple. We will start with a reception for the special people in your life, who are still alive or with us in spirit. Everyone you have ever known, or thought you knew, will attend. Even those who are no longer with us will be there. And when we are finished with the reception, we will have a really big chew."

Berk stares at condor and speaks slowly, emphasizing each word when he says, "So what will it be, schmuck!" Condor does not reply.

So, the guards, led by Berk, take Condor back to the Mormon Temple to face the music.

CHAPTER 21
SHOWTIME

Inside the Mormon Temple, the spacious assembly room is set up for Condor's roast. Slave workers are putting the final touches on special stage area that makes use of the three pulpits that were already there, removing many of the original theater seats to make way for food service and banquet tables.

Berk, an old movie buff, installed a back-screen film projection system to show clips from old Harold Lloyd movies on flammable colloid that survived Cybergeddon. Standing on a stool, Berk barks the final instructions to the catering crew guys, who are setting up long tables with pitchers of mead and snacks. He has ordered nut clusters especially for the Greeks.

The sounds of motorcycles and trucks announce the arrival of the Goths, led by Mad Moxie and his burly boys. They are followed by a motorcycle procession of the G-Spot Biker Femmes decked out in their identical black skin-tight leather jumpsuits that sparkle in the sun.

Brandishing their swords and knives, the Goth thugs are admitted by the worried guards to the huge assembly room. A lineup of topless Goth maidens greet the mostly male guests, offering them drinks and snacks as they mingle, surrounded by flickering images of Harold Lloyd clinging to the minute hand of a clock suspended from a building over a busy city street.

"Welcome to the homecoming," Berk shouts out to the Goths.

"We need more honey-dripping snacks." Moxie yells back looking in Berk's direction.

Berk replies, "Hold your horses. Do not spoil your appetite. Wait for the pig roast. We are roasting a pig especially for you Goths." Berk grins because roasting pigs is one of his favorite things to do, even though he claims to keep kosher.

"We here to party, bring on your mead." Moxie shouts loudly. His companions raise their swords in agreement. "But is it truly IPA?" Moxie asks Berk, who assures him that it is.

Berk turns around to greet John Smith, the jolly rancher, and his dour wife, Conchita. Berk stands on his tippy toes to shake John's hand.

"Glad you could make it. We need your expertise as a Techie. We are going to have a full house, and will need your help with the AV and the avatar part of the program."

"You better have some guacamole ready for me," John Smith growls. Meanwhile, long yellow school buses pull up to disgorge the Greek guests, who queue up to enter the Temple.

The guards escort Medea and Thor into the assembly room. Medea is wearing a glittering studded black pants suit, a large picture hat, white gloves, and oversized sunglasses. Thor sports a regal crimson robe with embroidered occult signs. Memory and Meditation make their entrance, each wearing short shorts and too tight t-shirts, emblazoned with a picture of their dead sister, Song, over their breasts.

Medea looks around the room and waves to everyone, even those, such as Berk's guards, whom she has never seen before. Thor gives a clenched fist salute to his compatriots. "Power to the People!" The Goths cheer him with their arms raised high.

Berk makes a motion to his guards to move the group to the banquet area in a large assembly room. The Goths follow him to their seats.

 Gregory and Margaret are the first to settle in. Gregory whispers to Margaret, "They used to hold the anti-technology purges here. They killed anyone who had anything to do with Xtremus."

Margaret responds in a monotone, "I heard they singled people out and executed them on the spot."

Gregory agrees with a sigh, "Tough measures for tough times."

"We have not seen the end yet," Margaret says, finishing the exchange.

The lights flicker after all of the guests arrive in the assembly room. The room darkens momentarily until a spotlight locates Berk standing up on a stool behind the pulpit, banging a gavel too large for his hands.

"Everyone, silence, please. Welcome to our special reunion. Please move towards the front of the stage and take your seats." John Smith cranks up the AV system to provide red carpet background music typically used during the old Oscars to accompany the seating of the dignitaries. After the music fades, Berk continues. "We have come here to celebrate the life of The Real Condor, also known as Siegfried, Jason, and Condor to those who are present. Condor, please step forward."

The guards bring fat old Condor up to the stage.

Berk looks down on Condor's shackled feet and asks, "You have come here of your own free will for your reward, have you not, eh?"

"I am here as the result of my quest."

"We appreciate your dedication to your quest, but today is all about truth and reconciliation. Condor, do you think that the unexamined life is worth living?"

This comment gets a laugh from all the Greeks in the crowd.

"What good will it do me to examine it now?" Condor asks.

"Does it matter so long as you are successful in your quest? Is not your quest to die for? We are here to help you with that," Berk grins.

The Goths cheer loudly and raise their fists. The Greeks smirk as Berk continues with the introduction.

"Before we go into the multimedia portion of our presentation, which will include shared hallucinations from The Well, let us begin this convocation with some choice words. The Goths have come to read some of their doggerel, uh...poetry. Let us give a rousing hand to the Goths."

The Goths come up onto the stage, acknowledging the applause. Mad Moxie steps forward and bellows out in Gothspeak, "Siegfried, or should meh call ya Condor, we haz a rap fo' ya. Moxie starts his doggerel as his fellow Goths cheer him on. Berk signals his staff to turn the spotlight on Moxie, who clears his throat and begins to chant.

You said you wanted to be one of us
All for one of us
To join our band
To fight for Tara's hand
But you betrayed the Goth cause
Without the slightest pause
You hid under Greek skirts

You wore their fancy shirts
And you learned their big words
So death be to you
Condor, Siegfried, Jason
Death to all of you Freemasons!
Let us put a rubber hose
Into your upturned nose
Let us put your head on a spit
Let us throw your body in a pit
Let us put a sword in your gizzard
You bloody Bionican lizard.

Mad Moxie finishes his performance with a bow to the audience. The Goth crowd cheers madly while the Greeks clap politely.

"God bless oral poetry," Margaret murmurs sarcastically to Gregory.

Berk thanks Moxie and encourages the other Goths to return to their places in the audience. Then he introduces Medea, who takes her place at the pulpit and bangs the gavel to get attention.

"Ladies and gentlemen, thank you for joining us on this most auspicious occasion. We have come here to bring power to truth and truth to power. We have come here to review the life of Condor and his various aliases. I have known this person since he made his way among the Goths and then the Greeks. It was our hope that he would help us make use of the wisdom of Bionica. Most of you are familiar with him and his quest. Our purpose here today is to help Condor achieve closure and to help him understand what his quest is all about. And in learning about his quest, may we all know a little more about our own."

Thor joins Medea on stage and puts in his two cents worth.

"I concur with Medea. We are here to testify and to unify. We are here to speak and to listen. We are here to think and to feel. We are here to bring everything together to make things right. We are..."

Medea, impatient, interrupts him. "I think we got the message. Let us move to the next phase of our program – the testimonies. Bring on the girls who devoted so much of their time trying to help Condor see the light." She turns to Condor, who is squirming in the spotlight, with guards at his side to restrain him. Berk signals John Smith to play the recorded fanfare. Medea shouts out the cue, "Come on girls."

Meditation and Memory appear on the stage. Meditation steps forward into the light to introduce herself. "I am Meditation. This is my sister, Memory. We have come here to bury him, not to praise him. My sisters and I spent countless hours trying to introduce this person whom we now know as Condor to the finest denizens of Greek civilization."

Meditation takes a long sigh and says, "We dialogued

with him."

"We read to him," Memory adds.

"And we played music for him," Meditation says, her face covered in tears. "When that person, who was then called Jason, came to us, we taught him everything we knew about truth, beauty and the Greek Way. And then he betrayed us." They begin to sob.

Memory composes herself to say, "And our beloved sister, Song, is gone. She gave him everything. He used her body, and he broke her heart; now she is lost to us."

Meditation looks in Condor's direction, staring straight at him. "Do you not see? Do you not see?"

Condor has no idea what is he supposed to be looking at.

Medea leaves the pulpit and joins the two sobbing sisters on stage, consoling each in their grief.

Berk returns to the pulpit and introduces John Smith. "John Smith, as you know, was on the team that created The Well. He has since then become a proponent of free will, living the good life on his ranch, Esperanza, with his lovely wife, Conchita. He is our virtual reality expert."

John sports a suntan and a huge white-toothed smile. His gray hair flows to one side. He moves to the pulpit as Berk steps down.

"Thank you for inviting me. I had the privilege of meeting this young man when he started out on his quest. I knew then that the road would be hard and rocky for him. As you know this project, which we call Project Pygmalion, started out as a bet between me and Berk." They exchange looks and laugh. "And thanks to Medea and the cooperation of the Goth and Greek communities, we were able to pull it off."

Confused, Condor recalls hearing about Project Pygmalion, but never realized that it applied exclusively to him.

"We kept the details about Project Pygmalion a secret from Condor to see what he would do with the greatest gift of all – free will. He always knew that we were watching and that we cared what happened to him."

Condor screams, "I never had free will. There was a voice in my head. She, uh, it told me what to do. I never had free will." The guards move violently to shut Condor up.

"Ah, my dear Condor, you *had* free will. The voice in your head disappeared whenever you wanted it to. You had opportunities to love and to be loved, to form friendships, to be loyal. What you did with these opportunities is the result of, uh, free will. We would like you to take responsibility. Freedom is not something that is given to you. It is something you have to seek out and embrace. Don't you know that *freedom's just another word for nothing left to lose?*" The audience cheers loudly and Smith takes a deep breath and continues his talk.

"Project Pygmalion grew out of a long tradition of

reality programming that took place when technology reigned supreme. There were thousands of reality programs then, but since the Plague, we no longer had the energy nor the resources to mount them. So this project is something special. I would like to thank all the actors in this great venture, especially those who so valiantly gave up their lives – especially Little Eddie, the Bead Lady, Eric, Olin, Song and Simon, the old man by the river, and all the innocent men, women and children. These wonderful people enabled us to learn more about Condor and what he would do with his precious gift, free will. I want to thank all of you who participated without divulging the nature of this project to Condor, thereby safeguarding the nature of this noble experiment."

Condor manages to loosen the grip of the guards. "I protest, I protest. I want a chance to be heard."

Smith nods to the guards. "Let Condor have his say, but I assure you that he will sing a different tune when we are done with him."

Condor is brought to the center of the stage in his chains. "Here is your chance to be heard," Smith says as he hands him a wireless microphone, the best that Berk can provide.

Condor takes a breath, stands up straight, and pauses before speaking. "I was Condor. I was Siegfried. I was Jason. Now I am Condor again. I lived my life as I was taught to live it. I was on a mission. I did it without complaining. Now I am being told that my life is a reality program. I consider this an invasion of privacy. You never had my permission. This is entrapment. I object to being an object."

Smith responds, "We beg to differ. You went along with the program. We gave you plenty of clues. Anyone with half a brain would have picked up on them. Apparently the light never went on in your head. You are the object of your obsession."

"I did what I had to do," Condor mutters in protest.

Smith wonders, "But why did you kill people who also had quests? If you knew that you had your quest, wouldn't you know that others have their quests, too? I would have thought that you might have been more sympathetic to theirs."

Condor's face goes blank.

Medea interjects, "Moral education was not featured in the database of The Well. When the medium was the message, it was easy to confuse the means with the ends. I guess we should allow him extenuating circumstances. Or maybe not," Medea finishes with a grin.

"Kill him, kill him, kill him!" the Goths shout out in unison. "We want poetic justice. He does not have a poetic bone in his body. He deserves to die."

Medea steps up to the pulpit as John Smith goes backstage to resume his AV duties. Medea bangs the gavel again.

"We have to respect due process. This roast is about truth and reconciliation." The audience is restless. They want blood.

"Perhaps there are things we can point to that would show that Condor discovered morality. Condor, maybe you can help us out here."

"What about the Institute of Character Correction for the Young? ICKY was my landmark achievement. I did that to help the children."

There are boos in the audience. Moxie, who has kept quiet so far, steps up from the front row with his fist in the air, livid. As he struggles to find his words, everyone in the room strains to listen.

"Education ...is the last refuge of a scoundrel," he blurts out.

"I thought it was patriotism," Gregory whispers to Margaret, who tells him to shut up.

The Goth contingent goes wild upon hearing their leader use an epithet.

"Down with education. *We don't need no education*," they shout with their fists in the air.

"Originality is not a Goth calling card," mumbles Margaret.

"They are such innocents," adds Gregory.

"Morons. And besides, is that not a double negative?" Margaret always has the last word.

Medea hushes the audience and announces the next

phase of the program in hope that light entertainment will keep things calm.

"Let us hear from the Bionican dancers," she shouts out.

The room becomes quiet. A steady drumbeat begins, and the curtain rises to reveal dancing Bionicans keeping rhythm to the drumbeats, more or less. Among the dancers is Pericles, completely nude with his eyes closed. His jerky hand motions and body movements are out of step with the others. Margaret and Gregory look at each other bemused.

"Look at that kid. He does not seem to have any rhythm."

Gregory responds lamely, "Oh, he is just following the beat of his own drummer."

Pericles moves to the front of the stage and looks away from his father.

Condor shouts at him. "Come back, you fool. You were destined for great things. I want the best for you. Son, you do not belong here."

Pericles stops dancing as the others continue. He faces his father and says, "You are my father in name only. I was destined to be here, and I am happy to be here. I want to be where the music is. I'm in my groove!" He bellows as he rejoins the dancers, proudly strutting with his member fully erect.

"It's been more than four hours he has been dancing

in that condition. Maybe he ought to see Medea for help," Gregory wisecracks, giving a knowing look to Margaret, who is too captivated to care.

"You will never be free. You will never be free by overextending yourself," Condor shouts at his son.

"Order, order, order!" Medea tries to reclaim attention. "Be quiet, Condor, this is your life. *This* is your life. The show must go on."

Medea then turns to the audience to get on with the program as the dancers finish their number and quietly leave the stage to scattered applause.

"We have with us the entire Bionican hacker core led by no other than the great Digi Diva, the only female hacker in the history of Bionica." Digi takes a bow, flashing her teeth that have become her signature. "We also have among us the members of her troupe, including Pengo, Draper, Jimmy the Greek, and Phiberoptik." There is applause as her colleagues step forward.

Digi Diva begins. "Thank you very much. We are proud to have been invited to your show. I only want to say how much we miss our old buddy, Condor."

One of the Bionican hackers shouts out sarcastically, "We *miss* you, Condor. Why *did* you ever leave us?"

Medea raises her arm to get attention.

"But before we continue, your son would like to offer you a special drink." Pericles, who emerges from backstage, carries a large beaker, which he places in front of

Condor.

"What is it, hemlock?" Condor asks sarcastically.

"No, it is our highest grade of Daytrain – the very best." Pericles assures him. "Let me show you." Pericles takes a sip to prove it is not a hemlock.

"I do not touch *that* stuff, not ever," Condor protests.

"We cannot go on with the show unless you imbibe," Digi says. "Be a sport old chap, drink up."

With the guards threatening to force his mouth open, Condor reluctantly drinks from the vessel. His acquiescence elicits scattered applause and rude shouts from the Goths. Everyone wants to see what this drink will do to him.

"He is again one of us," one of the hackers shouts.

The Goths shout in return, "You can have him. You can have him."

Medea puts a stop to this by banging her gavel on the pulpit.

"I am sure Condor will want to tell you his story in his own words now that he is fully lubricated, but before we get there, let us hear it again for the Bionican dancers."

The drums pick up, and the Bionican dancers return to the stage, moving in front of projected images depicting scenes from Condor's quest that took him to the Goths and to the Greeks. Now the dancers include some familiar user faces like Ty, Maya, Nellie, Jennie, Frank,

Bill, Gertrude, and Martha. Like Condor, they have aged. Digi Diva continues, "Some of our dancers have gone to the great beyond – Lenny, Phil, George, Suzie, Sasha, Nancy, and Tom. Here they are by special request."

The deceased users appear as holograms for all to see, moving right along with the live Bionican dancers. Condor catches the eye of the late Simon Girty, who is clutching a crucifix with one hand, while throwing a kiss in Condor's direction with the other. His body morphs into a tap-dancing skeleton singing:

Toe bone connected to the foot bone
Foot bone connected to the heel bone
Heel bone connected to the ankle bone
Ankle bone connected to the shin bone.

And then, after finishing up "Oh 'Dem Bones" ditty, Girty's skeleton disappears into the mist.

"Everybody lives forever when they are dancing," Digi shouts out optimistically. The dancing by the other avatars continues, and some of the audience members join in with heavy arm waving.

Medea takes the microphone from Digi. "Thank you. Thank you. This show would not be possible without our sponsor. You guessed it – the substance of all substances, the elixir of the imagination…"

Everyone shouts, "Daytrain! Daytrain! Daytrain!"

Digi calls back, "Things go better with Daytrain!"

"Train the Day with Daytrain!" the crowd roars.

The dancers pick up their tempo, thrusting their hips in all directions as they work up another round of applause.

Medea shouts, "Thank you, thank you Digi." Digi takes a bow. "We come here courtesy of The Well, the fountain of knowledge for everything. If you cannot find it in The Well, it is not worth knowing," she says with a wink.

Medea turns to the audience and slowly raises her hand to get attention. "I am glad there is so much enthusiasm. I can feel the love. Enthusiasm is a good starting point for everything. But before we continue with our event, we have a special treat in store for you."

There is a hushed pause in the audience. Even the rowdy Goths pretend to behave.

"We have for you some special guests and I am sure Condor will remember them. First let us remember crazy Little Eddie." Medea pauses and looks in Condor's direction. "Remember what he said?"

Little Eddie's apparition is stage center. Nearby, on top of a red cushion, is the Emergency Hammer that Condor once used to execute him.

The apparition of Eddie starts the religious rant that cost him his life, *"And God said, Let us make man in our image, after our likeness. And let them have dominion over the fish of the sea, and over the fowl of the air, and over the cattle, and over all the Earth, and over every creeping thing that creepeth upon the Earth."*

Condor is defensive. "I had to kill him; it was my job. He was creating a problem for the rest of the users." He tries to grab the Hammer to use it on Eddie again, but a guard restrains him.

Digi Diva defends him in a mock tone. "He was only doing his duty, but...maybe he enjoyed it too much."

"I have been set-up, betrayed." Condor cries out.

"You wasted your life. You could have been somebody. Instead, you chose to be you!" Digi laughs back at him. "Heck, we could have made quite a pair." The hackers laugh at this quip recalling the days when Digi humiliated herself to get Condor's attention.

Medea whispers to Berk, "Hell hath no fury like a woman scorned – something he should know."

While Digi continues to berate Condor, there is an apparition of Simon, the old Christian man whom he executed in cold blood.

"I was the last true witness on earth, and you took that away; may God forgive your sins. You murdered the innocents, and now they have come to sing for you and to forgive your sins."

The other Christians whom Condor murdered appear as a choir out of the mist, each holding a candle, chanting the Lord's Prayer. First adults line up on the top row and then the children file on the stage, first the taller ones and then the smaller ones. As they settle into position, the room becomes quiet, except for the pounding of Condor's heart. They all sing "Amazing Grace," and before they have a chance to finish, some of the Goths in the crowd jeer, demanding that Condor die immediately. The leader of the dead Christians, Paul, raises his hand to quiet the rowdy crowd, "Please allow our brethren to finish their holy song."

Amazing Grace, how sweet the sound,
That saved a wretch like me.
I once was lost but now am found,
Was blind, but now I see

They finish up and then fade away. Simon turns to Condor and points at him, "Sinner, repent!"

Medea turns to Condor, "I see that there are some rather strong feelings out there about the way you behaved. Maybe you were out of your depth, perhaps too literal in your interpretation of things. After all your education with us, you should have known better."

"I followed orders to kill the Christians. I have no regrets."

The crowd remains quiet as Medea addresses the crowd, "Well then, let us meet some of the women in Condor's life." She turns to Condor, "Certainly they could shed some light on your character. Let them come in the order you met them. Remember Beadina, the Bead Lady? She was widely beloved."

There is a long silence and a hush in the audience. Everyone has been waiting to see the wondrous Bead Lady and finally to hear her story.

"I am sure you remember her. Everyone knows her." Media stares at Condor.

"How would I have known that? I never heard of her before we met."

"You were not supposed to know. She was introduced to everyone after you left Bionica. Before you arrived at her house, we were all expecting you to arrive there. We were hoping that you would fall for her. You destiny was that you two were supposed to be together, forever."

Digi Diva joins Medea at the pulpit to continue the accusations. "Condor, you did not fall for me, and I can understand why. We were just buddies, but the Bead Lady was different; she was a treasure. She loved you passionately. We thought that she would be the girl for you and that you would fulfill your quest with the guidance of true love."

"I thought she was a witch with the power to stop me on my quest," Condor protests.

Digi Diva interrupts, "But did you have to kill her? You took her treasure. You could have let her live."

"I had to kill her because she wanted me to kill her, because she knew too much about me and about what I was going to do. It was her fault that I killed her. She even sang about it *before* we met."

Suddenly, Bead Lady appears, dancing like Isadora

Duncan entwined in beads, surrounded by her birds. Her head generates a golden aura as she speaks, "Siegfried, I mean The Real Condor, I loved you so. I wanted to make you happy forever. I warned you that you were heading for a fall. I told you that I was the only one who could save you, but you did not listen."

The birds fly away, and the Bead Lady dissolves into Teresa, the old woman he met when he was a Bionican hacker. She says, "We all grow old before our time. You missed your one chance," and then she disappears.

Medea steps forward and turns to Condor, "We are not finished with you yet. So you think you were not a lady-killer, huh? Later in your life, with my help, you were introduced to your Tara, your dream girl. She enabled you to become leader of the Goths; but you failed her miserably, both as a husband and as a leader."

Tara appears, wearing her favorite Disney Snow White dress and layers of jewelry. "I could have made you happy because I knew you wanted the good life, but you rejected me, and you rejected it. You used me for my name and my power. I gave you a child, and you broke my heart."

Standing next to her is Tara's father, Olin, pointing his finger at Condor.

"You were never worthy of my daughter, you Bionican scum!"

Tara and Olin disappear while Medea continues, "Do

you remember, Condor, the muse in your dreams? She was just *dying* to meet you."

Song appears and says, "If I had known you were a lady-killer, I would have kept you away from my heart. Little did I know that you were the cold-hearted murderer of little, itty-bitty children. I gave you all of me and in return you broke my heart."

Condor protests, "But that was collateral damage. You should have understood what I had to do. Instead, you wanted me to indulge your fantasies. I did not make you kill yourself. You cannot blame that on me!"

Song does not answer him and so Medea steps in. "How long can you say that? If you had any decency left, you would at least pretend to take responsibility. All you say is that the devil made you do it."

Song starts to cry, and Medea goes to comfort her. Medea goes to put her hand on her shoulder but since she is not there, her arm passes through thin air and Song disappears.

Berk is now in the audience jumping high to make sure Condor notices him. "You are a misogynistic mumsa. I am ashamed of having mentored you."

The crowd becomes unruly and yells out, "Kill him, kill him, kill him. He is a phony!" the Goths scream, raising their knives into the air. Medea holds up her hand to nip further unruliness in the bud. Meanwhile, the show goes on.

"You all have betrayed me," Condor cries out. "Mother, where are you? Why have you forsaken me?"

Condor's mother appears, but then turns her back on him and disappears.

Medea lowers her voice. "Do you not get it? There are many people who would prefer that you were dead. Does that not clarify things for you?"

"I want to live," Condor shouts out, hoping that his mother hears him.

"This is getting mawkish," Margaret whispers to Gregory, who quickly responds, "The banality of evil, how boring."

Medea continues to lecture, "*Condor, no, you can't always get what you want. But if you try sometimes, you just might find, you get what you need. Didn't you know that *when the going gets tough, the tough get going*?"

"But I want to live," Condor pleads as the crowd boos, impatient with what they regard as a breach of protocol. They want Condor to man up instead of seeing him jollied along by Medea.

"Think about it. This is the reality show. There are expectations, and we have to manage them. Your survival is in your hands, and the show must go on. We have invested a lot in you. It is payback time."

"But people need to know." Condor protests.

"Know about what?" Medea asks.

"About weapons of mass destructions and whether

the Greeks could ever use knowledge from The Well to build them."

"Tell us what you think."

"It has happened before and it can happen again."

Medea looks at Condor with disgust. "Is this the way you want to end your life, like a fool? We gave you every chance to get things straight, but you acted on bad intelligence even though you were warned. Not only did you not measure up to our expectations, but you also limited the growth of your son, to the point that his liberal education went completely to waste. And now, again, we give you the opportunity to become part of the solution, and you reject us. *Have you no sense of decency, sir, at long last?*"

The room becomes silent. The drums stop beating. The Bionicans stop dancing. Medea gives Condor a disdainful look from the pulpit.

"Now it is time for Condor's mother. She has something to say to him." John, the rancher, gives the cue for the next apparition. Condor's virtual mother, Julia, rises from a giant seashell, her hair blowing in the wind. She is more beautiful than ever. Surrounded by angels and musicians she makes her way forward to Condor. He is excited to see her.

"Mother, I want to touch and I want to feel you."

She comes slowly towards him. Her hips move with the oohs and aahs coming from the audience. Julia puts her hand on his head.

"Son, it is your duty to embrace your fate. This is what Xtremus is all about – living large outside the body. It is not about getting fat and old like you have done. They are right. We cannot afford to rewrite the script because the production is almost over. There can be no re-shoots. This is reality. It is your destiny. You had your chance, and it is time for you to ante up, to pay the piper."

Condor recoils in anger and says, "It is not natural for mothers to want their children to die. You were never on my side. You were never my real mother. You just used me! All you ever cared about was your legacy."

"This is not true; I cared about you."

"You lie. All you ever cared about was Xtremus," spits Condor

"You had plenty of chances to know the truth. Maybe it is time for you to consider your legacy as I did mine. Like me, I want you to live forever."

"I never had a chance because I was a motherless child," Condor whimpers.

Julia disappears, and Medea steps forward to resume her role as mistress of ceremonies.

"Condor, even when you committed the greatest of all sins, the premeditated but thoughtless murder of innocents, we stuck by you because you sincerely believed that your quest, and our project, should not be challenged. But that could only go on for so long. Your evil has outlived your innocence and usefulness. Our purpose today is not to revile you, but to understand you as best as we can. You might even say we are here to love you."

"Kill him, kill him, kill him!" The Goths scream.

The guards move on the Goths to quell their outburst.

Again, Medea tries to calm the audience, this time with food. "Quiet, please! It is time for the next phase of the program. It is time to eat.

Medea continues her announcement. "And now, to show how much we appreciate you, Condor, we will grant you one last wish, something that you never did for your victims. For your last wish, we have organized this sumptuous last supper in your honor. Will the Goths and the other special guests, who have been close to Condor, please come to the head table to join Condor in this repast?"

"But a last meal is not my last wish. I want to live," Condor protests.

Medea responds, "Too late, the show must go on, but first we must eat."

Mad Moxie and the other Goths proceed from the buffet table to seats at the head table that has been set up on the stage. Plato and Aristotle follow, taking places next to Meditation and Memory, who are next to Xantippe and Socrates, who keeps muttering his barely audible, but trusty mantra, "Know Thyself."

Meditation and Memory beckon Song's apparition to join them. All three are laughing and trying on hats brought by Tara. They are reenacting Condor's reoccurring dream in which eco-terrorists unleash the Great Plague as an act of revenge for the destruction of wildlife. "Lions and tigers, and bears, oh my." The sisters turn around teasing and feigning laughter. Condor now recognizes that the three women in his reoccurring dream are Meditation, Memory, and Song. The old woman's voice in that dream is his mother, Julia.

Among those at the head table are others who have figured in Condor's life, including the Bionican hackers led by Digi Diva; and Goths including Otto and Thor. The avatars of Olin, the Bead Lady and Tara, as well as Condor's best friend, Eric, join them as well. Medea escorts the bound Condor to the table, and he sits down between her and Berk. He reads out the names of each of the guests at the head table.

After the dignitaries are seated, Medea commands, "Bring on the food for the last supper."

She claps her hands once. On the side of the enormous huge assembly hall, another curtain is pulled open by guards to reveal an extra-long table stacked with food. Huge platters full of edible delights and delicacies surround a gargantuan roasted pig on a spit with a red apple in its mouth.

Berk reappears standing on a chair near the buffet table and announces, "There is plenty here for everyone. Please help yourselves. Today's feast includes fingerling potatoes, organic leeks, tomatoes, and the finest omega-3 ALA kale that Daytrain can buy, and some vintage French wine. And in the spirit of this occasion, we proudly serve our best and most beloved Pig 311."

As Berk speaks about today's menu, the virtual Pig 311 scampers across the room out of a mushroom cloud and approaches Condor. It looks like his favorite pig, Google, whose body had been served up years ago because Condor failed to protect him. Condor tries to hug him, but the ephemeral pig slips loose and runs away, and disappears into the real roasted pig, waiting to be served to the guests.

As the commoners scramble for food at the buffet, a busty Goth maiden carves and serves pieces of the porker to the VIP's at the head table. With a big smile, she gently plops down a juicy slice for the "guest of honor" who pushes his plate away while the others, who have already been served, are eager to dig in.

Condor looks much older than any of the guests, who suddenly look as young as they were when he first knew them. It appears as if not a day has passed over the last twenty years that he has been on his quest. He looks uncomfortable and squirms, tries to get up, but is restrained by the two guards posted behind him.

"Eat, drink, and be merry," Medea raises her goblet to the crowd. The Goths begin to gorge themselves. Condor refuses to eat.

Medea presses her mouth to the mike. "Do not eat so fast; you will get indigestion." This crack gets big belly laughs from the Goth warriors who are grabbing at food with their hands.

Condor hears his mother's voice, "I am your mother. I am your mother. Do as I say."

Condor cups his ears to drown her voice out, but she becomes increasingly shrill, "You have failed miserably." The blind old lady from Condor's early days takes her turn in this attack, pointing her gnarled finger, mocking and cursing Condor for violating womankind. The Bead Lady follows, dances slowly and sings, *"All you need is love. Love is all you need,"* as her sparkling hair changes color continuously.

All this is too much for Condor, who scrambles for words, "I wanted love. I could have used some," he pleads to no one in particular.

The Bead Lady, however, hears him. She stops dancing and turns to Condor. "But you never loved in return. Love is not something you can possess, nor is it something that you just put on, like a piece of clothing." She throws him a kiss.

"I never asked for it," Condor says in a monotone.

"Oh, you asked for it," she says and fades into the

background.

At this point, Condor's Pericles reappears, naked and sweaty, dancing a solo while the audience claps in encouragement. He addresses his remarks to his father. "It is the music, man. Music is love. You have got to be in synch with the rhythm. You have got to be lost in it to find it. Love is now, man."

Condor expresses his hurt and anger, "They are all against me. I do not have a friend in the world."

His dead friend, Eric, appears momentarily. "Wait a minute, you had a friend. I did everything for you and you took my life. Now whose fault is it that you do not have a friend in the world! It is your fault. It is all your fault."

"But I had to do what I had to do. It was my destiny!" Condor begs.

Medea steps up to Condor, "Perhaps now you are getting the point. It is not only about you. Even this roast is not just about you. It is for them, too. All these people here are part of it. Have you ever loved?"

"I know what love is about. I loved my quest. I was true to my quest, and I loved every moment of it with my whole being."

"You were enslaved by your perverted idea of the future. It was never about taking the world as it is and embracing it. It was always about changing it," lectures Medea. "This is the best of all possible worlds."

"I did my duty to protect The Well to prevent weapons of mass destruction and to save the environment. I did what I was told."

""You fool! The Well is obsolete. The time for saving the environment has passed, and our days are numbered. All that we can do is run out the clock until doomsday when there will be nothing more for your vultures to eat."

"Why me? *Why is everybody always pickin' on me?*"

"You are the scapegoat. The joke is on you, and we have the last laugh, you post-apocalyptic party pooper! Admit it, you have been a stupid scoundrel looking for your last refuge, always hiding under the skirts of your many lovers, myself included. If you were smart and inner-directed, you would have been more successful. You would have seen things for what they are."

"Maybe I can still learn," Condor pleads.

"Too little, too late. Your probationary period is over. You have had twenty years. Your time has come my boy toy." Medea says as she turns away from him.

"Why are you turning your back on me? I was always faithful."

Medea sneers, " Every dog has its day."

"Kill him, kill him, kill him!" the Goths shout in exasperation. "Put him out o' hiz misery!"

Medea quiets them down again and turns to Condor, puts her hand on his shoulder and says with exasperation, "Why don't you just sit down and mull this over so that we can go on with the show?"

Instead, Condor conjures his own hallucinations. He sees Google eating out of the hands of Moxie. His son Pericles is dancing too close with Song's ghost. His mother Julia is running off with Gunnarr on a motorcycle. And, the Bead Lady reappears, beckoning him to join her on the other side.

"Come, come away with me; I can still make you happy," Beadina intones loudly.

The Bead Lady suddenly vanishes and another apparition fades in. This time it is Condor's deceased wife, Tara, surrounded by a virtual tornado of luxury goods. Her sister, Gonorrhea, takes her by the hand to confront Condor. Tara shouts at Condor's face, "Siegfried, is that really you? You were to be my life's partner." Tara disappears to make way for the next ghost.

Song, with naked Pericles standing by her, plays a sad song on her lyre, not saying a word. She starts to weep upon making eye contact with Condor. She continues to strum the lyre and invites Pericles, to sing with her. A choir – the G-spot Biker Femmes led by Gonorrhea – lines up behind Song and Pericles, humming the spiritual, "Sometimes I Feel Like a Motherless Child," led by the piercing soprano voice of Gonorrhea, concluding the solo:

Who's got a shoulder when I need to cry?
I feel restless and I do not know why

Cry for help, but still feel alone
Like a motherless child a long way from home
Lord I am lost I cannot find my way
I am dealing with the struggles in my day to day
My soul is weak and I wanna be strong
I try to run away but I've been running too long.

"Thank you, girls." Moxie gives the nod to the biker choir and shouts out to the crowd, "Let's hear some *applauso* for Song and Gonorrhea and the G-Spot Biker Femmes." As the audience bursts into applause and whoops, Song disappears while Aunt Gonorrhea and Nephew Pericles roar off together on a motorcycle joyride.

Moxie thumps his knife on the table, "We want a roast...I mean a toast. Siegfried, give us your poetry, man."

There are voices of mock encouragement in the audience as guards come for Condor, who has yet to touch his food.

Two guards drag Condor out of his chair and lead him reluctantly away from the table to a podium on a riser. Medea brings over a stool so that Berk can climb up to adjust the mike for Condor's height. She whispers into his ear, "We've all been waiting a long time to hear what you have got to say in a poetic way."

Hunched over, Condor stops hallucinating and cries out in desperation, "I cannot stand it. I want to be free."

"Poetry will set ya'll free." Moxie shouts out

Medea offers Condor a sip from the beaker that she spiked with Daytrain.

"Just drink more of this to make you feel better."

Condor sits down and drinks the Daytrain. He rises slowly and extends his arms to the audience. At first, Condor babbles inaudibly and the crowd becomes restless. Moxie shouts, "Kill him. No poetry in his blood. Get this over with." Other Goth voices shout in a chorus to egg Condor on to die like a poet.

"Ya'll owe us. Owe us. Owe us.."

""Let us hear ya'lls verse." Moxie shouts out, making his signature throat-cutting gesture.

Again Medea tries to calm the Goths, "Gentlemen, let us have some due process here. We are no lynch mob."

Condor steps up and addresses the crowd defiantly, "I will give you what you want so that you can do what you want:

Anointed by you

To see my quest through your eyes

It is now a sham.

Condor finishes his haiku, and the audience is silent. They expected more words.

"Short an' sweet, no way a bad poem fo' a Bionican," Moxie opines "but maybe he haz more fo' us."

After a silence marked by indecision and indifference, Condor shuffles his bound feet and steps up to take control over his body. He slowly raises his arms in the direction of the audience and looks over defiantly at Digi with an ironic smile. He quotes from Genesis the exact same words that provoked him to execute crazy Little Eddie a long time ago, *"And God blessed them, and God said unto them, be fruitful, and multiply, and replenish the Earth, and subdue it; and have dominion over the fish of the sea, and over the fowl of the air, and over every living thing that moveth upon the Earth."*

Hearing the Biblical rant, Digi and the other hackers automatically spring into action. Following the procedures of their hacker profession, they first try to silence Condor and to bring him back to reason.

Digi faces Condor in a last ditch effort to save him, pleading with him to recant, "Please don't leave me again. I never wanted anything else from you. I only wanted you." She smiles revealing once again her buckteeth in the hope of rekindling what was once between them. "You know what I have to do, so please stop so that I can save you. You have my word."

Condor ignores her and keeps on quoting scripture with his crazed eyes now turned upward.

"To think you were once one of us," Digi yells at him, as contempt washes over her in a knee-jerk reaction to the Word.

Condor's religious rant is now in full throttle, leaving Digi no choice. She wipes her brow and prepares herself mentally for the next step – the final go-for-it.

Condor covers his head, falls on one knee, and reaches to heaven. He continues to quote scripture, *"And God said, Behold, I have given you every herb bearing seed, which is upon the face of all the Earth, and every tree, in which is the fruit of a tree yielding seed; to you it shall be for meat."*

The word "meat" hits a nerve in the hackers. They know that this is the cue to bring the deep-red cushion and the Emergency Hammer.

Digi Diva carefully examines the jagged edge of that huge golden hammer and lifts it up to get the feel of the serration on her skin. As Medea looks on in silence, Digi approaches the genuflecting Condor from behind. There is not a word from the audience, which is finally about to witness what they had wanted all along. Berk blows his nose to break the silence.

Digi lifts the sledgehammer high above her head and emits a hefty grunt as she slams it down on Condor's head, but miraculously Condor manages to rise and stand his ground for several minutes in silence. Tears of red nectar fall from his eyes and fill the air with the sweet scent of ambrosia.

As Condor slowly extends his arms to Digi and Berk, a stream of bright light from his eye sockets and gaping mouth covers the gathered crowd with golden brilliance. Then yellow Butterflies flutter out of Condor's cracked skull, at first a few and then hundreds fly out and land all over his body; soon they too fill the hall – yellow butterflies everywhere. Then, while the invisible chords of his life are being cut, a final tattoo message flashes on his arms, "Always listen to your mother!" Condor acknowledges the message with a knowing smile as he crashes facedown to the floor. Spilling his last breath, Condor whispers inaudibly to his fading tattoo, "Mission accomplished!" Digi and Berk turn away from Condor's crumpled body to face the audience.

Berk clears his throat and adjusts the mike for his height. His deep voice echoes as the audience starts to shuffle out. "I would like to thank all of you for coming to bear witness. Please give a round of applause to the Bionicans for putting on such a wonderful show. We all have gained a lot from examining the life of Condor, who found out that the unexamined life is truly not worth living."

There is a hearty applause as Berk and the guards prepare for an orderly exit. Meanwhile, Digi Diva and her hackers remove Condor's body from the stage while the audience exits from the assembly hall. The Bionican drumbeat tempo slowly picks up, and the sweet aroma of nectar permeates the air as the Greeks and Goths move through the temple to the exit. The crowd disperses as the smoke and noise of the rumbling motorcycles and trucks fill the outside air.

Moxie and Thor scamper off to the Temple gardens where their hot air balloon is waiting for take off.

"My wish has come true," Moxie says, hugging Thor as they rise into the air to the cheers of the onlookers.

Emerging from the crowd, Aristotle and Plato have a competitive tête-à-tête, each quoting the wisdom of their namesake to shed light on Condor's roast. Plato begins the exchange.

Plato, *"Death is not the worst that can happen to men."*

Aristotle, *"It is the mark of an educated mind to be able to entertain a thought without accepting it."*

Plato, *"The object of education is to teach us to love what is beautiful."*

Aristotle, *"Educating the mind without educating the heart is no education at all."*

Plato, *"The first and best victory is to conquer self."*

Aristotle, *"He who has overcome his fears will truly be free."*

Medea approaches Plato and Aristotle and says, "I hate to interrupt your dialogue, my esteemed colleagues. Looks like our Bionican did not pass the orals. Contrary to what I believed at the start, he just did not have the right stuff. I am sorry to have failed you."

"Too bad. Maybe you will have better luck with your next protégé, Pericles," Plato says sarcastically, cupping his ears to muffle the Bionican drumbeat that is still audible.

Medea laughs, "I am afraid Pericles is totally devoted to dance and music. I doubt even I could interest him in a quest after his joyride with his Auntie, Gonorrhea, who is offering him an opportunity to sing with the G-Spot Biker Femmes."

"Whatever it takes. Chew on this: *Musical training is a more potent instrument than any other, because rhythm and harmony find their way into the inward places of the soul.*"

Aristotle quips, "You cannot go wrong with music."

Medea agrees. "That is the plan. Let young Pericles get it out of his system. Then we can see what he can do for us," Medea says confidently.

Aristotle rolls his eyes and says, "The Well is deep, and Gonorrhea's reach is wide. He might just fall in and drown for good, but we will leave that up to you and to Digi, our gal in Bionica. Remember this always: *Time crumbles things; everything grows old under the power of Time and is forgotten through the lapse of Time.*"

Medea, not to be outdone, tries her favorite bard. "Let's hear from Sappho: *There is no place for grief in a house that serves the Muse.*"

"Enough wisdom for today," Plato shouts pointing to the departing buses, not wanting to miss his ride. Catching up with the other Greeks, Medea, Plato, and Aristotle get on a yellow school bus that will take them north to Polis. Medea is the last to board, wiping her brow, relieved that the ordeal is over.

"There they go." Medea points to the far-away hot air balloon carrying off Thor and Mad Moxie to the wild blue yonder.

"Maybe something good will come from this," Aristotle says casually to Plato.

"Cannot expect much from human sacrifice," Plato responds dryly.

Digi, with Berk bringing up the rear, leads a small funeral party out of the temple to the Bionican boneyard in Silicon Beach. Guards load Condor's body onto a truck driven by a familiar driver, Otto, the Goth. There are no words, no tears. They drive down Santa Monica Boulevard, careful to avoid the huge potholes that are never repaired, passing by empty and abandoned office buildings and stores that were ravaged by mobs long ago. As they approach the Pacific Ocean, they pass by a line of huge damaged stone monuments facing the ocean like the mysterious statues of Easter Island. The California versions are replicas of silicon heroes. Inscriptions emblazon each stone likeness with names such as Bill Gates, Mark Zuckerman, Larry Ellison, and off to the side, Meg Whitman. Alongside each name, numerals indicate the net worth of the moguls when they died.

The funeral party arrives at Silicon Beach near the ruins of Santa Monica Pier and its rusted Ferris wheel. The mourners arrived at a place where they have been many times before – the Bionican boneyard by the sea, surrounded by a wall of scrapped hummers that the eco-terrorists confiscated in the name of earth justice.

Digi and her hackers hoist Condor's corpse over the boneyard wall, dropping it unceremoniously on top of the bones of Little Eddie and all the other users Condor and his colleagues executed years ago. She blows him a kiss.

A large moving shadow swoops down on Condor's body. The vulture is ready for him. It has been waiting a long time.

ACKNOWLEGEMENTS

I would like to thank my editors, Charlie Franco and Michael Duncan, who understood the intent of this somewhat "transgressive" satire and worked with me to realize its potential. I also extend my gratitude to Badger McInnes and others at Montag for bringing this work to fruition.

Writing this novel took a lot of time, not just my own. My wife, Linda, provided valuable ideas and suggestions for this quixotic venture. Many thanks to my family and friends for providing the generous feedback, support and encouragement that helped move this work forward.

We hope you've enjoyed the story. Please help us share this story with other readers by letting us know what you thought with a review on either **amazon.com** or **goodreads.com**.

Thank you kindly,
Montag Press Collective

Peter Wiesner was born in South Croydon, England, spent his childhood in both East and West Berlin, and immigrated to the U.S. in 1954, settling in Santa Monica, California. He studied History at the University of California at Berkeley and earned graduate degrees at both the University of Pennsylvania and Rutgers University. In addition to several positions in higher education, he spent twenty-three years with the IEEE, an international professional association for electrical and computer engineers, for which he developed courseware and video programs for engineers and the general public. His lifetime interest in films led him to produce numerous television documentaries on social as well as environmental issues, including urban renewal, literacy, nuclear disarmament, and post-modern architecture. Recent projects have focused on the social and environmental implications of technology, such as e-waste, green engineering, ethics, and renewable energy. He is currently working on writing and video projects in Bucks County Pennsylvania where he lives with his wife, Linda. They have two grown sons and four grandchildren.

www.ingramcontent.com/pod-product-compliance
Lightning Source LLC
Chambersburg PA
CBHW032251020726
47495CB00001B/60